CW01660607

FAR FROM OVER

L. J. Hutton

Contents

Introduction

A brief word before we start: even nowadays, it is still traditional for Scottish women to retain their maiden name once married, while any children take their father's name. So one of our heroines is Elspeth Allen, with her father being Johnne Allen, but in the historical records her mother would be Jonet Clark – confusing to us, but your family history was in your name. It is also traditional for women to take their mother's maiden name as their second name, so for example you might get, Janet McGregor Fraser, McGregor being her mother's surname. But her husband and children's name could be something totally different, which adds to the puzzle when chasing people through time!

I have retained the seventeenth-century spellings of first names, if only to separate characters out. So, by separating Jannet from Jonet or Janet, rather than using the modern spelling of Janet for all of them, it at least allows readers to have some idea of who is who. And many of the people in the past in this book are real and taken from the records of the time, so I've kept them as they are in case anyone wants to go and look them up. Unfortunately, that does mean that there are two sets of sisters called Margaret and Agnes, for which I apologise for any confusion.

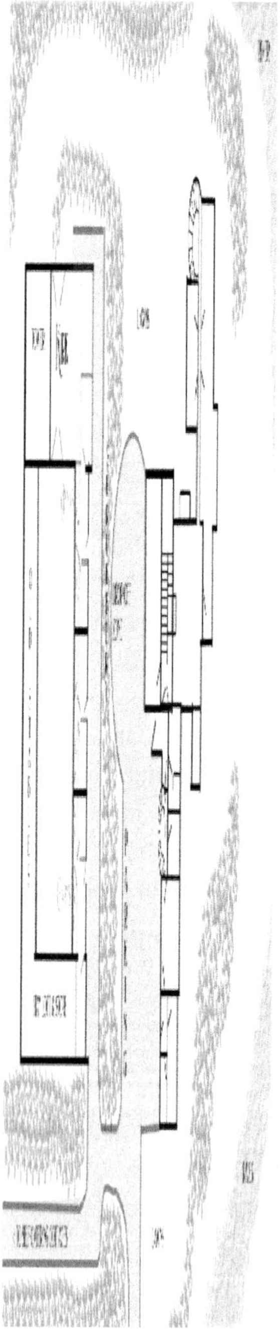

Nuns' Kirk Haugh Hotel and grounds

CHAPTER 1

The ghost of Gideon Corsan was furious. How dare they! How dare they have the almighty nerve to think that they could expel him from his own home? That wretched old Scottish witch was bad enough, shoving her nose into his business. But to be driven out by a Sassenach as well…unthinkable!

Perched up in his new eyrie at the top of the main stairs, which in his day had been the way up to the attic rooms of his tower-house, Gideon was now plotting his revenge. As far as he was concerned, the rooms that *Nuns' Kirk Haugh Country House Hotel* nowadays called their Rosemary suite, occupied the space that had been the master of *Blackpark House's* bedroom. And once his villainous old wretch of a father, John Corsan, had died, the title of master had become his as the oldest son. Therefore that space was his, and his alone, forever and always.

That other people had occupied it down the centuries since his death in 1685, had been a considerable irritant, but historically none were as bad as the succession of vile creatures who flitted in and out of it in its current guise of the honeymoon suite for the hotel when weddings took place. How he hated them. All their giggling and laughing. All the pawing at one another and rutting. Once upon a time – a very, very long time ago, in his youth – Gideon had dared to hope that he too might someday have something like that. What a fool he'd been. With a father like his, there'd been no chance of that ever happening, he'd swiftly realised. And never more so than when he'd met the woman his father had demanded he would marry.

Even now, the thought of her could chill his blood. Pious in the extreme, and even more bitter and twisted than his father, in the few years they'd been together, she had made his life a living hell. *That's* what marriage was like in reality, except these fools hadn't realised it yet. And since they were doomed to end in disaster too, why did he have to have a succession of them disturbing the peace of *his* room?

It was those damned women's fault. All of them! The ones still in the flesh here, and those witches who had burned back when he too had been alive. Those curses of theirs, which they'd flung at him as they died, clung to him like spiders' webs around a trapped fly, never releasing him from his torment. Well if he was witch-cursed for eternity, he wasn't going to linger alone – and that included his age-long sworn enemy Hugh Ferguson.

And that was a final insult he'd felt only recently. How had his old enemy connived to get one of his descendants to own this house again? How many times did he need to chase these bloody Fergusons out? Well he'd sent people running in fear before, and he was going to do it again – or at least he would once he'd worked out which of the men who'd arrived here recently it was, because after so long, time was something Gideon had trouble measuring. Damn them! Those Fergusons were clever at hiding themselves from him, but he'd find him. Oh yes, he'd find him! And then they'd all be sorry.

In the hope that they had won a reprieve from the dramas after despatching the spirit of John Coleborn to the Afterlife, Anna decided that Cameron was right, she really did need a few days off. And it was a sharp reminder that she was dealing with much nicer people these days when none of the other staff objected to a last-minute change of rota to accommodate it.

"Good grief, Anna!" exclaimed Polly, the receptionist who'd been there the previous night when Anna's soon to be ex--father-in-law had succumbed to his fatal heart attack. "I know the man had been vile to you, but you are allowed to be shocked and upset, you know. Yes, of course I'll do

Wednesday's shift for you, and the Friday one Cora was supposed to do."

Indeed, Anna was more than a little shocked at the way most of them responded to Cora's flouncing out before she could be out-ed as the one who'd booked Anna's father and soon to be ex--father-in-law, John Coleborn, in at the hotel under false names. Gemma simply gave a sniff and a roll of her eyes and said, "*Hmph*! Makes a change to be covering for someone with a genuine crisis rather than Cora's love-life going down the pan *again*. No problem, Anna, take whatever time you need."

Even Harriet, the new second chef alongside head chef Emilio, who'd only been with them a few weeks and had barely known Cora, said, "There have to be nicer girls locally than her."

All of which alerted Anna to the fact that Cora had become a problem she would've had to sort out sooner than later, anyway.

Another matter which was bothering her, though whether she could call it a problem was something else entirely, was Cameron Wiseheart – the recently-arrived new owner of *Nun's Kirk Haugh Hotel*, and therefore her boss. The spark between them was something which scared her, because she didn't trust her own feelings as yet. Having had her marriage to Jensen end in disaster on the day of the wedding, she was nothing if not wary of getting involved again.

And though Cameron was a lovely person, as best she could tell – which, given her inability to spot the problems with Jensen, didn't fill her with confidence – she also knew he had more than a few issues of his own. That lovely lingering kiss they'd had last night when he walked her back to her staff cottage had at least confirmed that he felt the same way about her as she did about him. But that wasn't the same as knowing if it would last between them.

You really do need that few days' break, she told herself firmly. *And make sure you get out on your own a bit, so that you can think without everyone else telling you what to do.* That was a bit of an exaggeration, because Gary – night porter, would-be love interest of her Aunty Rita, and well on the way to becoming her new best friend – hadn't been like that at all. In fact, it was Gary who was encouraging her to take everything slowly. But Rita herself could be a force of nature, as she was discovering.

Going up and visiting Rita three times a year for a week hadn't really given her time to know her half-aunt as well as she thought, and Rita was turning out to be every bit as strong-willed as Anna's own father. That shared mother of theirs must have been quite a woman, Anna had come to realise, though her father Gordon's father was where he got his bullying nature from. With Gordon, that fire from his mother manifested itself solely in getting his own way. With Rita, it came out as genuine love and concern, but that didn't make it any easier to deal with when Rita got the bit between her teeth.

Such as now. With the issue of the two rowdy ghosts in the hotel causing problems, Rita was pushing Anna hard to develop her own psychic skills. Yet as Gary had so astutely observed, Rita had grown up with a mum who supported her all the way. Whereas Anna's mother had eroded her self-confidence at every step, and Anna felt that she needed to get a bit better at sticking up for herself with real people, before she got into arguments with stubborn ghosts.

And so with everything as sorted as it could be, Anna put herself in the rota for four days off through from Tuesday to Friday, only going back in on the weekend when Cora's disappearance left them really in the mire. To her surprise, she went to bed very early on Monday and only surfaced midmorning on the Tuesday. Never one for lazing in bed once she'd woken up, nothing prodded Anna to realise what the traumatic couple of days had taken out of her more than that. She must have been truly exhausted to crash out so completely.

However, it was a lovely morning, and so after a couple of mugs of coffee and some toast, Anna decided that what she needed was a head-clearing walk out in the fresh air. Having got up later than intended, she was only going to do her usual morning walk around the grounds, rather than going further afield today, which was when she came upon Hugh Ferguson's memorial tomb in the grounds again, and reread the inscription.

"Oh no!" she gasped aloud as she realised the implication they'd all missed before. "Somebody buried Hugh Ferguson as a Covenanter dissenter. But he was on the other side!" Hugh being one of the ghosts who had proven to be so difficult to dislodge from *Nun's Kirk Haugh Hotel* in recent days, not least because of his centuries old feud with the other ghost, Gideon Corsan, meant she hurried to Gary's cottage to tell him and Rita, "I think I've found some more salt in Hugh's wounds!"

Straightaway, Gary and Anna took Rita out to see Hugh's 'tomb', which lay just under the tangle of the huge rhododendron bushes in the hotel's grounds. Once upon a time, the memorial tomb would have been easily visible, because it lay in a direct line from the staff cottages and remains of the old kirk over to the main building. However, first someone had planted a line of trees in front of the cottages – formerly a stable block – to hide it from the wealthy owners' view, and then a couple of hundred years ago rhododendrons had gone in too, and they were now virtually tree-sized too, with thick trunks and roots. Therefore, since Rita had come to stay and help them with their ghostly and unwanted 'guests', she'd been told of the tomb, but hadn't been there yet.

The carved, rectangular, stone box lurked in the shadows of the great rhododendrons, meaning it was hardly visible from the hotel, which was why it was ignored by most guests. Anna had only spotted it in the first place because she'd been coming up from the river on a different path, and even then it wasn't exactly out in the open. Nor were Anna and Gary that sure that Hugh's remains were actually buried *in* it. Memorials of this type littered the counties of Dumfries and Galloway, but few had the original bodies within them, having been erected many years after the events, all of which added to the problem of where and what Hugh was anchored to.

"Hmph! You can see where the confusion set in," Rita observed. "A full century passed between when Hugh died, and when this was made. *'Murdered by Col. James Douglas'*, I don't think so, do you? No matter how guilty Colonel Douglas was of persecuting people who were Covenanters, we know he wasn't involved in this case. You were right, Gary, if we'd taken this stone as gospel, we'd have been on totally the wrong track."

She referred to the fact that Gary had already told them about eighteenth-century memorial creators, who had possibly never even met so much as the close families of those whom they assumed were martyrs from the religious strife which had afflicted Dumfries and Galloway in the seventeenth century. The ghost of Hugh Ferguson, as named on the tombstone, had been haunting *Nuns' Kirk Haugh* since 1685, along with the man whom he hated, and who had died at the same time, Gideon Corsan; but which man had died where, how, and exactly when, was still a puzzle which needed solving.

"But do you see what I mean?" Anna asked anxiously. "Can Hugh get outside? And if he can, does he pass by this and read, *'for his adherence To the Word of God and Scotland's Covenanted Work of Reformation'* and think, 'No I bloody wasn't!' Or if not, has he heard people down the years talking about the tomb and still been unable to do a thing about it? In his shoes that would be the final insult, foisted onto him and those whom he loved and who had died horrible deaths as witches, when he'd been trying to right those wrongs that already lay a century in the past by the time this was made."

"We really do need to know more about how Hugh died," Gary decided. "I don't like the idea of distressing Hugh all over again, but we can't exactly ask Corsan, can we? And I think if Hugh's mum knew, she'd have told us by now." Hugh's mother, Jannet Corsan, was one of eight women who had died an excruciating death in Dumfries in 1659, executed as witches by strangulation and then burning at the stake – plus another woman who had died of shock witnessing that, and another who had committed suicide rather than burn – and whose deaths Gideon had been an accessory to, even though he'd been too young at the time to have been fully responsible.

"But do you see where this is?" Anna pressed them to see. "We had to come the long way around from our cottages because of the rhododendrons, but actually, we're in line with my cottage and with the hotel, and therefore with the kirk. This lies on or just in front of what was the old kirk's nave floor!"

Nuns' Kirk Haugh had been built out of the remains of a medieval nunnery, and its kirk now only had the nave up to where the chancel arch had been, but once upon a time, an elongated horseshoe-shaped apsidal end had continued on in the direction of where the hotel now lay. But that had long gone and the stone reused in the hotel building. Below the apse as the ground fell away towards the river, there had been a crypt, now filled in, which was where the remains of the tortured women had been thrown, and which now would defeat any attempt by Anna, Rita, and Gary to have their bones buried in proper graves. The ghosts of the last nuns were amongst those whom they had managed to contact, alongside the witches, in what remained of the old kirk's nave which these days adjoined Anna's cottage, and laying them to rest was another problem they needed to solve.

"Now, didn't Gideon say something about the original house not being completed enough for him to enjoy it at the time when he died?" Anna continued. "Because if so, then we've got a few possibilities. If there was much of the old kirk floor still in place, then Hugh might have died outside, but bled out onto those flagstones which then got reused within the house when whoever it was finished it, and him 'travelling' inside with them.

"Or, when the fight happened, did Hugh take a fatal wound somewhere inside what was then the tower-house? But while Gideon crawled away to what we now think might have been his own room to die, Hugh made it outside far enough that whoever found his body *thought* he'd died in a fight outside? Or another alternative is: did Hugh maybe die in the tower, and then his body fall from an incomplete wall, or some wooden scaffolding, to be found outside? Because somewhere along the line, the folk memory or idea of Hugh dying, and his body lying not far from this tomb and *outside* of the main building, had become part of local lore by the time this memorial was made."

Gary sighed. "And if I've learned anything in these last weeks, it's that that's going to matter, isn't it?"

"I'm afraid it is," Rita admitted, "because if his spirit is loitering inside solely because Gideon is inside, then I might have to come out to where he *did* die to help him pass on. We know he can't get much beyond here, because he's not been able to communicate with the ghosts in the remains of the old kirk, but that's not that same as not being able to get this far. If I'm not careful, I could expel him from the house, but then leave him in a horrible kind of limbo out here."

"And we don't want to do that to him," Anna said emphatically, though there was no argument from Rita or Gary.

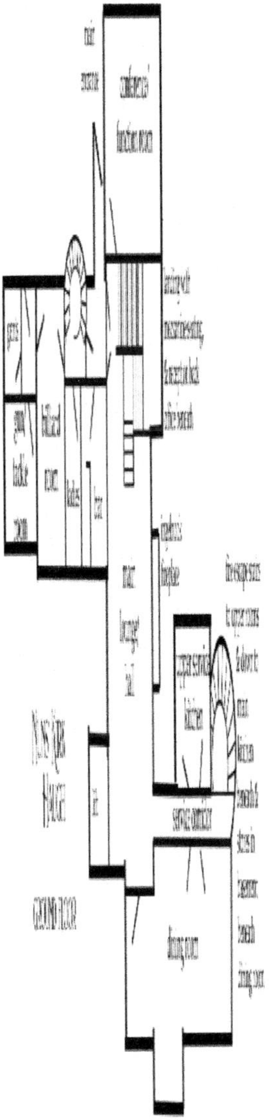

conference/ function room
gents
billiard room
ladies
bar
main lounge/ hall
kitchen
service corridor
dining room
GROUND FLOOR

CHAPTER 2

It resulted in them returning up the housekeeper's stairs for what were starting to feel like friendly chats with their ghost, rather than the kind of psychic battles they'd had with Gideon.

"What happened to you, Hugh?" Anna asked him when he appeared. Once again they had asked Cameron, the newly-returned hotel's owner, to come with them, if only so that he could see the difference between what he'd seen in the hall when they'd chased the ghost of Anna's father-in-law out and Hugh. "I'm sorry it's taken us so long to make the connections, but we've realised that the memorial to you out in the garden is hopelessly wrong. You weren't a Covenanter at all, were you?"

"No! I wasn'a!" Hugh replied vehemently, and out of the corner of her eye, Anna saw Cameron frown in concentration as he tried to follow Hugh's archaic, and therefore stronger, local dialect. "I wasn'a one o' they! They persecuted my ma."

"When your ma, Jannet, was killed," Gary began carefully, "were most folks around here following the Covenant? And were they different to the kind of men who later on hounded Isobel, and the lass called Grissell, who you tried to save? I'm sorry if we sound like we're asking the obvious, but we're so far in your future, the differences aren't clear."

It was well put, because they saw Hugh's ghostly features relax a little. "Aye, I can see that ye' wouldn'a ken the difference if ye're that far down the years. …So tell me this first, what are yon strange boxy things that folk sit in which make that terrible racket? The ones that come right up to the hoose?"

"Ah, those are called motor cars," Gary told him with a grin. "They're a machine that's replaced the horse and cart."

"Ye' don't say?" Hugh replied with a raising of his eyebrows, such as they could see, anyway. "Well, well, things have changed, have they no'. …Machine horses and carts, who'd ha' thought it? …*Hmph*! …Well in that case, I suppose I can forgive ye' for not knowing the differences in ma ain time."

Listening to his responses, Anna couldn't help but think that it was such a shame that she was never going to meet Hugh in the flesh, because he was the kind of person she would have loved to sit down and have a chat with, and talk over all the changes he'd seen come and go. It made her cast a glance Cameron's way, and she was pleased to see him gripped by Hugh's narrative.

"Well then," Hugh began. "When Ma and ma Grandma Grissell were hauled in fer questioning back in 1658, pretty much all o' the folk in these parts were following the Covenant in a rough kinda way. None saw the reason for having some bishop sitting in his fine hoose, laying down the law to us ordinary folk about how to say our prayers. Having a minister saying we could make our ain peace wi' God was something we felt made more sense for us out here in the west.

"But as time went on, things changed. It was, 'thou shalt no' do this', and 'thou shalt no' do that', to the point where a lot o' folks began to think that the presbyters and their Session meetings were actually worse than the bishops. At least we didn'a see the bishops from one year's end to the next! They didn'a bother wi' the likes o' us. The bluidy Kirk Sessions were in our ain backyards, or as near as made nae difference. And they kent us! Kenned us all. Made it too easy to use the Sessions to settle auld grievances, ye' see?"

"Oh, we do!" Rita confirmed. "Nothing like arguments between people who know one another to bring out the worst in them, because of course, you know what will hurt them most. A stranger wouldn't know. But a neighbour would."

Hugh's ghostly head nodded sorrowfully. "And it was the avarice of John McCartney and John Corsan that did the damage. McCartney couldn'a wait for his cousin's widow to die in order for him to get his grubby hands on their croft; while Corsan wanted our croft, and ma aunt and uncle's too. They did a deal, ye' see? Each bringing accusations o' witchcraft to the ones who stood in the other's way. To a court in Edinburgh, if they looked at the papers wi'out knowing the folk involved, there was no collusion, 'cause the names weren't the same."

Gary leaned in to Cameron and explained quietly, "The young widow he's talking about is the ghost called Agnes Clark, who died alongside her sister Margaret, who's also here."

"So did any of what went on in Dumfries get reported to Edinburgh?" Rita asked. "Were their trials that legal, I suppose I'm asking?"

Hugh gave a sniff of disgust. "Ye've hit on the big problem. The Kirk Sessions were a law unto themselves. Edinburgh heard about ma Aunt Marione's case, but only because ma cousin Alex rode there and told them. For the others it was all over with afore any in the capital knew aught of it. That was the danger in the bluidy Covenant. It gave too much power to local men like Veitch, Corsan, and McCartney with nae accountability."

"Was that different later on from when it started?" Anna wondered.

Hugh's sigh may have been in the Other Side, but they still heard it and the sorrow behind it. "By the time ma Ma and the others died, most folk had had enough o' the bluidy Covenant. I ha' nae idea why it clung on so long down here in Dumfriesshire, Kirkcudbrightshire, and Wigtownshire, but it did. Elsewhere, folk just wanted things to go back to the way they'd been. Going to kirk on a Sunday, listening to the minister, and then getting on wi' their lives for the rest o' the week. Here? Even to this day, wi' all these years to think on it, I'm still no' sure who truly believed the Covenant and that nae other way was right, and who was just too scairt to admit they'd had enough in case their neighbours turned on them."

"That's terrible," Anna sympathised.

"Aye, it was. At least in Grandma and Grandpa's day, we kenned who the enemy was. It was that bluidy Presbyter, Veitch, and his like – and he'd been known as a right bastard for years already. But later on, any woman who had a bit o' knowledge about healing and the like, was in danger from both sides, and worse, so was anyone who'd consulted her or traded wi' her. If yer neighbour was taken in to be questioned, ye' could be in danger for havin' done nothing more than speak to her of a morning! The Episcopalians were determined to take a hard line wi' any deviant, and that included those they thought might be witches, as well as Covenanters. And the Covenanters were convinced that a witch, alongside a Catholic or supporter of bishops, were just two sides o' the same Devil's coin, and both were bad."

"Good grief," Anna sighed. "And yet I'm guessing it was a different story when someone's wife got into difficulties giving birth, or someone got sick and never got better by themselves?"

"Ye' have it exactly."

“Hugh,” Rita said gently, “which side was your enemy, Gideon Corsan, on?”

“Him? Oh! He was a Covenanter! nae doubt about that. He was ever heeling Veitch and his guard dog McBurney, fawning around them.”

“So you were very much on opposite sides?”

“Aye! I saw him at the battle at Bothwell Bridge wi’ the rest o’ the rabble. Sword in his hand, baying for blood! You dinna do that if ye’re half-hearted about something. Damn near got him that time too. Put a musket ball in him for certain, though clearly I didn’a kill him that time. There’s something warped and cruel about Corsan, just as there was in his cursed faither.”

“Good grief, it’s very personal for you, isn’t it,” Anna observed sympathetically, yet thinking that from Gideon’s point of view, his hatred was also now a bit more understandable knowing he’d been shot by Hugh. “So he was a soldier too?”

“Him? *Hmph!*” Hugh snorted. “No’ in any official capacity, o’ that I’m sure. Those he fought wi’ were naught but a crowd o’ men and lads spoiling for a fight, and most turned tail and ran when they realised just what they were up against. We took over a thousand prisoners that day, ye’ ken, but five times that just disappeared. Went to ground and didn’a show their faces to any who might ha’ recognised them from Bothwell. The rabble-rousing ministers never got an army like that together ever again. Only the real fervent believers carried on actually fighting, though many still crept out into wilds to hear them preach.”

"And was Gideon a true believer?" Rita wondered, but Hugh could only shrug and say,

"I dinna ken. I never saw him actually fight again, that's for sure. Not until here. Not until *that* day."

"The day you died?" checked Rita and got a firm nod this time. "So where in the house did you die, Hugh? Only we're now pretty sure that Gideon died in the first-floor bedroom we've chased him out of. Yet we meet you up here in the tower room. Was it here?"

She thought it was a simple question, yet Hugh seemed uncertain.

"I took ma last wound on the stairs below here," he began. "And I recall crawling up here into this room wi' the blood pumping out o' me, though it wasn'a a proper room back then."

"In what way?" Anna gently prompted him.

"Well, there was the doorway to the stairs up to here, and a fair bit o' wall, but none o' the window panes were in, though the frames were done, nor was the roof fully done on the inside at least, though the tiles were on. I think I leaned on the wall, but then I have the briefest feeling o' going backwards, though no' far."

"That's why they thought you'd died outside," Rita said, thinking that they'd answered the question, "because you did. You were wounded up here but died out there from the fall."

But Hugh only looked perplexed. "I have nae recollection o' falling, much less the landing killing me."

Yet it was Gary who made sense of it. "I think you *did* die here, Hugh, but in your last moments, you either fell out of one of the window spaces, or you put your weight on a section of wall where the mortar possibly wasn't dry, or not that good, and it gave way. That could be why you have no recollection of falling. You'd already passed over by then. Or it could be that by the time the tomb was made, they simply assumed that you – as someone not of the gentry – would never have been allowed inside the house anyway, therefore you *must* have died outside."

Hugh considered this and then nodded. "Aye. I think ye' have the right o' it." He looked around him. "'Tis a bonnier place nowadays than when Corsan built it. When he's nae around, I quite like it up here. 'Tis peaceful, and I like watching the birds perching on the roof and the squirrels in the trees I can see. And the ladies who come in here…they're pleasant souls. Nae arguing and fighting. There was, once upon a time in the years in between then and now, young lassies who all had to squeeze in here to sleep, and all fighting for the beds away from the windows on account o' the cold."

"They'd have been the servants when this was a big house," Anna guessed. "Yes, I can understand that. I didn't spend that long in the other tower where the servants slept, but even with our modern heating, I was very glad we didn't have a cold winter. And they'd have had no heat up here at all. It must have been perishing!" Then a thought struck her. "Did any of them ever die up here?"

Hugh's expression became sad. "Aye, a few. A few did. I stayed wi' them while they passed. The feeling o' someone leaving this world always brought Corsan to the door, ye' see? And I couldn'a bear the thought o' him tormenting some poor lass in this in-between space the way he did Elspeth, Isobel, and young Grissell in life. I could always hear him a hammering on the door, calling to them to no' stay wi' me but to come away wi' him. How he'd make them a queen in their ain castle. Bluidy loon! The best thing for them was to be gone to the Light as fast as possible, no' lingering around here wi' us two knocking each other about."

Rita carefully suggested, "It sounds as though you wouldn't mind moving on as long as you knew that Gideon was gone too, and that your mother and the other ladies had as well?"

He didn't have to say a word for them to read his face. Hugh had long ago had enough of being in limbo. It was only his need to protect others – and women specifically – from Gideon Corsan which was keeping him here.

"Bear with me, Hugh," Rita told him gently. "I'm working on releasing his grip on this place. But would it salve your soul a little if we could get that inscription amended to tell the truth? That you were no Covenanter, and were killed by Gideon Corsan, not Colonel Douglas?"

This time Hugh's smile was brighter. "Aye, that would be grand. Yon Douglas was no bluidy soldier, ye' know. No' half the bonnie fighter that Claverhouse was. Douglas was a political animal, always playing on his family connections, but wi' no thought for the suffering of the ordinary folk. So it's no' that I care about Douglas being blamed for a killing he didn'a do – because God knows he got away with killing many who didn'a deserve to die. No, it's that it galls me that Corsan does no' get the blame he deserves! And no' just for my death, but for the others, too."

Leaving Hugh in his eyrie, the four trooped down the stairs and took refuge in the bar area, which was not one of the areas that had been part of the original tower-house that Gideon and Hugh had known, and therefore was a place where they weren't likely to unwittingly summon Gideon. Since he'd been ousted from the hotel's Rosemary suite, they didn't know where else he might linger, though the stairs were looking like a good candidate at the moment, since that was where he'd appeared from when John Coleborn had died.

"I see what you mean about this being very personal between them," Cameron said, as Gary went in search of mugs of coffee for each of them. "Not having been here when you did the deed, I didn't realise quite how stuck in the hotel they've become."

"They have," Anna sighed, "and we think they've virtually barricaded different parts against one another in that in-between world in a way they couldn't do in reality. That's why everything Aunty Rita tried the first time – thinking that they were just regular ghosts a bit attached to somewhere they'd once known – didn't have the effect it should have. It's not just the house, it's each other that are keeping them here."

Gary returned with the coffees at the end of what Anna was saying and added, "I hate to be the voice of gloom, but that memorial tomb – which almost certainly doesn't have a body in it at all – is of itself a late-Georgian artefact in its own right. I can't see the local authority letting us whack lumps off it, because how on earth could we explain that we've been talking to the man it commemorates, when he's been dead for over three centuries?"

"Would we need permission?" wondered Rita. But Cameron was already nodding at Gary's words, adding,

"I'm afraid so. And I know that because having recently looked at the deeds to this place, I can tell you that there's an add-on about that tomb, and the requirement to keep it in good nick, and not let it crumble away."

"Bugger!" Anna said with feeling. "That's really made life complicated."

"I don't mind paying for a nice brass plaque," Cameron offered. "Something we could stick on a post beside the tomb, putting the history right for anyone who goes to look at it." And he was rewarded with an approving smile from Anna.

"Oh yes! That would be a really good start. Thank you, Cameron. That's a really generous gesture." But he noted that he wasn't yet back to being called Cam. That familiarity was something he was going to have to prove himself for.

1661

Elspeth

Elspeth held the hand of her young niece, Jonet, as they watched the men folk carrying her sister Mailie's body to the kirk for burial. While wee Jonet was understandably sobbing, for Elspeth tears were harder come by. She hadn't seen Mailie since the day she'd left their croft in Dumfriesshire all the way back in 1645, until Elspeth with her new husband, Alex, arrived with Sorley McAllister in the village last year. Fifteen years was a lot of time lost, but worse for Elspeth, while Mailie had been delighted to be reunited with their father, Johnne Allen, her reception of her younger sister had been very lukewarm.

"Don't go bringing any accusations o' witching to our door, sister!" had been the first hissed warning, before Elspeth and Alex had barely set foot through the door. It was hardly the loving embrace of family that Elspeth had been praying for every step of the long walk up to Argyll. And for her lovely Alex it had been no easier. He'd hated being called Sandy, which was the normal shortening of Alexander and which all the locals immediately called him, and although he'd helped his own mother and father on their previous croft, farming in the Highlands was an altogether tougher prospect. About the only thing that could be said was that Mailie's Niall had been glad of an extra pair of hands to help work the thin and stony soil. Niall's main croft land was not down on the fertile soil of the valley but up on the slopes, though he had his share of the runrigs – shared strip fields – and only later was Elspeth to learn why.

Had it not been for the generosity of Sorley McAllister and his family, Elspeth dreaded to think what would have become of Marione Corsan and Samwell Black, Alex's parents, because from the first day it was made clear that there would be no room found for them in Mailie's home – and they soon discovered that Niall might be the man of the household, but he did what Mailie said inside the house. Marione was an accused witch, even if she'd never been found guilty, but that didn't matter to Mailie. The accusation was enough to turn her against Marione, fearful that once again accusations would be flung at herself. Mailie had become a very paranoid woman, yet wouldn't open up to the newcomers as to why.

That lack of welcome was something that Sorley was less than happy about. After all, he had been the one to promise them all a warm welcome, and Sorley and his extended family had been the ones to support Mailie and Niall when they'd first arrived with nothing but the clothes on their backs, and had helped find them the croft. As the months went by, and Mailie's welcome got no warmer, Sorley became more and more disgusted with her and Niall.

"This is no' our way," he was often heard muttering as he cast disgusted looks in Mailie's direction. "None but the lairds are rich up here. We all work together or we all starve together."

It didn't take long for Elspeth to learn that that didn't apply when clan rivalries came into play, but the days of pitched battles between clans were long gone, though a spot of cattle thieving was still considered fair game. And it was Sorley who found a place for young Hugh Ferguson in the militia of the local Campbell laird, for which Elspeth was very grateful. Hugh had been such a staunch helper when she had needed one the most, alongside Alex, who was Hugh's older cousin.

Without both of them, Elspeth knew that her much-loved and now departed mother, Jonet, wouldn't have lived as long as she had. Though these days, Elspeth sometimes wondered whether it might not have been better for Jonet to die in the cellars of Irongray Manse, rather than see her two nieces strangled and burned as witches at Dumfries Tolbooth along with the others. That horrific day was forever seared into Elspeth's memory, and even now, over a year on, she still woke from her nightmares screaming. That was another thing Mailie had had no patience with, yet Elspeth wondered how she would have fared had she seen that dreadful sight.

It only took a year to the day of arriving in Argyll for Samwell and Marione to quietly tell Alex and Elspeth that they were leaving, for Hugh's father James – Marione's brother-in-law – had died on the journey north, having lost the will to live when Hugh's mother had been strangled and burned alongside Elspeth's cousins. Only Johnne Allen, Elspeth's father would be left of that generation now, but Marione had wept, "We'll be forever Lowlanders to these folk. If we live here ten years or more, we'll not be one of them. I'd rather take my chances further south where we're not treated as outlanders all of the time."

Samwell had had a more practical reason for leaving, telling his son, "I've the chance of a job at a grain merchant's not far from Edinburgh. It's not Dumfriesshire, but at least it's back in civilisation," and Elspeth recalled him looking in dismay at the ragged children running barefoot around the runrig fields.

"Don't leave it too long to come and find us, son," Samwell told Alex as he and Marione shouldered the packs with their few rescued belongings in. Somehow the family pony had become subsumed into the village ponies as some kind of payment for keeping them this long, and so some of what Samwell and Marione had brought north had to be left with Alex and Elspeth.

All of which brought Elspeth and Alex to a new quandary now that Mailie had died. Niall desperately needed Elspeth to care for young Jonet and James, who was only a couple of years older than his sister, and too small to do much of the work in the fields. Yet Alex was a man, eating a man's portion of the food, but with no prospect of ever being able to do more than use the strength in his arms on Niall's croft. There was no unclaimed cultivatable land where they might find a place for themselves. And Elspeth could see how day by day that lack of any kind of respect was eating away at Alex. Moreover, with Mailie now dead, there was little familial obligation on Niall to keep his late wife's sister and husband, and Elspeth feared that sooner or later he would be asking them to leave, especially once the two little children wouldn't need her constant care.

As Mailie's body in the winding sheet was lowered into her grave, Elspeth took the hands of Jonet and James once more and gave them a tug.

"Come on," she said gently. "You're both frozen in this wind. Let's go home and get you warm." She could see closer to the grave the older two sons standing supporting their grieving father, but somehow the younger two always got excluded from this close trio. It was most bizarre.

For Elspeth, who had long been craving to have a child of her own, it was hard to see these two young ones disregarded, and she'd had no hesitation in stepping in to look after them right from when they'd arrived – one thing which Mailie hadn't complained about, strangely. For a woman who was as territorial as Mailie, it struck Elspeth as odd that she was almost glad to have her take the two youngsters off her hands. Yet Mailie fussed over Callum and William, the two older boys, who almost seemed to resent her affections. That was even more peculiar. Did Callum and William somehow hold Mailie responsible for something? But nobody ever seemed willing to speak about what had gone on, and Sorley was away too often for Elspeth to find a chance to ask him.

Autumn turned into winter and the year changed, and yet the harvest was poor. Nothing Alex was capable of could help Niall stretch the meagre grain and vegetables any further. Almost worse, after waiting and hoping and praying for so long, Elspeth finally found herself with child, with a tough pregnancy rendering her incapable of helping in the fields when she was sick from dawn to dusk. However, when the longed for baby girl was born in the late spring of 1662, even that was tainted with sadness, because Elspeth would have loved to call her after her own mother, Jonet, but they already had Mailie's little Jonet in their single-roomed cot with them. By now the two youngest had been expelled from the main cottage, and were in what had previously been a byre with Elspeth and Alex. Two Jonets in the same generation in the same house simply wasn't practical. And so the baby was called Marione, after Alex's mother, and Elspeth tried to be happy for Alex's sake. It didn't dull the ache in her soul, though.

However, she did finally discover why Niall seemed to become ever more detached from his two youngest children. As soon as she could walk that far after the birth, Elspeth had gathered winter foliage and made a wreath to take to her sister's grave. She had seen Niall walking out of the village to the kirkyard on Sundays with a posy of whatever flowers were growing at the time, and so she felt guilty that she'd laid none of her own.

Yet when she got to Maillie's grave there was no sign of any flowers ever having been there. Indeed, the path to her grave was overgrown and looked as if nobody had been there since it had been filled in. And then she saw him. Niall was standing weeping at another grave with another token of his affection, which he bent and put on that grave, before turning and striding away.

Suddenly furious, Elspeth stamped over to the other grave. How dare he disrespect her sister like that! It had puzzled her ever since she got here how her sunny-tempered sister had turned into the crosspatch they'd met, quietly blaming the tough life her sister had led in those years in between. But now it occurred to her that if she discovered that her husband's affections were elsewhere, that might account for a lot.

The little kirkyard served a cluster of small hamlets, none of which was large enough to have a kirk of its own, and Elspeth knew that Niall had originally come from the one north of the kirk, whereas they were south of it. So no wonder she had never come across whoever this woman's family was. And there it was on the simple wooden cross:

Jonet Fraser
Loving wife of Niall Munro
And deeply missed mother
Of Callum and William

"His *wife*?" Elspeth almost screamed with rage. Her sister had been second best! "Oh that is the bitter end! He doesn't love Jamie and Jonet becau…God in Heaven! The bastard! …He named their daughter after his dead wife, not our ma," and she sobbed. How could she ever tell her father this? And now, of all times, when Mailie had gone to join their mother, leaving Johnne heartbroken all over again.

Then another realisation dawned. "Oh God! Callum and William aren't Mailie's. They're *hers*!"

Then a woman's voice came from beside her,

"Ye'll be Mailie's sister, then?"

Scrubbing her tears away with the heels of her palms, Elspeth looked around to see a grey-haired woman.

"I see ye've found my daughter's grave," the woman continued with a bitter sigh, stunning Elspeth before she could reply. "We thought when Niall brought yer sister home as his new wife that it was proof of what we'd always thought o' Niall – that his passion for our Jonet was a lad's passion that wouldn'a stand the test o' time."

"You were against the marriage?" Elspeth managed to choke out.

"Oh, verra much so," the lady said without hesitation. "Niall came to our farm as an orphaned boy to become our ploughman's help. To my man Angus' and my eyes, he had no prospects, no chance to improve his lot. And what parents would we have been if we'd not wanted to stop our only surviving daughter wed into what amounted to poverty?

"But Jonet adored him, and he her, and by the time they were old enough to wed without our consent, we knew they would. So we gritted our teeth and welcomed him into the farmhouse. And Callum and William came along pretty fast after they did wed, and we couldn'a see them going wi'out."

"How old were they when their mother died?" Elspeth asked gently.

"Oh, five and six, but Jonet had had two miscarriages after them before the bairn who took them both. Well, Niall was inconsolable. So much so that I had to intervene and take on the care o' Callum and Willie or the poor lads would ha' starved. Ach! The man was no use to himself or anyone else.

"My Angus told him, 'ye' have to pull yerself together for the sake o' yer sons,' but it did no good. A year on and more men were being rounded up to go and fight by the Campbell's bailie, and I'm no' ashamed to admit we shoved Niall into Bailie Murchison's hands, glad to be free o' him."

"I can see how you would have been," Elspeth sympathised. The poor woman had to be nearly as old as her own parents, and she herself would never dream of leaving her children solely in Johnne's care at his age. He loved Mailie's two youngsters dearly, but she saw how they wore him out with their boundless energy, even after they'd helped out around the farmyard.

"He was hopeless around the boys, ye' see," Goodwife Fraser expanded. "One moment he was spoiling them rotten, the next weeping all over them. And no discipline, no discipline at all. I'm no' one o' those who believes in beating children for no reason, but sometimes ye' have to stand firm for their own good."

"And Niall wouldn't?"

Goodwife Fraser shook her head with a shiver at the memories. "No' at all. They were well on the way to being uncontrollable, causing trouble wi' others, no' just us. So wi' him gone, Angus was able to put his foot down more. 'Twas hard on them, and as hard on us, for we didn'a do it to be cruel."

"I'm sure not," Elspeth sympathised. "Children have to know not to mess with fire and other things for their own safety."

Goodwife Fraser looked at her with relief. "At least you see it. And from what my friend Mary tells me, ye've been a good influence on young Jonet and Jamie."

"I try to remember how my own ma was and take that as guidance," Elspeth admitted, "though in truth I was the youngest, so I never saw her deal with anyone younger than me, only older."

"Well ye' do yer ma proud," the older woman said warmly, with a smile. "Back when my Jonet was alive I saw how poor that croft was that ye' now work with Niall. Sorley McAllister has a good heart, and he did Niall a better turn than he deserved when he helped him take on that croft when old man McAndrew died wi'out anyone to succeed him. But the intent was always that Niall would try to better himself, no' just plod on wi' the place as it was," and she gave a snort of disgust.

"Wi'out Jonet there to push him onwards, he's become as stagnant as the old mill pond now that the mill's moved. When he came back from the war wi' yer sister, I was shocked that he asked for Callum and William back. ...Wondered, in truth, what yer sister was thinking to be saddled straight away wi' two boys she'd no' had chance to get to know.

"Then I heard about how she'd lost two weans of her own on the road – two girls, mind – and I hoped that maybe she was feeling the need to be a mother, even if it wasn'a to her own. Sorley had told folks that she'd had a rough time o' it being dragged down to England by the girls' father, and I wondered whether she feared she might no' be able to have more. Well she got wi' young Jamie after a while, and we prayed it might settle Niall down. But then the flowers started appearing on our Jonet's grave, and even afore young Jonet was born, my friend Mary started telling me about how things were no' so good between him and Mailie."

Elspeth gave a sigh of her own. "I'm guessing that once he was back here, Niall kept seeing Jonet's ghost at every turn? Or at least his memories of her. And perhaps while he'd thought he could replace Jonet with Mailie when they were far away, once here, all he ended up doing was comparing Mailie to Jonet, and finding her wanting?"

Goodwife Fraser nodded sadly. "I didn'a want to see my daughter replaced, but I didn'a want to see Mailie treated like that, either. She loved him all right, or at least she did when they first arrived, and when wee Jamie was born. But it was the way that Niall never seemed to see past Callum and Willie to Jamie that fair broke my heart. And then he went and named the wee lass Jonet, which I though downright cruel."

"Our ma was Jonet," Elspeth told her and saw her surprise.

"Oh! So maybe it was no' the only reason that name was chosen?"

Yet Elspeth felt the tears flowing unbidden again. "No, I think it was doubly a slight. You see, my ma' was accused as a witch, taken in for questioning by a vile presbyter named Veitch. That was when Mailie and our older sister were still small. After that, Ma was never quite the same, but I was born a couple of years after that, so I only ever knew Ma the way she was after she'd been broken. But Mailie left home as soon as she could, because our oldest sister Joan had married a fire-and-brimstone Covenanter, and she filled Mailie's head with how we were cursed by association with

Ma. There's no way she'd have named her daughter after Ma. Mailie's first words to me when we arrived, and I was alone with her, were not to bring any such damnation down on them here."

"Ach, that's wicked!" Goodwife Fraser gasped, coming to wrap a motherly arm around Elspeth's shoulders. "What a thing to accuse yer ain sister of! Yet ye're the one loving and caring for wee Jonet and Jamie, while Mailie only rejected them and instead tried to show Niall what a good mother she was being to Callum and Willie."

"Mailie always loved the boys," Elspeth managed to sniffle, "but I never thought she'd favour a man over her own children. And certainly not enough to stand back and let him call *her* daughter after his first wife."

"Some women are strange that way," sighed Goodwife Fraser. "I'm Clara, by the way."

"I'm very glad to have met you, Clara," Elspeth said warmly. "You've made so much clear to me. Alex and I have already talked about leaving, but it was the leaving behind of Jonet and Jamie that bothered us most. But now I see that Niall won't even notice if we take them. Callum and Willie are almost old enough not to need a mother's care for the most part, and they have you close by, but Jonet and Jamie aren't your responsibility if Niall stops taking notice of the world."

"Ye'll do right by the two weans, then?"

Elspeth nodded.

“That’s a huge relief,” Clara Fraser said from the heart. “Ye’re a good woman, Elspeth, and I won’t hear a word said otherwise.”

Yet Johnne Allen’s health took a turn for the worse, and for the next few months all Elspeth could do was stay and nurse him.

CHAPTER 3

Anna didn't have time to do much more on Tuesday, but Gary was very firm with her, saying,

"You're supposed to be taking time off. That means from the ghost hunt too, you know. A few days aren't going to make any difference right now. We've no big weddings in for a couple of weeks, so take yourself out somewhere and relax."

"Yes, Dad," she said, throwing him a mock salute and a grin. After a lifetime of indifferent parents, it was lovely to have someone genuinely caring about what happened to her without trying to overwhelm her.

And Gary's affectionate reprimand of, "Cheeky bugger!" even as he was grinning back at her, was so different to the way anyone else had responded to her, but in the best kind of way.

She was then surprised that Cameron appeared at her door the next morning, and was greeted effusively by Harris and Lewis, his two hounds whom he had abandoned with Anna and Gary while he went to Edinburgh to pack up his flat there.

"Would you like to take a run down to Wigtown?" he asked warily, clearly wondering whether he'd overstepped a line when he'd kissed her. "Gary says there's a lovely walk along the estuary a bit further down the coast at the Isle of Whithorn, and I thought with it being a dry day, the lads might appreciate a longer walk."

Phrased like that, it was hard for Anna to refuse, and in truth, travelling in Cameron's rather nice Mercedes estate was going to be more comfortable than her elderly Fiesta. Indeed, Anna was rather worried whether the Fiesta would even pass its next MOT, so she was grateful not to put any more wear and tear on it than necessary – just in case she had to use it to leave and go somewhere else. It was a daft thought, she knew. Cameron had made it plain that he thought she was doing a first-class job as manager of the hotel, but having spent so many years working for derisory bosses, who used her when it suited them, but then denied her any promotion, she hadn't quite managed to shake off the dread of disaster looming.

So, armed with plenty of old towels in case Harris and Lewis went into the water, they set off for the lovely little town down on the Solway estuary.

"I'm dead keen to see the place," Cameron confessed. "I feel like I missed all the fun when you and Gary and Rita came here. Packing up my flat wasn't half as interesting."

Anna smiled, but said, “I wouldn’t call it fun. Kirkcudbright was just Gary and Rita, so I haven’t seen it yet, either. And Whithorn is a bit too far for me to risk taking my old car, so I only saw it briefly with Gary and Aunty Rita.” She didn’t feel up to explaining about Rita having a massive hissy fit that day, meaning they’d hardly spent any time there. “Anyway, I had to work because of the impending wedding, so I missed out as much as you.”

“Oh. Right.” Clearly Cameron hadn’t quite got his head around how stressful that run up to her first wedding as the organiser had been, not least because of the danger of Gideon Corsan’s ghost invading the bridal suite. But he covered it well by adding, “Really well done with that wedding by the way. We had a letter from the bride’s mum and dad this morning singing everyone’s praises. They’re over the moon at the way you all made adjustments for the bride’s disabilities. It’s so good that I’m hoping they let us use some quotes in promotional advertising. Reviews by real guests like that are worth their weight in gold. …But I hadn’t realised that you haven’t been to explore Kirkcudbright either. Somehow I thought you were with them that day?”

“Only later that day, when we all went to try and put Geillis to rest in Irongray kirkyard,” Anna explained, “but the atmosphere there was still too toxic for her to leave the others. Rita wasn’t able to call Grissell McCartney home to rest in Kirkcudbright when she tried earlier, either – that’s Hugh’s grandmother, in case you’d lost track.

That's part of what makes this ghostly feud so toxic. Grissell's father was a first-cousin to the awful John McCartney's father, so they were family."

"And John McCartney is one of those who brought the poor accused witches to their deaths, wasn't he?"

"That's right. John wanted his own cousin Donald's croft, when Donald died and his widow Agnes was still young enough to have lived on for many years yet. He was hand in glove with John Corsan, who had his own agenda, and to my mind was the even greater villain – and who, by the way, was Hugh's *grandfather*'s cousin, so poor Hugh has both villains on each side of his maternal grandparents' family.

"I've now found that John McCartney had his own land at a place called Senwick, which is near Kirkcudbright and a little place called Borgue, meaning in those days it must have been a bit of a jaunt for him to get up to Dumfries for serious business. We think that's why he was keen to get his sticky paws on a place closer, where he could travel there and back to Dumfries in a day. But there's no doubt that he knew who the women from Kirkcudbright were whom he threw accusations at, even if their deaths directly benefited his co-conspirator, not him. There's no excuse for him – he knew he was taking what he had no right to, and was as good as committing murder to get it."

"Wow! No wonder things are so acrimonious between Hugh and the other ghost. That's a lot of family bad blood to get over."

"It is. It really doesn't help that poor persecuted Grissell McCartney married William Corsan, first-cousin to the dreadful John Corsan. With generations often overlapping one another in those days, Gideon – as one of John's sons – was only a year or two older than Hugh, from what Hugh's said, even though they were technically a generation apart, since Gideon was Hugh's mum's first-cousin, rather than his."

"So, it's Hugh's Grandma Grissell who Rita wanted to lay to rest at Kirkcudbright?" Cameron checked. "What about his mum? Grissell was his maternal gran, wasn't she?"

"She was. And yes, Jannet Corsan, who was married to James Ferguson, is Hugh's mum and also Grissell and William's daughter, and her ghost is still hanging on in the old kirk at *Nuns' Kirk Haugh*, unable to let go until she knows that Hugh is okay. So you see, we really do have to settle everyone down and get rid of Gideon, at which point I think Hugh will gladly move on. But he has to know that Gideon has gone, and none of the women in his family are lingering here to be persecuted if Gideon sneaks back."

"Can he sneak back? Is that even possible?"

"Once he's gone to the Light, no. Or at least, not according to Aunty Rita. She's the expert here, not me."

"That's a relief. So when we've done it once, we shouldn't have to do it again?"

"No. Not as far as I'm aware."

They drove on in comfortable silence for a while, though Anna's mind was still whirling as she watched the tapestry of farm fields passing by. For a couple of days now, she'd had the feeling that she was missing something vital. Something which could be key to getting the ghosts to leave, yet it wouldn't come forward no matter how hard she thought.

Yet one thing she did realise was that she needed to know a lot more about what had gone on in Kirkcudbright. Nine women had died in Dumfries on that day in 1659, though of the nine condemned to be burned, the one called Bigis Cairnes had committed suicide the night before, according to the records she'd seen. Meanwhile, she now knew that Jonet Clark – mum of Hugh's beloved Elspeth – had collapsed and died at the scene from the shock of seeing the burnings, bringing the number of actual women's deaths back up to nine on the day, because even though she'd been accused of being a witch, she'd not been put on trial that time. But that left eight women who had gone through the horrific trial of strangulation and then burning, and she only knew anything much about Agnes and Margaret Clark, and Jannet Corsan, Hugh's mother. Were the others relevant to the story, and if so, how did they connect to it?

"Penny for your thoughts?" Cameron said, bringing her back to reality. "You were far away there."

"Yes, I was. I was thinking that I need to know more about the other women who died with Hugh's mum, and who of them were from Kirkcudbright. Why all those deaths from there? Why them?"

To her surprise, Cameron seemed to be taking her more seriously than she'd expected, but his next words really shook her. "And you have to learn how on earth they connect to you, don't you?" He glanced away from the road and saw her shocked expression. "You'd forgotten that, hadn't you? Who was it, of the lady ghosts in the old kirk, who said they could feel a connection to you?"

"Erm, it was Jonet Clark, who is…was…Agnes and Margaret Clark's aunt and our missing Elspeth's mum, but yes, they could 'feel' me too. It was a bit creepy to be honest, which is why I think I kind of blocked it out once we were done that time."

"But I don't think you can ignore it," Cameron said gently. "Truly, I'm not trying to freak you out, but of anyone, I think you might be the one who can sort this out. Somewhere along the line, pretty much all of the ghosts except those of the original nuns, relate to you on an emotional level, if no other."

He didn't want to labour his growing belief, given how much it seemed to be bothering her, that both male ghosts had some ancestral link to Anna. And who wouldn't be a bit freaked out, knowing that two ghosts who'd fought down the centuries might yet end up fighting over you?

"I meant it when I said we should start looking at your family tree, Anna. On both sides! If your dad has links to this part of Scotland through his father…"

"…*Urgh*! The dreadful Dennis the Menace."

Cameron laughed. "Appropriate though that nickname might be, what was his actual name? I mean, what name are we searching through the records for?"

"Oh. Dennis Arnold Gracie, the same surname as my maiden name and the one I've never stopped using."

Cameron rolled his eyes. "Okay, I'm a twit for asking that, because Gary told me that you never took on your married name. And of course we sorted your father's surname out when we booked him into the hotel under his own name of Gordon Gracie, didn't we? And anyway, the fact that it was your father-in-law who died, John Coleborn, ought to have told me that you'd be Mrs Coleborn, but you're being paid as Anna Gracie." He shook his head with a good-natured laugh. "Clearly I'm not HR management material!"

Anna laughed with him. "You're excused. Dealing with your own family stuff, and then coming back to ghosts all over the place and a dead body is enough to throw anyone off kilter. …But seriously, it's really thrown me too. I had no idea that Dad had connections to here through his father."

"Did you not know him, then? Only you never refer to him as 'granddad'. Did he die before you were born?"

"No. He was just what they'd call up here 'crabbit'. Couldn't stand kids. Never wanted to have anything to do with my older brother and sister, let alone me. And with me being Mum and Dad's 'afterthought', it meant that I never really questioned it when I was later told he'd died when I was about five or six. There was nothing to miss, you see.

"But what I'm now realising is rather more peculiar are Mum's parents. With Dad's parents both being dead once I was old enough to take notice, I kind of assumed that Mum's were too. The only one of her family I ever encountered was her maiden aunt – the one who left me the money which became the deposit on my flat. Great-Aunty Morag was someone I met a few times, but only because she'd come to live down in England with her job, I now recall. But it's just come back to me that when she died, I overheard Mum and Dad talking, and them saying something about her being Mum's father's much *older* sister. So if that was the case, and she died in her late eighties, it should have made me wonder how old my maternal grandpa was – I mean, how much is *much* older? Eight years? Twelve years? And where the heck were he and my grandma?"

"Did you never question it before?" Cameron asked in surprise.

"Errr… No. Actually I didn't, even though I was coming up twenty at the time. I think because Mum and Dad were so wrapped up in being a couple that even us kids were something of an intrusion – something we were made very aware of – I was kind of indifferent to the rest of their families, assuming that they'd be more of the same.

With them having had my brother and sister in their very early twenties…" She suddenly clasped a hand to her mouth, looking shocked.

"Anna? Are you okay?" Cameron asked anxiously, wondering if he was going to have to slam on the brakes for her to dive out and be sick.

She took a deep breath. "God, I'm so stupid!"

"No, you're not. Why do you say that?"

"Because I've never done the basic maths. What an idiot! I knew that Mum was only just twenty when she had Heather. But they must have *had* to get married, and I've suddenly worked that out because I remember their silver wedding anniversary coming around, and how old Heather was at the time. …God! How did I not spot that?

"And then Nigel came along just two years later. So with there being twelve years between me and Heather, Mum could only have been thirty-two when she had me. I was nowhere near being a *menopause* mistake, though that was kind of implied if I ever asked why the long gap between me and the other two." She tutted. "You accept so much of what you're told as a kid, don't you? Especially if asking questions gets you grief from your parents. But more than that, Cam, Mum's only in her early sixties *now*, so potentially her parents could still be alive if they too married and had her young. Okay, they might be into their eighties, but these days that's not unusual. And even if they died in their seventies, how come I never heard about it? I was an adult by then."

"And your parents never talk about them?"

"Never! It's like they cut all contact with that side of the family even before I was born. It was different with Aunty Rita, because she's on Dad's side and she made the first move. *She* wanted to know *me*, rather than me going and seeking *her* out."

"Yeah, I see what you mean," Cameron said, skilfully manoeuvring the Mercedes into a parking spot in the central square in Wigtown, right outside a rather imposing building and a war memorial. "If your parents were *that* detached, why wouldn't you assume that the rest of the family didn't give a damn about you?"

"That was exactly it."

"So do you know anything at all about your mum's family?"

"Beyond the fact that her maiden name was Clarke? No. Great-Aunty Morag was Morag Clarke, because of course, she'd never married, so kept her family's name regardless of any conventions about married women keeping maiden names up here. And let's face it, it's a common enough name pretty much anywhere, isn't it?"

"Right. So we're really going to have to trace your mum back right from the point of her marriage certificate to your dad to make sure we've got the right person." He looked at her enquiringly.

"What?"

"Well what is her name? Mrs Gracie isn't going to get us very far, is it?" though he said it with a laugh, and not criticism of her for not having told him already.

"Oh! *Duh*! Silly me. She would have been Euphemia Clarke before she married Dad."

"Euphemia? Bloody hell! Which century did they dredge that one up from?"

Anna laughed. "I'm told it's an old family name." Then she stopped in surprise. "In fact, that's about the only thing I was ever told about Mum's family. That the oldest girl always had Euphemia as her first name, even if she didn't use it. Mum always used one of her middle names – Belinda."

"*One* of her middle names? Good grief, Anna! How many did she have?"

"Euphemia Belinda Grier… Oh fucking hell!"

"What?"

"Grierson. Her last but one name was Grierson!"

"That's not so odd in Scotland, you know. My maternal granny was Flora Bruce McCall, Bruce being her mum's maiden name. It's quite normal up here. So your mum's mother's family were Griersons – that'll help."

"But…!" Suddenly Anna remembered that Cameron hadn't been with them at that point either. "Oh shit! You don't know this bit, do you?"

"What bit?"

"Well, the two women who Hugh tried to protect later on in his life, and after Elspeth had left, were Isobel Milligan – daughter of Elspeth's cousin Margaret who burned as a witch, and who is the link to Wigtown – and a younger girl called Grissell Asman. And they were prosecuted – and I do mean *pros*ecuted, not *pers*ecuted, though you'd be forgiven for thinking he did that too – by the Laird of Lagg, which was a local big estate not far from Dumfries, and he was the local justice of the peace called Robert Grierson."

"Good grief!"

"Oh, it gets worse than that. Grierson has gone down in local legend as Cruel Lagg, and when he died, not only did the horses bearing his hearse collapse and die – a very bad sign witch-wise – but a crow alighted on his coffin, and wouldn't leave until it went into the ground. Crows are witches' birds, Cam! It would no doubt have been seen by some as the so-called witches taking their revenge on him in death."

"Bloody hell! That's…" Words failed him as he sat aghast.

"Admittedly, Cruel Lagg also persecuted local Covenanters, which is the context where the nickname Cruel Lagg originated, but there's no association between Covenanters and crows like there is with witches. The only other thing I can tell you is that *Robert* Grierson the justice wasn't involved in the witch trials in 1659, but his predecessor as laird might have been. His father, maybe? Or an uncle or cousin? I don't know.

"But more than that, Gideon Corsan was involved in forcibly bringing Elspeth's cousin Isobel and Grissell Asman here to Wigtown, where he *knew* Grierson headed the court hearings. It was Grierson who ordered the women to be flogged through the streets here – an ordeal that Hugh's much-cared-for Isobel didn't survive – and it was

Grierson who ordered young Grissell and Isobel to join two other supposed Covenanter dissenters in death. Yet unlike the men who died, they were given witches' deaths, by being tied to stakes out there in the Bladnoch estuary," – she waved her hand to where they could just see the edge of the water – "to be drowned slowly by the incoming tide."

Cameron looked horrified at her for a moment, too shocked to speak. "He did *what*? …Tied them to posts out in the estuary? To drown slowly? With the tide?"

Anna nodded with a grimace. "Yep. What a bloody cruel thing to do, eh? And poor Hugh was following too far behind them to get to either woman in time, and save them before they died. But he saw Grissell drown from a distance."

"Christ!" Cameron gulped, genuinely shocked. "Poor Hugh. …And poor them too. …What a bloody awful way to die!"

Anna looked slightly sick. "So you can see why I'm keeping everything crossed that the Grierson name in my family doesn't link directly to him. Because that would be too grim for words. To be a descendant of the victims of the witch murders, *and* to the bloody man who killed two more innocents, just on the say-so of a few bigoted men accusing them of being witches, would be beyond awful!"

"Oh, Anna," Cameron gasped sympathetically, taking her hand and holding it tight. "Oh, God! I hope not. I hope there's not *that* connection, for your sake as well as theirs."

"Thanks."

Then a thought occurred to Cameron. "But if there were other Griersons, wouldn't it be likely that they would be around here? Isn't it the case – as far as I know, anyway – that clan connections make for a clustering of various clan names? So why not Grierson as a clan name down here if there's a local laird?"

Anna breathed a sigh of relief. "Good point. Yes, I'd not thought of that. At some other point, can we go and have a look at the Covenanter memorial at Dalgarnock, in the churchyard near Thornhill? Because I'm sure that I saw online the surname Grierson amongst those commemorated on there, and they surely can't have been the Laird of Lagg's close relatives to be persecuted in that way? Not unless he was even more wicked than I thought, anyway."

Cameron was instantly in favour. "Yes! Absolutely, let's go and do that. Nothing is going to prove that there were Griersons on both sides of this horrible time better than that." He paused, then added, "I'm still offering to fund you doing the whole Ancestry family tree and DNA thing, though, Anna. You need to know who the heck you are, for your own sanity's sake. Even if it comes back that you're nothing to do with them – and to be honest, I hope that is the case – then at least you can move on with your life without that worry dogging your heels at every turn."

"But what if it does?"

"Then we deal with it here and now. This ends now, Anna. It's not bloody fair making you suffer for something that went on so many generations in the past. Christ! You didn't even know that you were related until now, did you? So why should you be held to ransom over something someone did over three hundred years ago?"

Anna gave him a watery smile. "Thanks for that, Cam. I think I needed to hear someone put it like that. Aunty Rita is a bit too focused on all of the hocus-pocus, and it all being about the ghosts."

But she also thought, *I daren't tell you that you might have a connection too, with your mum being a Ferguson! Not when you're being so understanding of me.* Instead she said, "I think that's what Gary's been trying to get me to see when we're away from Aunty Rita – that I have a stake in this too, and to not suppress it just for the sake of getting shot of the ghosts."

"Wise advice from Gary, then," Cameron said approvingly. "And he's right. I know you told me that he was advocating you easing off on the ghost hunt for a few days to give you breathing space, and also that that's not easy for you to do. But I think changing tack and trying to find out about your own family might be the tonic you need."

1664

Elspeth

That spring was wet and the winter grain crop poor; Johnne declined through the summer; then as the autumn came around, Johnne died, and it was another poor harvest, which was when Alex made a decision.

"We're leaving, Elspeth," he announced upon coming in filthy and cold from the fields one day. "I've had my fill of this! I and that poor lad Dougal have broken our backs today for Niall, getting in the last of what grain has grown, and he's still not satisfied." Dougal was little more than an orphaned boy who was all Niall could afford to pay to help him, and the lad was getting thinner by the month for want of decent food. "We're going to find my parents, Elspeth, and that's the end of it. If Niall wants us to take little Jonet and Jamie with us, I'm happy to do that, but Dougal has already said if he can't leave with us then he's running away."

Elspeth knew that that would be viewed very badly by the locals, but she couldn't blame the lad.

Here he had no future at all, indeed might not even survive, if he didn't do as Hugh had done and joined the militia, and he was neither big enough nor strong enough to fight. Dear Hugh himself was gone more than he was here nowadays, so although Elspeth missed him and wished she would still be able to catch up with him, in reality that had only been for a few weeks in the depths of each winter.

"We'll leave word for Hugh and take Dougal and the children," she decided. "When do you want to go?"

"Michaelmas is coming up soon, so I think we go then," Alex said, referring to the date when most rents and dues were still paid for the year. It was a good choice because they could leave owing nobody anything.

"I want to tell Sorley, though," Elspeth insisted. "We owe him that. If not for him we might have died soon after Ma and your aunt."

Yet Sorley wasn't at home but away with the laird, and so the best Elspeth could do was leave word with Sorley's niece, who was a good deal more understanding than she expected.

"Ye've no' had the help from yer ain family that my pa expected," Sorley's niece said with disgust. "And yon Niall is no use to himself, let alone anyone else. I dinna blame ye' for going to try yer luck elsewhere. God go wi' ye', and may ye' all find the peace and happiness ye' deserve."

It probably wasn't the wisest decision to leave just as the weather was getting worse, but Alex had been right about leaving at Michaelmas, for with their share of the rent paid, Niall didn't even bother to come and see them leave. Elspeth had firmly repossessed the pony she and her father had brought north with them, and also Marione and Samwell's pony, which had been given back far more willingly by the McAllister family. It meant that they could take what remained of Alex's parents' things with them, and have the three small children ride on top of the baggage. Young Dougal had his paltry worldly possessions tied up in a hessian sack thrown over his shoulder and beneath his rag of a plaid, which was his only garment. The poor lad had never had a pair of shoes, and walked barefoot beside the ponies, never giving a backward glance to the tiny croft which had been his last of many homes.

"We are getting him some clean clothes and a pair of shoes as soon as we can," Elspeth said firmly to Alex and got no argument, but for now what little coin they had had to be spent on food along the road.

And they needed every penny, for the trek towards Edinburgh was long and arduous, made worse by a persistent drizzle which turned every road into a quagmire, and slowed them down terribly. Most of the time, they spent their nights in farmers' barns, allowed in because the various farmers' wives took pity on the shivering children. But as they got out of the Highlands, the endless wet gradually faded to occasional showers, and by the time they reached Edinburgh, they were at least halfway to being dried out instead of sopping wet.

Sadly, it wasn't the joyful reunion they had envisaged. The address that Samwell gave them turned out to be a burned-out ruin, and the neighbours told them that the fire had been a year ago, so clearly Samwell and Marione had long since departed for somewhere else. Nor could any of the neighbours help them. A few remembered the poor couple who had come to work there only months before the fire, but none had any idea of where they had gone.

In the end, it was Elspeth who found work, not Alex. They had crossed the Firth of Forth to the tiny but prosperous town of Culross, with its medieval palace, and still wealthy houses – or at least compared to anywhere else Elspeth had been aside from Edinburgh. But at least it cost less to find a place to stay just outside of than the capital. Doing the laundry for a trio of moderately well-off families wasn't much, but it was enough to allow her to rent a tiny single-room cottage on the outskirts of the town instead of just a room, and close to a stream where she could get water to heat up, with plenty of wood to scavenge to fuel the fires with. Dougal made himself useful as a general stable lad and in the fields, and brought in enough to feed himself, and had as much spare to hand on to help Elspeth feed herself and the children. But it was Alex who failed at every turn.

All he did was walk miles and miles, searching for his parents, and though Elspeth understood his worry, she was also angry at him. Why could he not see that he needed to find a man's work? Something which would bring in a proper wage, and allow them to have more than a single-roomed cott with a leaky roof and wind whistling in through the walls?

"I have to find them!" Alex told her over and over.

It meant that by the time three months were out, Elspeth was wishing she'd sent a message to Hugh Ferguson for help while she was in Argyll. She knew that Hugh had adored her. Indeed, she had been very careful not to flaunt her love for Alex in front of him. But every time he'd come home from fighting in the militia, Hugh had brought her a purse of money. Not a lot – he wasn't that well paid – but it was money!

He'd understood her need for money to get things for the children with, not just crops or fleeces which might or might not sell. Actual coins, with which she could *buy* stuff. Things like some cloth, because her own clothes were starting to get threadbare, and though she could cut them down and make them into something the children could wear, she was getting very short for herself. Not that Alex noticed.

And that was what began to grate on her nerves. She didn't expect miracles from him. But she wished that he would open his eyes and look at her. Properly look at her, not simply notice that she was putting food in front of him and then ignore her. His disregard had been too easily attributed to exhaustion while he worked with Niall, but now she was starting to wonder whether her life wasn't starting to echo her sister's with her indifferent husband. And in her own mind she began to wonder whether she had made the right choice? Hugh might not have been around often, but when he had visited, he spoke to Elspeth directly, instead of barely seeing her as he gazed off into a distance only he could see.

It had been so easy to fall into a companionable relationship with Alex, who was her own age, rather than the younger Hugh, but she'd begun to question whether had it really been love on Alex's part. At the ages they'd been back when Jonet was being persecuted, the few years between Hugh and her made a difference, but not now, not as full adults. It meant that in those last months up in Argyll, after she'd discovered Niall's first love, Elspeth began to wonder whether Alex had proposed to her because, as one witch's son to another witch's daughter, he knew she wouldn't turn him down? Had he loved *her,* though? Or like poor Mailie, was she just a substitute for who he really wanted, though in his case he'd not met whoever that was yet? Or so she thought.

On the other hand, she had no doubt whatsoever that Hugh loved *her*. Back in Dumfriesshire, she had thought it just a young boy's infatuation, not real love. Yet as time had gone by, and Hugh had grown up – rather faster than Alex had, if she was now being truthful with herself, because of what he witnessed off fighting with the laird – he'd never once wavered. And if he was tactful enough not to declare his love out loud and in front of Alex, the things he did made it clear that the boyish infatuation had grown into something more long-lasting and deep.

Yet when she sent a message back from Culross via Sorley for Hugh, it transpired that having come home and found Elspeth gone, Hugh had signed up as a permanent soldier, seemingly having nothing left to come back to the village for. And that was when Elspeth had truly broken down and sobbed for a whole day, until exhaustion and the need to care for the children had got her briefly onto her feet before collapsing into the rough bed she'd long since ceased to share with Alex for anything except sleep.

Her mother and father might have been barely getting by, but at home there had been love within their little trio. And while Johnne Allen had lived, there had been love from him for her as Elspeth, as herself. But now? Now there was nothing and nobody. Why oh why hadn't she woken up to Hugh's devotion and loyalty sooner, instead of treating him like the boy he no longer was?

Nowadays, she was struggling to keep some kind of maternal control over Jamie and Jonet, because she was permanently exhausted from working so hard at doing peoples' laundry. And even little Marione was suffering for want of her mother's attention. The only person who was working as hard as she was was young Dougal, and how long would he keep bringing back to her what he earned once he caught the eye of some local lass? For Elspeth was not so oblivious not to notice that sometimes Dougal came home later than others, and with a gleam in his eye. Yet without him, there was no way that she could even afford the place they had now.

Then disaster struck in the August, barely a year after they had moved east.

"I'm going to go back to Dumfries," Alex announced.

"Alex, no!" Elspeth cried in horror. "I cannot go back there. You know I can't! I barely got out alive when we left. You can't ask that of me."

"I wasn't asking you to," was the reply which froze her blood.

"You're going *without* me? Without *us*?" She looked to where the two older children were watching intently, knowing that something was wrong.

"For heaven's sake, I'm making a trip back there just to see if anyone has heard anything of Ma and Pa," he said with exasperation. "I shall come back. Hopefully with them, or to take you to them."

Yet Elspeth had a dreadful feeling of foreboding of the kind she'd not had since they'd fled their old homes. Suddenly she knew that she would never see Alex again. And it wasn't just because of all the dangers of travelling alone such a long distance. Once he was back in familiar territory, would he really want to trek all the way back her just to fetch them…to fetch *her*? She thought not. Alex had never settled anywhere else, whereas she rather liked it here if only life wasn't quite such a struggle. It had been family problems which had made Argyll less than home, not the other people around her or the place itself. No, Alex would never face leaving where he called home a second time.

Nor did she have time to talk him out of it. With the next dawn he was walking out of the door with a pack, and loading his father's tools onto his family's pony, making Elspeth glad that she'd been allowing Dougal to use her family's pony to get to and from some work he'd found a few miles down the road, and he too was leaving for work. If he hadn't, Elspeth thought that Alex might have made some excuse about it being faster if he could ride, and taken both, leaving her really stuck.

Any faint hopes she might have had that Alex would change his mind after a day or so on the road were dashed, and after he'd been gone a week, she knew that her intuition had been right – Alex had abandoned her and not even had the grace to tell her the truth. Suddenly she felt a deep kinship with Mailie and Isobel, her cousin Margaret's unfortunate daughter. Like Elspeth now, Isobel had been a victim of the tides of chance, forced into a marriage with a man who had never loved her, because Elspeth was seriously doubting whether what Alex had felt was true love for her, or only the need for the companionship of someone whose family was going through the same torment as his.

Oh Isobel, Elspeth thought with genuine grief, *I wish I'd kept in closer touch with you. Is this what you felt like all those years ago? And if you did, did you ever get away from that man and find someone who truly cared about you? I pray you did, because then it might give me some hope, instead of feeling so very alone.* And it was then, in that cold, long night, with Dougal snoring on the other side of the room, and little Marione snuffling in her sleep beside her while the other two slept on a makeshift bed nearer the fire, the Elspeth heard her mother's voice come to her.

'You know all of my remedies,' Jonet's voice said in her head. 'You came along with me time and again to difficult births and to treat the sick. Start finding the herbs and brewing the cures. Folk will pay for those. Not much, but they will pay – or at least they'll give you in kind, like eggs and bread and cloth.'

And the more Elspeth thought about it on getting up the next morning, the more it made sense. Indeed, she'd rather people paid her in kind. That way she couldn't be accused by those who didn't make a miraculous recovery of robbing them of money.

There was also another benefit of Alex being gone. The food went further. On the random days when he'd done a day's casual work, he'd brought home enough to feed himself for a day or two, but then would go off on another wild goose-chase, come home hungry, and eat whatever he found. That Elspeth had been eking food out to last several days never occurred to him. And once she could have a little more food for herself without leaving the children short, Elspeth found that she had more energy to go foraging. If she walked out first thing in the morning with the children and her basket to gather herbs, by the afternoon they were tired, and she could get on with the laundry with fewer interruptions while they played or napped. And then at night as they slept, she could use the last embers of the cooking fire to brew up her potions.

A quiet word with Dougal had him keeping an eye open for cheap, small pots in the markets while working further afield, and so soon she was able to do more than hanging bundles of plants and herbs up to dry from the rafters. In this first batch, she made only pastes and salves, for small clay pots were cheaper come by than bottles, and anyway, she would need something like oil or wine to top up bottles with to make drafts that would keep, adding on an expense. But one of the unexpected but best outcomes of her hunting down specific plants was that she met other local women out doing the same. There were only a handful of them, but they recognised in her a fellow healer and welcomed her into their little group. Finally Elspeth had friends.

CHAPTER 4

Getting out of the car and pulling on waterproofs over their fleeces against the suddenly cloudy sky that threatened a heavy shower, Cameron locked it and then turned to look at the imposing building behind them.

"Wow, this is quite some edifice for a little place like Wigtown to have as its Town House, what in England you'd probably call a town hall," he observed, "the place where civic business took place."

Anna nodded. "But Victorian, I would guess, if I've learned anything about architecture from Gary. From what I've read, Isobel and Grissell Asman would have been held in the tolbooth, which in these small towns north of the border seem to have served as town hall and local jail all rolled into one in that era." She turned around in a full circle. "I don't see anything that looks like it might be the original tolbooth, do you? Nothing looks quite that old. Let's go and have a walk around the town and look, shall we?"

It didn't take long for them to stroll down one side of the main road with the dogs, briefly look into some of the side roads, and then come back on the other side of the road to get to the car.

"Well the tolbooth is either somewhere well hidden," Anna said with a huff of disgust, "which I reckon is unlikely given the status of the place back then, or it's long buried in the foundations of this Victorian pile."

"I'd say the latter," Cameron said. "Look at the commanding view this has got down the high street. I don't imagine the worthy gents of late Georgian or early Victorian Scotland plucking this site out of thin air, do you? I reckon something prestigious was here before it, and it just got upgraded in the latest fashion."

Anna nodded. "And that would explain why I don't feel anything creepy coming off this place. Nothing happened *here*. But something tweaked my cat's whiskers when I was here at the memorial up the hill, Cam. I don't know what it was, but I've got this strong feeling that it's to do with Isobel."

She reached into her fleece's pocket and pulled out the piece of paper she'd made notes on. "Okay. So it says here that there's another one of those Covenanter graves in the churchyard here, although I'm betting that it's like those others that Gary was telling us about, which date from probably a hundred years after the event. Shall we go and try to find it?"

They put the dogs back in the car, not wanting them to disgrace themselves in the graveyard, and took the side road. Given that the Covenanter graves were signposted, it wasn't hard to find the parish kirk and its graveyard, but to Anna's disappointment, once again the graves were far from original.

"I don't feel a blessed thing here," she complained to Cameron. "It's sterile, that's what it is."

"Is there anywhere else here that's associated with those two women?" he asked, reaching out to take her list from her. "Oh look. It says that there's a memorial out in the estuary where the women are supposed to have died." And as they came back out of the kirkyard, hoods up against a sudden squally shower, he pointed to a signpost leading downhill. "Looks like it's that way."

Feeling a slight dread that even there she wouldn't feel a thing, and beginning to doubt herself for what she thought she'd felt up on the hill, Anna tagged along, half of her praying that she'd find an answer, and the other half dreading yet another connection. Yet when they'd walked down the steep slope and found the signposts to the stone pillar out on a wooden walkway above the tide line, Anna had to admit that there was something chilling about the place quite apart from any spooky tingling on her part.

"Regardless of your connections," Cameron said with a shiver, "this is a pretty grim place to die. I mean, there's no doubting that it's beautiful. Look at the view towards those huge rolling hills to the north. Glorious! Especially with dramatic clouds like we have today. But at the same time, looking down into those reeds and rushes, and imagining that that's your last view of anything on this earth, when you are soaked to the skin and cold beyond feeling much of anything of the bits of you that are in the water to boot…" and he gave a shudder.

His words only emphasised everything Anna was feeling, but then as she turned around on the first wooden platform, away from the estuary to look back at the town, she gave a gasp which made Cameron spin to look at her.

Pointing with a shaky finger, she said, "Look! Even with these recent trees and bushes in the way, you can still see straight up to the church. Only the tower's visible now, but back then…? The 'good folk' of Wigtown didn't need to come down to the water's edge to watch the witches drown – they had ringside seats from the kirkyard!" and then the world around her went black.

Instantly Anna was aware that she was somewhere else. Or rather, some*when* else. Looking down at herself she saw thick, homespun woollen skirts, and that her hands were rough and reddened by hard work.

Struggling to hold back her rising nausea, she turned her head, and realised that she was standing near to where in the modern day there was an information board about the women's deaths. In this time, though, there was no duckboard walkway, and her feet felt wet. Uphill in this other time, she could see many more people, none of them in modern dress, some of them looking at her with pity and dread, and others with smug expressions as though she deserved what was coming to her. And then she felt it. The trickling sensation down her back. And when she put her hand around there, and then brought it back to look at it, she saw blood. A lot of it!

Her head swam, and something in her said, 'you're dying', and that this strange light-headedness wasn't just at the sight of her own blood, but something far worse. Yet as she gasped, desperately trying to suck in more air in the hope of clearing the growing fog, she saw three women being led past her. One was an old lady, visibly so even through her battered appearance, for the trickles of blood on her face were running down the creases made by her wrinkles, making weird highlights of them. She, at least, seemed resigned to her fate, but a young girl – probably not even out of her teens – who came behind her was screaming, "Father? Father? Where are you? Help me! Help me!" as two rough-looking men, in what she vaguely realised were soldiers' uniforms of the time, hauled her on past and out towards where she now saw a causeway leading into the mud flats and reed-beds.

They weren't alone, though. A second young girl was also being led towards where Anna's now fading vision saw that there were posts in the water beside the causeway. This girl was sobbing, not screaming out, as if she knew that there was nobody here who might risk all to help her.

"Grissell," Anna heard herself say, but the words weren't hers but whoever it was she was sharing this moment with. "Grissell! Stay strong. Hugh will come. I know he will!" But in that moment it all went black again for Anna.

When she came around, it was to find herself sitting on the ground with Cameron propping her up and holding her so that her head was between her knees.

"Anna! Anna! ...Are you all right? Anna...can you hear me?"

"What happened?" she asked him groggily.

"You looked up the hill and then you fainted," Cameron said, the relief that she'd come to clear in his voice. "You mumbled something before you came around, but I couldn't hear what it was." She felt him move and then a hip flask was held up to her lips. "Here. Have a nip of this. It'll help bring you round."

The strong whiff of whisky by itself was enough to wake Anna up more, but she gratefully took a couple of sips of it, after which she felt strong enough to say,

"Oh God, Cam. I was there. I was there when Isobel died! I saw Grissell Asman and the older of the two young sisters we know of from the information board, Margaret Wilson, being led to her death with the old lady. She's the other Margaret who's named on the memorials." She didn't dare say that she'd been within Isobel – that was still freaking her out enough by herself without having to handle how Cameron would take it.

"Shit! I don't like that," he said worriedly. "That implies that you have some kind of link to that Isobel, too, as well as Elspeth."

Anna eased herself into a better position then asked, "Help me up, would you? I can feel the damp seeping through my clothes." Then she heard Cameron's gasp of dismay. "What's the matter? What is it, Cam?"

In answer he brought the hand which he'd placed on her back around to where she could see it, and for a second she thought she might faint again, because it was damp with blood.

"That's not mine," she managed to warble, and then as she saw him looking like he might faint alongside her, began undoing her waterproof. "Help me get this thing off and I'll show you."

With his hands shaking as much as hers, Cameron helped Anna out of the waterproof and the fleece underneath it. Yet when she'd shrugged out of the sleeves and turned to show him her back, his gasp was of a different kind.

"Bloody hell! There's not a mark there."

Anna lifted the back of her t-shirt up too, showing him that there wasn't a mark actually on her body.

"I'm not in any pain, Cam. That wasn't my blood. It was Isobel's!"

"Well it's made a right mess of your waterproof," he said, still shaken by what he'd seen. "Look!" He held it up for her to see the red smears down the back of it in streaks which looked as though they'd echoed cuts on Isobel, and snags in the cloth along them.

"Is it on my fleece?" she wondered, bending down to pick that up, and glad to see that there was nothing on that. "Thank heavens for that! The waterproof will wash off. I wasn't relishing trying to get blood out of the fluffy inside of the fleece." She was trying to sound practical, as much for Cameron's sake as anyone's, because inside she was still shaking like a leaf from the experience.

"Please tell me that you don't want to walk out to the actual site itself," Cameron said worriedly.

Yet Anna felt certain when she answered, "I don't think the same will happen out there, Cam. It was Isobel I went back to, and she never died out there."

She could see that he was still far from happy, and he followed her closely as she walked out on the wooden duckboards to the stone memorial. Yet out where the fresh air off the river estuary was blowing, she felt her head clearing dramatically.

"Dear God, Cam, stood here you can see the impossibility Hugh faced. He wasn't exaggerating when he said he couldn't get to young Grissell. Look at it! There must have been people lining that lane down to here, and others watching from up on the embankment by the kirk. It was more like a freak-show entertainment with ringside seats than an execution. Horrible!"

She saw Cameron give a shudder before he said, "And there's not much room to manoeuvre here, is there? It's not like Hugh could have come around another way to get to the girl. There would have been the causeway and then nothing but treacherous mud flats, where he'd have sunk in up to his neck at the wrong time of the tide. Do you think he knew this Grissell well?"

That made Anna pause to think. "Actually, he probably didn't. If I've understood him, he'd met young Grissell briefly when he was still a soldier – her and her family. And it was the whole family he'd intended to try leaving Isobel with for a few days to recover from her ordeal with the questioners. It was terribly bad luck that young Grissell's father wasn't as supportive of her as he should have been, and had her tied up in the family barn waiting to be handed over to be questioned, as her mother had been at some time in the past. So at that point, Hugh was suddenly on the back foot. He's never said so explicitly, but taking Isobel back to her father – who was the equally dreadful Thomas Milligan, who testified against his own wife, Margaret Clarke – was not even considered.

"You can't blame Hugh for that, can you? He knew by then that bloody Milligan had shoved poor Isobel off onto a brute of an older man, just to get her out of the way when she was probably not even out of her teens. And then, when she'd been widowed, he'd sent her to possibly the most feared man in the county, Presbyter Veitch, at Irongray. God alone knows what Isobel suffered there. Aunty Rita thinks at best he probably tried to 'beat the sin out' of her. At worst Veitch repeatedly raped her."

She found herself giving a hiccupping sob. "Poor Isobel. She was given less thought than the family goat by the men in her family, and then just when she thought she was escaping all of this with the man she thought loved her, he let her down."

"Hugh let her down?"

"Oh no! No, the man she tried to run north with, and with Hugh's help, was the son of John McCartney, Edward. It sounds as though Edward was a very different personality to John. He was appalled at what his father had done, and wanted no part of it. But Hugh says he was as weak as water when it came to standing up for them.

"Edward pretty much caved in the moment he and Isobel got caught, and that was down to him wanting them to be married in a kirk where the Covenant still held – though heaven only knows why! John McCartney had been hand-in-glove with Presbyter Veitch, who was about as ungodly a churchman as you could imagine, and it sounds as if a lot of people in his parish were scared to death of him. But for whatever warped reason which only made sense to him, Edward brought Isobel back south, but only got as far back as close to Sanquhar before they got picked up."

"If they were on foot, Sanquhar's a fair bit north of here on the way to Ayr," Cameron observed. "How did they end up back here?"

"Well *they* didn't. Hugh was a soldier still at that point, and his unit – his patrol, or whatever they were – met up with those who were guarding Edward and Isobel at Sanquhar's tolbooth. They'd been found elsewhere and brought there, you see. Edward died under questioning in there, spouting some nonsense that only dug Isobel deeper into the mire. It was pure luck that Hugh ended up there at the same time. So Hugh made a run for it with her. But he said that he knew that after traipsing most of the way north of the Clyde and back, she was exhausted and needed rest. His idea was to hide for a week or so a bit north of Dumfries, around where his old farm was, and where he knew every molehill and tussock of grass."

"And I can see how that would have made sense," Cameron admitted. "Those hunting them would presume that they would be high-tailing it *out* of Dumfriesshire as fast as they could, so to come further in would be a good deflection. As long as they didn't make contact with any of her wider family, who might give them away, even if it was inadvertently, they should have been safe."

"If it wasn't for Gideon getting wind of Hugh going AWOL, they would have been," Anna sighed. "It was dreadful luck that he knew exactly where the ruin of Hugh's home was, and that he'd had this obsession with Isobel. I won't call it love. I don't think Gideon ever grasped what real love was. But he has all the hallmarks of what we'd now think of as a stalker, incapable of giving enough of himself to have a proper relationship."

Cameron gave a snort of disgust. "I know that these days we'd probably regard Gideon as the classic case of an abused child becoming an abuser, because he never knew any different. But bloody hell, he had a knack for trashing the lives of everyone he came in contact with, didn't he?"

"I know what you mean. At times, I can feel quite sorry for him. He's not a likeable man, and I get that from quite a young age he must have suffered awful isolation from the youngsters he should have had friends amongst, not because of himself necessarily, but because of his father. Let's face it, if you were a mum of the time, would you have risked having Gideon over to play in case he let something slip to his old man? Let alone parents being scared to death that if John Corsan could do that to his own family, what he might do to their child if they went to his house."

"But he never grew into being his own man," Cameron added thoughtfully. "Some people go through similar, but decide to get out and make a new life. He didn't."

Anna nodded. "And it was possible, even back then, because Hugh did it."

"Do you think that's part of the problem?"

"He's jealous of Hugh? Well, yes he is."

"I meant not just for Hugh having the trust of Isobel. He might not acknowledge it, but Gideon might have been very jealous of Hugh right from when Hugh ran away with Elspeth and their families. Hugh got out, Anna. He got out while he was still young enough to choose his own life. In those years *before* Hugh came back, how warped do you think Gideon's perceptions of him became? There must have been a point when he made the connection between Hugh and his family going, and the woman he obsessed over – Elspeth – vanishing out of reach. That can't have gone down well."

"Oh good grief!" Anna gulped. "I hadn't thought of it in quite that way when Gideon said Hugh escaped justice. I only thought of Hugh and his dad, along with the others, eluding John Corsan's twisted punishments. But my God, you've got a point! *Gideon* was the one who stayed and got 'punished', wasn't he? Punished by association, not for anything *he'd* done. Oh well done, Cam. That's something else we can tell Aunty Rita and Gary tonight."

CHAPTER 5

They returned to the car and collected the dogs to walk up to the memorial on the hill, but as they did so, Anna observed, "You know nothing highlights to me what a poor state Isobel must have been in than seeing how small Wigtown had to be in those days. When Hugh said the women were whipped through the town, I was thinking of a substantial distance – not that that diminishes what they went through in any way. It's just that looking at the short walk from the kirk to where she died, and then the equally short walk from the kirk to where we think the tolhouse would have been, that's a fraction of the distance I thought they'd had to go. Being whipped must have been appalling, but I'd had visions of it taking over an hour just in terms of how far they'd have had to walk."

Cameron nodded. "Yes, 'whipped through the town' to me conjured up something like being marched the whole way through the centre of

Dumfries as it is now, but you're right, this wouldn't have been anything like as long."

"And to a woman used to hard work and walking everywhere, the actual distance shouldn't have been as wearing as it would to most modern people. So yes, her back would have been a bloody mess, and she'd have probably been scarred for life, but would those handing out the punishment necessarily have expected her to die from it? Because it doesn't make sense to me for them to have added on another punishment, if they hadn't expected her to survive the first."

Cameron, who had had to stop to get his breath from the short, steep climb to the monument, gave her a rueful grin. "…You aren't even breathing hard! …I really have to get fitter. …And what you say makes sense, because why would they have ordered the drowning if they'd thought the women would be dead before they even got there?"

They walked around the memorial's huge stone pillar and gazed out over the estuary.

"Did you get no sense of your connection when you were here with Gary and Rita?" Cameron asked. "No hint of feeling faint or anything?"

Anna could see how worried he still was by what had happened, and realised she truly did have to explain.

"It was all a bit tense right then. Sally was stripping all of the soft furnishings out of the bridal suite so that Aunty Rita could go in full bell, book, and candle on Gideon. But Aunty Rita made a mistake. She contacted Gideon that morning without properly warding herself. Honestly Cam, she was as prickly as a hedgehog that day! Snapping Gary's head off at every turn. She had to go and have a strong salt bath with heaven knows what other herbs to sort herself out. But it meant that while we were here, I didn't really get chance to just pause and work out what it was that I was sensing, because Aunty Rita was already storming off back down to the car."

"Well that fits with Gideon," Cameron said with a worried gasp. "If he somehow influenced Rita at that point, he wouldn't want to be reminded that this was all *his* fault, would he?"

Anna turned to him, eyes wide with shock. "Oh hell, Cam. That's it! That's why she was in such a foul mood – it leaked through the connection to her. Oh dear, I'm going to have to tell her about that, aren't I?"

Turning to look at the view out over the estuary again, the wind whipped away Cameron's quiet response, meaning she didn't hear him say, "And I don't like that he got under the skin of an experienced psychic like Rita. If he could do that to her, I don't want him anywhere near you."

By now, the tide was going out, and they could see the mud gradually appearing, and how far out the shallow water ran.

"My God, it would have been a slow process." Cameron said, appalled.

Anna felt the tears welling up. "Those poor women. …And poor Hugh, too!"

"Do we know if Gideon stayed to watch?"

Anna whipped around to stare at Cameron in horror.

"Well that would be another raw wound if he did," he said, his voice choking up with emotion. "The Gideon we're coming to know wouldn't be able to face that he was the cause of Isobel being here in the first place, would he?" Anna shook her head. "He'd have felt the need to blame someone else, and who better than his old enemy? What's the betting that in his eyes, it all started when Hugh brought Isobel back into the area? The fact that he himself was every bit the idiot Hugh said he was for bringing Isobel and Grissell to Wigtown would be something he'd blank out."

"I really think we need to ask Gideon why he did that," Anna said with a grimace. "Might be better if you or Gary asked the actual question, though, because from what Aunty Rita said, he doesn't take much notice of women."

She turned and looked southwards. "The Isle of Whithorn is down that way, isn't it?"

"Yes."

"Well I don't give much for our chances of walking the dogs down there today. Not with the way those dark clouds are building up. Shall we drive back to Kirkcudbright instead?" Cameron nodded, but silently prayed that there Anna wouldn't make the same worryingly personal connections, and that she wouldn't faint again.

The drive as far as Kirkcudbright didn't take too long, with Cameron pulling in at the quayside car park. Donning waterproofs again, though it looked like the rain clouds might miss them here, the walk along the estuary shore with the dogs was refreshing and calming. Harris and Lewis loped along, investigating interesting smells, and occasionally had to be called back from going too far afield by Cameron, but by and large, they were simply happy to be in the fresh air, as Anna was.

What the walk did illustrate to her was just how small the town was even now, let alone what it would have been like in the past. In no time at all, they had left it well behind as they did the walk along the estuary. Coming back, this time watching the approach to the town, made Anna realise that the core of the modern town hadn't grown that much, as illustrated by the visibly older buildings and their chimneys poking up over the roofs, and the tower of the castle right in the middle.

"Gosh! It must have been a tiny place in the seventeenth century," she observed.

Cameron nodded. "And suspiciously, too small to have produced quite so many 'dangerous' women, at least without somebody deliberately stirring the pot and slinging accusations. It really brings it home to you that someone was on a persecuting spree. I mean, take away the modern houses, and you have that core of stunning old cottages and houses on the streets around MacLellan's Castle, and how many families would they have realistically held? I know that back then, families were probably rammed in several to a bedroom in a way that would be appalling to us now, but even so…"

Anna pulled out her phone and tried to do an internet search. "About the only thing I can find is that by 1831, so very roughly a hundred and fifty years on from when stuff happened that we're interested in, there was a population of 2,690, and it's only about a thousand more than that now. Phew! So I think if we said that in 1659 the whole administrative area covered by Kirkcudbright might have had less than two thousand people all told… How many families might that have been? They had much bigger families than now, so each family would have been far more people than our conventional 'mum and dad and a couple of kids'. Because I think these statistics cover not just the town proper, but the other side of the river, and possibly even up to that little place at the start of the estuary, Tongland."

Cameron was doing some swift mental arithmetic. "I'd estimate we're looking at not much over two hundred multi-generational families, and that's spread out across the local farms, too. I think we can also assume that on a farm you might have the farmer's own family in a small main house, but possibly a couple of workers' families in tiny cottages. Whereas the little crofts or smallholdings would have just had one family, albeit an extended one. But back then the farms themselves would have been way smaller than modern ones. They would have been what one family could reasonably manage to plough and harvest, plus looking after whatever livestock they had, and all without any kind of modern machinery."

"So a lot more farms, but all of them small?" Anna queried, looking around at the gently rolling landscape on either side of the estuary. "And presumably, since there's still some fishing going on here, the families within the town might have included several who made their living on the sea?"

"I think that's a reasonable assumption."

She gave a huff of disgust. "Then given that not every woman who was accused from here got murdered – because that's what it was – even so, that's still several women from the Kirkcudbright area whom I found reference to in the witch trials of 1658 or '9. Granted not all died from *capital* punishment, but you have to wonder how many died just from being 'questioned'."

Cameron's mental arithmetic was faster than hers. "So maybe up to ten percent of families having women accused, let alone what percentage of local women that then works out to. And they're just the ones we know about. As you said, how many others got questioned who we know nothing about? *Sheesh*! That's surely abnormal for a little place like this? If you think of them as the mature women at the head of a household, and there were how many accused women in the area…?"

"Accused? Oh, probably twenty or so over the years."

"Jeez! That really is potentially something like one in ten, then."

"And that's just the ones who whose records have survived. Heaven knows how many others in their families got the black looks and nasty words thrown at them which never went any further."

"Good grief. That means that everyone in Kirkcudbright at the time must have known at least one of the families affected. It must have felt like a reign of terror for those whose women were known to be good at things like healing."

Anna nodded sadly. "That makes a lot of sense of what Hugh said, doesn't it? That people didn't speak up in defence of their neighbours because they were terrified of being tarred with the same brush. And maybe, for some weird reason just down here in south-west Scotland, the reason the Covenanters' hold on people hung on so long was because there had developed this culture of informing on others. The soldiers might come and go, but your neighbours were always there, and you'd never know who was watching you."

"That's as bad as Nazi Germany," Cameron said with disgust.

"To be honest, any regime that's like that is," Anna agreed. "It applies to any setup where the authorities reward informants – because there's always some avaricious so-and-so who'll do anything for money, or some kind of advancement. And once it's started, it's awfully hard to stop. It's too easy for it to descend into settling old scores, which I think is a fair chunk of what happened with our women. It wasn't necessarily even their generation where the animosity began, it was just where it sadly ended."

"Blimey! That's enough doom and gloom for one day. Especially when it's supposed to be your holiday day, Anna. Come on, let's go and find a pub with a bench outside and have a drink and some crisps, though I warn you, you won't get many of the crisps with Harris and Lewis with us!"

Yet before they reached the hotel, they walked past the church where Rita and Gary had failed to put Grissell McCartney to rest.

"Heavens, I see what Aunty Rita meant," Anna sighed, as they walked the loop around the circular remains of Greyfriars' kirkyard. "It's not a graveyard anymore, just a patch of grass around the kirk. There was no way she could start lighting incense out here. Sooner rather than later, someone would come up and ask what the heck you were playing at. There's not as much as a bush to sneak behind anywhere. It's a peaceful enough spot – not like at Irongray – but how we're going to call Grissell back here to rest I do not know." Then as he frowned in confusion she added, "That's Grissell *McCartney*, Cam. Hugh's granny, not the lass who died back down in Wigtown."

He clapped a hand to his forehead. "*Duh*! Of course! Jeez, I wished they'd been a bit more adventurous with their names back then. Too many Grissells, Margarets and Agneses!"

Anna laughed, but pointed out, "Doesn't that illustrate, though, why Hugh kept making those connections? His adored Elspeth lost her cousins

Margaret and Agnes at the witch trials, then he comes back here and witnesses two girls of the same names being persecuted who were also sisters. And then there's a girl with *that* young Margaret, who has the same name as his grandma! The poor man must have felt like he was in some seventeenth-century Groundhog Day."

They found *The Selkirk Arms* from *The Good Beer Guide* that Cameron kept in his car, and took a seat outside to keep Harris and Lewis with them, where the limited outside seats were in a sheltered recess leading to the main door, and out of the stiffening breeze. Cameron went inside and bought himself a pint of coke, on account of driving, and Anna a large glass of red wine, and for a while they just chatted, Anna wondering why she had felt such a connection to Isobel. "It's not like she's one of our ghosts, so what made me react like that?"

"Well if I'm keeping up, she was Elspeth's cousin. Perhaps the link to your family connects to her too?"

Anna sighed. "Or is it that she evokes such strong emotions in both Hugh and Gideon, that now that I've made a connection to their ghosts, I'm somehow closer to her?"

They couldn't decide, but it was something Anna resolved to ask the witches when she got a chance. Then she noticed that his gaze was riveted somewhere over her shoulder, and she wondered whether he'd heard a word she'd said in the last five minutes.

"Cam? …Cam!"

Turning, she expected to see some luscious blonde in skimpy clothing. Instead, she realised he was staring fixedly at a menu on the wall, making her smile. Food, not some glamorous woman, was a distraction she could cope with.

"Yes, Anna, I was listening to what you were saying about Hugh, even if I was drooling a bit at the same time. The more I hear of what happened to him, the more I feel sorry for him. That's not how I feel about bloody Gideon, though. The man needed to grow a pair, or whatever the equivalent saying was back in the 1680s. Yes, he got a rough deal growing up, but what on earth was the matter with him that he never got even a bit of the way past that?"

"He really is our fly in the ointment," Anna agreed, as they got up to head back to the car. Laughing, she asked, "Did you get like the dogs? Or they like you? Because you're looking at that menu like Harris and Lewis do the shortbreads!"

"I'm so sorry," Cameron apologised with a rueful grin. "It's all this walking in the fresh air! I'm not used to it and I'm bloody ravenous. And damn it, we've missed the lunchtime serving and we're too early for dinner. We should have come here and eaten first, then taken the lads for a walk."

"I'm not sure I'd have got any of you beyond here in that case," Anna giggled. "What is it that takes your fancy?"

"All of it!" Cameron said without hesitation. "My God, we have to get Emilio to put some dishes like this on our menu. Do you fancy coming here one night next week when you're not on duty and trying it?" He hoped that sounded somewhere between asking her for a date – which he wasn't sure she'd accept as yet – and professional curiosity. "What do you fancy from this lot?"

"I don't know," Anna admitted. "I've not had much experience of eating out. Are scallops nice? The times Emilio's done them, they get snapped up so fast by our customers, I've not had the chance to try them."

Rather shocked, Cameron asked, "But surely What's-His-Name took you out for meals? Sounded as though he wasn't exactly broke. He must have taken you to some nice places?" Then wished he'd never opened his mouth as Anna blushed and looked embarrassed.

"We didn't go out much," she said, attempting to be blasé about it.

Cameron couldn't help himself. "Then I'm with Gary – the man's an idiot! If I had a lovely girlfriend…no, *fiancée*, like you, I'd be wining and dining her at every chance."

"There wasn't much time…"

"Time? You *make* time for someone you truly value!" He could feel his heart breaking for Anna, and at the same time a building anger towards the fool who had treated her as some kind of disposable add-on. But how to convince her that he wouldn't be the same, and to come out with him without scaring her off? He'd already put his foot in it mightily once already and been lucky he hadn't wrecked his chances. "Right, that settles it. We are looking up all of our competitors in the general area, and once a week, you and I are going to go and sample their fare. If we don't even know what they are serving, how can we hope to compete?"

With relief, he saw Anna's colour return to normal, and a smile appear on her face. He really must not go too fast for her with that much emotional baggage, and it emphasised to Cameron that it was also important for Anna to be able to separate out who she had a connection to in the past. Given the way the living men in her life had treated her, a link to some of the ghostly women was one thing. But he was getting ever more concerned that she potentially had a link to Gideon, let alone that judge bloke who'd done the sentencing down in Wigtown.

He was so deep in thought about this that Anna's small yelp of shock almost made him jump out of his skin.

"Anna? What's wrong?" he asked, then followed her pointing finger to the massive old building they were passing as they tried to find their way back to the car.

"*That's* a *tolbooth*?" she gulped, aghast.

"You didn't know?" Then Cameron felt an idiot for stating the obvious. Clearly by her expression it couldn't have been. "What were you expecting?"

Swallowing hard, Anna managed to wring out, "In England, old toll booths – and we even spell their name differently – are usually cottages by the side of some main road. The places where the money was collected for taking goods on that particular road, yes, but hardly a whacking great place like that! These days, most of the surviving ones are really cute little buildings that make lovely homes." She cleared her throat, managing to say in a more normal voice, "I realised pretty fast that yours up here must be more substantial if people were held in them…"

"But you weren't expecting it to be like this?"

"No."

He stood back and looked at the wonderfully preserved tolbooth. These days there was an artists' centre on the ground floor with a glass door into it, but originally, access would have been up the massive sandstone steps which led up to a solid door on the first-floor level. Down here at the ground floor, there would have been few windows, and those that survived were very small squares with iron bars at them to prevent escape. There was a blocked original ground-floor door arch in the stonework beyond the modern shop, but that might have been where tolls were collected, back in the day, and totally separated by thick walls from the cells where people were held.

With an impressive tower at the one end, if you didn't know otherwise, you could be forgiven for thinking that this was a converted medieval church of some standing, because that was the size and heaviness of it. The one thing that might make you think twice about that was the fact that the windows high up on the first floor were obviously original, square, and domestic, not pointed or rounded and ecclesiastical. There were no residual outlines of defunct pointed windows in the stone walls, either, and right up under the eaves on the second floor, the windows were tiny squares, not like clerestory windows at all.

"God!" Anna said shakily. "Can you imagine being one of our women and being dragged through the town to here? Especially if you lived in some turf-roofed cottage on a farm. You'd never believe that anyone was going to break you out of this place. It's the seventeenth century equivalent of Barlinnie!" Barlinnie being the huge prison she'd passed one time as she'd driven on the M8 through Glasgow, and which Rita had told her was the largest prison in Scotland, housing some very serious offenders.

"Well not quite the Bar-L," Cameron said, giving it one of its nicknames, "But yes, I see what you mean. To a woman who'd lived her life in a thatched one-roomed cottage, being brought into here would have felt…"

"Like going into the gates of Hell itself," Anna finished, and to his horror, Cameron turned and saw she was rather glassy-eyed.

CHAPTER 6

Grabbing her arm, he commanded her urgently,

"Anna? Anna! Stay with me! Don't let them take you over." and was relieved to see her focusing back on him.

"Ooh! That was weird," she admitted. "Just for a second I could hear someone else in my head." Then she realised how worried Cameron looked. "It wasn't like down at Wigtown. Then I had no control. That was like *wham*! I was back there, and it was Isobel dying that broke the connection. This was more like someone whispering in my ear. I could hear you. I knew where I was. And I could feel Harris' cold nose being stuffed into my hand. I was definitely *present* in the here and now."

"Thank God!" Cameron said, trying not to show how rattled he was over this. "Please, move away from here. Come on. I think the car is down this road."

Yet Anna couldn't stop herself giving glances back over her shoulder to the tolbooth. Walking away from it only emphasised the size of it, and how imposing it must have been, back when the women from Kirkcudbright had known it. Its huge greyish-brown sandstone blocks, mortared together in irregular lines, looked menacing against the pretty rendered and painted houses.

How many of the women had been held here? Had any of them been questioned here? Suddenly she felt she had to know, because even if not all of them had been here prior to that final trial in Dumfries, she was now wondering if they'd known other women who'd been brought here who'd never lived to be tried. And did any of it have anything to do with why some of them couldn't rest?

Cameron didn't waste any time in pulling out and heading back for the hotel, but on the way back Anna observed, "They're very careful to say that *criminals* were held at the tolbooth on the information board, aren't they? Yet from what *we* know, sometimes ordinary people got swept into there. Because I can't help but think that some of those Covenanters who got caught, might simply have been people who went to the prayer meetings with their families. In fact, the hard-core dissenters were almost certainly more practiced at avoiding capture. *They* wouldn't have been dragged into a dark room with iron bars at the window."

"No," Cameron sighed. "From what Gary's said, they'd be more likely to be shot where they were found."

"Which might be cruel and unjustified to our eyes...but don't you think they got off lightly compared to the women who got taken into that same prison, and possibly kept there for months? For the men, it was over and done with fast, probably in minutes. Who knows how long those women endured torment?"

She could see that Cameron didn't really get it, but when she went around to speak to Rita that evening, knowing that Gary was on duty and that they would therefore be able to talk in a different sort of way, she got a more receptive hearing.

"They don't get it, Aunty," she said with a sigh.

Rita nodded sagely. "Aye, hen. I know. But even in this day and age, it's a different experience being a woman. Both Gary and Cameron are big lads. I doubt they've ever walked through a town in daylight and felt unsafe. Aye, at night after going out with the guys, and being a bit worse for wear at two in the morning – *then* they might think it no' so wise to go down a dark, narrow street. But in the normal way of things? No.

"So it's asking them to put on a different thinking cap to see how it must have been for those poor women. Whereas for us, it's an extension of how we've lived all of our lives. We may not spend every waking hour in fear and dread, but by God, we can put ourselves in their shoes without having to work so hard at it."

"I think I'm going to have to try to find some more out about those other ladies who died."

"The other ones who haven't said much to us when I made contact with them, you mean?"

Anna nodded. "I was having a look at my notes before I came over to you. Jonet Clark – who was Hugh's much-loved Elspeth's mum – is actually the odd one out who died on that same day. If I've pieced together what they've told me correctly with the information from the admittedly sparse records, she probably died of something like a heart attack at seeing her nieces strangled and then burned at the stake."

"And who could be surprised at that?" Rita said with a shudder. "Jings, it makes the shivers run up and down my spine just at the thought of witnessing something like that. Let alone if it was *you* I was watching!"

The realisation of what Rita was saying slammed into Anna, and she actually dry heaved at the thought. "Oh my God! Oh my God! …That's what Elspeth saw, wasn't it? …She saw her mum and her own Aunt Geillis after they'd been questioned. After Geillis had been *tortured*! And later she saw her own cousins after they been put to the question, and then had to watch them die the most vile and excruciating death. …Oh God, Aunty! I know I *knew* what had happened to her and to Hugh, but until this moment, I don't think it really sank in…sank in in my *heart*, what that did to both of them."

Rita came and sat on the same sofa as Anna and wrapped her arms around her shaking shoulders.

"It's been quite a day for you, hen," she said softly, hugging Anna to her and feeling more than a little mortified as she realised that in part this was what Gary had been badgering her to wake up to. This was hitting Anna even harder than it might, because she was completely unaccustomed to having such emotional links to the past. It wasn't comfortable for Rita to be making the connections with women who had been so badly abused in the past. But at least doing that psychic thing of linking to another time was by now as easy as breathing to her, having done it ever since her mum had thought her able to handle it. For Anna, it was a bolt from the blue to discover that she could do this, and to have such an emotionally rough first time was making it even harder.

"I'm so sorry, hen," she murmured, as Anna sobbed her heart out. "I'll watch over you, I promise I will."

Rita was true to her word, coming around the following day with a rather large bag which turned out to be full of all sorts of things.

"Good grief, Aunty! How many crystals have you got here?" Anna teased. "You could open up a gem shop with this lot."

Rita had the good grace to laugh with her, but was quick to say, "They all have their properties, and I'm going to take you through the ones you might use for protecting yourself from incoming influences from the Other Side. I can't say exactly which ones you'll use, because the best will be ones that call to you personally."

"Did our 'witches' in the old kirk use crystals, then?" Anna asked, and all by itself that was a warning to Rita of how little Anna really knew.

"No hen, they didn't. Not crystals in the way we use them." She picked up a beautiful purple stone. "This is amethyst. Very good for all sorts of things. But back in the time when women like Grissell McCartney and Jonet Clark lived, they were jewels only rich ladies could afford. And of course, a lot of the lesser gemstones we use nowadays come from the New World. It wasn't until explorers got right into the interior of places like Australia, Africa, and South America that some of those came to light."

"So what would they have known and used?"

It was a question which Rita realised she'd not fully asked herself before, and given that they were trying to settle seventeenth-century healers and mystics – if not witches in the sense that they could perform magic – to their final rest, it was one she ought to have asked long before now.

"Well, they'd have known of incense, but probably had little experience of using it themselves, because stuff like frankincense and myrrh were too expensive," she told Anna, after a pause for thought. "And you make a good point, Anna, because I'd not considered for a moment that incense, all by itself, would reek of the Catholic Church to a man like Gideon. It might work for us in our modern and very secular age as just a prompt to the more spiritual side of life, and without any underlying connotations. But I should have considered that for Gideon, even just a whiff of it would make him angrier than he already was. And that's not what we've been trying to achieve."

"So would the nuns who appear with the witches be more comforted by smelling incense?"

Rita sighed, though not at Anna but at her own assumptions, hesitating before saying, "You do realise that with every one of these questions you are showing how much of an absolute natural you are?" Then as Anna stiffened and looked worried, she explained, "*I* should have taken all of this into consideration, but didn't. I'm used to dealing with rather more modern ghosts, where things like the difference between being Catholic or Protestant wasn't a matter of life or death to them, and wasn't such an issue. But good grief, Anna, you're absolutely right! Some of the modern, more perfumed incense sticks wouldn't feel 'right' to the nuns. But something like frankincense resin burning on a disc of charcoal in the old-fashioned way…*phew*! That would definitely be something they would associate with a priest of a higher level coming to say mass for them."

"So equivalent to something that we'd consider a real treat to experience?"

"Oh yes!"

"But which might be something that our witch ladies, though not rabid Covenanters themselves, would find a bit alien? Didn't the Covenanters renounce all such 'papist' practices? And wouldn't incense be one of those? Would it make our witches fear they'd be spiritually compromised by using it, or even by merely accepting it?"

Rita's stunned expression told Anna that she'd hit upon something even before Rita replied, "I don't know about me teaching you stuff, you're making me stop and think a lot harder about what I do than I have in ages. …No! Don't apologise, Anna. What you're asking is absolutely right on point…was I not Catholic *enough* for Geillis? Who, if she wasn't from around here, as you so rightly suggested, might even have been brought up Catholic?"

Rita shook her head in disgust at her own presumptions. "I've only ever dealt with ghosts for whom I've know a certain amount of family history, and none of them have ever come from an era when there was so much religious turmoil. But that's no excuse for me having come blundering in like a bluebottle in a meat store, making assumptions, and then cussing a blue streak when I got nowhere with the ghosts concerned.

"And nowhere is that more proven than with you instinctively saying that maybe Geillis wasn't a local lass at all. That trying to call her 'home' to Irongray kirk was just ridiculous. Both because, as you and Gary rightly said, it was the place of her torment – so why on earth would she ever want to return there in spirit – but also I'm now realising, because that possibly wasn't even her faith? I wouldn't expect you to have picked up on her intonations, even with her 'voice' in your head, but by the Goddess I should have after all of my years up north. Geillis was a Highlander!

"And in those days, there were a lot more Catholics in the Highlands than the Lowlands – although not all Highlanders were Catholics, either, and many were vehement Protestants. If we want to lay Geillis to rest, we may be looking at getting a Catholic priest to come and say a Latin mass for her in Irongray kirkyard, not just me pissing around with a bit of incense. What was I thinking? *Phfaa*!"

"I think you're being a bit hard on yourself, Aunty."

"No, I'm not, Anna. At least give me the solace of being able to admit that I was wrong – unlike my bloody half-brother who's treated you so badly. And what you've made me see is that I've been trying to apply modern Wiccan practices to ghosts who lived over three centuries in the past, and who wouldn't remotely recognise what I was doing. If I want to call to them, then I have to use something they can understand. It's like speaking to someone of Shakespeare's day in modern English, and expecting them to understand modern colloquial speech and references. Never going to happen!"

"Okay, so what are we going to use of this lot, and for whom, then?"

Rita sighed. "Well, the crystals for protection will still work for *you*. We can still go ahead and get you well and truly warded against ghostly interference. And nothing makes me realise that you need this more than your experience with Isobel. There's some connection there, but I should have taught you how to control it, not leave you to be knocked out by it. But no wonder Gideon fought so hard against us in the main bedroom. To him it must have been as though he was being expelled from his personal space by those he thought the worst kind of Christians, if even Christians at all."

"It was that bad? I mean, that he wouldn't have recognised Catholics as Christians?"

Rita sighed. "Well, you're more in Gary's territory than mine, asking that. But from what he's said on reading up on the period, quite possibly not. That whole thing of the vehement Protestants belonging to what we'd now term the Low Church, regarding anything even vaguely reminiscent of Catholic Church as being 'the Whore of Babylon', certainly isn't made up. That was a very real opinion at the time, and well recorded."

"Good grief! That sounds worse than the Troubles in Northern Ireland, and then some."

"I know. And it's something *I*, again, should have taken a lot more into consideration once I knew that Gideon was a Covenanter. By the Goddess! Archie told me enough of the strife he witnessed over in Belfast when he was a young squaddie. Religious strife among neighbours can get very toxic very fast."

"But what about Hugh? He isn't – wasn't – a Covenanter, but by the same token, I haven't heard anything from him that suggests he was a Catholic, either?"

Rita nodded thoughtfully. "We'll have to check with him, but I think Hugh was what we'd now call a religious moderate. Someone who was probably raised with a church which followed the Covenant's guidelines, but who personally wasn't that deeply committed to only one set of observances. I don't know about you, but I got the impression that Hugh was more of a believer in God and Jesus, than in any specific way to worship either of them?"

Anna agreed. "Yes. That sounds very much more like Hugh. Someone who tried to live his life as a good Christian as the Bible he read – or had read out to him – 'spoke' to him. After all, we are talking about a time not long after the King James Bible got printed for the first time, and was made available to more people, aren't we? But he could still be repulsed by people such as the local Presbyter of Irongray, who could torture women like his own mother in the name of a dour and restrictive reading of the Bible that only they understood."

She paused and looked at what Rita had emptied out onto her rickety old dining table, or at least what passed for one until she could go and get her own stuff up here. "So, is there anything here that we can use that our seventeenth-century ghosts will recognise?"

Pulled out of her mental self-berating, Rita nodded and pointed at the herbs first.

"There's nothing here apart from basil and bay leaves which the women from around here wouldn't know. Granted, some of the more Mediterranean herbs would have only been used in very small quantities, because they wouldn't grow up here in the colder and wetter climate. But seventeenth-century Britain wasn't totally divorced from Europe. And pedlars would have brought dried plants like lavender and rosemary this far north. They weren't that cut off up here."

"So no crystals, and careful with who we use the incense on, but otherwise there's quite a lot we can use? What about tarot cards? Would they have known them?"

Rita was a little cagier over that. "Did they use tarot cards as divination cards in that time? I'm not so sure. What we call tarot cards were certainly around by that time, but they were very much works of art owned only by the very rich. You have to go more than a century onwards to get the first surge of popular interest in them, and Continental printers producing decks at a price that more ordinary people could afford."

"Maybe not such a good idea, then, to try to use the cards to actually communicate with our ghosts?"

Rita took the point and scooped the tarot decks back up and put them back into her bag, along with many of the crystals, adding, "I'm guessing here, but I think we're okay making smudge sticks out of herbs which could be found or bought locally. I know that our concept of smudge sticks comes very much from the American First Nation peoples, but I can't think that it was utterly unknown for wise women here, even in the period we're talking about, to burn herbs in rituals."

However, she did look enquiringly at Anna, as if expecting someone in the Beyond to communicate with Anna to tell them otherwise. Yet if the ghosts had any opinions, they were keeping them to themselves, and so for an hour or two, Rita took Anna through the crystals and other items she might want to use.

To her surprise, Anna was actually wary of warding herself too vigorously. "I don't want to make it impossible for them to contact me if it's urgent," she told Rita. "After all, if I'm the one with the supposed connection to some of them, surely it stands to reason that if anything really bad starts going down, it'll be me they want to warn?"

"That's a very valid point," Rita admitted. "But just be very sure that it is one of the women and not Gideon! He's trouble."

They left it at that, not least because Rita didn't want to overwhelm Anna now that she was beginning to realise what an absolute beginner she was. But it did give Anna a bit more confidence, and with that came the realisation that every time they spoke to the ghosts, Rita very much took the lead. That was great at first, because Anna hadn't had a clue where to start, but now she was starting to have some questions of her own that she wanted to ask. There was no way that she would risk trying her hand at contacting Hugh, though, not least because she suspected that one whiff of her being there on her own and open to that portal – or whatever it was – would draw Gideon like an angry wasp to honey. Indeed, trying anything within the hotel seemed foolhardy, if not downright dangerous.

Yet she did want to know if she could now control contact with someone long gone, after being so overwhelmed by Isobel. And thinking back, she was increasingly coming to the opinion that it was Isobel's *fate*, rather than Isobel herself, which had hit her so hard. She'd been opened up – tuned in might be a better way of thinking of it – but Isobel hadn't tried to speak to her. Isobel hadn't wanted her to actively do anything. It was more as if she had been given some kind of weird 3-D imager through time to bear witness to Isobel's fate, and having done that, it was enough. Would telling Hugh and Gideon what she'd seen help or hinder getting them to leave?

1664 – 1670

Elspeth

Elspeth's new friends weren't without their dangers, or at least dangers which Elspeth with her bitter memories soon spotted. Jonet and Agnes Hendrie were cousins, both widows, and rather worse, had small crofts close by one another which might not have been anything special on their own, but if put together would make a desirable holding for their shared other male cousin. A cousin who, like the dreadful John Corsan and John McCartney whom Elspeth had known, was already married, and so in no position to marry one or other of them to get his hands on at least one of the crofts legitimately.

And it was this, along with local news, which made Elspeth confide in them about her mother, aunt, and cousins' fate on one frosty spring morning, as they were trying to get the frozen village pump to work before the other women arrived.

"It was so cruel," she told them. "Poor Agnes had done nothing to warrant such accusations. Her sister Margaret and my Aunt Geillis were less guarded about what they said in public, but some of the things they got accused of were just ridiculous. Agnes' neighbours were bullied into making accusations, saying untruths that they'd had to appease her or she would curse them. As if poor Agnes could have made cows wander or faggots of firewood suddenly disappear! And the worst you could say of Margaret was that she threw a large stone at the bailie when he came and wrongfully tried to take her fleeces – not her best idea, but hardly worth making a fuss over. The stone only gave him a bruise, yet in court he made out like he'd been seriously wounded."

"I hear you, Elspeth," said another of her new friends, Katherine Sands. "Thirty years ago, my mother was murdered like your family." She gave a shudder. "'Tis a terrible thing to witness. I'm lucky I was recently wed then, and not at home when they came for her, and my John has always stood up for me. But even so, I get looked at sideways by some every time the Presbyter preaches against witchcraft. Be warned, there are some around here who like to cause mischief just as you had in Dumfries. Those who think to ingratiate themselves with those they think have power, even if it means doing true evil to those they accuse without proof."

"And it makes me cringe every time I hear of that," admitted the fourth of the women, Elizabeth Huiton, "because the bailie in question was my uncle, Edward Ezat, who used witchcraft as an excuse to get rid of his first wife, my aunt Margaret."

"That's just what happened to *my* cousin Margaret," gasped Elspeth. "Thomas Milligan had never been faithful to her, but then he met a widow with money, and that sealed Margaret's fate and that of her mother and sister!"

Elizabeth nodded. "Sadly, not that uncommon. For my uncle, may he rot in Hell, 'twas because he was so taken with the Covenant, and had just risen to be an elder in the kirk. 'Twasn't good for him to be known to have a respected healer for a wife once that happened. The chance to creep around the Council in Edinburgh soon had him making up accusations against her, though given how far back he went with them, 'tis a wonder nobody asked him why it had taken him so long to come forward. I was too young to go to the trial, but my ma said that for a big man like him, he still managed to imply that he was afeared his wife would hex him – as if my poor Aunt Margaret could *ever* have done such a thing. Nor her sister Elizabeth, after whom I'm named, who also ended up tried for things she wouldn'a have dreamed of doing."

Elspeth took a deep breath, knowing that what she was about to say might condemn her, but praying that with women who knew all too well what accusations could bring, that they wouldn't betray her.

"Do you ask for money for your cures?" she asked, aware that her voice was shaking. "My ma only did when it was for obvious things, like a cough soother. For any other help, she was careful to only take a gift of food, or something like seeds which we could use. 'Take nothing more than one neighbour might lend another,' was what she told me."

"Your ma was wise," the last of the women, Isobel Inglis, agreed. "We all need to take care. Have you heard? They've taken seven women in for questioning at Torryburn not a week past."

Elspeth felt her blood running cold again, as it had when she'd heard the news in the market place. Torryburn was the next small town to the east on the Firth of Forth, halfway to the larger town of Dunfermline, and even less of an important place than Culross was.

"I thought when the King came back to the throne, the witch hunts would stop," Jonet Hendrie said mournfully, referring to the return of King Charles II a little over five years earlier in 1660. "I thought with him and his ministers wanting the Covenanters gone, that their righteous Presbyterianism would get watered down. That there'd be fewer Presbyters baying for the blood of women like us."

Her sister gave a snort of disgust. "Instead it got us a massive witch-hunt in the two years after! What's wrong with these men? Can they no' leave women alone?"

"It's not 'women'," Katherine said bitterly. "It's those of us who they see as having a bit of power."

"But we haven't got any power," protested Elizabeth.

Yet Katherine shook her head. "No' the kind of power you're thinking of, Eliza. But we bring forth life, do we not? Without women there can be no more men."

"But the same holds true for us," Elizabeth riposted. "We need men to have children just as much."

"We do," Katherine agreed, "but for some who want and need earthly power in a way that few women I've ever known do, it's not a welcome realisation. Not for these men who've grown up with some minister or presbyter telling them that they no longer need a bishop to tell them and their kirk how to speak to God. In their minds, God is practically sitting on their shoulders and whispering in their ears…though 'tis strange how he always tells them just what they want to hear. So you see, my friends, those witch-hunts of a couple of years ago were those same men panicking that they were going to lose all if the King's men thought they were fomenting rebellion."

Agnes Hendrie nodded. "I said at the time it was as if they were trying to say to the King, 'Look at all these witches! You need *us* to be watching out for them. Your grandfather, King James, hunted down the witches who were poisoning his reign. You need us to do the same for you.' Though thank the Lord that this time around, many were questioned, but few went to trial. There weren't the hangings and burnings of our last King James' reign."

"But questioning can be as bad," Elspeth said mournfully. "We must prepare what healing salves we can, and be willing to take them to our sisters in Torryburn when they get freed, even if it's under cover of the darkest nights. Do any of you know their names?"

Jonet Hendrie said, "I heard that Christian May, Agnes Broun, and Margaret Cowie got taken in."

Her sister Agnes adding, "And Elspeth Guild and Margaret Dobie."

Katherine sighed and added, "I'm sure that Grissell Anderson is another and also Margaret Horne."

"Oh, I don't like this," Elspeth said, choking up. "Seven women? That sounds too like what happened in Dumfries with my cousins!"

To Elspeth's great relief, in the end, none of the women from Torryburn went to trial, but all of them bore the marks of their questioning when eventually seen in public again. Of her new friends, only Katherine Sands and the younger woman called Isobel Inglis dared to come with her to take salves to the seven women of Torryburn, though all of them made healing potions. On those nights when the moon was hidden by clouds, or during new moons, they would creep out and make the three mile walk to Torryburn to make the deliveries. Katherine had a bold streak and would knock on doors to hand over the little packages, and somehow

Isobel became enthralled by her daring and went with her.

Elspeth wasn't as foolhardy, always insisting that she leave their gifts in places where only the women would go and find them, such as by the nanny goat or the hens, or tucked behind a butter churn. She never woke anyone. Knocking on someone's door loud enough to wake them in the depths of night was likely to be loud enough to wake a neighbour, and once seen, who knew who might testify as to what they had seen if under pressure? Therefore nobody saw Elspeth, and nobody knew whose brews and mixtures were in which of the cheap pots that could be bought in any market place. Elspeth had learned her lessons the hard way, and she intended to survive for her children.

What saddened her was that the children still sometimes asked where Alex was. If Jonet and James had any memories of Mailie or Niall, they never mentioned them, and Elspeth had gradually come to realise that in their minds, she and Alex were their parents, and little Marione their full sister. In one way that made life simpler for her, for the children never let anything out in public that might cause queries. She never had to give awkward explanations as to what she was doing with her sister's children when she could barely provide for them. Not that it was odd for one sister to be bringing up another's in an age when women all too frequently died in a late pregnancy, but generally the village knew who had died where and when – they didn't just turn up out of the blue with children in tow.

Time passed, and Dougal married a local girl and found a position as a groom to one of the big houses on the outskirts of Dunfermline, but he never forgot Elspeth and her kindness to him. He couldn't bring much money, but when there was an abundance of vegetables from the kitchen garden, he would often ride over in an evening on one of the work ponies to bring her some. She also sent messages when she could across to Argyll, and for a long time she wondered whether they ever got there. She had to find someone to write them for her, and so she had to be circumspect in what she said, never fully trusting her scribe not to go straight to the kirk if he thought something was amiss, and of course she could never tell if the address was right.

She had never forgotten Hugh, though, and if her letters went to the McAllisters, he was nonetheless always included in them. Then slowly a few letters came back, which she discovered were from Sorley's daughter, Ishbel. Hugh was still soldiering, but with Sorley's sons, for Sorley himself had had to take a role up at the big castle since he was too old to ride out anymore. But then in 1670 a letter came that said that Niall was dead, found hanging from a tree beside the graveyard where his first wife lay.

According to Ishbel, in the years since they'd been gone he'd become a drunk, and the two boys – Callum and William – were back with their grandparents and working their fields for them in their old age. Not that Elspeth told Jonet and Jamie, as he was now known as far and wide. What was the point when they didn't remember Niall or their older brothers? And in a way it was a strange relief to know that that connection was now fully broken.

"Why am I staying here?" Elspeth wondered aloud, the week after the news about Niall had come. "Who am I waiting for? Alex is never coming back now. I missed my chance with Hugh. And Katherine, Jonet, and Agnes, are reckless with their craft. They're going to bring someone down on us sooner or later." In reality she was talking to Bessie, the old pony who'd come with her and her father all the way from Dumfries up to Argyll and then here. Indeed, Bessie was proving to be more of a constant companion than any human being, and sometimes Elspeth thought she understood more too. "What am I going to do, Bessie?"

As if in answer, Bessie suddenly began tugging her away from the road that led to the coast and home. They had gone into Dunfermline market – something Elspeth rarely did since she couldn't afford much, but she had needed specific seeds from the apothecary there to sow in her little garden – and so they were on a road they rarely used. So it was odd that Bessie should be so insistent to go a different way. There were no particularly lush patches of meadow for her to graze as far as Elspeth knew…and then she saw them. Standing stones.

"Oh Bessie! You clever girl."

Blessing the fact that it was a chilly March evening, and therefore few folk were abroad at all, Elspeth felt safe to go right up to the stones. She hadn't seen a soul for the last mile or two, and so she dropped Bessie's reins, knowing that she wouldn't stray, and went up to the largest of the stones. It was a huge thing with four deep furrows running down its length on the western side, and five on the eastern one, and a groove running up and over its top. The holes which were bored into it on either face, about a hand's width wide, lay too high up for Elspeth to look in, but there seemed to be no light shining through, which made her think that they didn't go all the way through.

"Well aren't you a beauty," she breathed in awe. Unlike the Apostles' Stones that she had known over near Dumfries, she couldn't even see the remains of a circle, but three other stones lay clustered a short way away. Yet she could hear her mother's voice in her head telling her about ancient fertility symbols, and if the three stones represented the male, for one stood more upright than the others, then this one definitely felt more female. Was that what the circular hole alluded to?

She went and put her arms around the stone from the side, so that she was touching both faces of the stone with her hands, and was surprised at how warm it felt. There was an energy to the place that revitalised her, but in a warm and familiar way. For the first time in years, Elspeth felt more like her old self.

"What do I do?" she asked the stone. "Do I stay here, or do I leave?"

'Go!' a voice in her head said. This time, she didn't see any fae, but there was something about that voice that was familiar enough for her to think that it came from one of them. 'If you stay, you will die. Leave now while you can.'

"Where do I go?" she asked, but this time there was no answer.

Yet that was all the urging Elspeth needed. Her instincts had been nudging her to do this for weeks already, and so she opened the precious parcels of seeds and placed one of each into the hole in the stones as thanks. Then, wrapping them up securely again, she picked up Bessie's reins and, bracing herself against the chill wind which was now blowing in off the Firth, turned for home, with Bessie now eager to get back to the warmth of her little lean-to stable at the cottage. Yet up on the hillside she saw a fox illuminated in a bean of moonlight, as the clouds passed away, and she was sure that like the fox who had rescued her back at the Apostles' Stones, he was watching her.

"I heard you, and I thank you," she called out, remembering the need to thank the fae, and saw the fox stand up, bow his head, and then vanish with a swish of his bushy tail.

For the next few days she tried to make plans, but couldn't seem to find a direction to go in. Then Dougal appeared with happiness written all over his face.

"I'm to be one of the new under-grooms at House of Duns!" he declared with pride. "'Tis up by Montrose, Elspeth. The family are the Erskines, and Lord David has just inherited the house. He's a judge and a commissioner to Parliament, so he'll be wanting to do more entertaining, and that means more servants. My Meg and me will be living in one of the stable cottages, but there are other wee cottages on the estate, and they need more women to do things like the laundry. I've told them about you, and there's a wee place close enough that you can walk in to do the laundry. Please say you'll come, Elspeth. 'Twill be a better cottage than this, and on the laird's estate ye'll be safer than here."

Elspeth's sigh of relief and immediate 'yes' took Dougal somewhat off guard. Clearly he'd been thinking that he was going to have to do a lot more persuading.

"Marione is eight and old enough to do some helping out," Elspeth explained, "and Jonet and Jamie will soon be looking for proper jobs of their own. If we go now, the chances are that Jonet can go into service and Jamie join you in the stables. I'm as good as a widow, Dougal, and soon to be forty, though I've forgotten exactly when. I need security in my old age, not endlessly waiting for men who never come. Jonet and Marione are good girls. They'll not leave me to starve once I'm too old to work, and working within a big house won't be as rough as dragging the linen to and from the big houses here. I'll come and thank you for remembering me, bless your kind heart."

“Nay, Elspeth. ’Tis me who’s grateful to you. I know who it was who insisted I come with you from Argyll. If I’d been left with Niall he’d have beaten me to death when in his cups or left me to starve. You saved me. ’Tis my chance to pay you back.”

Yet as Elspeth said goodbye to her friends, part of her still called out, ‘Where are you, Hugh?’

CHAPTER 7

With Cameron needing to make some business calls, Anna was quite glad to have had a day's respite from the ghosts, but on the Thursday, Cameron appeared from the self-catering cottage Anna had installed him in with the dogs, inviting her out again.

"Shall we go and look at that graveyard with the big memorial in?" he asked, and somewhat recovered, Anna felt up to saying yes. Some retail therapy in Dumfries yesterday afternoon, plus the consumption of quality coffee and sticky cake, had done much to restore her equilibrium.

Yet having agreed to it, finding Dalgarnock Kirkyard turned out to be harder than they expected. They went in and out of the tiny village of Thornhill without ever finding the way to it. Twice. And in the end, Cameron resorted to going and buying an Ordnance Survey map.

"Gary will laugh his socks off at me for this," he said ruefully. "The man never seems to lack a map, and he's pulled my leg several times over relying on the sat nav. Well this is the proof that he's right."

They spread the map out across the bonnet of his car and at last saw where they had gone wrong.

"Good grief, it's up that little track there!" Cameron said in disgust. "No wonder we couldn't see it from the road."

Yet when they went that way and found a signpost, they still ran out of road, finding the way blocked by a gate, and ended up turning around to attack it from the other end of the tiny track of a lane. Finally pulling up in a small parking area that was more rough ground than anything purpose built, they got out and looked around.

"You'd think that all churchyards would be much the same," Cameron observed, "but they're not, are they? Some of them give you a right dose of the creeps, while others are positively friendly like this one, and often you can't say why."

"That's exactly it," Anna agreed.

While Thornhill itself was busy with a lot of through traffic – being on the arterial A76, which headed off north-west towards the Ayrshire coast – away from the village's central crossroad it was very quiet, and the cemetery was out in open fields beyond there. In the distance, they had a perfect view to the low, rolling foothills to what they knew were the higher, smooth-domed mountains beyond, so very different to the jagged peaks of the west coast or parts of the Grampians. The atmosphere was of peace and tranquillity and very different to what Anna had felt at Irongray.

Looking at the map, Anna observed, “We’re right by the Scaur Water. I bet these fields don’t half flood in winter. I wonder why they put a cemetery here? Not exactly the obvious place, is it? You wouldn’t want your granny getting washed away by the winter floods.”

“Maybe they didn’t get as many bad floods as we do now with climate change?” Cameron suggested. “Or may be this is just far enough away from the river to be safe?”

Anna gave him a baleful look. “You wouldn’t say that if you’d lived down where I did. Where the River Severn meets the River Teme, we got a *lot* of floods, and you soon realise how fast and how far a river can rise. I mean, really fast! People used to get caught out parking on Worcester racecourse in the morning and come back to find that they couldn’t get to their car when they left work!”

Cameron was searching on his phone while listening to her and suddenly exclaimed, “Hey! I’ve found a YouTube video about this place.”

Leaning in so that she could see and hear too, Anna watched the video with him.

“Wow!” she gasped softly as the presenter told them that the parish church had ceased to exist in 1606. “So do you think it’s significant that this was almost what you’d call a redundant burial ground even by the time the witches died in 1659 – or if not necessarily redundant as a graveyard, then at least not next door to the church anymore – and even more so by the time of the Killing Times in 1685? Was it a 'safe' place to bury those who might offend the great and good of a normal modern parish church, do you think?"

"You have to wonder," Cameron agreed, "although not everyone on the memorial is buried here. But if you wanted to put a whacking big memorial up to people who died for a version of the Kirk that had fallen from favour, then this is isolated enough not to offend the worthies of any parish."

They listened on, Anna then hitting pause as the presenter told them that fifty-four men and three women were represented on the memorial cross.

"Hang on, doesn't that sound a bit lopsided to you?" she asked Cameron. "Wouldn't you think that things like religious attendance of service would go by families?"

He shrugged. "I suppose it would all depend on personal faith?"

"No, Cam! Not back then. You're taking a very twenty-first century view on that."

"What's so different, then?"

"What women wanted, to be blunt!" Anna shook her head. "Honestly, it was a revelation to me – not being a historian – as to how little say most women would have had in things like that. The more I read, the more I'm so bloody glad that I wasn't born then. Truly, if your old man was a rabid non-conformist of the Covenanter kind, then like it or not, you went to the conventicles – those were prayer meetings that would do a Southern Baptist in the States proud – and sod what you wanted, I tell you! Fervent praying. Calling on the Lord when the spirit moved you. All of that sort of thing went on here when the USA was still in its infancy."

"Good grief!"

"I'm not kidding," Anna said with some passion. "My heart goes out to those poor women, because regardless of how they had been brought up, if their husbands got the bit between their teeth over the Covenant, then they had damn all say in the matter. They went! Even if it choked them to do the responses, they went. And not least because back then it was perfectly socially acceptable for a husband to beat the crap out of his wife if she didn't obey him!

"Okay, I suspect that most women weren't *that* easily crushed, especially about things within the home and to do with the kids. Not every woman in the seventeenth-century was a doormat, not remotely. But when it came to how a family was perceived by their neighbours and the outside world, then yes, it was very much a man's world. Far more so than anything we know these days, except for the women abroad who live under things like Sharia law."

Cameron looked at her aghast. "That bad?"

"Well in terms of what went on in public, yes, my interpretation is that it was. As I said, there must have been more give and take within most marriages in the home. But you've got to remember how much influence the local ministers had. And it was considerable!

"A man might have had very little say in the matter himself as to which prayer meeting or kirk he attended, or at least not if he didn't want to be shunned by his neighbours, and possibly even worse, by his employer or landlord if he was lower down the social scale, as the majority of men were. So what choice would a man like that have had, if his wife started kicking off and saying she wouldn't go to *where*ver for *what*ever? If it was make the missus toe-the-line, or lose the roof over the family's head, he'd have little choice in the matter. And that's why the temperament of the local minister was so critical back then."

"I had no idea," Cameron breathed in astonishment.

"So then knowing that, don't you think it's weird that you get only *three* women mentioned on this thing? Three out of fifty-seven names?" By now they were standing in front of the memorial and reading the names. "So from the top down, we've got the obvious Elizabeth H. Ferguson, Margaret Gracie, and Elizabeth G. Hunter, and that's it!

"And what these people are saying online doesn't exactly marry up, does it? How do they *know* – according to the Covenanter memorial website I went onto, at least – that the Elizabeth H. Ferguson on the memorial really *is* the same as an Elizabeth Hunter Ferguson of *Holland*? Holland is a bit distant to be making that strong a link, don't you think? Especially when none of the names is exactly uncommon. Margaret Gracie of Penpont, which I now know is a local village, I get. People must have known who she was around here, or at least who her family was by the time any gravestone got erected, let alone this twentieth-century monument.

"But these guys are saying that Elizabeth Hunter *must* be the same person as Elizabeth H. Ferguson, without saying how or why they think that? Let's face it, *we* know of two sets of sisters both called Margaret and Agnes, so how can anyone make such an assumption about that H. middle name? Even on this stone we've got Harkness and Heron as surnames, let alone if she had Helen or Harriet as a middle name."

"So who is their third woman than?" Cameron asked. "If they think the two Elizabeths are the same woman, who is the third they refer to?"

"*Huh*! That's 'M. Jas. Forsyth', which they read as being *Mrs* Jas. – presumably Jason – Forsyth, who, again according to them, died all the way over on the east coast near Aberdeen at Dunnottar Castle. But why on earth would she be remembered over here? Let's face it, the records from that time are scant to say the least. I think it's really dangerous to presume that just because you've got two women of a similar name – and common names at that – that they *must* be the same person. If we had the equivalent of the comprehensive records we have these days, with dates of birth and parentage, you could be fairly certain, but not in time when over half of the records haven't even survived."

"Point taken," Cameron sighed. "It really is a leap of faith, isn't it? But looking up and down this list of names on the cross, I really do see your point about the women. They're vastly under-represented, aren't they?"

"Exactly! It was supposed to be a hotbed of dissent around here. Where are all the local women? None apart from Margaret! Yet you look at the men, and overwhelmingly they're all from around here. Yes, there are a few who died further afield in places like Edinburgh – so probably went to trial over there – but the rest are local men, even if you allow for a bit of wishful thinking on the part of those who had the memorial made."

Cameron was beginning to grasp that Anna was making a particular point here. "Okay…I know I'm missing something else here. What is it?"

"Well, the Covenanters had to be tried according to the law, or at least were supposed to be. In truth many of these men on here got shot where they were caught or entrapped. Look at them, Cam. There are a host of tiny villages which couldn't possibly all have had their own jails, or at least tolbooths, and therefore somewhere in which a trial could have been held.

"The ones who died in Dumfries or Edinburgh…they went to a trial, even if it wasn't quite as particular in finding the truth as we'd like, but I bet the others in the villages didn't. They were either shot where they were found, or there are those who must have been transported or put on prison hulks. I don't know what 'Pitlochy's ship' was that's on here, but two men died on it, which can't have been good.

"But my question still stands – where are the local women? Where are the wives? And the thing that keeps coming back to me is that it was probably much easier to try *them* as a witch in the *local* courts, where they could get away with less justification for a violent 'questioning' which the woman might not survive. Witches went against *everyone's* religion, Covenanter or Episcopalian or Catholic, or any shade of grey in between. So it was much easier to allow – or perhaps it's better to say that no *man* in a position of authority *objected* strongly to – a witch trial, in the way they might over a fellow *man* being unfairly tried for his faith?

"Dumfries might never again have seen a mass witch killing like our ghosts suffered in 1659, but there are people on this memorial from 1667, which is only eight years on from then. In ones and twos, I found more on the website in Dumfries itself, let alone anywhere else, in 1661, 1664, and 1671. It didn't completely stop with our ghosts!"

Cameron could hear her outrage making her voice shake, as Anna continued,

"*That's* what incensed Hugh – the knowledge that men like Grierson were using the excuse of witch trials to allow them to kill women like Grissell Asman and the others who died in Wigtown, for whom they would otherwise have had to justify a formal trial which conformed to civil laws. When the Covenant was at the peak of its power and influence, the Kirk Session were virtually a law unto themselves, especially where women accused of witchcraft were concerned, and later, when the Covenant was as good as outlawed, the prohibitions against witches still stood. You could drag some poor soul in front of a local court and incarcerate her to be 'questioned' without having to justify why you were doing it as late as the early eighteenth century. Women got a raw deal for nearly a century and a half, Covenanter or not!

"A man praying wildly out on his own the soldiers hunting them might get away with shooting on the spot – because *all* preachers were men in the Covenanter Church, and they could use that excuse for a shooting, especially if he was particularly vehement and refuse to recant when caught. But the women stayed closer to home, from what Aunty Rita was telling me. So it must have been that much harder to drag a woman out of her own farmyard, probably in front of her neighbours, without much greater proof of her attending conventicles than if they found some man praying or preaching on a hillside, clearly trying to keep what he was doing *covert* if not exactly hidden. That's a big part of it with the men, that they were deliberately trying to do things out of sight of the law. But what could you accuse a woman of doing that wasn't visible to others when she was at home? Making charms and spells!"

She stepped back and scanned the monument up and down. "There are fifty-three men on this monument, from all around this area, but if you take the online database records for the half century from

1650 to 1700 which covers this same period, twenty-two women were 'investigated' in Dumfries itself *alone,* let alone the wider district. And just because they all didn't go to a full trial, doesn't mean they didn't die from the 'questioning', very much as Hugh's grandmother did. They were of such little consequence to the men in power that *their* fates didn't get recorded. *They* don't appear on any marble memorial!

"And it works both ways, Cam. Where are the husbands on the witch trial database? Because in an era when a woman was scarcely allowed to sneeze in public without her husband's say-so, if a woman could be murdered for simply praying as her husband ordered her to, where are the men being accused of – and punished for – not keeping their witchy wives in order? Looking at our ladies, only one of them – Margaret Clark – had a husband who testified against her, and none seem to have a husband on trial alongside them. So why target widows so hard? If it was because no husband was keeping them in order, then where are the men in the witch trial records? Because, while widows are overly represented, they aren't all of the women by any stretch of the imagination.

"Yes, there are men accused of witchcraft themselves. But I went and looked. Just ten in a whole century-and-a-half in these shires. In the same period, there were *thirteen* women accused within tiny Kirkcudbright itself, and though most of them never went to a trial, it was for things as simple as healing someone. But *these* men," and she waved her hand in disgust at the memorial, "who openly defied the *government,* no less, andthe *King, and* the Kirk...and *publicly*...these *men* get a bloody monument!"

Her mention of the names, though, gave Cameron the opening to distract her back to what they'd come here for. "Grierson!" he proclaimed triumphantly, pointing to a name on the memorial. "See? And he can't be of the family of the laird, can he? Not if he's on here as having been martyred."

"But look at the surname of the name before him," Anna gasped in stunned tones as his distraction worked. "Gracie! Both of my family surnames are on here."

"But no Clarkes," Cameron reassured her.

"No, but that's the surname of three of our ghostly witches," Anna reminded him. "So maybe there's a reason why they aren't on a memorial to the very people who hunted *them.*"

"Ouch. Didn't think of that. ...There's a Cor*san* and a Cor*son* on here, though. That's Gideon's family name, isn't it?"

Anna nodded. "Corsan with an 'a', but that could just be down to spelling hardly being regular back then. I think some of the modern histories I've been ploughing through modernise them all to Carson, so you'd have to be *very* sure from other sources that you were talking about the same family, or not."

Cameron had been using his iPhone to take shots of the different names as a record of what they'd found, and suddenly gasped as he checked back to make sure he'd got them all. "Do you remember that weird pyramid thing in Dumfries that Gary took us to see?"

"The Dumfries martyrs' memorial, you mean?"

"Well one of the names on that was a William Grierson. We didn't take much notice of it then, because we were trying to identify our ghosts, and that wasn't one of the names we were looking at. But William died earlier than some, in 1667."

"Not earlier than the witches, though. Their date of 1659 is burned into my brain permanently." She looked over his shoulder at the screen and realised what he'd seen. "…Oh! Then that must be him here on this monument, too, because the William Grierson on here is 1667 as well. Surely there can't have been two men of the same name killed in the same year *and* in the same area? That would be a bit too spooky."

Cameron agreed. "I wonder who the Robert Grierson was who is on here, too? He died later in 1685, in what Gary tells us are the main Killing Times. A son, perhaps? Ingliston isn't that far from here, so it looks like he was as local as William."

"Come on," Anna said with a shiver. "This is starting to creep me out. Let's go home."

CHAPTER 8

However, once back at her cottage, with the log burner lit against a chilly spring evening that was threatening frost, they sat at her rickety table and looked at the Covenanters' website, while drinking warming mugs of soup. Anna got up to shake the chips she had cooking in her air fryer, and to turn the gammon steaks over under the grill, when Cameron called across to her, "Hey! That other church Gary took us to? One of the men who died alongside the blokes buried there was Robert Grierson – the one from today's memorial! And listen to this, Anna, this website says that those five men were shot by Colonel James Douglas. Apparently, he sentenced them to death where they were caught, and they were shot in front of an old thorn tree – a bit biblical isn't it? Wasn't the True Cross supposed to be a thorn, and that's why the Glastonbury thorn is so revered as an offspring of that tree, brought over by Joseph of Arimathea?

...Seem to remember reading about that somewhere.

"So how accurate is this? Is that later wishful thinking, pointing a finger to their devout adherence to what was thought to be the 'true' path of righteousness? Where is that thorn tree, and why isn't *it* a memorial to the men? If they were remembered down the years, you can't imagine that the locals would have let someone just hack it down. These are the same men who weren't allowed time even to pray before being shot, meaning we know they weren't easily forgotten, so what about where it happened?"

She came and looked at the laptop. "There's a lot of similar phrasing to what's written on Hugh's memorial, isn't there? Not identical, but the drift is the same. Interesting what Hugh said as well – that Colonel Douglas was a toy soldier, and good at parading around, but with little experience of hard fighting. Whereas Claverhouse he spoke of as being very much a soldier's soldier, and you don't read of him being maligned in the same way on these memorials, do you? Later, maybe. Gary says he became known as Bloody Clavers eventually. But at this point, it sounds like Douglas was getting the bit between his teeth and going outside of the law, because he knew his family would protect him from prosecution."

Cameron smiled up at her. "And it makes sense of Hugh saying that he was less bothered by Douglas being accused of killing him when he didn't, than Gideon getting away with the crime.

Sounds like this Colonel Douglas was a pretty unpleasant bloke – especially if he wouldn't even let men pray before dying. That would have been something of a no-no whichever side you were on, surely?"

"I think so, but you'd be better asking Gary."

The timer pinged on the air fryer, and Anna served up their gammon, eggs, and chips, rendering further conversation difficult while they tucked in. Quite often Anna ate at the hotel, meaning that she'd had leftover portions of some superb dishes by Emilio, but after a while she'd also begun to hanker for something a bit more basic. And today the fresh air had given them both an appetite.

So it was only as they collapsed into Anna's sagging sofas, a hound with each of them, that Cameron woke the laptop up and began typing.

"What's your email address?" he asked.

"My email? Why do you need that?"

"Ancestry!" he declared with a grin. "I'm signing you up. No excuse now, Anna! Let's find out who you really are!"

It didn't take long to set Anna up with the basics for her account, after which Cameron suggested letting the system do its own thing for a day or so.

"You'll hopefully have some people who'll have done a bit of the work for you," he told her, as he went to make his way back to his own cottage. "Don't expect miracles. We won't go straight back to the seventeenth century in one go, but you'll hopefully get more of an idea of where your ancestors lived."

She spent her last day's holiday going shopping for clothes in Dumfries, and then joining Cameron and the dogs for a walk down at the pretty coastal village of Rockcliffe, very consciously not engaging with Covenanters or ghosts. The only blot on the horizon was a nasty letter from Mrs Coleborn's solicitors, saying that they would be investigating the possibility of bringing a civil case against Anna for the death of Mr Coleborn. Apparently Mrs Coleborn also intended to reclaim the cost of transporting her husband's body back down to Worcester, and was threatening to drag Anna through the courts for the distress and harm she had done to Jensen. However, Cameron was swift to get his own solicitors involved in defending Anna, and after a long phone call to Mrs Coleborn's legal representatives telling them just what had happened, they in turn told her what Gary and Rita had already said to Anna, which was that she didn't have a leg to stand on. They did warn Anna and Cameron that the likelihood of Mrs Coleborn leaving at that was slim, and she would undoubtedly come up with some other claim, but for now, at least, her claws had been cut.

However, it did make Anna's mind up about one thing.

"I honestly can't see me ever going back to live in Worcester now," she told Gary, Rita, and Cameron, as they sat in Gary's cottage after a late

Sunday lunch following a busy weekend. "I'd be forever jittery that I was going to walk into one of theirs or Mum and Dad's cronies. I don't think I can face a shouting match in the frozen aisle when I'm just trying to do my weekly shop. I think I'd be better going and emptying my flat and selling it."

"There's no rush to do that, though," Rita said firmly. "Take your time. You ideally want to sell your flat and buy somewhere up here, so that you have your own place in the future when you retire. You can always let it out for now and get some income. Start looking at the property market before you jump."

Anna gulped. "Heavens, Aunty! I'm not that close to retirement. I've got a good thirty years to go before I can do that." Then she remembered what Gary had told her had happened to Rita when her husband had retired from the army, only to lose everything to his gambling debts.

So she forgave Rita when she responded with, "You can't be too careful!" and saw Gary catching her eye and winking.

No, she would not argue with Rita over that. Not knowing where she was coming from with those worries. Her late husband's hidden gambling debts were the reason why Rita was finding it so hard to fully commit to a relationship with Gary, and having lost everything once, it was a very sore spot for Rita.

Desperate now to change the conversation, Anna grabbed her laptop and switched it on, saying,

"By the way, Cam was right – someone has started a family tree on Ancestry!"

"Great!" Cameron enthused. "Come on then, what have they found? Please tell me you're not related to royalty and worth a fortune, because I don't think I can face having to find someone as good as you to run the place." He was joking, but Anna appreciated that he was trying to lighten the mood for Rita, Cameron having been brought up to date on why Rita was so cagey about relationships.

"Err... No," Anna laughed. "Not a drop of even faintly noble blood as far as I can see as yet."

"That's good then...isn't it?" Cameron said hopefully. "No links to the Griersons of Lagg?"

"Not that anyone has come up with. Mind you, we're only back to the 1800s here, not the 1680s, so it's far from certain."

"Don't keep us in suspense," Gary said, "what have you got, then?"

Anna sat back to turn the laptop towards them. "This is Mum's family tree as far as we've got. Heaven's they were rabbits! How many generations did you estimate in three hundred years, Aunty?"

Rita paused, then answered, "An average of ten, but it could be nine to twelve."

Anna gave a laugh, "Well the Clarkes knock that out of the ball-park. I thought my sister was the black sheep for getting pregnant in her late teens. But having belatedly realised that my mum was only two years older than that when she had Heather, I was relieved to find that my gran on her side had Mum when she was thirty-two. ...Except

Mum wasn't her oldest child, as I initially presumed, but her *youngest*, with the oldest being born in 1959. She started her family early too. Mum had, or has, two older brothers and two sisters!"

She took a deep breath. "So that's my gran, Euphemia Jean Howarth Grierson, born 1939…and I can't find any record of her dying!"

"Good God," Rita gasped. "Your grandma is still alive?"

Anna nodded. "I think so. And so is my grandfather, Davey John Clarke, I think, because I can't see an entry for him having died either."

"Great," Gary enthused. "So there's a chance we might be able to trace them. Of anyone, they ought to know something o' the local connections. But you said they were rabbits, Anna. What did you mean by that?"

Anna groaned. "Okay… so according to this, Gran was born in 1939 in Ayr. But *her* mum's mother – that's my great-great-grandma – must have been celebrating the return of her soldier from World War One, because Great-Grandma was born in early 1919! So she was only twenty when she had Gran. And *her* mum in turn was born in 1898 in Selkirk – which is almost on the English border, isn't it? – making her only twenty when she had Great-Gran. See what I mean? Knocking kids out like rabbits!

"So Great-Great-Gran wasn't from immediately around here, which is a bit of a relief. The next generation back was born in 1869, and the mother before that in 1840, because that 1840 great-whatever crops up as a child in the very first census in Carlisle. Gran and my great-gran were the oldest kids in each generation, with their mums barely twenty, but in the next couple of generations back, the ones I relate to were the second or third kids in line, and a whole tribe followed on from each of them!

"If you count my mum as generation one, I've got seven generations there and I haven't even got back to 1800 yet. Granted there's a question mark over that last lady's mum being the person born in 1818 in Carlisle, but I need another hundred-and-twenty to hundred-and-thirty years to get back to where we want. Oh, and it also makes it a load of old tosh that Euphemia is the name given to the oldest girl, doesn't it? Not with Mum having two older sisters. God, what a load of lies my parents told me!"

"But that sounds like you – or rather whoever did this tree – focused very much on going back in the female line every time with that line," Cameron pointed out.

Anna nodded. "Yes, those are for the Howarth family as best I can tell, but they did the male line from…" she had to stop and count on the screen "…my great-grandfather, the World War One soldier. He's a McKinley, but going back in Cumbria at least four more generations before him." She sighed. "So in that line I'm not seeing any connection to around here. Nothing that would connect me to our ghostly families, anyway."

"Steady lass," Gary said, sensing her despair. "All o' us have four grandparents and eight great-grandparents, whether we know who they are or no'. You've only told us about two so far. You don't have to track every one o' them back to around Dumfries for you to have a connection. And by the way, McKinley is a good Scottish name if ever I heard one, and Cumbria is only the other side o' the Solway Firth. It's no' as far as the Outer Hebrides! So come on. Deep breath. Davey John Clarke – where does he hail from? Because at least he has the right surname for one o' our ghosts."

"Sorry," Anna apologised. "I'm just a bit overwhelmed with all of this. I thought I was nobody and no connection to anyone, and all of a sudden I have ancestors coming out of my ears!"

"You were never 'nobody', Anna," Gary said affectionately, coming to give her a hug in passing as he went to replenish the coffee pot in the kitchen.

"Let me have a look," Cameron offered kindly, sensing that it was all getting a bit much for Anna. "Okay, so this is how you move to another part of your family tree…" With a click of the mouse and a gasp of surprise from Anna, a whole new tree appeared. "Anna?"

"Yes."

"What's your brother's name?"

"Nigel."

Cameron looked up and grinned. "Then I think this is your brother's work, because the 'owner' of this tree is Nigel Gracie, with an address in Australia, but he's working on his British family."

"Oh my God!" Anna gulped. "So everything in there for him applies to me as well?"

"Sure does," Cameron laughed. "My guess is that he wanted to tell his own kids about their family heritage, but wanted to avoid discussions with your parents as much as possible, so what better way to do that than dig into the more distant past? So high-fives to Nigel, and let's see what else he dug up, shall we?"

With Cameron's greater familiarity with websites, at the great-grandparent generation they quickly discounted on Anna's mother's side both of her great grandma Howarth's lines as having local connections, and to Anna's great relief, the male line through the Griersons too. But an Ellen Allen who married a George Grierson in the 1890s started to look a lot more promising.

"She's a Kirkcudbright lass," Cameron announced triumphantly, "and the generations are a bit more spread out in this line. When she marries George in 1892, her father is shown on the marriage certificate, which there's an image of here, as being a fisherman. That's good, Anna, it's really good! Because fishing boats tend to get handed down through the generations. I know this from holidaying on the south coast of Fife where Dad's parents lived, where there are still coastal fishermen with small boats. So going back through Ellen's folk, I'd say that there's a fair chance that some of her ancestors were always in Kirkcudbright."

He looked up at Gary, willing him to back him up on this. "Wouldn't you agree that in a small town like Kirkcudbright, and especially back in the time we're talking about, if you checked far enough, everyone would be related in some way to everybody?"

"Oh aye," Gary said without hesitation. "In every small town and its hinterland – for want o' a better word for it – you'll get a lot o' families eventually meeting up wi' a connection o' some sort. And the more rural, the more that's the case. The wee villages which got swallowed up when Glasgow started to sprawl out would be different by the end o' the nineteenth century, o' course, but you get up into the Campsie Fells and out towards Argyll, and also down here between Dumfries and Ayr, and that'll be so. You dinna have to go to the wilds o' the Highlands to find those kinds o' family links."

Cameron shot him a covert look of thanks and got the almost unnoticeable nod of recognition back. Both of them were clearly trying to make this as easy for Anna as possible, which took Cameron hoped had taken him back up a notch in Gary's estimation.

From Gary's perspective, the younger man might have been a bit of a dobber for not phoning them during his several-weeks' away in Edinburgh, sorting out his flat and other problems, but Gary could forgive him that on account of his dreadful upbringing at the hands of his mother. Gary's final opinion on Cameron's father had yet to be made, having not yet met the man, but from what Cameron had said, he seemed to be as much a victim of the mother's manipulations as Cameron was. And if Cameron was making this much of an effort for Anna, then he couldn't be all bad in Gary's books.

"What about bloody Dennis Gracie, then?" Rita asked, rather bursting the bubble of optimism that Cameron had fought to create. It made Gary wince, because he saw how Anna went from being perked up to downcast again.

"Jeez, Rita! Give us a chance," was all he said, but when she whipped around to stare at him, caught his annoyed glance towards Anna.

"We've got to face him sooner or later," she riposted, only for Gary to snap back,

"Aye! But just because he was the bane o' *your* ma's life, he doesn'a have to be the focus o' *Anna's* search."

That made her blink, because clearly Gary was thinking along very different lines to her.

"We haven't done with Anna's mum's side yet," Cameron added, though with less force. "And there's another line here which looks as though it's coming back to Dumfriesshire." He enlarged the image for Rita and Gary, sat on the other side of the table, and began scrolling down pointing out names. "Now at first, it looks as if we have a dead end here, because Davey John Clarke was born over in North Berwick, by Edinburgh. Granted, that's in Scotland and south of the Highland line, but that's not saying much, is it?

"But look here – Davey's *grandfather* might have wed in North Berwick, but he was born south-west of here in Castle Douglas in the late 1850s, right on the road to Kirkcudbright! And he and the great-grandfather didn't spell their name with an 'e'. Your brother got almost as far back with the Clarks as he did with the Howarths, because their generations were a bit more spaced out."

He sat back and said thoughtfully, "You know, Anna, I think you got a bit rattled by thinking that you had to have one solid line of ancestors going straight back to our lost lady ghosts. But in fact, it's far more likely that several strands of your family tree share that link."

"Aye, that makes more sense," Gary instantly agreed. "It's a bit o' a link from here and a bit from there, but it's pure coincidence that all o' those strands have come together in you. Because let's not forget that this is just your *mum*'s side o' things, and we've already got two lines which look verra like they're coming from around here. If there's even only one or two on Dennis the Menace's side, that still makes for quite a strong link when they all come together."

They could see that Anna was looking more than a little relieved at that, and Gary surreptitiously kicked Rita's ankle under the table when he saw her take a breath to speak. As she turned a startled gaze to him, she picked up on his glare, but before she could ask why, Cameron had tactfully drawn Anna over to the bottles of whisky he'd brought with him, asking her, "Have you tried either of these? I thought that since I depleted Gary's supply so badly, I ought to replace a couple of bottles."

It gave Gary a chance to hiss at Rita, "For the love o' God, woman! Give the poor lass a chance. *You* grew up wi' all this witchy stuff and a loving mum. She had that pair o' psychos, and had never even picked up a bloody tarot card before she met *you*! And did you no' think to start giving the lass some o' this training you're now shoving down her throat a bit earlier on?"

"Well thank you, Mr Expert!" Rita hissed back. "And how much could I do with her when I only saw her three times a year at most, and then only for a week at a time? She needed holidays back then, and I wouldn't be pushing so hard now if it wasn't that her job might hang on it!"

Gary growled softly. "Ach! So she needed a holiday *then*, but no' now, when she's scarce had chance to recover from that shit wedding, and then working non-stop since Christmas? And I'm sorry, Rita, but now Cameron's all in wi' us, I dinna think Anna's job is in the balance anymore, is it? I've no problem wi' you giving her some instruction in this stuff you do. I think it's pretty essential, in fact, given what we've come up against. But will you please get your head around the fact that no matter what talent you think she has, she's still a total novice compared to you, and you need to no' be scaring the pants off her at every turn!"

Rita looked slightly abashed at that, making Gary feel glad that he'd got that out in the open between them. At last she was beginning to see what had been obvious to him from the start – which was that Anna was more than a little frightened by this link to the past. Leaning in he added softly, "And you didn'a exactly help by no' taking your own advice, and having to go and stick your bum in that salt water bath because you let yon Gideon get to you, did you? That *really* rattled Anna! …So wi' that as a pretty dramatic example o' what can go wrong, why in God's name would you expect her to be over the moon about a bunch o' seventeenth century witches lurking in her soul?"

He saw his words genuinely shock Rita. Clearly, she was used to doing these psychic battles every now and then, and had never stopped to think how it would look from the outside to someone like Anna, witnessing it for the first time, and who had nothing else to measure it by. Rita's silent, 'Oh!' and stunned expression made Gary turn away from everyone so that he could roll his eyes in exasperation. He loved Rita dearly, but sometimes her talent for going in like a bull in a china shop without thinking things through infuriated him.

And more and more, he was starting to think of Anna as the daughter he'd never had the chance to raise, but to whom he could now be everything her father should have been. Rita might or might not ever come around to living with him as he wanted. But there was no doubt that Anna would welcome him as a surrogate dad with open arms, and he was surprised by how that overrode his feelings for Rita at times.

CHAPTER 9

Meanwhile, Anna had been tempted into trying an Auchentoshan malt by Cameron, and they were coming back with glasses for Rita and Gary too.

"Cam's just been saying that a potential connection on my awful grandfather's side to the witches doesn't need to be the same DNA strand that made Dennis such a nightmare," she said cheerfully. "Phew! What a relief."

That earned Rita a pointed look from Gary, though Anna didn't spot it, Anna continuing with, "I was getting a bit freaked out at the thought of a nasty grandfather who was also a male witch. I mean, after all the wicked things he seems to have got away with – at least from what you've told me, Aunty – it was starting to feel as if he had something spooky up his sleeve."

"Great Goddess!" Rita gasped. "No, no! My mum always said that her ex – your grandfather –

didn't have a 'sensitive' bone in his body. Not a glimmer of talent."

Cameron spoke before Anna could regarding the same question. "But if there *is* a DNA link back to the witches in that line, it *has* to have come via Dennis. That's science, Rita. You get fifty percent of your DNA through your mum, and fifty percent through your dad. Absolute fact. So if Anna has a link back to here on Dennis' side, it's impossible for it *not* to have come *through* him. It doesn't have to be the bad strand, which clearly hasn't been handed on to Anna in her fifty percent of him, but it does have to be *his*. He *has* to have had it within him, do you see, regardless of whether he consciously connected to it or whether your mother recognised it?"

Gary was almost pleased to see Rita thoroughly rattled by this, because now she might be a bit more sympathetic to how Anna felt.

"But the big thing," Cameron continued, "is that his nasty side may have come from one of his parents, while the link came from the other. Do you see? It could be either his mother or his father who was the nightmare in his past, and the other one who has the link? They *do not* have to be the same genetic line. At Dennis' parents' or even grandparents' generations, we could be looking at strands with totally different characteristics."

Rita was clearly uncomfortable with this. "But it *must* be her mum's line. The talent goes through the female line. Ma always said so."

"Did she *know* that?" Gary asked. "Or after the dreadful time Dennis gave her, did she no' want to believe it? ...Do *you* no' want to believe it?"

Anna nodded. "It's a point, Aunty, because you know that database I looked at where I found our witches? There were *some* male witches who were executed listed on there too! Nowhere near as many as the women, and there was a lot more 'proof', or at least of the kind believed in in those days, demanded for the men than ever there was for the majority of the women.

"But if there were male 'witches' in the seventeenth century, why couldn't there be more recent ones? Dreadful Dennis might not have been a practicing one or even have believed in it, but that doesn't mean his father or grandfather couldn't have. Why *can't* one of my great-however-many-grandfathers have been a male witch, closely descended from one of our ladies? I could have great-great-grandparents on both sides who were female *and* male witches – though I'm praying not too many!"

"Then I think," Gary said pointedly, looking at Rita, "you need to give Anna some more coaching on how to *protect* herself before she goes digging any deeper."

"Oh, I will," Rita promised. "Gideon Corsan is bad enough. I'm not having bloody Dennis sticking his oar in here as well!"

As far as Anna was concerned, it was therefore something of a relief that they had a hectic few weeks ahead after that, meaning there was limited time for Rita's intense coaching sessions. The second wedding was swiftly followed by Easter, when the hotel was full of families making the most of the slightly cheaper rates outside of the main school holidays, and so everyone was just glad to collapse into chairs and beds after busy shifts. Rita took the opportunity to return to her cottage to get fresh clothing and make sure everything was all right up there, which was even more of a relief for Anna. She hadn't realised quite what it would be like virtually living with such a force of nature as Rita, and if she didn't actually say so to Gary, he still understood that at times it was a bit like being back with her father. Rita might act out of love, rather than Anna's father's rampant self-interest, but the overall effect could sometimes be very similar.

And it made Anna appreciate what Gary had said to her about standing up for herself with Rita at times. It didn't mean she should be disrespectful, or unappreciative of the lifeline Rita had thrown her in finding her this job. It was simply having the confidence to say, 'I really don't want to do that,' and have Rita believe her.

It was also a relief to find over the following weeks, that the haunting of *Nuns' Kirk Haugh* had died down again, even if Anna – as the presumed ghosts' trigger – was still here. It meant that Anna felt she had a little bit more time to work out whatever it was she needed to know about to deal with them. And a flurry of weddings in May managed to pass without Gideon causing trouble, and with the newer members of staff finding their feet and becoming more of an asset. Chef Harriet seemed to be happy in the middle cottage, and if she heard anything strange from the ghostly nuns and witches, she certainly never said anything, which Anna hoped meant that she'd been right to take the end cottage for herself, though even for her things were quiet there.

Cameron moved fully into the smaller self-catering cottage with Harris and Lewis - Anna having always kept one of the cottages booking-free in case of accidental double-bookings, meaning she could swop booking around which now worked in Cameron's favour – but took seriously what Gary and Anna had told him about the hounds pining for him when he went away. And so every so often, they would come and spend the night with Anna or Gary. It meant that when Cameron subsequently did have to go away on business for a day or two, the dogs were a lot more settled, but his distress at having caused them upset had done much to make Anna think that he hadn't been deliberately unkind, but just unknowing. And in its turn, that meant that she wasn't quite as worried by the fledgling romance between them. Both of them were taking this slowly – Cameron in particular after a couple of carefully worded pieces of advice from Gary about how easy it would be to wound Anna at this point, and to a point beyond repairing the relationship.

And in terms of relationships, Anna was just getting worried that Rita had headed for the hills, and was now getting cold feet again about coming back to Gary's cottage, when her aunt turned up.

"Sorry I didn't come back sooner," Rita immediately apologised, "but I wanted to have chance to chat to a few of the ladies in what you might call my witchy circle. ...To get an outside perspective on the situation, if you see what I mean."

"And did you?" Anna wondered, suddenly feeling faintly worried about what she might be expected to do, then was surprised to see Rita blushing – quite a rarity. "Aunty?"

Rita had the good grace to meet Gary's eye as she said, "My friends have said exactly what you did. That I was expecting too much from Anna all at once. That I needed to give her time to get used to her talent, especially after a lifetime of having my arse of a half-brother for a father, and his hopeless wife not having the gumption to stand up for her own daughter."

Anna glimpsed Gary smothering a smile as he said, "I'll put the kettle on," and vanished into the kitchen. But from where she was sitting, Anna saw him punching the air triumphantly, even if Rita didn't. So Gary had been quietly standing up for her had he? That was a pleasant novelty for Anna.

It was even more of a shock for Anna when Rita had brought in her bags and sat down to tell her and Gary, "My friend Lois is a bit of a family history wizard, and I asked her to do a deep dive into Anna's family on Dennis' side. Couldn't stomach doing it myself, you understand – too close for comfort. Not after the way he treated my ma. But after what Cameron said, it made me realise that *somebody* needed to do it, and it was too much to ask Anna to make it a priority when she's working as many hours as she is."

"It *is* getting easier, Aunty," Anna said, not wanting Rita to think that she was sinking under the strain. "We've got a barmaid now, who comes in Friday and Saturday, so that helps. Emily has small kids, so she only wanted weekend work, and preferably in the evenings so that her husband can take his turn watching the kids, so this suited her and us perfectly. But it's been such a relief for Brenda and me not to have to man the bar on the two busiest nights. It means I can get on with more of the proper manager's jobs, even if I'm doing them at the reception desk rather than in the back office."

"Don't distract her," Gary said with a grin. "Come on, then, Rita. What has your pal found out? Only you look like you're about to burst if you dinna tell us."

This time Rita grinned back. "Cameron was right! …Okay, Gary, don't overact," she laughed as he mimed astonishment. "I can admit to being wrong, you know. He was right that just because Dennis didn't choose to acknowledge his talents, it didn't mean that they didn't exist in his family.

"But more than that, do you remember, Anna, that I told you that I'd got interested in the

Covenanters because of the witch trials which went on in the same era? Well I wanted to go back and have a dig in my own records, and have a chance to look better at that database you found, because I had a feeling that I'd looked at that myself some time ago – though without my own notes, I couldn't be sure." She gave a smug grin. "Do you remember when we were talking to Jannet and Grissell's ghosts?"

Anna nodded. "We're talking about Hugh's mother and grandmother, aren't we?"

"That's right. Do you recall them talking about the other daughter, Marione, and how she was the one who escaped with her husband? And what his name was?"

"Oh heck, I'm getting the feeling that this is important," Anna sighed, "but at this distance, no, I don't."

"Samwell Black," Rita told them, "And at the time I wondered why that name sounded vaguely familiar. Well I've found him! On the database. He was arrested as a witch, too, but set free. Cameron was right that men got given much more of a chance both to prove they *weren't* witches, and that witch hunters needed a lot more evidence for a case to stand up. In Samwell's case, they hadn't found sufficient. And it was exactly the same for another man who was accused within a year in 1659. Robert Short's son protested and said he needed to be tried or bailed, and officials agreed with him, saying that whoever it was that was detaining him at New

Galloway, had to let him go or pay to move him to Edinburgh. He was let go."

She managed to look a little rueful as she added, "And finding him made me think that I was wrong to dismiss Dennis' heritage for you, Anna. My ma was right, of course, in that with him not being my pa, his line has nothing to do with *me*, but it does you." She produced a long roll of paper and proceeded to unfurl it across Gary's table. "This is your family tree, Anna, as best we can get it, and obviously with quite a few gaps in it."

"That's not a family tree, that's an ancient oak!" Anna gasped with a laugh. "Good grief, Aunty! How many lines did you have this poor woman working on?"

However, Gary was nodding sagely. "Of course, the number o' people doubles with each generation you go back. But even with the dead ends and the ones whom she couldn'a trace, this is an awful lot o' ancestors. The potential for even one o' them to be linked to our witches gets bigger with each generation you go back."

"And it's not just how many," Rita pointed out. "It's *where* they are. I'd dismiss these various lines a lot more if they'd been from places as distant from here as Aberdeen or Fort William or Inveraray, for instance. But in the early nineteenth century, Anna, you have *seven* lines linking to either Fife and southern Perthshire – which is another area notorious for witch trials – or that bit to the east of Edinburgh around North Berwick and that cluster of villages and small towns which lead to Edinburgh, which are just as bad. Now that might not mean much to you until I show you the map of where the witch trials were focused…" She produced a piece of A4 paper on which was a map with lots of tiny figure symbols around the coast east of Edinburgh, and on the other side of the Firth of Forth facing Edinburgh.

"Heavens!" Anna exclaimed. "That's a lot of witches!"

"More like a lot of *accused* witches," Rita corrected her, "but yes, there are a lot. But it's this one that really made me gasp." She pointed to a figure on the map who she'd circled with red ink. "Here… His name is John Black, and he gets accused in 1683 in Berwickshire near to Duns. As far as we know, he's not likely to be Samwell's son if he's adult enough to be hauled in in 1683, given that Samwell and Marione left Dumfries in 1659 as fairly elderly people, but he could be a younger nephew. Maybe he's a family member whom they ran to?

"Now Black isn't the most uncommon of surnames, but with an accused man called Samwell Black in our witches' family, John Black on the east side in Duns, and with you having a great-great-great-great-great-grandfather called Adam Black just over on the coast at Eyemouth in the 1840s, it's getting a bit too close for coincidence. And Adam's father is recorded as a shepherd from Ayton – that's out of Eyemouth on the road towards Duns – called Samuel Black, who would have probably been born at the turn of the nineteenth century between, say, 1800 and 1815, so…?"

"Aye," Gary sighed, "you do have to wonder whether Samwell and Marione ran that way, no' into Argyll."

"They did go to Argyll," Anna said with certainty, then clapped her hand over her mouth as she wondered where on earth *that* had come from.

"Got a wee message there, did you, hen?" Rita asked with a smile.

"Just a bit," squeaked Anna.

Rita reached across and took her hand. "Go with it, Anna, don't fight the message."

Shaking like a leaf, Anna managed to croak out, "They did go to Argyll but they didn't settle there. …*Oof*! …I think… No…I'm sensinging that Marione and Samwell didn't stay. I think it was their son and his family who lingered! Then *they* – that's the son who I think was Alex and Elspeth? – came south again. But not to… to…" She jabbed a finger at Duns on the map. "Down here first…" this time pointing to the name Culross on the map, just across the firth from Edinburgh. "But something went wrong."

By now Anna was shaking badly, and Gary came around to wrap her in a hug.

"Oh God," she gulped. "I thought being haunted was bad enough, but this is worse," and she saw Rita's shock at her response.

"I told you Anna wouldn'a see it in the same light as you," Gary told Rita in a growl which said he wouldn't stand Anna being frightened all the time.

"Anna, it's a gift!" Rita protested.

"Doesn't feel like it!" Anna threw back at her. "Feels more like some creepy, dirty old man invading my head."

"It's a *man's* voice you're hearing?" And for the first time Rita sounded concerned, and presumably worried that this was another of Gideon's attempts at control.

To her great relief, Anna shook her head. "Not an actual *voice*. It's just like that feeling you get the moment when some slimy creep of a bloke begins following you around for no apparent reason, and you start wondering when he's going to turn nasty."

"Anna!" Gary was appalled. "Tell me that didn'a happen to *you*? Who was the bastard? I'll leather the living shit out o' him!"

"It's okay, Gary," Anna managed to say a bit more calmly. "It happened a long time ago. I was still in my late teens, and it turned out it was the son of someone Dad knew who'd simply got the wrong end of what he'd overheard." She gave a shaky laugh. "My bloody father implying that he was going to have to find a 'suitable' husband for me to his damned friends, of course," she said, rolling her eyes wearily.

"It's just that at the time it really freaked me out. Enough that I ran into the local police station and pointed the lad out to them, at which point the WPC could see how shook up I was, and they detained him." She gave a shaky laugh. "Dad was bloody furious at me for doing that. His 'friend' gave him hell over it, and of course Dad took it out on me in turn."

"Bloody hell!" Gary seethed. "If I'd ha' known he'd done that, Gordon would ha' left here wi' his balls in his hand and walking bandy-legged. And dragging his sodding man-bag on foot to the station. I wouldn'a have had the bastard in my truck, but kicked the shite all the way down the drive. No, Anna. No! There was no way in which that was okay. Never! And you did exactly the right thing in going to the polis, so never hesitate doing it again if, God forbid, anything like that ever happens again."

Anna let him continue hugging her hard, but looked to Rita and saw that she was speechless with shock.

"I never realised it was *that* bad," Rita finally managed to croak out. "With Gordon as a father, I mean. …Oh Anna, I'm so sorry! Gary's been trying to get me to see how different your childhood was from mine, but until now I don't think it sank in just how bad it was. Did your mother say *nothing*? Even over *that*?"

Anna shook her head. "She always went along with what Dad wanted. She'd never cross him."

"Is she afraid o' him?" Gary asked suspiciously, but Anna replied immediately,

"Oh no. She can give as good as she gets when she wants to. It's just that my mum likes the easy life, and letting Dad have his own way suits her when it gives her all the fancy stuff that she thinks makes life worthwhile. She never has to beg Dad to throw cash around if other people will see it. And anything that happened to me was never important enough for Mum to rock the boat over."

"What a bloody pair," Gary growled in disgust, finally letting Anna go, but continuing to hold her hand as he sat back down.

Rita nodded, looking deeply ashamed. "I'm truly sorry, Anna. I should have listened more and thought harder. I should certainly have prepared you better for this. It never occurred to me that you wouldn't welcome your talent being woken up. My ma had been talking to me about messages for so long I was nothing but thrilled to have it finally happen. I wanted it more than anything else by the time it happened – had spent most of my teens eagerly waiting for it, to tell the truth."

Anna's disbelief at her words, only hammered it home for her that for Anna it was a very different proposition.

"Right! Enough for one day." Gary ordered. "Rita, go and unpack your bags. Anna, get your boots on, we're going to take Harris and Lewis for a nice walk away from all o' this…" and he waved a hand in dismissal at Rita's paperwork.

It said much for the way Rita had been shocked as much as him that she didn't argue, and ten minutes later, Anna, Gary, and the hounds were striding off across the field at the back of the hotel, Cameron being in Edinburgh for the day. Gary set a brisk pace, and Anna had the feeling that he was burning off his own anger over her father, which was proven when they stopped at the far field gate and he turned to lean on it, giving Anna chance to catch her breath.

"Sorry lass," he apologised. "It's just that I've been saying for weeks that Rita needed to stop and see all o' this from *your* perspective, and time and again I've felt as though I've been talking to the wall for all the good it did."

"It's okay. No harm done," Anna said, not wanting to be the cause of dissent between Rita and Gary, but he was having none of it.

"No, no, no!" he declared firmly, reaching out to take her hand and hold it affectionately. "I felt how hard you were shaking back there. Nobody fakes shock like that, and certainly not *you*. Rita *has* to stop making assumptions about you like you're her 'mini me'!"

Anna laughed. "I'm certainly not that. I can't be half as fierce or brave."

"I think you're more than that brave," Gary told her, absolutely serious. "Every bit as brave as Rita and more. She had a lovely mother, a father who cared even if he wasn't around a lot because o' his job, and she was adored by Archie. Just because the daft bugger got into debt, it doesn'a mean he didn't still think the world o' Rita, even at the verra end. Please believe that – Archie worshipped the ground Rita walked on, even if he was a daft bastard in other respects. She's had disappointments, but had one, and only one, true set back, Anna. Okay it was an awful big one, and at an age when none o' us bounce back like we did when we were younger.

But since then, life's been on an even keel for her again, and it only lasted a few short years.

"*You*, on the other hand, have had shite handed to you from day one. You were the third kid your daft parents had by mistake, and they seem to have never let you forget it. And what I find unforgivable is that they haven'a stood up for you even when they should – like with that incident wi' the polis. The polis believed you, but your own parents didn'a? Unbelievable! When your father rolled up here wi' bluidy John Coleborn, it should have been to stand *between* you and him, no' against you!

"When I first met you, I was surprised that you never expected anyone to be in your corner. But it gradually sank in that it was because you've *never* had anyone back you up. Oh, Rita did in as much as she took you in when you ran north, and she found you this job, but it took a while for me to grasp why that was such a huge thing for *you*. That maybe, it was the first time anyone had personally lent you a supporting hand, and that's why you were letting Rita boss you around so much. But worse, it dawned on me that *Rita* didn'a see that that was *why* you let her – that it wasn't because you were enthusiastically going along wi' her, but felt you owed her that much."

Anna had never seen her life in quite such stark terms. "I'm not that much of a victim," she protested weakly.

"No' a victim. A child," Gary corrected her. "Year upon year o' being treated like shite, when you were no' old enough to know that it shouldn'a have been like that, nor old enough to do anything about it. That's the difference, Anna. I'm no' saying you're going around an emotional cripple, but it is going to take you a while to learn how to handle someone like Rita. And she really ought to know better after all the work she's done wi' battered wives and stuff. She should ha' seen long ago that you need as much help as they did – no' from your man but your father, who let's no' forget, she kens well enough to be a full blown fud o' the first order – no' to be dragging you headlong into her psychic stuff without warning you first."

Put like that, Anna couldn't protest further, but Gary was already opening the gate, and then offering her his arm to walk alongside him. He said nothing more on the subject for the rest of the walk, which all by itself was different to what she was used to, Anna belatedly realised. When Gordon Gracie wanted to make a point, the whole family got it on endless repeat until he ran out of steam, even if Anna, her mother, and – when they were still at home – her brother and sister, had long since got the message.

Back at the cottages, they found that Rita had vanished off somewhere, but as Anna and Gary were due on shift for the evening, they had to assume that Rita could take care of herself, and went to work. So it was only as Anna walked back to her cottage at coming up midnight that she saw that the light was still on in Gary's lounge. With him on as night porter tonight, it wouldn't be him, so it had to be Rita, and feeling a bit guilty that Rita had taken the brunt of Gary's chastising, she went and knocked on the front door.

"Oh good!" Rita said when she answered. "I really hoped you'd come around before you went to bed. I won't keep you long." She ushered Anna into the lounge, immediately saying, "I owe you an apology, Anna."

"No, Aunty, it's all ri…"

Rita waved her to stop. "No, it's not. And Gary has been right all along. I haven't even started to face up to what it must have been like for you to spend years with my bloody half-brother. I've been so absorbed in what I wanted for you, I never saw what was *happening* to you, and for that, Anna, I'm truly sorry. Not for one second did I ever think that you wouldn't grab your talents with both hands. I thought I'd be having to hold you back once you realised what you could do. The fact that you hadn't a clue what that might be didn't occur to me, never mind that you might *not* want it."

"Honestly, Aunty, there's no damage done. Well, I'm maybe a bit shaken, but I'm not that much of a wilting flower that I can't cope with a shock or two."

"That's very kind and very generous of you," Rita sighed, "but I'm still ashamed of myself for how I've tackled all of this."

Anna walked over and hugged Rita, getting hugged back in return.

"We were rather in a crisis when we called for you," Anna reminded Rita. "If you hadn't come and done what you did in such a short space of time, that first wedding could have been a disaster. Can you imagine what might have happened if Gideon and Hugh's ghosts had started battling it out with that particular bride and groom?" She shuddered at the thought. "No, Aunty, you did what had to be done." Then couldn't resist a teasing, "But can you please pause to explain stuff from now on, or at least warn me a bit more?"

Rita summoned a smile. "I can definitely do that! And starting tomorrow, I'm going to give you a much more comprehensive lesson on how to psychically protect yourself. If messages are going to start coming through to you, you need to be able to control when you pick them up, not be jumping out of your skin in front of customers."

1675-80

Elspeth

Elspeth sent a letter to Ishbel to tell her that she was moving on, but no letter ever came to find her at Duns. Then five years later, she discovered she had been right to leave Culross. Katherine Sands, Isobel Inglis, and Jonet and Agnes Hendrie were all taken for questioning in Culross and then moved on to Edinburgh for trial. Her new household were well-informed of goings-on in Edinburgh, and so she heard that in the July of 1675, her four friends were taken to Gallow Lea on the Leith Road and strangled and burned, just as her cousins had been. And so one Sunday, when she and Dougal could slip away for a few hours, she rode pillion behind him up to the Keithock standing stone and offered up her thanks once more.

"I've taught my girls to respect you," she whispered to the stone. "They know there's more power in the land than just in kirks. But I would love to see Hugh again just one more time. There's nobody else from home who would know me or care, but I owe him thanks and much more."

Yet when word came of her old home five years on again in 1680, it was from the most unlikely of sources.

The laird and his family were entertaining again, meaning Elspeth was kept busy washing things like tablecloths – the rich, she was discovering, might have money, but they could mess up a table like the pigs in the sty on the home farm. So she had been working in the laundry, and was just taking a pile of clean sheets and tablecloths in for the housekeeper, when she realised that the servants' hall was heaving with strangers.

"Elspeth!" the normally dour housekeeper greeted her with relief. "Excellent! Can you give those tablecloths to Big Jeanie, and take away the ones she's just stripped off the tables from lunch?"

There were so many Jeans and Janets working there that inevitably they ended up with nicknames to distinguish them from one another. Big Jeanie was a Highlander by birth, a tall, flame-haired lass who towered over everyone else, hence her name. She was also someone Mrs Murray, the housekeeper, could safely send into the dining room alongside the footmen and butler if needs be, knowing that she wouldn't come out with her bottom bruised from repeated groping when the 'gentlemen' were in their cups after the port or whisky had done a few rounds. One glare from Jeanie's feral green eyes, and even the hardiest of drunks kept their hands to themselves.

Yet as soon as Jeanie discovered that Elspeth had lived in the Highlands for a while, she decided that Elspeth was her new best friend. And so they were standing at the bottom of the servants' stairs leading upwards, with Jeanie telling Elspeth about a particularly obnoxious guest, when they heard a voice. It was a visiting maid with a gaggle of others around her, all hanging on her words, but it was what she was saying that made Elspeth's blood run cold.

"My ma's cousins were strangled and burned as witches!" she said with salacious glee, and got gasps and giggles in response.

Jeanie immediately put her arm around Elspeth, for she knew of her past, and why she had gone so pale. What Jeanie hadn't picked up on, but Elspeth had, was the local accent from her home, meaning that unless there had been some other poor souls who had gone through that hellish death since then, the girl was talking about the time when Elspeth's mother and cousins died.

"Ma? Are you all right?" Young Jonet asked as she came past with an armful of clean crockery for Jeanie to take upstairs to start laying the dining table ready for dinner.

"Shhh!" Elspeth hissed softly. "That girl. She's from home…well, *my* home. I think she's talking about your grandma and our cousins."

Jonet's eyes went wide, but she dumped the crockery on the nearby dresser, and shrank out of sight of Mrs Murray and Cook on the other side of Big Jeanie to listen.

"Oh, *my* ma was a good Kirk-going woman," the lass was bragging, obviously enjoying being the centre of attention, the maids having all come down to eat now that their ladies were out for the afternoon. "But she said her own ma was a fool who believed in the fae and the like." Her forced laugh of derision was echoed in the giggles of her audience. "Well God paid her back for that. Struck her down right in the square where the others burned! Ma says it was a judgement on her. Her own sisters paid for their folly too. One ran off with a soldier and died, and the other stayed with the old witch and got hunted as one herself."

Before she could stop herself and before the gasps of fascination had died down, Elspeth found herself barging into the group and giving the girl a hard slap across the face. And with her years of hard work, Elspeth had rough hands and a lot of muscle in her arm to deliver it.

The girl went down on her bottom and landed up against an old dresser in the hallway where they stood.

"Don't you dare speak of my mother and sister like that, you ignorant little trollop!" Elspeth blazed, oblivious to the silence that had dropped over the outer kitchen and hall. "Do you think it funny to watch a woman you love being viciously strangled before your eyes and then set alight?"

There were gulps and gasps of horror amongst the other young women as the truth sank in.

"You have to be one of our Jean's daughters," Elspeth raged on, "but let me tell you this, young miss. Your ma turned her back on her own ma years before any accusations came against her, or our cousins. And Jean wasn't the daughter of my lovely pa, but the bastard got on our ma when the local Presbyter raped her! Well she proved herself the daughter of that evil man over and over, and he was a so-called man of God who took women into the cellar of his manse, and then beat them and raped them to supposedly turn them back to God…just because he could.

"I for one am glad that the Covenanters have been outlawed, because I never want to see that cruelty inflicted on another soul. But you should be careful, young missy, because I know for a fact that your ma and pa were fanatical Covenanters themselves. So you be careful what you brag about, because it could come back on you threefold the way the tables have turned now!"

"Goodwife Allen!" Mrs Murray's shocked tones broke the spell. "Did you just strike this maid?"

"Did I give my own niece the reminder to keep a respectful tongue in her head when talking about my ma, my sister, and me?" Elspeth flashed back. "Yes, I did!" Meanwhile, the lass was still making fish-out-of-water noises and unable to refute Jean as her mother. Claiming to be her aunt gave Elspeth an authority to deal with this beyond the household here.

Mrs Murray blinked and took a step back herself. Elspeth had always been the most polite and calm of women under her control, and Mrs Murray had the wit to understand that some real offence must have been given for her to lash out like that. Had the maid been a stranger to Elspeth, that still wouldn't have saved Elspeth from a docking of her pay for causing trouble. However, Elspeth's words had shown this to be a family matter, and that was a different thing altogether. Everyone knew that you didn't disrespect your parents, and if Elspeth was this maid's aunt, then that gave her a measure of authority within the family too.

"Take this outside to the stable yard," Mrs Murray ordered, "and you, young miss…when you've learned to behave towards your own elders, I expect you to come back in and continue with your duties without any of the scurrilous gossip you've been handing out. His lordship doesn't approve of below-stairs scandals being paraded about."

Quite what the girl would have said was lost as Big Jeanie hoisted her to her feet with one hand and marched her outside in Elspeth and Young Jonet's wake.

"You all right to deal wi' this wee besom?" Jeanie asked, and getting Elspeth's nod, headed inside, saying to the maid over her shoulder, "Dinna be a fool, now. Elspeth's no' one fer tolerating fools."

Luckily, Young Jonet was looking towards Jeanie, so her blink of surprise wasn't seen by the maid, and then she caught on as Jeanie turned the other way and winked at her. Ah, so Jeanie was instilling a bit more fear into the maid, was she?

And Jonet turned around and adopted a crossed-arm, disapproving stance and scowl alongside Elspeth, doing her best to look suitably intimidating.

"Now then, you wee fool," Elspeth was growling, "who are you, *heh*?" And as the girl just looked bug-eyed at her, prompted her, "Well…what's your name?"

"I'm Aggie Henryson," she replied, her bottom lip now starting to wobble. This had all gone so wrong so fast, and if she didn't fully understand why at the moment, she was sure that this fierce old woman – who she belatedly realised did look rather like her ma when in a temper – was going to make sure she did.

"*Hmph*!" Elspeth snorted, her time with Highlanders having imbued her with the same ability to invest that one sound with a world of meaning. "So if you're a Henryson, which one are you? One o' Jean's or one o' George's family's?"

For a moment the girl looked blank. "My ma is Jean…she's married to…"

"No, ye' puddin' heid!" Young Jonet snarled, rolling her eyes. "We dinna need to ken the whole rabble o' you. You! Which one are you?"

"I…I'm…I'm the youngest one," the girl stuttered out.

"Ah, the youngest," Elspeth said with a sniff. "Aye, we heard about your oldest brother. Nasty wee boy prone to carrying gossip home to your pa if it would get someone in trouble. Looks like you're an apple that didn'a fall far from the tree, either.

…So who are the others? Did our Jean have more than the five I last heard of?"

"I'm Aggie, and my older sister is Meg. My brothers are George and John, then there's Meg, then Archie, and then me."

"Agnes and Margaret?" Elspeth echoed, turning to give a glance of surprise at Young Jonet as the names of her sister's girls she'd never met sank in. Her ma had probably known the names, but Elspeth had been disinterested in a sister who had shunned them long ago. Turning back to Aggie, she said, "You do realise that you are both named after the so-called witches in our family? Albeit from before the trial. So someone had a guilty conscience about turning their back on everyone after all."

Young Aggie's face drained of colour. "I'm named after a witch?"

Relenting and realising that this silly girl had only been repeating what she'd been told, rather than thinking about it, Elspeth grasped her arm and walked her over to where they could perch on one of the stone mounting blocks.

"Actually, my cousin Agnes was as good and kind a woman as you could wish to meet. You're named after a good and Christian soul."

"Then why was she burned as a witch?"

"Because her husband died before her, and his cousin was a wicked man called John McCartney, who wouldn't wait for Agnes to die to inherit their croft. That's all it was, Aggie. Plain old-fashioned greed. Her sister Margaret had upset a few people, but not by trying to turn them into toads or anything. She just stood up for herself. But when another evil man, John Corsan, decided that he didn't want to wait to get his hands on land, he and the other John plotted to get rid of the ones who stood in each others' way. Poor Margaret – my cousin and your ma's – was unfortunate enough to have a husband who had met a rich widow, so getting her out of the way by accusing her of being a witch suited him, too."

Elspeth shook her head sadly. "Thomas Milligan, for that was Margaret's husband's name, was a cruel and godless man for all o' his creeping around the Presbyter. He all but sold his own daughter, Isobel off to get her out o' the way. I sometimes think o' her and wonder if she's survived."

"Isobel Milligan?" Aggie repeated. "Oh! I heard about her! Ma and Pa were talking about her with George and John, saying she got what she deserved. They said that Master Milligan had been right to send a witch's get off before she could mate with another's…'cause the son o' the witch that got away was sweet on her…and Master Milligan and Master Corsan thought that the Black's son was too clever, and might find a way to get Master Milligan's old witch o' a wife off if she was his ma-in-law. And Master Milligan couldn'a let that happen.

"And he did!" she gabbled on, totally oblivious to the thunderbolt she'd just launched at Elspeth's heart. "…Get her off. …No' the old Milligan witch, ye' understand, but his own ma who was a witch.

He got her off. She disappeared wi' the Black man and Ma's sister, who was another witch..." Her voice trailed off as she finally woke up to Young Jonet's furious expression and the way that Elspeth had gone grey.

"You stupid wee besom!" Young Jonet snarled. "*This*," and she jabbed a furious finger towards Elspeth, "is your ma's sister you're calling a witch!" Given that Jean Allen had had her youngest child not that long before Mailie had had Young Jonet, Aggie was only two or three years older than Young Jonet, but the difference in maturity was vast. Young Jonet had seen what real hardship looked like. Aggie had grown up the spoiled youngest one in a comfortable house, even if it was nothing special. If her mother and father had been overly righteous, by the time Aggie had been old enough to rebel, Jean and George were having to be more circumspect in their practices as the political climate had shifted.

Taking a deep breath to try and calm the way her heart was pounding, Elspeth told her, "I'm your Aunt Elspeth. And yes, I left with Samwell Black, his wife Marione, and their son Alexander, along with the Fergusons and my father. We left because we were in fear for our very lives thanks to the connivances of John McCartney, John Corsan and his son Gideon, plus the old bailie's nephew, Thomas McBurney, and vicious old Presbyter Veitch. I pray men like that never set their sights on you, because it's a terrible thing to live your life in such fear all of the time."

Aggie's eyes were getting wider and wider as the reality of who this woman was sank in. The truth was turning out to be a lot more complicated than her ma had made out to her and her sister.

"Why did Ma name us after her…her…"

"Cousins," Young Jonet supplied with some asperity. "For goodness' sake, keep up, Aggie!"

Elspeth was barely holding back the tears as she answered, "Your ma used to go with our ma to visit Margaret and Agnes when they were still unwed and living at our uncle's home. Margaret especially, used to always have some little treat for her. A bit of ribbon for her hair, or a posy of dried flowers. And for our middle sister, Mailie, too. That was before our ma got questioned by Veitch for the first time. She was never the same after that. Never dared to walk to market with Aunt Geillis anymore."

She heaved a great sigh of regret. "I never understood why your ma was so taken with George Henryson. He was hardly the most ardent of suitors, and she wasn't that short of options. The only reason Ma and I ever came up with was that he was such a righteous man, she maybe felt safe from her natural father's attentions with him."

"Natural father?" Aggie asked in a whisper.

"Weren't you listening?" Young Jonet demanded with scant patience. "Veitch! The God-curse-him Presbyter who raped Grandma and got your ma on her."

"Jean always acted as though she was proud of having that connection to the most feared man in the neighbourhood," Elspeth said sadly, "but I wonder now whether that was just a show in public to make sure he never bothered with her. He was the sort of man who would have taken it as a personal tarnish on his soul if even his bastard daughter had failed to be the best of Covenanters."

Suddenly Aggie burst into tears.

Looking at one another in bemusement at her great gasping sobs, Elspeth and Young Jonet could only wait for Aggie to recover enough to be able to explain, "M…Ma said she w…was sending me into service like…like she did Meg f…for our own good. I di…didn'a understand. B…But auld Presbyter Veitch was talking to Pa when we went into Dumfries for the fair, and he said he needed a new lass to do for him now that Isobel had gone to do for auld John Corsan. Pa said on the way home that Presbyter Veitch kn…knew how to deal with unruly women. M…Ma went awful pale at that."

She had to pause to snuffle before adding. "Ma sent Meg away within the week. I…I thought Ma had got it all sorted beforehand. I was surprised Meg had never said anything to me, b…because she was all interested in William from two farms over. She was all angry with Ma one moment, and then crying and packing her bag the next."

"Oh Lord," Elspeth sighed, feeling her chest tightening even further with grief. "Poor Jean. She realised that George was sending Meg to Veitch where she'd be endlessly raped. No doubt she had to tell your sister why when she began arguing about going. Poor Meg, too, to have to leave a lad she was fond of just to preserve her reputation and stay safe. ...But you say our *Isobel* was with Veitch? When did *that* happen?"

Aggie had managed to calm down enough to be a bit clearer. "Why do you call her *our* Isobel? I'm still not sure who she is? Is she some cousin?"

Elspeth was saved the pain of reminding a niece who should have known this by Young Jonet chipping in with, "Did your ma never tell you? Isobel is the daughter of Margaret, the cousin of *my* Ma, here, and your ma's. The woman whose sister, Agnes, Ma's just told you you're named after."

Aggie gulped, it finally dawning on her just how personal all this should have been to her. "Oh! Oh my goodn...so if my ma was given gifts by this Margaret, then did Ma actually know Isobel?"

"Knew her well enough to have cradled her in her arms as a babe," Elspeth told her, feeling tears welling up at the memory. Now Margaret and Agnes were long gone, and by the sound of it, Isobel had had a pretty wretched life. One even harsher than her own if it had included being raped by Veitch. "Aggie, how did Isobel end up with Veitch?"

"Isobel and her man were sent to help Edward McCartney on the Black's old croft." The penny suddenly seemed to drop with her that there was something she needed to tell her aunt, because her eyes flew wide open. "Oh! Edward didn't want the Black's croft. I heard Pa saying that Edward was a fool to give up a gift like that from his pa, but then we heard that the croft wasn't worth cultivating."

"Oh it most certainly was," Elspeth corrected her. "It might not have been big, but it was productive."

"Well the McCartney's never had a day's luck with it. And Isobel's man died there. I do know that. I heard that Isobel was sweet on Edward, but her father and the auld Presbyter colluded with Thomas McBurney to send her to Veitch, the croft got sold, and Edward went somewhere else."

"And Hugh Ferguson and Alexander Black…did anyone ever hear anything of them?" Elspeth asked, trying to sound as if her whole world didn't hinge on the answer.

"I've never heard of anything about any Hugh Ferguson," Aggie said, screwing up her nose as she thought hard. "But I'm pretty sure Alexander Black is dead. He went off somewhere and then came back a few years ago. I'm sure it was him who got into a fight with Thomas McBurney, and McBurney brained him wi' a hammer. I think it was a fight over a woman, though I've never heard of McBurney taking much interest in women, not even his poor wretch of a wife."

"You said earlier that Alexander Black been fond of Isobel?" Young Jonet asked, always swift to put two and two together, yet not quite daring to say that Alex was the man she knew of as her father. "Was it because McBurney sent Isobel to Veitch? Was that why he fought McBurney?"

"Might ha' been," Aggie said, her brain struggling to keep up. "After what you've said about Veitch, I suppose Black must ha' known about his dirty ways?"

"Oh, I think it was more than that," Elspeth said faintly, wishing that the vice-like pain in her chest would ease up. "Veitch was the one who instigated the witch hunts along with McCartney and Corsan. Alex hated Veitch with a vengeance. Veitch was the one who killed Alex's aunt and nearly killed his mother, even if it wasn't by his own hands."

But inside she was screaming, *You got into a fight with an evil brute like McBurney for Isobel, who you hadn't seen since you were both little more than children, but you couldn't come back for the mother of your child? Damn you Alexander Black! Did I mean so little to you? Why couldn't you have left me alone once we escaped our homes? Why didn't you go for a soldier like Hugh, and let me have a chance of a life with Hugh when he came home?*

As a soldier you could have made your ma and pa's life in Argyll easier, and they might not have left had there been your wages to help them out. It wouldn't have made my life with Mailie any better, but she and Niall would only have had Pa and me to look after, and if Hugh had seen us in need when he came home that first Christmas, might he not have taken us on instead? You let me believe you loved me, but was that ever true? I hope you rot, Alex. May you rot in the deepest pits of Hell for leaving me to struggle with your child, only to die fighting for a woman you scarcely knew. ...And Hugh, oh my dear Hugh, I've so missed you. You were my guardian angel and I never even saw it until it was too late. Yours was a true love I squandered without thought, foolishly thinking that what Alex felt was even close to a match for your feelings. I hope we meet again in the afterlife and I get to tell you how sorry I am.

Because Elspeth's heart had given up with the stress and strain, just as her mother's had all those years ago, and she slumped to the floor, with Young Jonet's screams of, "Ma! *Ma*!" going unheard. For she was gone before she even reached the ground.

1673

Gideon

Gideon Corsan knelt by his mother's grave and let the tears flow. Not for his mother, God rest her soul, for she had died some eleven years ago and had always been a quiet, distant person whom it had been hard for him to connect with. No, his tears were for himself and the nightmare of a life he was living.

Back when he had been in his teens, and his father had been party to the terrible conviction, strangling, and burning of the witches in Dumfries in 1659, he had thought that his family was untouchable. His conniving and often brutal father always seemed to find a way to get what he wanted, and the young Gideon had been impressed by that, never realising what a price would be paid. Initially it had been his mother who had paid it, he belatedly realised. Only now and looking back, did it dawn on him that she'd never had the company of other women. The Corsans weren't so high in society that she couldn't have mingled with the other farmers' wives, yet although those other wives frequently visited each other's homes, maybe under the pretext of exchanging preserves or recipes, but in reality staying longer to chat, nobody came to their house.

Gideon could almost pinpoint the moment when his mother lost the will to live, and it was at that trial at the tolbooth in Dumfries, the flames rising around the remaining eight of the nine convicted women tied to the stake, and the curses that were hurled out of the smoke in their agony. Some he had understood, some had been in what he now knew was Gaelic, and like the foolish boy he'd been, he'd just laughed them off along with his father. But his mother had turned white and ran from the scene. When they got back to their townhouse, she had locked herself in the little hut in the yard that acted as their dairy, and didn't come out until night-time.

That was the first night she did not share his father's bed, and never shared it thereafter, preferring instead to sleep in the second main box-bed out at the croft, and she never again went to the townhouse in Dumfries. Young John was ejected from the truckle under it, and sent across the room to the truckle bed from under their father's bed, which had been used while their sisters and Matthew had been at home in the days before the townhouse had been bought. Gideon had to give up the second main and was relegated to the truckle his younger two brothers had once used, tormented by his mother's night-time weeping which she dared not do in front of his father.

"Thank the good Lord both Katherine and Jean are away from here," Gideon heard his mother saying often from that day onwards. Both had gone into service as mere scullions before they'd even reached their teens – their father unwilling to support what he saw as useless females – with families outside of the district. At the time Gideon hadn't understood why their mother had sent them so far afield, and by now had almost forgotten that he even had sisters as he'd still only been in his teens himself when Katherine, the younger one, had left the year before the witch trials, never to be seen again. But it hadn't taken much for him to understand why his mother was so glad after the trials. Lads who had once joined him to go fishing, or hunting the foxes which preyed on the lambs, excluded him. The only ones who seemingly could tolerate being with a Corsan were Thomas McBurney, who was Bailie William McBurney's son, and if forced, John McCartney's younger son Edward, though Edward had always been a more bookish lad like Gideon's own brother Matthew.

Even so, he didn't fully understand until he came home dejected after being thoroughly rebuffed by a yet another girl he'd had his eye on, and asked his mother, "Why do none of the girls want me?" at which she'd replied,

"They don't trust your father. What girl of any sense would want to come to this house? Do you think that the women who saw your *cousin* burn wouldn't wonder just what your father would be capable of, even to one of his *own* family?"

"M…m…my *cousin*?" Gideon had spluttered. "Who was *my* cousin?"

His mother shook her head in exasperation. "Why do you boys take so little notice of family when your sisters understood it from when they were small? They understood they'd never marry a decent man around here, not coming from this family. That's why they left willingly. We've had good times over the last decade, Gideon. No crop failures. No famine. Even the plague that hit so much of England has left us alone up here in Scotland for the most part. But in bad times we all need our families. We need to band together sometimes just to survive.

"That's why people hereabouts know who is family to whom, and no longer trust your father. His *own* older cousin, and a first cousin no less, William Corsan, married Grissell McCartney, and she makes a connection that…" She sighed heavily. "…Well it just makes everything that much worse."

"I'm sorry, Ma, I still don't understand."

"Oh, Gideon, try to keep up. William and Grissell's daughters are…were…Jannet Corsan who burned at your father's behest, and her older sister, Marione Corsan, who mercifully escaped with her husband, Samwell Black, and their son. Do you grasp it now? Your father sent his *own* cousin's daughters to the stake! And all for greed."

"Greed? Ma, what did we get from their deaths? I know John McCartney got his cousin's croft after Donald's widow was proven a witch."

"No, no, no," his mother protested sadly. "Proven? No. Poor Agnes Clark, who was Donald's widow, was beaten and tortured, but *proven* a witch? No. That was just the opinion of men who had other motives for condemning her."

"Ma, you're not making sense."

"Am I not? Then think on this, Gideon. Your father sat as the commissioner in Agnes' trial. He swung opinions towards her needing to be burned. Meanwhile, *we* now own the croft that was Jannet Corsan and her husband James Ferguson's, plus the one that belonged to Marione Corsan and Samwell Black – because both the Fergusons and the Blacks left and were deemed to have forfeited their ownership. But they left because they knew they would never survive otherwise, and that was because McCartney swayed things on your father's behalf to come out *our* way. We have the crofts of those cousins, not because your father properly inherited them, but because he took them at the expense of at least one cousin's life, and the exile of the other.

"Deals were done in dark rooms, my son. Deals which condemned decent women I grew up knowing, to a vile and horrific death. In his turn, John McCartney wanted the crofts of those women down in Kirkcudbright to expand his holdings around his land at Senwick, so your father made sure he got them, while he reciprocated by making sure your father got what he wanted. So do you see? People hereabouts aren't blind or stupid. They know your father wanted those crofts, and it hasn't taken long for them to work out how he got them, either."

As the dreadful truth pounded in on Gideon, his mother finished with, "I don't blame the other women for not wanting to come near me now. In their shoes I wouldn't either, because I'd never know when the most innocent of overheard remarks might condemn everyone I love. But what goes for me goes for you and Young John too – no family will want you wed to their daughter in case your father sees what they have, and wants it for himself.

"I'm only glad that dear Matthew went away to St Andrews less than two years after the trials, and when he finished his studies went into the Kirk and is now off in his own parish. And your sisters are far enough away and sufficiently forgotten that they won't instantly be tarred with the same brush as us. I bless the day that I sent them away and told them to use my name of Heyman, not Corsan, because your father had crossed one of the family Jean went to, and I wanted her to start afresh without his trouble hanging over her. So then Katherine did the same, meaning to anyone who asks – and few will trouble over a mere kitchen help – she's Katherine Heyman." She reached out and gently patted his cheek. "But you, my son, you're going to feel the full weight of the local hatred for your father, and there's not a thing you can do about it."

Thereafter, Gideon's mother had become ever more withdrawn until she simply faded away, and they never spoke about those things again. Yet when old John Corsan came home and announced that Gideon was to wed, and to whom, Gideon knew that his mother had been right – his father would use any of them, and no matter how cruelly, if it got him something he wanted. John Corsan didn't give a tinker's curse for any person, only money and property, and like some malevolent spider, cast out his web to ensnare whoever and whatever he could.

It meant that 1669 turned into a year Gideon was never likely to forget. Sir James Dalrymple, Lord Stair, whose estates were north and east in Ayrshire, found even his daughters being accused of witchcraft, and the more vehement members of Presbyter Veitch's congregation had celebrated wildly. At last, they declared, even the nobility could not escape God's wrath for such practices! The Solemn League and Covenant's time had come, they avowed. No more bishops. No more prayer books imposed from that bunch of heathens down at the King's court in London, which no longer existed.

"The Kingdom of God has come!" Veitch roared from his pulpit on many a Sunday that year, but if this was God's kingdom, then Gideon found himself wishing for the first time in his life that God might have waited a few years longer. Because in the fervour which gripped their local parishes, finally John Corsan had come back into favour for his hard-line religious views, and had found a bride for Gideon – and what a bride!

Euphame Watt had been presented to him as if he was being blessed with one of the saints themselves. All Gideon saw was a sour-faced stick of a woman, some five years older than himself, who had been short on suitors for good reasons, one of which was that the woman never smiled. The first time they were alone, she rounded on him saying, "I will not have you practising your filthy habits on me! Know that! I've heard what Presbyter Veitch does with his housekeepers in the absence of a wife, and I'll not stand for it, d'ye hear me? You may come to my bed when I *tell* you, and I shall be keeping a sharp carving knife under my pillow to make sure you don't sneak in to have your evil way with me, when I've not had chance to pray for my soul beforehand."

Poor Gideon had been too stunned to even protest. He hadn't expected love from such an arranged marriage. But equally, he hadn't remotely anticipated such outright hostility clad in prayers and righteousness. Nor could he go to Presbyter Veitch and ask what to do about it, not when he'd have to reveal what had been said about the man, and when he also had many years' prior knowledge of what Veitch was like in a rage.

The old man would be more likely to beat *him* around the head with the blackthorn stick he had taken to walking everywhere with, and call him a liar, rather than questioning the words of the daughter of a friend and fellow Presbyter. And he knew what his father would say – throw her onto the bed and take her like a man! Something his father had done to his mother, Gideon belatedly realised and recalled, and wished he'd been more sympathetic over. It was something which his own body singularly failed to let him do.

Gideon was well and truly trapped.

Night after night, his wife would wrap herself in so many layers it would have taken the very Devil himself to fight his way in through them, and would take herself to the curtained-off box-bed which sat to the right of the fire in the croft which Gideon had been compelled to take on, forcing Gideon to retreat to the one on the left and sleep alone. It was the croft which had belonged to Marione Corsan and Samwell Black. A croft which by rights should have passed to their son Alexander, had they not fled in fear. And a croft which wouldn't allow him to lie easy in his bed any more than Euphame did.

"Leave me in peace," Gideon would beg the shade of an old woman, who seemed to follow him around the yard at night as he put the chickens into their coop, and made sure the cow couldn't get out. He could guess who she was. Grissell McCartney, Marione and Jannet's mother, who had died before she could be put on trial.

"I know Veitch questioned you hard," he often said, out in the chill of the night. "I know you blame my father for your Jannet's death. But I was only a lad. I couldn't have stopped him. Please, leave me alone. I've got enough problems with her inside without you haunting me." Then he thought how ridiculous it was that he found it easier to talk to the ghost of a witch and tell her off, than speaking to his flesh-and-blood wife.

A year passed and then another, with Gideon able to count on one hand the number of times Euphame had let him into her bed. But talk in the district of the lack of a child seemed to do more to thaw her resistance to him than anything he could have said and done.

"You may come to my bed once a month," she told him sternly as their third year came around, and so once a month Gideon went out to old man Crauford's place up in the hills, and bought a bottle of his home-distilled rot-gut whisky. It left him with a vile head in the morning, but getting absolutely staggering drunk was the only way he could nail his colours to the mast enough to tackle Euphame in bed. The fact that the whisky did as much to hinder his performance as help wasn't lost on him, but then miracle of miracles, she declared she was with child.

"At last!" was his father's snide comment upon being told, with not a word of congratulations. But then congratulations didn't match how Gideon felt once he realised what this pregnancy would mean. For a start off, Euphame was violently sick day after day, not just the mornings, and long after the local women said it ought to have passed. Moreover, Euphame made it clear that she wasn't doing a thing until the babe arrived, forcing Gideon to get someone to come in to clean the house and see to things like feeding the chickens and making the butter.

That brought with it a whole new raft of dangers, for although he picked the simplest girl he could find, he still feared what she would say when she went home of a night. Therefore he staggered through the months putting on the bravest performance he could manage, trying to pretend that having this child was his deepest heart's desire. In truth he was coming to the conclusion that it might be his bane, for Euphame made it clear that it would be brought up to her standards, not his, and that in essence he would play no part in the raising of his child.

Strangely, that bothered Gideon more than he ever expected it to.

"What if it's more like me?" he asked God when he went out for his evening walk, which he did to save being forced into Euphame's company any longer beside the fire, and which somehow often ended up at his mother's grave. "Ma, I now see how you protected us children from Father's wrath. How did I not see that so often you took the beating for us? Yet Euphame is like Father in women's clothing, and I'm turning into you – the bystander trying to do my best, and yet never making a difference."

And so on the fateful night when he woke in the early hours to Euphame's agonised screams, two months too early, he couldn't help but think that his prayers had been answered. God would not allow some poor child to come into the world to be at the mercy of a cold, unfeeling mother like her. And after he'd run for the local old wives who did all the birthings and laying-outs, he gratefully escaped to the barn and waited for the news. That they came to him full of sorrow, telling him that Euphame had died, was such a weight lifted off his shoulders that he had no problem weeping copiously – he just never let on that it wasn't in grief but relief.

Moreover, although they couched it in hints and cloaked phrases, it turned out that what had swelled Euphame's belly hadn't been a child but a great growth, which had burst on that fateful night. That had Gideon weeping all over again in relief, because that meant that he hadn't even lost a child of his own. Not that he ever said a word of that to anyone, and for once, the dread the locals had of the family ensured that if the old wives spoke, it was only between themselves and to folk who never broadcast it to others.

Yet if being a widower had eased Gideon's private torment, in the wider world he still suffered from being John Corsan's son.

CHAPTER 10

As June arrived with the first true burst of summer, Anna decided she needed to start with a softer approach than Rita's, even if now Rita was more understanding of her caution. Popping down to Dumfries one afternoon, she went to get more fresh flowers for the hotel's public areas, and in the process, bought some for the old kirk. Peonies were fully in flower at the moment, and she found some of the lovely deep-red, old-fashioned ones, which the witches at least might have known as Apothecaries peonies. They wouldn't last long in the warmth of the hotel, but in the cool atmosphere of what remained of the old nave, Anna thought she might get a week out of them.

And so once she'd gone and handed the flowers for the hotel over to Brenda – who was a master at making lovely displays for the reception area and the bar – she went back over to her cottage and unpacked the pair of pretty vases she'd found in a charity shop. Nothing like as smart as she would put into the hotel, instead they had a homely feel about them. Once upon a time she could imagine them sitting on either end of somebody's mantelpiece, with cut flowers from the garden in them, and it was that homeliness that she wanted to evoke. This had never been a grand church. Just a wee kirk attached to a small and rather insignificant nunnery. So the nuns wouldn't have had any fancy decorations, even of the ecclesiastical kind.

With the vases sitting on the blocked up windows' sills, and a trio of lavender tea-lights burning in a little holder up as near to the east end as remained of the kirk, the place suddenly took on a different atmosphere. And so when the next morning dawned on a lovely early summer day, warm and sunny, Anna nipped out of her kitchen door and across to the inner ones of the two big stable doors which had been put in. Opening up the double doors, she propped them open with a couple of hefty bits of stone, so that if the wind picked up, they wouldn't start banging. And standing there under the doors' arch in the early sunshine, she could have sworn she heard the sighs of happiness from the ghosts.

She carried on opening up the old kirk's doors in the morning, and then closing them up at dusk, simply out of respect for the women who had died, and to try to ease their afterlife for a while by letting in the sunlight. By the time the inevitable shower of rain came by the weekend, the inside of the kirk smelled a lot sweeter, fresh air having completed what Gary, Rita, and Anna had started with their sweeping out and scrubbing, and the slightly manure-like whiff that had percolated through the place was fully gone. An old table destined for the recycling yard had been repurposed up at the altar end, and Anna had found an old-fashioned white tablecloth which had also been revived by a couple of trips through the washing machine with some stain remover. Carefully folded to show its best side, it wasn't quite a standard altar cloth, but it was certainly clean enough to appear respectful – especially as this was hardly the original site of the altar, which lay somewhere out towards the tomb.

"There! That's better," Anna declared as she stood back to survey her handiwork a week on on the following Sunday, and she could have sworn she heard murmured agreements. She'd rearranged the four old dining chairs they'd used when Rita had led them in contacting the women last, and turned them around like two pairs of pews facing her makeshift altar. So all in all, the place now looked more like what it had originally been – a place of worship. There might not be a cross on her makeshift altar, but a fresh vase of flowers with a nice beeswax pillar candle on either side gave what she hoped was the impression of a sacred area.

Anna had never really thought much about her faith in the past. She'd spent too much time just trying to survive her parents and her job. But now she sat on one of the chairs and gave it some real consideration. Finding an old Bible and putting it on the altar might be nice for the ghostly nuns, she thought, but would it actually be off-putting for the witches? It certainly wouldn't make any difference to her. Having never been a church-goer, it wasn't as though that was the way she would instinctively go for support over things spiritual, and she thought that strengthening her link to the accused women was what she needed to do above all else. And with it just being flowers and candles, she hoped it would appeal to the witches as well as the nuns' ghosts.

She also thought it was about time that she summoned up the courage to face up to the abilities that Rita said she had. *Burying your head in the sand like some psychic ostrich isn't going to solve anything*, she told herself sternly. *You don't have to try to do everything Aunty Rita says straight away. But you do need to face up to the fact that this isn't just going to up and go away. So maybe trying baby steps on your own instead of the great leaps and bounds Aunty Rita wants, won't freak you out as much?*

She took a deep breath.

Time to give it a go.

"I don't know if you can hear me?" she said, addressing the empty space. "But I'd really like to get to know more about those of you who *aren't* directly connected to our ghosts." Then she thought that given that Gideon's father had had a hand in several of the deaths, hurriedly added, "By that I mean other than Hugh's mother and grandmother. Can one of you tell me more of what went on in Kirkcudbright, please? Only we need to know who amongst you would even want to be called to rest there. I can't find out enough of your ordinary lives in the surviving records to know, you see?"

She sat back in the chair and took some deep, steadying breaths as Rita had now taught her. She was clutching the little linen bag in which Rita had put her protection crystals, hoping like mad that they worked, while on her other knee she had a notepad with a pen in her hand to write down anything important. In truth, she wasn't expecting to contact anyone this first time around, not having much faith in her abilities. So it was something of a shock to feel the temperature drop around her, and then to feel a definite presence with her.

When Rita had done this they had actually been able to see the ghosts, but whatever the connection to Anna, it wasn't strong enough to fully manifest them. Yet that turned out to be a blessing of the kind she hadn't anticipated.

'I'm Agnes,' a voice more in her head than heard out loud said, 'and I'm so glad you've come alone. When that other lady calls to us, she opens the way wide enough that my sister Margaret comes bustling through so strongly, I struggle to find a way to speak to you without her interrupting me.'

"She's my Aunty Rita," Anna explained, "and she's a very experienced psychic. I'm only just learning how to do this, so please don't expect too much of me as yet."

She took a deep breath. "Can we go through who exactly is with you again?" Looking down at her notebooks she asked, "Am I right in thinking that Hugh's aunt was Marione Corsan – Jannet's sister – and that it's her and her husband, this man called Samwell Black, and their son who I presume is Alexander Black, whose fate nobody knows?"

'You are right,' the ghostly almost-voice replied. 'Marione was badly questioned, the same as the rest of us, but Alexander had the wit to ride to Edinburgh and get her case delayed. It gave Samwell and Alexander time to get her away.'

"And you think they went up to somewhere in Argyll with their rescuer, this Sorley McAllister?"

'Yes. He was a good man. He took them, along with Jannet's poor broken husband James and Hugh, and my cousin Elspeth and her father, Johnne Allen.'

"And Elspeth is Jonet Allen's daughter?"

'Well Jonet was always known by her maiden name, ye'understand, but yes, Elspeth was Jonet Clark's daughter, and Jonet is here with us.'

"So where did they live? Elspeth, Jonet, and their family, I mean?"

'Oh, they had a croft not that far from mine, though they were closer to Dumfries.'

"Not Kirkcudbright, then?"

'No.'

"So where does the Kirkcudbright connection come in? Only I'm getting a bit lost over that."

Anna thought she heard the ghost's soft laugh as she answered, 'Aye, I can understand that ye' would. It's *my* sister, Margaret Clark, who lived in Kirkcudbright wi' her evil man, Thomas Milligan. But I ken what's confusing ye' is that Margaret was accused alongside other women from Kirkcudbright who died wi' us. I was the outsider in that sense.'

"Ah! Now I begin to see the pattern. And did those other women's remains get thrown into the old crypt here alongside yours?"

'Aye, they did.'

"So are they amongst the ghosts we see when all of you are present?"

'They are.'

Anna felt a surge of triumph. At last she was getting somewhere! "So can I ask you this: how many of those women have no family connections to our two ghosts? Can we lay them to rest by giving them a proper funeral service or whatever, *without* dealing with Gideon and Hugh?"

She was thinking that the fewer women's ghost left here, the easier it would be to get Hugh to let go, and therefore Gideon would have no reason to stay either. "I can't promise re-interment of their bones, because that would involve a massive digging up of some of our modern stuff, and I can't see the owner wanting to pay for that much deep excavation because that would be expensive. That crypt is probably a long way down by now by our modern measurements."

'I understand,' Agnes replied. 'Yes, I think that it would do much to soothe them, but ye' have to understand that because Gideon Corsan is John Corsan's son, and the father was instrumental in *all* of our deaths, everyone o' us has *that* connection to him. And Gideon was present at our trial, laughing and joking wi' Presbyter Veitch.'

“Ouch! I hadn’t realised it was quite that personal for you all.’

There was a sad, ghostly sigh. ‘Oh aye, it’s personal, so it is.’

“So can I ask you, who of all these women have a connection to Kirkcudbright?”

Agnes seemed to have to think about this, which as far as Anna was concerned was quite understandable after all this time. It took Agnes a moment, but then she said thoughtfully, ‘Jean Thomson and Janet McGown lived at a wee place called Borgue, just west o’ Kirkcudbright, but they got dragged into Kirkcudbright once accused, ye’ understand, as the nearest place where they could be held in a tolbooth. We’ve been thrown together for so long now it’s like we were always like that, but thinking back, I’m sure Jean and Janet were friends in life as well as death.’

“And they’re here with you now? They got thrown into the crypt?”

‘Aye, they did.’

“So if we can find a local church in or near Borgue, even if it’s more modern, they might be called home to rest?”

‘Ach, lass, Borgue even in our day had a kirk o’ its own, but the minister was all fer the Covenant, and awful harsh against witches. Then when they thought he’d finally left them in peace, it turned out that he was taking over in Kirkcudbright parish kirk, so overseeing the ‘spiritual care’ o’ prisoners in the tolbooth, ye’ ken. Thomas Wylie was awful harsh for a man o’ God, and Bigis – another from

Kirkcudbright – often calls his name out in fear, even now on this side. It's as if the man haunts her.' Anna could hear the stress in Agnes' voice.

"Did this Thomas Wylie rape her?" she asked gently.

Agnes' ghostly voice was almost beyond a whisper as she replied, 'Aye, I fear so. Poor Bigis is never right i' the heid, because whatever yon man did, it's stayed wi' her long after her body failed.'

"Oh Lord. …Thank you for telling me, Agnes. We'll have to give poor Bigis some extra thought. But for the others, might we lure them to rest in some other kirk? One without bad associations?"

'Aye, ye' might at that. That's a bonny thought, lass. Aye, resting in a wee kirk wi' no bad memories might bring them some peace at last.'

"Great! That's a good start. So who else had a connection to Kirkcudbright?"

'Aside from Marione and her ma, Grissell? That would be Helen Moorheid, though she's no' lingering around here quite like the others. Kind o' flits in and out, if ye' get my drift? But then she had an awful wallop on the heid when she was a bairn, and she was never quite right. Always talkin' about chatting to the fairies, so she was, when she walked the earth. I reckon it wouldn'a take much to settle her down. Then there's poor Bigis Cairns who I just mentioned. Ach, she's a poor haunted soul! The poor woman was a bit simple, if ye' ken my meaning? She was first a servant to Janet McGown.'

“That’s one of the ladies from Borgue?” Anna checked.

‘Aye, she was, and it’s nice that ye’ dignify her by calling her a lady. Poor Janet fell on real hard times when her man, Willie McGuffic, died – though she wasn’a that old herself. So she had to earn what she could, doing healing and selling a few charms to those who wanted them. Ach, she did no harm to anyone, but once those evil men started hunting for anyone they could thrown the dirt at – and that wicked swine John McCartney in particular, because she lived close by his lands – she was a ripe target for them. Nae respectable man to speak up fer her, ye’ see. By the time they’d done wi’ her, she didna ken what year it was, much less who was a witch and who was no’.

‘But I’ll be confusing you again if I’m no’ careful. …So after Willie’s death, Janet went around begging folk to take in poor Bigis, on account of Janet scarce able to keep herself, and Bigis no’ ever likely to get a husband to take care o’ her, and being an orphan wi’ nae family. It was Grissell and her William’s kindness that made them take Bigis in, though they were by no means rich themselves. They couldn’a do much more than keep a roof over her head and feed her, but she made herself useful around the croft and helped where she could.’

“That was kind of them,” making Anna think what it must have been like in a world where there were no Social Services for someone who these days would be classed as having at least learning difficulties, if not being fully mentally disabled.

Yet Agnes' sigh hinted even before she spoke that things hadn't been that simple.

CHAPTER 11

Her voice full of sorrow, Agnes continued,

'Kindness was to be the undoing o' Grissell. Ye' see, when her William then died young as well, it was Grissell's turn to be left too short o' money to be able to keep Bigis on. And that's where my poor sister comes in. Margaret's husband Thomas – may God rot his miserable soul in perdition forever! – fancied hisself the big man around town. Not that Kirkcudbright was that big a place, ye' understand. But initially, it tickled his fancy for his wife to take on a servant.'

There was a ghostly snort of disgust from Agnes. 'Took us all far too long to work out why he was happy to take on a simple soul like Bigis! The wicked swine was having his evil way wi' the poor woman when Margaret was confined, miscarrying her last child late in life, and nearly dying along wi' it.'

“*Euw*! That’s really nasty,” Anna agreed. “And doubly ‘poor Bigis’, if she’d already been raped by the minister, and then found herself being abused by Milligan as well. That’s too cruel. …How many did your sister lose?”

‘I dinna ken that even she can remember at this distance,’ Agnes admitted, ‘but I’m fairly sure she lost three or four between her sons and Isobel, the daughter and youngest who survived.’

“Poor Margaret, that’s a lot of miscarriages to suffer.”

Again Agnes gave that sniff of disgust. ‘No’ all were natural miscarriages either! Thomas was awful free wi’ his fists when in a temper.’

“That’s horrible. He clearly wasn’t much of a man if he beat up his pregnant wife.”

‘Oh, he did worse than that. He was the one who bore testimony to her being a witch.’

“Oh my God! I remember now. You said that one of you had been betrayed by her husband, but I hadn’t got to grips with who was who at that point. Good grief, poor Margaret. No wonder she’s so angry.”

‘Aye, well she has more reasons than even that. ’Twas *her* daughter, Isobel, who Hugh tried to save. And ’twas Isobel who Gideon caught up wi’, plus the other young lass, and took to Wigtown to be judged by Cruel Lagg.’

“Good Lord! So *Margaret’s* Isobel was the lady who Hugh told us about, who got whipped through the town?”

‘She was. And though Margaret was long dead by then – as were we all – we all felt her pain and passing too.’

“But it must have been ten times worse for Margaret if she recognised her own daughter. Bad enough to be betrayed by your husband – even if you didn’t love him – because she should surely have expected to be able to depend on a bit of loyalty from him towards herself? But to then witness, albeit from afar, your own daughter being treated so brutally? Heavens, it’s a wonder she’s even half-way sane!” And Anna recalled her recent conversation with Rita about personal connections. Jonet and Elspeth had seen their nieces and cousins die horribly, but Margaret had actually suffered that fate herself and then witnessed her own daughter die horribly. No wonder she was so full of fury and hate. Even three centuries wouldn’t be long enough to lay that much pain to rest.

‘There was a long time when I wasna’ entirely sure that Margaret was sane,’ Agnes confessed. ‘Ach, but she was fair mad wi’ grief and fury, and no’ helped by the fact that she couldna’ feel Isobel in our afterlife. The nuns did their best, ye’ ken? But they couldna’ reach all the way to Wigtown from here.’

It made Anna realise how different their perception of distances must have been. For her, the run to Wigtown was no great distance in the car, even if she hadn’t wanted to risk it in the Fiesta. But in the days when it would have to be done on foot, or at best riding on a farm cart, even the bit over a twenty-five-mile run between Dumfries and Kirkcudbright would have taken a very long and full day, and that only in the summertime if the roads were dry and there was daylight for longer. In winter, even that must have been a two-day journey, necessitating an overnight stop somewhere, because Gary had told her that the reason why so many market towns were about fifteen to twenty miles apart, was because seven or eight miles there and then back again was as much as most folk could comfortably do in a day on foot. It meant that each town had a radius of ten to fifteen miles for their own markets without competing with one another, but for special markets in the big towns it was a very long trek.

Therefore then adding on the extra thirty miles from Kirkcudbright to Wigtown – because the great loop of the coast road was the only way to avoid struggling through the narrow twisting passes of the foot hills of the mountains to the north – Anna suddenly realised how unrealistic they had been in thinking of what Hugh could cover in a day to catch up with Gideon. No wonder he'd been days behind Gideon if Gideon had taken the women on ponies with over a day's lead, not to mention that Hugh could hardly have stopped folk to ask which way Gideon had gone. Had Hugh expected Gideon to take the women to his home – to here, in other words – and then had to turn and start chasing him all the way to Kirkcudbright, only to find he'd gone onwards to Wigtown? That was something she suddenly felt they must talk to him about, because she had this gut feeling that someone being understanding of why he'd been too far behind to save anyone might be a great comfort to him.

Now, though, it made Anna stop and think hard, eventually saying to Agnes, "So would I be right in thinking that of all of you, Margaret is the one who won't leave here until Gideon does?"

And to her credit, Agnes seemed to give that as much consideration before answering, 'Aye, I think ye' have the right o' it. None o' us ha' any affection for Gideon. He had nae sense o' right and wrong as a lad, ye' ken? Couldna' see the level o' hurt and disgust his father had roused in the ordinary people. But I and others observed from here that, as time went on, he came to understand more just what his father had cost him.

'Even in life, it didn'a make Gideon a likeable man by any means. Too full o' his own grievances, if ye' ken my meaning, and not enough o' what hurt had been done to others. And at an age when he should ha' been a wee bit more alert to what had gone on. But there's nae doubt in my mind that Gideon suffered for grievous sins that were no' his own. Whereas Margaret canna' comprehend any kind o' sympathy for what it must ha' been like for Gideon, even if she kens all too well what a vile brute his father was.'

"I hear what you're saying, Agnes," Anna sympathised. "We know by now in our age that sometimes the damage done to children results in those who've been abused becoming abusers to their own children. They just don't know how to be anything else. And that's a terrible tragedy. Some people manage to overcome a childhood like that, and resolve that their own families will never suffer the same. And others never quite get over being so warped by a vicious parent. There's no magic pill that cures or doesn't. It just seems to depend on the personality of the person involved. So I can't hold it against Gideon that he never overcame what his father pounded into him – probably with his fists."

'Oh aye, 'twas wi' his fists, nae doubt about that,' Agnes agreed. 'And it turned out he was no' the worst of John Corsan's sons in the end. The next son down was a real Holy Willie, running to the kirk as fast as he could to escape his father.' Anna heard or maybe felt a shiver from Agnes. 'Young Matthew was the next son down from Gideon, ye' ken, but whatever it was he learned at university at St Andrews, it had aye-all to do wi' the love o' God, and much to do wi' smiting!'

"Smiting? Oh, the, 'spare the rod and spoil the child' kind of smiting, you mean?"

'Ye' have it exactly. John Corsan was a grand man for beating the sin out o' his children. His two daughters got sent away young by their ma to try and save them, but auld John kept his sons close. If Gideon got warped in one way, Matthew got warped in another. He was no' shy of using some very…' Agnes seemed to struggle for the words until Anna supplied, "…Muscular Christianity…?"

'Aye, lass, that's a good way o' putting it. …It was Matthew who finally put auld John Corsan out o' his misery.'

"Matthew killed his father?" Anna was shocked.

"'Oh aye. The auld man could ha' carried on for a few years yet, even in his state after the seizure. Gideon…aye well, certain folk heard him threaten to do for the auld man when in his cups wi' drink, but even he couldna' stoop so low in truth. Matthew? Well he thought he had the hand o' God on his shoulder."

"Wow! That was…strange, surely, for a man of the cloth? …Murder, I mean, and patricide, in particular? Ten Commandments and all that. I have good reason to loathe my own father, but to go as far as killing him? No, never that."

'Aye, but ye're a good soul, lass. Matthew? He saw himself above the law. Saw his ain faither as a wicked sinner beyond redemption, never once seeing that the same could be said o' him. He was as wicked as that evil auld de'il, Presbyter Veitch. Him that raped Aunt Jonet when she was but a lass!'

"Wha…*What*?" Anna squeaked. "Jonet was *raped* by the minister? Jeez, that's *awful*. To go through that and then lose her only daughter to who knows where, and after she'd been tormented to death…!"

'…Only daughter?' Agnes questioned.

"Yes. Elspeth. …The way she vanished out of Jonet's ability to sense her, I mean."

'Ach, lass, we've gi'en ye' an awfully wrong impression if ye' think that Elspeth was Jonet and Johnne's only child.'

"She wasn't?'

'No. She *was* the youngest, and the only one left at home by the time it all went so wrong. And Elspeth, poor lass, had got tainted by the accusations flung at her ma. She didn'a have any local lads courting her once that was well known. Their families wouldn'a risked it, ye' ken? Couldn'a risk having their ain families tainted by association, for to have the hand o' the Presbyter turned against ye' was something to be mightily feared. That's why it was such a blessing that Marione and Samwell's Alexander fell for her – he couldn'a get any more tainted than he already was, ye' ken?'

"So who else was there?"

'Well the next sister up was Mailie.' Anna heard Agnes' ghostly affectionate chuckle. 'If Elspeth was her faither's daughter in temperament – all common sense and kindness – Mailie was the double o' Jonet as a young lass. …I didn'a ken my aunt at that age ye' understand, but my ma…'

"…That's Geillis?"

'…Aye, Geillis. She met Jonet when they worked as serving lasses up at Lagg, afore either o' them were wed.'

"*Woah*! Hang on a sec'! …You mean Jonet and Geillis *knew* Robert Grierson? The one who ordered your niece Isobel's death?!

Agnes' 'Aye,' was filled with sadness. 'I no longer ken whether it was Robert or one o' the other wee ones in the family who Geillis was nursery maid to, because Robert was the auld laird's nephew, no' his son, but aye, she kenned him as a babe, and he her, though I doubt he stooped to recall it once a man.'

"God help us," Anna gasped, appalled. "I can't believe how every lead we find keeps coming back to someone else in this puzzle. Did everyone know everyone else in your day?"

'Pretty much,' Agnes admitted. 'Ye' might no' ken them well, but ye' kenned who they were right enough.'

That put a whole new level of personal acrimony into the mix in Anna's eyes, and it took her a moment to digest it, but then she recalled that Agnes had started to tell her about Jonet's family.

"So this Mailie. Elspeth's sister. You were starting to tell me about her?"

There was the sense of a smile, even if Anna couldn't see it. 'Mailie, aye. So much like her ma. Bonnie and full o' life. She had all the young lads eating out o' her hand just the way Ma said Jonet did in her time. But making eyes at the lads and swirling her skirts didn'a make up fer having an accused witch fer a ma, in Mailie's case, because ye' must recall that Jonet had already been questioned by Veitch for a witch at Irongray by the time Mailie was o' an age to be courting. Oh, they'd play along wi' her, but the moment it started looking like it might get serious, they backed away. Mailie couldn'a stand it. No' like Elspeth, God love her, who shouldered that burden and carried on looking after Jonet. No, Mailie ran away wi' a lad who was going fer a soldier.'

“And did Mailie have children?” Suddenly it dawned on Anna that she’d been focusing solely on Elspeth as the one and only one whose child or children could have been her ancestor, but this talk of other children of Jonet’s opened up a whole new field.

‘Aye, she did. In truth, we dinna ken if Elspeth had any child o’ her own. She was gone too far away by then, ye’ ken? But the oldest sister, Jean – a dour and twisted woman, just like the evil man who fathered her – came and told Johnne and Elspeth that Mailie’s first man Patrick had died, and so had the next man she took up wi’. But her third husband, though I ken no’ if she married him in kirk or no’, was the one up in the Highlands who Elspeth and our families went to, and the man who led them there said that by then Mailie had wee ones. Who was faither to which I canna tell ye’ either, but she had more than one, o’ that I’m sure.’

“Good grief,” Anna breathed, frantically scribbling this down on her note pad. “So you’ve no idea what Mailie’s husband’s name might have been? His family name, I mean?”

‘I canna help ye’ wi’ that, I’m afraid. …Jean? Aye. Jean’s man was a pious sourpuss called George Henryson, and they had five wee ones – three boys and two girls. They lived o’er Newton Stewart way. Far enough so that they were no’ tainted by gossip about her ma,’ and Agnes’ sniff of disgust told Anna everything about what Agnes thought of a daughter who worried about what was being said over caring for her own mother.

“Thank you so much,” Anna said gratefully to Agnes. “You’ve explained so much for me. I really have to go now, because I have to go to work, but I will try and come back to talk to you if you’d like?”

‘Aye. That would be grand,’ she said, and there was no mistaking the warmth in Agnes’s voice, ghost or not. But then, as Anna thought as she headed into her cottage to change, if you’d been cooped up for three centuries with the same women, some of them rehashing the same old bitter arguments over and over, it was hardly surprising that Agnes would welcome someone new to talk to.

It was only as she dumped her notebook onto the table beside the huge family tree that was still spread out and held down by some clean mugs, that it hit her. There on the tree was the surname Henryson!

“Oh no! Oh God! Please tell me I’m not genetically linked to the man who tortured some of these women?” Because if her link to Jonet went through not just Elspeth but Jean…and if Jean was the biological daughter not of lovely Johnne Allen, but vile Presbyter Veitch…and Veitch had been partly responsible for corrupting Gideon as a child… “Oh God! Does Gideon sense Veitch in me?”

the laird's
main hall
main
entrance
family
room
THE OLD
TOWER HOUSE
family
room
GROUND FLOOR
kitchen

1674

Gideon

It was a fine early spring morning at the townhouse in Dumfries when the fateful knock came at the door. As usual, Auld John simply bellowed at Gideon to go and answer it, their lone serving woman being too busy preparing Auld John's breakfast to go.

"Oh, it's you," Gideon said as he saw Thomas McBurney standing on the step and grinning evilly.

Oh God! What scheme's he up to now? was all Gideon could think, because by now he'd become embroiled in a few of Thomas' hare-brained antics, and they never came out well. Full of bluster and bullishness, Thomas might think himself another such as his uncle, the astute and worldly former bailie Alexander McBurney, but in truth he didn't even have the brains of his father William, and William had always been several steps behind his older brother. It had only been a couple of years since Alexander had relinquished the role of senior town bailie to a younger and more vigorous man, but his influence remained strong, meaning Thomas was still riding on the coat tails of his uncle's renown. *What's he going to do when his uncle's power fades from people's memories?* Gideon often wondered.

"I've got it for you!" Thomas was crowing as he shouldered past Gideon and into the room where Auld John was sitting at the table, a plate of steaming devilled kidneys in front of him. "I told you I could."

Gideon's heart sank. "Got what?" he asked, dreading the answer.

"*Blackpark House*!" his father said, giving him a filthy look. "Do try and keep up, Gideon."

"The old nunnery?" Gideon managed to choke out, horrified at even the thought of going back to that place. It had been just down the road from there that they'd found the body of Thomas' brother Rab at the Apostles' Stones, but Gideon hadn't forgotten what he'd seen back in 1650 when they'd pursued Elspeth Allen there. The ghosts of those nuns still haunted his nightmares. Why on earth would his father want that?

His father's laugh sent shivers down his spine. "Not for much longer," he chortled and grasped Thomas' hand as they grinned at one another. "Your brother will be revenged and those Whores of Babylon forgotten."

"And you are the right man to do that," Thomas flattered John with, making vomit crawl up Gideon's throat, forcing him to swallow hard and take deep breaths.

Oh God! O God! Here we go again! he mentally screamed. Then he realised his father was saying to him, “Stop gawping, boy, and take notice! Presbyter Veitch has wanted that place gone for as long as I can recall. Thomas and his father want it gone to avenge Rab – because even if nobody else believes it, we know that the ghosts of those damned witches had something to do with it. And Hugo Grierson has run out of money in his attempt to make himself a grand house that will match his cousins’ at Lagg.”

“Lagg’s a *castle*,” Gideon managed to croak. “Surely you don’t want a castle?” *Ever-loving-Christ! His father’s delusions didn’t run that far, did they?*

“God in heaven! What did I do to have such dolts for sons?” Auld John fumed as his youngest – also called John – came in and stood looking as puzzled as Gideon. “Of course I don’t want a bloody castle!”

It said everything for Auld John’s arrogance that he would swear in front of someone who wasn’t family, albeit in his own home. Blasphemy of any kind in public was punished with heavy fines, and even someone well-off like John McCartney couldn’t afford to keep paying those. So he had to be so deeply implicated with Thomas that neither would dare inform on the other to their other conspirator in most things, Presbyter Veitch, because Veitch issued such fines to the extreme with a true zealot’s fire.

Thomas turned to look at Gideon and Young John, adopting a patronising manner as he explained as if to men of little brains, "Grierson's made a start on what was the old gatehouse to the nunnery. It's solidly built and has good foundations. And there's plenty of stone in the nunnery buildings and kirk to use to make the extra wing of a house, which he's called *Blackpark*. It won't take much to pull the old stuff down and put a grand house up."

Not much? was Gideon's mental snort of disbelief. *Not for you, maybe. But I know who's going to be doing most of the hard work up there and it won't be Father! God, I hate you, old man. Will I ever be free of you and your schemes?*

His father's bark of, "What's up with you, boy?" made him jump, but realised that this time it was aimed at Young John.

"You promised," his brother managed to splutter out. "You promised that I could go and join Matthew over in St Andrews. Where's the money for that going to come from now if you're going to build a house?"

"A pox on you and your daft daydreams!" Auld John snarled. "What good would an education do a thick sod like you? Have I had any benefit from all I've paid out for Matthew? No! He was supposed to come back here and help Veitch once he qualified, not still be gadding about over in Fife! So no, John, you will not be going to join him. Instead, you are going to stay here and help Gideon build my house – because God knows, Gideon needs all the help he can get with just about everything!"

As Gideon watched Young John's face fall as he realised that his plan to escape their father had failed spectacularly, Gideon also felt the bite of their father's words about himself. Was that really how the old man thought of him? As some kind of imbecile who needed constant supervision and help?

Well, I'll bloody-well show you! he thought savagely. *I'm the oldest, so when you go, all this will be mine. And by God, if you want a fine house, I want one that will be even finer, and I'll do it on your money while you still live, not forking out from my inheritance, because I know you'll not leave me everything. You might curse Matthew, but he was always your favourite, and you're bound to leave him a tidy sum of money, even if you make me provide for John. So I'm going to have a house big enough that I can shove John off into another part and never see him from one day to the next. Not be sitting across some grubby croft from him day in and day out, listening to him bleating about how he wants to be a poet over and over.*

"You'd better come with me and show me the building work, then," he said to Thomas and felt smug when he saw Thomas go pale. Clearly Thomas wasn't any happier about going back to that place than he was, but if he had to suffer it, then for dropping this onto him, Thomas was going to suffer in part too.

In the end, all four of them rode out a week later to inspect *Blackpark House*, as Auld John and Thomas insisted on calling it, not that there was anything remotely house-like about it yet. For Gideon, it was going to take the complete removal of the still-standing parts of the old nunnery before he could think of it as anything other than the site of his former torment – and he included being deprived of Elspeth that very first time in amongst that. Young John had never been there, but Gideon felt smug when they rode in via the fallen walls of the enclosure and saw his brother shiver, and begin to cast about him as if expecting to see ghosts leaking out of the ruins. *Yes, you feel it too, don't you?* he thought with grim satisfaction. *Not so quick to take the piss out of me now, are you? It's different once you get here. Those other two have the senses of a plank, but you've enough of Ma in you to feel it like I do.*

Already Auld John was waving his arms in grand gestures as he declared, "I'll put another proper floor in on this tower. I don't care how high that current roof goes, or whether it's got a walkway around the edge. I'm not fighting off my enemies with muskets and swords. I want the bastards cowed in awe when they come here!"

"Please God Veitch doesn't hear him talking like that," Young John whispered fearfully. "He'll have us all before the Kirk Session if he did – and we know what can happen there!"

"We're men." Gideon whispered back to him. "They don't execute us for witches."

"No, but they can 'investigate' us, and you know what Veitch is like with that witch pricker's needle. I don't want that length of steel shoved up my manhood just to see if I feel any pain!" Young John bit back with, and the thought of what he'd just said was enough to have Gideon's balls shrivelling up even further than they were already.

As far as Gideon could recall, Samwell Black hadn't been walking funny when he'd been released from custody, but that signified nothing, because Samwell had been in the Dumfries Tolbooth, not out at Veitch's manse at Irongray. And he knew of only a couple of other men who'd been detained, both of them in proper tolbooths, not by men like Veitch. Robert Short had been questioned, but his son had appealed to Edinburgh, and he'd been set free; while Thomas Wilson had been detained back in the early sixties, but hadn't even got as far as the local trial that Robert Short had been through. Nonetheless, his brother's words sent a shiver down his spine, and he vowed to be extra careful about how he spoke in front of Veitch. His father might think himself above the local kirk courts, but Gideon went in fear and trembling of them just like everybody else.

"I'll have the domestic wing out here," his father was carrying on, and at this point Gideon summoned the courage to speak up.

"No."

"No?" His father rounded on him and glared. "Who are you to say what I will and will not have?"

Sighing, Gideon pointed out, "The ruins are in the way. The way you want to go, we'll be having to rip out the old buildings, find *somewhere* to store the stone, and only then will we be able to put the foundations in. And for a building as grand as *you* want, there *will* have to be foundations."

Auld John went puce at being publicly contradicted, but then suddenly seemed to see the sense in what Gideon was saying.

"So you do have a brain after all," was his snide response. "*Hmph*! Well in that case, take the domestic wing out towards the track."

"We'll need a builder," Gideon dared to say, almost shocked into silence by his father not shooting him down instantly.

"*Phfaa*!" Auld John snorted bullishly after a moment. "*I* don't need some *builder* telling me what can and can't be done."

"That's what Grierson thought," Gideon responded with silent glee, glad that he, of all of them, had thought to go and speak to Grierson two days before about what had gone wrong with the building. "Grierson thought he could do without a builder, and what broke him financially was having the whole of his domestic wing crumbling into dust the moment it got to putting the roof beams on. …Look! You can see the rubble over there! That's where Grierson's building fell down."

Auld John looked fit to spit nails through an oak door, but he couldn't disregard the evidence of his own eyes. There, just beyond where he needed to build his new servants' wing, was a huge, crumpled pile of sandstone blocks, some of them with what was clearly fresh mortar on them.

"Get me James Kennedy," he snarled, "and make sure he knows it's *me* who's after his services!"

"Already spoken to him," was Gideon's gleeful response. "He's ready to start next Monday when he finishes his current job."

The shock on his father's face was worth the wait. And yet even the simplest of words of praise seemed to stick in Auld John's craw. With nothing more than a snort and a nod, he heeled his horse and turned for home, Thomas McBurney hurrying to turn his horse and follow him, pouring oily words of congratulations in the old man's ear.

Turning in his saddle to look at Young John, Gideon saw awe in his brother's eyes for the first time.

"You challenged him…and you *won*!" Young John said breathlessly.

On that day, it felt as if Gideon had achieved a small victory.

He should have known better.

From then on, Auld John stuck his nose into each and every decision Gideon made. It didn't matter that, for all but a couple of insignificant incidents, Gideon had been right in his decision. All that mattered to Auld John was that he was *perceived* as being the one who'd had the last say. It got so bad that Kennedy and Gideon simply stopped referring things back to him, and in Gideon's case, even mentioning stuff at the dinner table. If they hadn't, the work would have slowed to a snail's pace, and that wouldn't have been right either.

For the most part, it ensured that the building work continued at a rapid pace, but when it came to the mullioned window Auld John wanted on the stairs' wall, nothing would dissuade him.

"I haven'a room to fit in a window of the size ye're wanting," Kennedy protested as Auld John was building up to another apoplectic rant. "Without taking all o' the ground floor o' the new wing out and starting again two yards over, it canna' be done."

And that was when fate stuck.

Gideon and Young John had both seen the shades of furious nuns as the builders tore down first the domestic buildings of the nunnery, and then began on the east end of the small kirk, which was the bit closest to the old gatehouse. At that stage, even some of the labourers, many of whom Gideon thought were the most unimaginative and dense men he'd ever come across, refused point blank to work on it. And though he would never have given the workmen the satisfaction of acknowledging that he too had seen the ghosts, Gideon fully understood why. The burnt and disfigured shades of the women he knew were the witches his father had contributed towards being burned at the stake, and had then had their mortal remains flung into the crypt here with singular disregard, flew alongside the ghosts of the nuns at any man trying to rip up the flagstone floor of the kirk.

The walls weren't too bad at first. It was only as they got down to the last course of blocks before the chancel floor that things turned truly ugly.

However, at that point it became outright war between the ghosts and the builders – or at least those who had strong enough nerves to stay on the job, and they tended to be dyed-in-the-wool Covenanters, who hated the very thought of the Benedictine nuns, even in ghostly form. There were a couple of truly hard characters amongst the labourers, who would dash in when others had loosened the mortar, and literally rip the stone blocks or pavers out and onto wooden sleds, which others would then haul on the ropes of from a safe distance.

"Mary, Mother of God," Young John whimpered the one time he tried to help, echoing their mother's oft repeated plea to the divine. "What did we do? Why do they hate us so?"

And in truth Gideon struggled to answer him, because to do so would have meant admitting to his own guilt. He shouldn't have laughed. Even at the time he'd been nauseated by the sight of burning flesh and its smell. But he'd been more frightened of his father, and the thought of yet another lashing of that heavy belt across his arse and back when they got home, if he hadn't made the appropriate responses. Since then he'd tried so hard to forget that he'd been coerced into being one of those who scooped up the partially burned remains, and brought them here to the old kirk. Veitch wouldn't hear of them being put to rest in *his* kirkyard. And the rest of the parish had been equally adamant that they didn't want the souls of the eight burned women haunting them if they *weren't* put to rest on hallowed ground. So at the time, the old nunnery seemed to be the perfect answer.

Why, Gideon mentally fretted time and again, why oh why did his father have to choose *this* place above all others to boast of his climb up the social ladder? But then it was so typical of Auld John. He couldn't be content with a simple victory. Oh no, he had to hammer his triumph home to all and sundry. Well now it was coming back to well and truly bite him, because not a week went by without another workman refusing to come back onto the job.

As the work slowed to a snail's pace, once again Auld John came out to the site on a weekly basis to harangue them all.

"What's the matter with you?" he bellowed at the terrified mason and his helpers. "Get in there and rip the place apart! I want more stone. I want my window! And if Kennedy needs to extend the house, then by God you *will* extend it."

He stormed over to where the farthest part of the apsidal east end of the kirk still stood two courses high. Pretty much all of the domestic buildings had gone, the builders leaving the worst to last, and until now, they hadn't needed to rob the last of the kirk itself to take the gate house higher, and to put the foundations in of the new building. But now they needed more stone, and proper blocks too, and because of the rubble from their previous robbing of blocks, the only way they could drag the blocks from the nave walls out was across where the old crypt lay, meaning that had to go first.

Because of the lie of the land, and the way it began to fall away towards the river, the old crypt had been partially above ground – or at least its top courses of stone had, even if much of it had been subterranean – and it had been taking up the blocks which had formed its ceiling which had really brought the ghosts' wrath upon them. Yet with scant regard for how stable the land was, Auld John stomped right to the edge of where a cave-like opening was appearing in the ground as the men got down to the crypt itself.

"Father! That's not stable." Young John tried to warn him, but it wasn't the land crumbling which got him.

"Rip it out! All of it!" Auld John was screaming, turning and flinging a threatening fist towards the men. But what he was going to say next never happened.

He saw the men before him blanch, and the watchers thought he believed it fear of himself. Instead, the men saw nine ghostly women rising from the hollow of the crypt, faces masks of fury – or as much as anyone could tell in their ruined state.

'Time to pay, ye' de'il!' several men later swore they heard, though in the real world there was no sound but a murder of crows in the nearby trees.

As one, they swarmed up and around him, battering at him with wisps of fists. In spite of their lack of earthly strength, Auld John reeled back and tottered on the uneven ground, getting ever closer to the edge.

“Not in the crypt!” Gideon yelped in horror, not because of what the fall might do to his father, but at the thought of someone having to go down there and haul his body out. There was no way that Veitch would let John Corsan’s body lie in a Catholic crypt, however sanctified the ground, and Gideon knew who Veitch’s wrath would fall on hardest – him!

Yet his words had the strangest effect, for the ghosts seemed to hear him, pause, and then instead start pushing Auld John hard away from the edge.

“God preserve us,” the mason intoned, and meaning it, not blaspheming. “The ghosts don’t want him in there with them!”

John Corsan took three or four wobbling steps away from the edge and then went down as if poleaxed.

The ghosts froze.

Then on the breeze, or in their heads – the men never did quite decide – they heard them. Cackling laughter, as if coming out of the witches’ ruined throats, and as one they turned and sank back down into the crypt.

“’Tis a judgement on him,” someone behind Gideon whispered into the silence, and neither he nor Young John contradicted that.

CHAPTER 12

On slightly wobbly legs, Anna made it into work for the late shift, but was very grateful that it was quiet enough for Gary to wander through and sit down for a chat with her. Rita, it seemed, was having a long video call with her Wiccanly inclined friends up north, and had shooed Gary out of his own cottage so that she could talk openly with them without his askance glances.

"It's a bit rich, chucking you out of your own place," Anna teased, albeit rather weakly, her sense of humour having taken something of a battering after her discovery.

"Oh, I'm just glad she feels enough at home to do that," Gary replied with a knowing wink.

Now Anna's laugh was genuine. "You crafty bugger! Letting her get her feet well and truly under the table are you? Good on you, Gary. Let's hope she realises that you're worth moving to be closer to."

Gary grinned, but became serious as he asked, "And what's got you all shook up? I know you by now, lass, and you look like you've just found out someone's died. What's happened?"

"Don't shout at me, Gary, but I had a go at talking to the ladies over in the kirk." As his eyebrows shot up, she hurriedly explained why she'd felt the need to do that, and was relieved when she saw him nodding in agreement by the end.

"Aye, well at least you had the sense to do it where you did and who you did it with," he praised her. "I reckon you should stick to the ladies for now, because they don't mean you any harm at all. And from the sound of it, Agnes is glad of a wee blether wi' someone new after three hundred years. That was a good thought, too, for us to chat wi' Hugh and show that we now get why he was so far behind Gideon on that chase across to Wigtown. I'll happily explain that these days we can do it in an afternoon, and that it's our fault that we've no' realised how long a journey it was for him. A bit o' sympathy will go a long way wi' him, I'm thinking."

"But it's discovering that Jonet and Johnne had *three* daughters that's freaking me out a bit," Anna confessed. "Elspeth I love the sound of. She seems such a kind person now that I know she stuck it out here for her mum and dad's sake. And if Mailie is what we'd now think of as a bit flighty, by the same token you can't blame her for wanting to get away to somewhere where people weren't always judging her by what her mum may or may not have done. I got the impression that there might have been a bit of a gap between Elspeth and her sisters, but that could be just me assuming that was the reason why Elspeth stayed at home.

"It's this oldest one Jean who freaked me out, though, Gary. She was the illegitimate daughter of Presbyter Veitch! And she married someone called Henryson. Well I've got Henryson as a surname in my dad's family tree, and it goes a long way back too on that huge tree Aunty Rita's friend did for me – as far back as she was able to get, so closer to Jean's own time. Jean went on to have two daughters who wouldn't have handed on the Henryson name, but three sons who would have carried the family name onwards. So if I could inherit this whatever it is through a male line, what's to stop it from having come through Jean's sons?"

"Which would mean you're connected, albeit awfully distantly, to that bloody Presbyter," Gary said sympathetically. "But Anna, Gideon wasn'a related to Veitch. It's a bloody grim discovery if you are from that line, but he's no' one of our ghosts."

"No," Anna conceded, "but from what we've heard from some of the women, he had his nose wedged firmly up Veitch's bum! And that's something I'm not comfortable with."

Gary shuffled his chair sideways so that he could put an arm around Anna to give her a hug, as they sat behind the reception desk.

"Don't get yourself too wound up over that," he said calmly. "I doubt Gideon can sense anything that faint in you after all these centuries. But speaking of things you don't find comfortable, I've been thinking about what we can do to try and discover stuff. How do you feel about phoning your mum?"

"Oh God, Gary, not great."

"Is there a night when you know your dad won't be there? Some evening he clears off to the pub? …Okay let me rephrase that, because he's too far up his own arse to mix with normal blokes. But does he sod off to the Masons or the Rotarians or something?"

"Er, yes, he goes to some meeting or other every first Monday of the month."

"And that's this coming week. So why don't you give him chance to get clear, and then ring your mum? Only I'm thinking that you might ask her about her own parents, and why she's never spoken about them? Because otherwise, to track them down, we'll have to hunt through things like electoral registers and pray that they haven't moved house very often."

"I doubt Mum would speak about them. And while it's a good thought, Gary, I don't think she'd speak to me. I've rocked the family boat too hard, and that won't be forgiven. …Oh! But I wonder if Nigel ever tried to make contact with them? He's so much older than me, there may have been stuff going on with him that I never picked up as a kid. I think I saw a way to contact him through Ancestry. I can try leaving him a message?"

"Great idea! But in the vein of speaking to someone, what about your sister? She's at least on the same side of the world as you."

Anna grimaced. "Heather? *Naah.* If there wasn't money involved, she'll never have remembered. She's like some neurotic mix of Mum and Dad's worst points. If I've upset them, she'll never speak to me in case they get mad at her."

Gary gave a huff of disgust but said nothing. What a family! However, he did go back over to Anna's cottage and bring her laptop over for her so that she could send Nigel a message. What neither of them was expecting was for the laptop to ping with an alert, just as Anna was wrapping up the accounts she'd been doing, and was about to unplug it at the end of her shift and head back home to bed.

"Oh my God! It's from Nigel! He must have just got up over there."

Gary leaned over her shoulder and read the message alongside her.

Hello little sis! So you broke free of the monsters too? Good for you! Stay away from them, they're toxic. Funny you should ask about Nan, because I'm back in contact with her and Granddad since getting out from under the monsters' shadows. It took me a while to track them down, but if you are in Scotland, you're not far from them. They're in their eighties now, but fit as fleas and still totally with it. This is their address and phone number –

he gave an address in St Andrews.

Great to hear from you! Keep in touch. This is my home address now and my email. Who knows, one day you might come over to Oz to visit us and meet the family?

"That really sounds like he's never coming back," Anna sighed, "but who can blame him?"

"Aye, but he seems genuinely glad to hear from you," Gary pointed out. "I think you have an ally there, Anna, even if he is too far away to do much."

"Yes, he does, doesn't he?" Anna said, brightening up considerably. "And now I've got a phone number for my grandparents! I'm actually feeling tingly and a bit nervous about phoning them, but excited at the same time."

She was doing a back-to-back shift the following morning, and so it was after lunch before she could do anything. Feeling that she needed some moral support, she took her mobile and laptop around to Gary's and sat at the table with him and Rita, and Cameron, who'd been informed about this development by Gary.

"This is great," Cameron said, giving her hand a reassuring squeeze after she'd put the number into her phone and with great trepidation pressed 'ring'.

Whatever she'd been anticipating, the bright and cheerful voice giving the number wasn't what she'd expected. Was this her gran? It didn't sound like an old lady's voice.

"Hello. Can I speak to Mrs Euphemia Clarke, please?" Anna was struggling to keep her voice even.

"Who's speaking please?"

"Erm, she's never met me, but I'm her granddaughter, Anna…Belinda's youngest child."

There was a clunk as the phone got dropped and they heard her move away a little, then yell, "Davey! Get in here! You'll never guess who's on the phone."

It made Anna giggle nervously, because her gran sounded suspiciously as if she was as much of a force of nature as Rita.

In the distance they heard noises, then Euphemia saying, "Well take your boots off, man! I've just mopped that floor. Jings! I don't want the whole veg patch in the kitchen."

Already Gary was smothering laughter with a hand, looking pointedly at Rita, who was nonetheless also grinning, clearly approving of this woman she'd yet to meet.

"There, now." The phone was picked up again. "I'll put you on speaker. Davey, this is wee Anna!"

"What? Belinda's lassie?" they heard a much broader Scottish accent say.

"Well who else do we know called Anna?" her gran said with a tut. "You'll have to forgive the poor old soul. He's no' as fast on the uptake as he used to be."

"Says you who's a year older than me," he fired back, but with mischief in his voice.

Cameron leaned in and whispered to Anna, "They sound like a lively pair!"

She grinned at him and nodded, but Euphemia was already speaking.

"How did you track us down? It can't have been that daft daughter of ours. Is she still with that god-awful stuffed shirt of a husband of hers?"

Rita leaned in and answered for Anna, "Oh aye, she's still with my idiot half-brother. I'm Rita, by the way, and I'm here with Anna giving her a hand with a little problem."

"Oh," Euphemia gasped, "I've heard of you! I remember Gordon cussing a blue streak about you and your mother back when he and Belinda first got married, back when Helen and Nigel were still small and before you came along, Anna. And of course, Morag used to write to me and keep me up to date on what was happening back then."

"You knew Great-Aunty Morag?" Anna gasped. "Oh God, of course! She was on mum's side, so she was *your* sister, Grandfather – oh heck, I don't know what to call you – but I didn't realise you were still in contact with one another."

Davey's gravelly voice answered, "Call me Granddad, all the others do. And aye, well our Morag was a normal person, no' worried about whether you wore the right brand o' bloody socks! So yes, o' course we were in touch. No' like Belinda, who was always the daft one o' our kids, but she got ten times worse after she took up wi' Gordon."

"Excuse me, interrupting, I'm Gary, a friend o' Rita's and Anna's and here to offer a bit o' moral support. But can you tell me how on earth the daughter o' a good pair o' Scots like you ended up married to him down in England?"

"Nice to meet you, Gary," Davey replied. "If you're helping our girl, then you're the right sort. As for how they met, my work had taken me down south for a few years. All the others o' our kids were old enough to stay up here, but Belinda was still at school, so she had to move wi' us. What a mistake! I wish now we'd left her wi' her oldest sister, Janice, because Janice had a good job and a steady lad she was engaged to. We could ha' left them in our house instead o' renting it out."

Euphemia was heard tutting again. "Ach, Davey, that's just wishful thinking in hindsight. You know that Belinda fought like cat and dog wi' all the others. I swear that child was crabbit from day one. She could fall out wi' her own fingernails if she'd nothing else to argue wi'."

"That sounds like Mum," Anna giggled. "I was so worried about phoning you in case you were the same as her."

"Ach, Jeez, lass! Don't wish that on us." Euphemia answered with a laugh. "No, she's nothing like any o' the rest o' us. It's like all the wee niggly bits in everyone else came together in one big package wi' her."

And at Anna's end, Cameron was smiling and waving the gene chart he'd printed off to explain inheritance. Yes, it was perfectly possible that Belinda had inherited all the wrong bits from both sides so that she was nothing like any of her siblings.

For a few minutes the conversation continued about families, Anna discovering that Phemie, as she preferred to be called, had been a much-loved great-aunt's name, and who her gran, and then her mum, had been named after. It had nothing to do with eldest daughters at all. Then Anna held up crossed fingers and started explaining to her grandparents just why she had gone to such lengths to track them down. She was praying that they didn't go all distant on her over this, or worse, put the phone down. So she was shocked to the core when Davey said, "Oh, then you definitely need Phemie to come over and gi' you a hand. This is right up her street."

"You're a psychic?" Rita asked, almost unable to believe their luck.

"Well I'm no' a practicing one, you understand," she answered. "Haven't had much need to be, if the truth be told. But the talent certainly runs in our family.

"You see, I was something of a going away present to my ma from my pa at the start of the war, and at that stage they hadn't got married. So after I came along, both my ma and my grandma – who was only in her forties then – had to work. But my great-grandma was still sprightly in her late sixties, and she lived with us in this great big rambling old farmhouse in Ayrshire. Ma and Nan ran the farm wi' the help of land girls, and Great-Nan looked after me. Even after Pa came home, they needed help, because Ma then had my two younger sisters, and if Great-Nan couldn't do any of the heavy work, she was still on the ball enough to look after me and two wee ones. And it was Great-Nan Sarah who was something of a witch.

"Of course in those days you still had to be a bit careful using that word. But she knew remedies for every kind of ailment, and she used to walk me over to *her* ma's cottage to check on the old lady. And Great-*Great*-Nan Mairie was an amazing woman. By then she was in her early nineties, crippled with arthritis, house-bound, and very frail, but her mind was still as sharp as a tack. Oh my dears, the stories I could pass on that those two told me! And they were the ones who gave me my training, though it was never spoken of like that, of course. You didn't in those days. But when the sixties came around, and some friends of our older girls got a bit silly with an Ouija board while smoking pot, I can tell you I was very glad I'd learned what I had!"

"Good grief, Grandma, I think I'm going to have to come over and see you the next time I get a couple of days off together," Anna said weakly, envisaging another training session like the ones Rita had been putting her through.

"Well that's no use," Phemie said briskly, "your ghosts are over there, not here. I'll come to you. If you're at a hotel, I presume you can put me up?"

Cameron was vigorously nodding, so Anna said, "Yes, that's no problem at all. …When would you like to come?"

The distant voice of Davey was heard calling across, "If this website is right, there's a train from here to Edinburgh at eight o'clock tomorrow morning, and you can catch the train to Dumfries with a change at Carlisle within half an hour of getting there. She can be arriving at just before three o'clock, Anna."

"I'll come and collect you from the station," Gary immediately volunteered.

"Grand! I'll go and pack my bags," Phemie said with as much glee as if she was off to the seaside for a holiday.

After she'd rung off, Anna leaned back declaring, "I feel quite weak after that. She was nothing like I was expecting. Good grief, I hope I'm as good as that if I get to my eighties!"

"You're looking very chipper about this, Rita," Cameron observed. He hadn't said so, but Gary and Anna both knew he was thinking that he hadn't expected Rita to accept another strong woman coming into her territory.

"Too right," Rita replied. "If she's experienced and talented, then that gives us three women who are all related and can work together. Gary, willing though you've been to help out, your talents don't lie in the psychic world, and neither do yours, Cameron. And it's reassuring to me that if Phemie is 'talented', that it looks as though your psychic abilities have come through the female line, Anna, even if your connections to the ghosts might be down both lines. Your mum might be a bit of a doormat for my bloody brother, but she's a lot better than the prospect of him and his dreadful father being powerful psychics. You know, time and again while dealing with this we keep stumbling across threes, so I think having three working to resolve the situation is going to be a very good thing indeed."

CHAPTER 13

Come the following day, Cameron showed a hitherto hidden steeliness when Rita declared that she would go with Gary to collect Phemie. Anna had been on the rota to do the late shift starting mid-afternoon, but without asking, Cameron had contacted Gemma and swopped her from the morning to the afternoon, ringing Anna last thing to tell her when it was already arranged. When it came to Anna, clearly he was determined to give her all the help he could. So feeling very jittery with nerves, Anna was about to climb into Gary's truck to head to Dumfries station when Rita came out clutching her handbag too.

"Anna needs to go and meet her grandmother on her own," Cameron said firmly when Rita didn't take more subtle hints. "This is someone she's never met before, so give her the chance to make first contact without juggling conversations between you as well." He didn't need to add anything about

Gary, because he knew he'd be the soul of discretion. However, Gary had mentioned prior to this that Rita could be prone to going in with both feet, tact not being her greatest talent, and that was what both of them had been a bit worried about. They didn't need Rita ruffling feathers before they'd even got Phemie here, because Rita had already implied that she would need to bring Phemie up to speed – something which in truth might not be required.

Indeed right now, Gary was smothering a smirk at the way Rita was bristling at Cameron putting his 'boss' hat on for once, but was swift to jump in with, "Aye, Cameron's right," when he saw Rita about to protest. "Give the lass a chance, Rita," he added firmly when she still looked like arguing. "This is no' your side o' the family, so it's no' like you can help make the introductions, is it?"

His pointed glare seemed to finally get the message across to Rita, and with an offended glare back at him, she stalked back into his cottage.

"Well done, lad," Gary praised when he saw Cameron give a huge sigh of relief. "It's no' easy facing down Rita when her mind's made up."

"I'm practising for when I next have to face my own mum," Cameron confessed, "though I don't expect that to go anything like as well."

"We'll back you up," Gary reassured him, and saw the look of relief. Facing up to someone else's family was always easier than your own, and having someone on your side could be the difference between caving in and standing your ground.

"I'll be with you too," Anna told Cameron, giving him a hug. "You've been great over my disaster of a family. The least I can do is help you with yours."

"Well for now, go and meet your granny," Cameron said, returning the hug and giving her a kiss on the cheek – about all he dared to do in front of Gary for now.

"There's a surprise," was Gary's reaction when he and Anna saw an older lady tugging a large, wheeled suitcase out of the station later on in the afternoon.

If Rita was a generously proportioned lady, who had never worried too much about her appearance, Phemie was clearly quite the opposite. Slim without being one of those desiccated older ladies perpetually trying to stay youthfully skinny, her silver hair was swept up in a casual chignon, and she could easily have passed for fifteen years younger if not twenty. Her flowing, knee-length dress had neat pleats on the bodice, which gave it shape without being figure-hugging, and even from a distance, Anna was sure she was wearing leggings under it rather than stockings. Closer to, Anna saw that she was also wearing the on-trend brand of trainers – very sensible for an older lady when navigating getting on and off trains, but without getting anywhere close to the kind of typical old-lady shoes Anna had seen advertised in the flyers which used to be stuffed in magazines, back when she'd been in supermarkets. Phemie was definitely in the twenty-first century and enjoying every moment.

"Gracious!" she exclaimed happily, as she spotted Anna. "I would have known you for family anywhere! You're the image of Great-Gran Sarah, though much younger, I hasten to add. I'd no' want you to think you looked ancient." The twinkle in her eye as she said this robbed it of any offence.

Laughing, Anna had no hesitation in going to hug Phemie. This was someone so far removed from her mother that she couldn't believe they could be mother and daughter. Why could her own mum not have been more like this lovely, affectionate lady?

Then when Phemie said, "Nigel has told me so much of what my dreadful daughter has done to you," Anna was nearly reduced to tears. She didn't think Nigel had even noticed, much less cared. That he would have bothered to tell their grandmother was something that utterly floored her. And unlike Rita, Phemie noticed that Anna had welled up and simply hugged her a bit tighter and gave her chance to recover.

"I'll take your bags to the car," Gary said with a smile after shaking Phemie's hand. "You two follow on at your own pace." And leaving them he thought, *thank heavens this isn't another woman who will make assumptions about Anna.*

There was no doubt that Rita loved Anna dearly, and would do anything for her, but she wasn't very good at recognising that not everyone could cope with the breakneck speed she sometimes went at problems with. Phemie, on first impressions, seemed as if she might be a good deal more intuitive over the bits Anna found harder to deal with.

The journey back was filled with conversations and laughter, meaning that when they pulled up outside Anna's cottage and Rita came out, only Gary noticed that she looked a bit dismayed at how well Anna and Phemie were getting on.

"Don't worry," he said quietly, putting an arm around Rita's shoulders as Phemie and Anna walked ahead of them. "Phemie's no' taking your place. You'll still be the one who was there for her when all this trouble started after her wedding. Just remember that you had the chance to know your mum's mum. You learned a lot from her didn't you? …Well Anna didn't even know Phemie was alive this time last week, so let her be excited to discover someone she can get to know. Phemie's in her eighties, Rita, around twenty years older than you, so who knows how long she and Anna have got. You two have still got donkey's years together."

He felt Rita take a deep breath, but then her smile up at him was genuine, not forced. "I'm being a silly sod, aren't I? It's just that I used to find it hard to let Anna go, back when she used to come up for visits, knowing that she was so on her own down in England."

"And she's the daughter you wished you'd had. I get it Rita, I really do, because she's become that for me too. But Phemie's no' going to take that away from you. Anna's mum has siblings, so I'm sure Phemie has more than enough kids and grand-kids to satisfy her without needing to monopolise Anna."

Rita nodded, and Gary knew that she wasn't far from tears as she said, "It just felt so harsh, you know? After all these years, getting what I'd dreamed of for so long, and now seeing glamorous granny of the year sweeping in. …Don't worry, Gary, I'm not going to rock the family boat. I'll put my big girl knickers on and smile for Anna."

And through that evening, Rita did exactly that, letting Anna lead the conversation as they all gathered for a celebratory meal in the hotel's front dining room, away from the other guests. Phemie seemed to be someone who did her best to get on with everyone, making Rita feel a little churlish for having taken umbrage without even meeting her. But best of all, Phemie was genuinely interested about the ghosts, listening avidly as they told her all of what had happened.

"There's one of them lurking around here now," Phemie suddenly said, making Rita say through gritted teeth while addressing the empty space in the centre of the room, "For the love o' God, Gideon! Bugger off and mind your own business!" She turned back to the others. "I should have thought of this sooner. This is part of the ground floor of the old tower-house, Phemie, which means it's somewhere Gideon can access. We think Hugh can too, but he's far more polite and less trouble. Gideon seems to enjoy lurking like some spectral spider up in the corner of the room, listening for gossip."

Phemie smiled. "Back in medieval times, they used to believe in a small devil called Titivillus, and he was supposed to do exactly that – lurk up in the roof beams listening to people and making them do things like mispronounce their prayers so that it would count against them and send them to Hell. He was also the demon of scribes, causing them to make errors, back in the days when scribes were inevitably monks copying Bibles and other religious texts."

"Good grief, how do you know that?" Anna asked.

Phemie laughed. "I have a friend who does calligraphy. You know, making people pretty phrases and stuff that they then frame and hang on the wall. She used to say to me, 'Titivillus has been at it again', whenever she made a mistake and had to start again, because it cost her time, and money at least for the special papers and inks she uses. Well your ghostly Gideon immediately reminded me of him, though being compared to a demon known in the Catholic Church probably won't go down well with him."

Crash.

They all near levitated and turned to stare at the wall which was between the front dining room and the back office.

"Sarah? Are you okay?" Gary called, jumping to his feet and making a dash for the office, only for Sarah to meet him in the doorway looking shaken.

"The map of the grounds with the fire assembly points on it just came off the wall," she told them shakily. "One minute it was there, the next, it was like it had been ripped off and thrown on the floor. It didn't just slide down the wall like the hook had come out. It's actually out in the middle of the office floor!"

"Oh crap, this is my fault for not thinking more," Rita said grimly. "In the excitement of realising we found you, Phemie, I totally forgot that it wouldn't be safe for us to talk openly in here."

Then they all jumped again as from the stairs there was an enormous bang and the faint smell of gunpowder.

'Leave the women alone!' an ethereal voice which all but Sarah and Phemie recognised as Hugh's, and the equally disembodied,

'I'll have none o' yer Ferguson spawn in ma hoose!' flung back, and another bang echoed around the reception area.

As startled guests began coming out of the main dining room at the back, wondering what all the noise was, Anna decided, "Upstairs! We need to go upstairs to draw them away from the guests."

"I'll stay and help Sarah calm the guests down," Gary volunteered, seeing that Sarah was looking more than a bit rattled herself. "Cameron, go with them, and if you need me, come and get me."

"Gottcha." Cameron replied, and took off after Anna, Rita, and Phemie, who had already got up as far as the mezzanine landing where Gary and

Cameron had felt Gideon listening in to them months ago.

Anna took them up through the first set of fire doors on the main staircase so that that would hopefully muffle any further sounds. Immediately, Rita began calling, "Gideon? Gideon, where are you, you bloody pest?"

'Don't ye' call me a bloody pest, ye' sour-faced old besom,' the retort came back from the next flight up, and through the door's glass they could see a hazy outline of him in the doorway to the second floor, above Rosemary suite from which he'd been ejected, and where on that floor Tulip and Crocus lay.

"Oh thank God I've been avoiding putting guests in those rooms," Anna breathed softly with a wince as they hurried up to confront him, and gave a brief explanation to Phemie of why.

Meanwhile Rita had adopted her sternest expression and was telling Gideon, "You're a bloody liability! Someone could have got badly hurt with you throwing glass around."

Perhaps because of both her and Phemie's abilities, this time they could see Gideon's face really clearly, and the petulant expression on it as he responded with, 'It's my hoose! I can do what I want in it!'

What none of them were expecting was for it to trigger Phemie's 'mum' instincts. Having brought up her own sons, she was an expert in teenage-like behaviour, even if Gideon ought to have long grown out of that by the time he died.

“Oh, it is, is it?” she said with the weary patience in her voice of someone explaining the blindingly obvious. “Well you won’t have much of it left if you keep breaking stuff, will you? If you want to keep it, you need to look after it, not go around wrecking the place. I thought you were supposed to be all grown up, yet here you are, behaving like a wee boy who’s had his toys taken off him. Dearie me, you’ve got yourself wound up into a right state, haven’t you? So why don’t you calm down and tell me what’s wrong, eh?”

Something in her tone got through to Gideon in a way that Rita’s confrontation hadn’t. It had been not just years, but centuries, since someone had spoken to Gideon in the soothing tones his mother had used, and it brought welling up all the feelings Gideon had forgotten he even knew how to feel.

‘It’s no’ fair,’ he blurted out, and they could swear that his lip started to wobble. ‘Bluidy Ferguson. He took everything I ever wanted. Him and my bluidy faither. What did I ever do to deserve even one o’ them, let alone both?’

“That sounds dreadful,” Phemie sympathised. “You’d better tell me about it, then,” and to Rita and Anna’s amazement he started to.

1674-78

Gideon

They got Auld John home, and for days he lay near insensible in his bed at the townhouse. Eventually he seemed to rally, and after a year, he was able to walk with the aid of a stout stick, but not far, and the stairs of the townhouse were impossible for him to navigate. And so to Gideon's horror, his father determined that he would go and live in the croft he owned nearest to the building site. That wouldn't have been as bad if he'd been content to live there with McKay, the poor wretch of a man he threatened into coming to care for him. But nothing would do but Young John and Gideon going to live there with him.

"I'll no' have you idling here in town when you should be working," the vicious old man snarled. "I'll no' have you leaving me to moulder there while you lord it back here!"

"This is hardly a palace," Young John muttered darkly to Gideon, as McKay grunted and staggered past them with the weight of Auld John in his arms, as he took him down the cramped stairs to where the dog-cart waited by the front door to take Auld John to the croft. And looking around him, Gideon could only sigh and nod. This might be a stone-built house, compared to the croft's cobbled walls, but it was a dark, cold, and cheerless place and always had been. The main room was well-appointed, but that was only because it was where visitors came. The rest of the rooms were as spartan as any impoverished crofter's, for John Corsan hoarded his money like a miser. And now there wouldn't be a penny spent on this place when the new house was taking all of their father's attention. They'd be lucky if he even paid for coal for the grate in the winter if he wasn't there to enjoy it.

Nor was Auld John the only one who had changed on that fateful day at the nunnery. Something in what he saw seemed to have shrivelled Young John's soul, too. Once a bright and cheerful lad – or at least he had been when away from his father – now he was eternally fearful, always glancing around him as if expecting an attack to come at him from out of the blue. And it didn't matter how many times Gideon explained to him why the witches had it in for their family, and that if they didn't antagonise them, then they might be content with having imprisoned Auld John within his own body, Young John was terrified that one day they would come for him.

Not that Gideon himself was wholly convinced that they wouldn't do so. Ever since that fateful day, a whole murder of crows seemed to have taken up residence in the trees around what would soon become *Blackpark House* in reality as well as name. And if they were mainly seen simply flitting in and out of the trees by the builders, it was when Gideon and Young John were on the premises that they seemed to set up their raucous cawing. It upset the builders, worried Gideon, and absolutely terrified Young John.

Progress was slow, but bit-by-bit, the tower itself was completed, and the family rooms attached to the main tower rose to second floor height. The servants' wing at a right-angle to it went in, built out of whatever Gideon could find, because there was no way that he was sending men in to get the rest of the stone from the kirk. Had he tried, he knew that the remaining workers would have walked off the job not caring what threats were made against them. As far as they were concerned, it was suffer in this life or suffer some dreadful torment in the hereafter at the hands of the ghosts, possibly for eternity, and none of them were taking a chance on that. Therefore what blocks were accessible got used on the main building, and the servants' wing was concocted out of what was left over.

Off-cuts of stone and any other building detritus got wheel-barrowed to the hollow of the crypt and unceremoniously tipped into it, with the men retreating at speed the moment the barrow was empty. In Gideon's mind, the sealing forever of the crypt and its grizzly remains could only be a good thing. Auld John rarely came to the site now, and since he had to be helped to reach whatever he wanted to inspect on his wobbly legs and walking sticks, it was easy enough to keep him turned away from the old kirk, so he never saw that his demand for it to be levelled hadn't happened. Gideon had every intention of panting a nice line of trees across that view once the building work was done, thereby permanently hiding the remains from his view. If he couldn't get rid of it, at least he wasn't going to look at it.

Therefore they staggered on until the fateful day when Thomas McBurney once again stuck his wretched snout into Gideon's life, by bringing Isobel Milligan to act as cook and cleaner for Auld John. The need for someone to come and help had been growing month on month, for while McKay did his best, the man couldn't cook, and when Bessie, a local woman who'd been coerced to come in daily to cook finally refused to set foot in the croft again, Gideon and Young John were well and truly stuck. Yet Gideon could never have anticipated the personal torment that would come with his simple decision to have a woman come to help, and live out in the former byre where McKay also slept.

The day cowed and frightened Isobel walked into the croft's yard behind the rough man who helped Veitch out, Gideon thought his heart might leap out of his chest. She was taller than Elspeth Allen – or as best he could recall from the last time he'd seen her – and not as bonny, but then a few years living in Veitch's house would crush the life out of anyone. And why Elspeth, of all women, should have had such a grip on his fantasies, even Gideon couldn't explain. All he knew was that nobody had made him lust after them like Elspeth Allen had, and God alone knew that he'd tried to replace her in his obsessions, but to no avail.

Isobel's father, Thomas Milligan, had been married to one of the women burned at the stake in Dumfries back in 1659, on the same day that Elspeth's mother had collapsed and died upon seeing that dreadful sight. And it had taken Gideon far too long to make the connection between Elspeth, her witch of a mother, and her cousin who had been Isobel's mother, and who had also died that day, in no small part condemned by the testimony of her own husband. Thomas Milligan had been in league with Gideon's wretched father and another equally villainous man called John McCartney. Corsan and McCartney had acquired property out of their collusion, just as Gideon's mother had tried to explain to him all those years ago, while Milligan had got rid of a first wife he'd come to loathe, leaving him free to marry a local widow who came with a substantial amount of money.

Now, the last thing Milligan wanted was his widowed daughter coming back into his house, and conspiring with his harridan of a second wife, who was proving even harder to control than the first, if only because she was an ardent kirk-goer, and generous with her weekly donations. This one he was never going to get rid of by accusations of witchcraft. The local presbyters would see to that. But Milligan was also not entirely sure that his first wife hadn't passed on some of her craft to Isobel, and the thought of what might get cooked up in his own kitchen to get rid of him was sufficient for him to have shoved Isobel straight into Veitch's hands. That he was judging Isobel by his murderous standards, not hers, never entered his head.

Why Veitch subsequently let Isobel go, nobody dared ask. In private, Auld John cackled on about Veitch finally being unable to raise a lusty stand for a woman, but given Veitch's advanced years, Gideon thought that that time had passed decades ago, not recently. Personally, he thought that the frustration of having a pretty woman like Isobel about the place, and yet being unable to do anything about it, might be closer to the truth. For all his lauded godliness, Veitch set a poor example of resisting temptation, in whatever form, and God alone knew that Gideon certainly found Isobel tempting.

Yet the trauma of living with Euphame for those hideous years of his marriage had left its scars on Gideon. In his dreams, he swaggered into the croft garden on a sunny day and had wild, passionate sex with Isobel beneath the apple tree, as blossom floated down upon them. In reality, he could never seem to summon the courage to lay so much as a hand on her arm, for fear of her turning on him with the same disgusted look that Euphame had possessed down to a fine art.

So it was salt in an already raw wound in his soul when he saw her gazing upon Edward McCartney with such longing.

"You be careful of him," he dared to warn Isobel the day after Edward had come bringing some missive or other for his father. "Auld John McCartney is every bit as dangerous as my father. He won't look kindly on his son having anything to do with the likes of you. He could make your life a living hell."

What he wasn't remotely prepared for was for Isobel to turn on him with tears streaming down her cheeks to snarl, "Living hell? What do you think *this* is for me? Washing your father's shit out of his small clothes. Bowing and scraping to him…and you…and your brother! Freezing out in the byre with only a sack blanket, and what hay the horse hasn't had to keep me warm. You think that's *living*?

"Damn you, Gideon Corsan! Edward might be the son of a man as bad as your father, but *he* didn't stand there laughing while my *mother* burned! The McCartneys might have been cousins to my aunt's husband, but they weren't *blood* relatives to *her*. Not like you and your father were to poor Jannet Corsan. You watched your own *blood* be strangled and burned, yet all *you* did was creep around Veitch, telling him what a righteous man he was. Well, I know what Veitch is. God help me, I know very well. And I hope that when his time comes, God will show him the error of his ways for all eternity."

And with that, she stormed off into the tiny orchard, where a rough rope line had been strung up between the apple trees for the washing. It left Gideon standing breathless and feeling as if his heart had just been ripped out of his chest. He hadn't expected her to love him…yet. But her level of disgust and hatred shocked him to his core.

'Unfair' was the word which kept rattling around in his brain. How unfair of her to hold him accountable for something that had happened when he was a mere boy. How bloody unfair that once again the actions of his father – over whom he'd had not a scrap of influence – had come along to destroy his scant hopes of happiness.

Therefore on that fateful day in 1678, when God-curse-him Hugh Ferguson rode up to what was close to being the completed imposing frontage of *Blackpark House*, Gideon was in no mood to be reconciliatory towards another who – in his eyes – had ruined his life. Already that month, he had seen Isobel talking to Edward in the market at Dumfries. And since it was a public place, he had no chance of forbidding her to do so. To try would have made him seem even more ridiculous in her eyes, and Gideon was far faster at reading such situations than his father had been. Auld John might have just bullied his way through such a confrontation, but Gideon knew that he didn't possess the temperament for that. Nor was he as immune to cutting comments and people sniggering behind his back – and making a fool of himself with a woman right in the busiest place in the town was the fastest way to ensure that that happened!

And worse, Ferguson was with some of those accursed Highlanders. Those filth who had been sent by the godless men in Edinburgh to make sure that law and order was kept in the shires of Dumfries, Kirkcudbright, and Wigtown, and the Covenant crushed. So it was little surprise that when a damned Highlander took it upon himself to speak to Gideon, Young John took umbrage at it. The musket was a mistake, Gideon couldn't deny that, but in his eyes, Young John had every right to order the four riders off their property.

Yet for it to be Hugh-bloody-Ferguson who took his boot to Young John, added the worst insult to injury. In his current state of mind, Gideon utterly refused to see that all that Hugh had been doing was booting the musket's shot out of line with the men he'd arrived with. That the shot had gone into the air, harming none but the bonnet of one of the Highlanders, was a blessing he could not find it in himself to be grateful for. Instead, all he could do was blame Ferguson for the fact that his brother had been thrown backwards by the recoil on the musket, smashing his head against the stones of the tower, and rendering him an idiot for the rest of his life. That Young John had repeatedly proven that he couldn't hit even a barn door at twenty paces with the damned thing, and should never have even tried to aim at the four soldiers, was neither here nor there, either. Nor that the fool of a lad hadn't braced himself for the recoil which by this time he ought to have known was coming.

No, it was Ferguson's fault. Another black mark against him in the growing list Gideon was mentally compiling against him for ruining his life. And Gideon swore that this time he would have his revenge upon that man, come what may.

CHAPTER 14

As Gideon ran out of steam on this part of his story, Rita stayed quiet and let Phemie speak, more than a little impressed with the way she'd handled him so far.

"That was a lot for you to deal with," Phemie said gently. "Your father sounds like a nasty piece of work all round. But can you see that maybe it was down to him that the ghosts of the women he hunted still haunt this place? They were as much his victims as you were, Gideon."

At least there was no arguing back from Gideon, though he did give a sort of petulant shrug of his ghostly shoulders.

"Why don't we give it a rest now," Phemie suggested soothingly. "You've given us a lot to think about, and it must have been hard for you to dig up the past like that." The way he deflated from building up to argue about the women being victims the moment the sympathy turned back to him was quite startling to the others, and even more so was the fact that he nodded and turned to trudge back into the landing space by Tulip, where he vanished from view.

"Go and tell Gary we'll meet him back at the cottage," Rita said to Cameron, with a twitch of her eyes towards where Gideon had gone, implying that they weren't going to try to talk more over here.

When she and Anna and Phemie had got up the drive and well on the way to the cottages, Rita turned to Phemie and said, "That was impressive! You really calmed him down."

"I've got three teenage grandsons who could give him a run for his money," Phemie laughed. "I just went on autopilot."

"Well, it's a damned good autopilot," Anna declared, linking her arm through Phemie's. "I think you've just got yourself the job of being our contact with Gideon, because you've got more out of him tonight than we've ever heard before."

When Gary and Cameron joined them, they brought Gary up to speed with all that Gideon had blurted out.

"I have to feel sorry for the poor sod," Cameron admitted. "What a bloody life his father gave him. And you can understand why local families didn't want their daughters anywhere near the Corsans and McCartneys, can't you. They must have been scared stiff what either of the old Johns would do if he set his grubby sights on one of their homes."

"But so harsh on Gideon that he never got to court any of the local girls," Anna agreed. "In those early days when he was just a bit of a pain in the arse young man, he'd probably have got over it and grown up if he'd been mixing with the others of his generation. A few scraps over who went out with who, but some fun times as well, and he'd be a different person. But it's like all of the joy got torn out of his life the day our witchy ladies died." She turned to Cameron specifically, adding, "And I think both of us can sympathise with him over the burden of parental pressures when still only a kid. What he did at the trial was wrong in every way, but *why* he felt he had to I can only empathise with – especially with what my dad put me through with Jensen."

Cameron was nodding, adding, "And I think that makes even more sense of what you and I said, Anna, about him not being able to cope with something being his fault. If he'd had possibly decades of being blamed for stuff he'd had no control over, to then be really at fault must have felt ten times worse than it would have to someone else. Suddenly there wasn't even his father to share the blame with."

Rita sighed. "Gideon may not be likeable, but I'm now seeing that he was shockingly damaged, and from long before he died. Even my psychiatrist pal Doctor Mac would have his work cut out treating him in the modern day. What we do about him, however, is a whole other question."

"It did sort of answer one of our questions, though," Anna said thoughtfully. "Do you remember what Agnes said about John Corsan having two daughters, Aunty Rita? It wouldn't have meant anything to you Nan," for Phemie said that was what all her grandchildren called her, as she had her own grandmother and great-grand-mother, "because you haven't had chance to read the leaflet about the history of the house. But in there it says that by the 1689 Jacobite Rising, what was then *BlackparkHouse* had passed to a Jean Corsan, who was married to a Captain Ferguson. Well if Gideon had a sister of his called Jean, that could be her. We'll need to get a few more dates out of Gideon to be sure, but if Hugh and Gideon died in 1685, if the Jean in the leaflet *is* Gideon's sister, it would make her the right generation to have inherited the place after he died. Heaven only knows who the Captain Ferguson was who it refers to, aside from being Jean's husband. He might have been someone not even from the area, but clearly Gideon thinks he was some relative of Hugh's."

"Aye, that does make sense," Gary agreed. "Gideon said his kid brother was an invalid, so chances are he died before Gideon did, and didn't one o' the ladies say that the middle brother was the one who killed their father?"

"That was Agnes," Anna reminded him. "And yes, she said that Matthew killed old John Corsan. What the outcome of that was we might never know, but it sounds very much as though either Matthew died, or had to go on the run and was no longer a legal heir if he was wanted for murder. Mind you, I can't imagine that even Nan will get Gideon to talk rationally about that. We might do better asking Hugh. If he was in the area, he may have heard talk of what happened."

However, Rita grimaced. "I get where you're coming from, Anna, but if Gideon is ear-wigging our conversations with Hugh, or as best he can, nothing's going to have him flying off the handle again like him thinking we're dragging his family through the muck with Hugh. I reckon Phemie's got a better chance of getting the truth out of him over that. He might get upset, but if she can keep him at the level he was at today, he's more likely to get weepy over it than start firing that damned musket off in a temper."

"Oh Lord, yes," Anna said with feeling. "In fact, I'd suggest we wait until all of the current guests have left. We'll have had a complete rotation of guests within three days of now. There's only so much soothing of frayed nerves that Gary can do. We don't want customers leaving and saying online that we've got a ghost problem – not least because of the undesirables who might suddenly start booking in with us to have a 'spooky' experience," looking pointedly at Cameron.

Since his return, Anna had been able to get him to see that offering ghost hunt weekends was not his brightest idea, and he had the good grace to look a little sheepish now.

"We could always divide and conquer," Gary mused. "If Anna and I go up to the housekeeper's room for a wee chat with Hugh, you – Rita and Phemie – could have a word with Gideon up on the second floor. If we have Cam as a runner between us, if Anna gets into difficulties, he can always come and fetch one of you and stay to watch over the other."

"That's a very crafty move," Rita said approvingly. "Yes, if Phemie and I get Gideon talking first, then he's less likely to notice you talking to Hugh, but are you okay with doing that, Anna?"

"If I know that Gideon's preoccupied with you and Nan, Aunty – and let's face it, he feels far more strongly about you than he does me, so he's likely to stay where you are – then yes, I think I can manage a chat with Hugh. And Gideon will sense me less strongly anyway, because I don't have your strength in opening up portals to reach them as yet."

Then the thing that had been niggling away at the back of her mind for so long suddenly came to her. "And there's something else we need to know!"

"There is?" Rita said dubiously.

"*When* did Hugh and Gideon die? It's been implied by both of them that in their last hour they fought one another, and seemingly delivered the fatal blows, even if they didn't expire on the same spot and together. But we don't actually know when that took place, do we? I know Hugh's fake gravestone out in the grounds says 1685, but by now I think we're all aware how wrong that could be. With 1685 being such a significant date around here, did the grave maker *assume* that Hugh had died with the other Covenanters who got shot or hanged in that year? Because we know he was wrong in thinking Hugh was ever one of those."

"And I hate to bring up a grisly subject," Gary said, looking grim, "but where do Gideon's bones lie? We keep worrying about Hugh, because he's the likeable one, but surely we need to know that Gideon was put somewhere too? Did the poor bugger even get a Christian burial? Because with that dreadful old Presbyter literally having put the fear o' God into him, if Gideon never got properly buried according to his particular beliefs, is part of the problem that he's terrified of what will happen to his soul if he lets go of his hold on this place? You know, that whole shift from the spiritual waiting room of Purgatory down to actual Hell. Is that part of his beliefs, and he's terrified of where he'll go if he leaves limbo?"

The others looked at him, momentarily lost for words as the implications sank in.

"To such a damaged soul," said Rita thoughtfully, "that might account for a lot. It could be something that has quite literally driven him mad with fear down the years. Oh dear. Phemie, do you think you could ask him where he was buried? Or perhaps better, ask him if his remains lie at Irongray? Because I think if he was properly buried, that's where he'd want to be called back to, and he's more likely to be happy to tell you that, than that his bones got chucked into a ditch somewhere. We might discover more of his fate by finding out where his remains *aren't*, I'm thinking."

Cameron cleared his throat. "Can I ask for us to clear up something else with him too? Hugh's shown no sign of recognising me, and to be frank, I doubt my mum's family, who are the Fergusons he currently rants about," he added for Phemie's benefit, "have any link at all with Hugh's, or even our unknown captain. It's a common enough surname, and I've met Fergusons I've no connection to at all. So can we please tell him that I'm not Hugh's descendant, nor his brother-in-law's, and that it was a different Ferguson who owned the hotel for a short while, but has now sold it? You don't need to tell him it was to me. Just say it was to a Mr Wiseheart – which unless he's been paying far more attention than we've given him credit for up to now, won't immediately click with him that it's me. Surely it will take some of the sting out of his tail if we can remove that misconception?"

"That's a fair point," Gary immediately agreed. He turned to Phemie. "The only reason we've not cleared that up is because he's never listened to any of us. He's been too busy ranting and raving for us to get that through to him."

She nodded. "I think I might open with that with him, you know. Calm him down first. If we can get that particular bee out of his bonnet, then it might be such a relief to him that he'll feel more willing to open up to me about how he died."

Mercifully, there would be no such inhibitions with Anna talking to Hugh about the hours leading up to his death, so the only thing holding them back now was ensuring that they had new guests in who hadn't heard the muskets going off previously. Therefore with Sally and her ladies changing bedrooms over on the following Monday morning, when the guests who'd come for the weekend had left, there was no better time to go and start questioning their two ghosts. The few people who were booked in for that night were all assigned rooms outside of the old tower-house's perimeter, and as far from the main stairs as Anna could put them, and most hadn't arrived yet. So with fingers crossed that this wouldn't all go horribly wrong, Rita and Phemie headed for the second floor, while Gary and Anna went up the old stairs to the turret room.

Taking her courage in both hands, Anna took a few deep breaths and then started following Rita and Phemie's instructions. Part of her didn't really expect this to work for her, believing that it was the link back to Elspeth which had made it work for her when she'd spoken to Agnes. So she actually jumped when Hugh appeared before her and Gary, and fairly visibly too.

Seeing Anna's shocked face, Gary decided to take the lead, beginning with, "Hello, Hugh. We're here again. I hope you don't mind us asking you more questions, but we'd like to start by explaining something to you," and then telling him of how they'd only just worked out how long it would have taken him to get to Wigtown.

'Ye can do it in under a day, ye' say?' Hugh said in astonishment when Gary finished. 'Aye, but that must be some speed those car things can go at.'

“They can,” Gary said with a laugh, “scarily so when it’s some young lad trying to impress his friends and going too fast even for our roads.”

Hugh nodded sagely, ‘We had a few like that soldiering wi’ us, though wi’ the ponies, no’ yer weird machines.’

“And poor Isobel, too, having to spend that long travelling with Gideon,” Anna added, “though I was surprised to see how small Wigtown is, or at least must have been in your day. We have vast cities nowadays in England that have more people in them than in the whole of Scotland in your day, so please don’t think I’m being derogatory about Wigtown, it’s just our modern perspective. But she must have been pretty frail if the whipping actually killed her – which is not to say that we don’t think it was serious, because it obviously was. So we were talking about it, and wondered why Grierson would have bothered with the second sentence of drowning, if a lashing always resulted in a death? And more to the point, if she was that weak, why was she running away with Edward? Why not try to find somewhere to hide more locally? Or have I got it totally wrong?”

She said the last because of the increasingly perplexed expression on Hugh’s face.

‘I’m no’ sure what ye’ think happened,’ Hugh said cautiously, ‘but ye’re right about the flogging. It wasn’a ever meant to kill. There was another woman wi’ them in the tolbooth, ye’ ken. Yet another Margaret who’d come before Grierson o’ Lagg under suspicion o’ being a Covenanter, but come the day o' *her* flogging, the good folk o' Wigtown stayed indoors and refused to come out and watch. But then that Margaret – Margaret Maxwell – was a servant to one o' the Earl o' Galloway's sons, so no doubt folk were in two minds as to who they were willing to cross, Lagg or the earl. Whereas our girls had nabody on their side o' any consequence, and a lot o' folk frightened o' Lagg and what he might order done to them when there wasn'a a laird involved.'

He gave a snort of disgust. 'I tell ye' this, the other poor young lasses were even charged wi' being at Bothwell and Aird Moss, two battles I was in. Young Margaret and her wee sister Agnes would ha' been mere bairns at the time. Utter nonsense. …But why did ye' ask why Isobel left here at all if she was in such a state? Isobel was hale and hearty when I sent her north wi' my Highland friends, or at least as anyone could be after years o' living wi' an old miser like Corsan.'

"Gosh, the road must have been even rougher than we thought if she went downhill so fast," Anna gasped, then realised that that was a modern turn of phrase which Hugh probably wouldn't understand. "I mean, even in your day, walking as far as Sanquhar would have been tough but not crippling, especially for someone used to walking a lot. So for her to be in such a bad state when they got there and then turned around and came back, something must have gone horribly wrong."

They saw understanding dawn on Hugh's face as he waved a hand saying, 'No, no, you have that wrong. Ye didn'a think all that happened within one year, did ye'?'

"We thought it happened within months if not weeks," Gary confessed.

'Ach, no! No, the Highlanders were packing up to go in early spring 1679. That's when I got separated from so many o' ma friends, including Sorley McAllister's sons. They went home to Argyll, and as far as I knew fer a long time, that's where I thought Isobel and Edward were. Oh, I kent that Elspeth and her family had left Argyll by the time Isobel was heading there, but that was twenty years on from when Ma died. I'd had word passed on to me o' Elspeth leaving, but ma belief was that Sorley's daughter knew where they were, and would pass on word o' Isobel arriving up there too. And once they knew that, I thought Elspeth and Alex would invite them to go and join them wherever.'

Hugh shook his head. 'I nearly keeled over when I went into Sanquhar five years later, and there Isobel and Edward were.'

"Five *years*?" Anna gasped. "Well that explains a lot! Had the poor woman being living rough all that time?"

'Aye, if ye' mean wi'out a proper roof over her head and food on the table. As far as I ever got to find out, they'd got across the upper reaches o' the Clyde before it got too wide and there were still bridges they could cross. And they were a way further northwards than that before Edward got…well whatever Edward got. Cold feet over what his bluidy faither would say, or over having to finally put his back into being the man Isobel deserved, or something else altogether to do wi' his faith, I dinna ken. Whatever it was, they left the army afore it reached Glasgow and started heading back south, but Edward must ha' had the brains o' a newt, because he somehow started following the Clyde south but going the wrong way towards the coast, no' upstream as he should ha' kenned.'

Hugh rolled his eyes in despair at Edward's failings. 'Isobel told me they spent some time in Ayr, but I never got chance to find out if that was for long, or even at the start or the end o' their wanderings. All I kenned was that she was a wraith of the woman I'd last seen when I found her locked up at Sanquhar, and half bluidy starved.'

"Now that does make sense," said Gary. "So confronted with a woman who was already weak, you had to make what plans you could."

'Aye, I did. I decided to head for our old croft simply because in ma soldiering around here for years by then, I'd seen that the roof was still on part o' it, and I still knew where the best places were around and about to forage for food. I only ever meant to give her a week or so's total rest there. Planned to cook up plenty o' rabbit stew and the like to build her up a bit, then get her over to the forest east o' Dumfries to hide up for a bit longer, maybe even over winter to gi' the hunt time to die down.'

"And of course that was after your plan to leave her with Grissell Asman's family all came apart,"

Gary sympathised. “You really were having to think on the move, weren’t you,” getting him a weary nod from Hugh.

Anna decided she needed to take the plunge and now ask the vital question. “So how long after you saw Isobel die did *you* die, Hugh? Was it a long time or…?”

Thankfully, Hugh didn’t take offence at the question, and Anna and Gary hoped that Rita and Phemie were having as much luck with Gideon.

“I reckon it was probably within the year,” he said pensively. “’Twas the following late summer, anyway. The problem by then was that it was known that I’d deserted from the army, ye’ see. I was already so damned tired o’ fighting, and fighting folk who were no’ soldiers, but it was where to go that always defeated me. What I really wanted was ma own wee croft, and Elspeth and me seeing out our old age together there. But that was never going to happen. No’ after I discovered ma stupid cousin had come back and left her over on the east coast.’

“So you knew where Elspeth had gone?” gasped Anna

Yet Hugh looked uncomfortable. ‘I heard from other folk, ye’ understand, so I was never quite sure how true it was.’ His sigh seemed to carry the weight of the world. ‘Alex came back. That’s ma cousin, Alexander Black, who went north wi’ Elspeth and who she wed. Right from the start we both loved her, or at least I thought he did, and him being closer in age to Elspeth, I understood why he was the one who caught her eye, though she was always kind and generous wi' me. And I did hear from the McAllisters that it wasn'a quite the joyful family reunion that Elspeth and her pa were expecting in Argyll. Jamie McAllister told me his pa was fair spitting feathers over the way that Elspeth's sister Mailie treated them.'

"Oh dear, Mailie wasn't exactly thrilled to have her sister join her?" Anna could imagine what her older sister, Heather, would say if she turned up at her door on the run, and none of it was good.

Hugh looked glum. "'Twas the accusations o' being a witch that came wi' Elspeth and her pa that I think Mailie couldn'a stand. I saw them a few times in those early years when I first went north, on those times when the Campbell didn'a need us out on the march. Sorley told me that Mailie had a terrible time o' it before he brought her to Argyll. The first man she married died, and then the second ended up dragging her south as part o' the last army to fight for the King in 1651."

"Ooh! Battle of Worcester!" Anna exclaimed. "I know about that. It happened just down the road from where I used to live."

CHAPTER 15

Hugh was astonished. 'Ye' came up here from Worcester too? Why did ye' go there?'

"I was born there,' Anna explained. "Both of my parents, I'm only now discovering, were from Scotland, but for various reasons ended up down in the Midlands as children. It's only since I recently came here that I've discovered how close my links are to this area. But to come back to what you were saying, I know that the very last battle fought in the English Civil War was fought just outside of Worcester at a village called Powick, and that the army on the King's side was pretty much all Scots. The English support for the King had melted away by then. And the poor Scots took a dreadful pounding, not least since by then they were half-starved and sick, because they were having to live off the land as they marched. They'd long gone beyond the point of being resupplied by their own.

There's a memorial to them at the bridge down there."

'Is there, by God?' Hugh gasped. 'Well then you'll be knowing that fer Mailie to be one o' the few women left straggling behind that army, and a Scots woman in England, it was disastrous.'

Gary quickly added for Anna's benefit, "The women weren't just whores, many of them were the only medics those poor soldiers had."

"Oh, that makes sense, then," Anna said. "If Mailie had remembered her mother teaching her about healing plants and potions, she wouldn't just have been unwanted baggage, she'd have been almost essential, even if it was only treating blistered feet and other ailments."

'Exactly. Ye' ha' the right o' it, Anna. But the real tragedy was that Mailie had two wee girls by then. One o' them died at some time around the battle – or as near as Sorley ever told me – and I believe the other poor wee one died on the road coming north, too weak to survive.'

"Poor Mailie," said Anna sympathetically. "To lose both children…"

'Aye, 'twas hard on her, and Sorley always thought that that was why she clung to Niall Munro on the journey, because Sorley swept up him and another wee lad from Argyll around the same time and was bringing them all north wi' him.' Hugh shook his head. ''Twasn'a to the joyful life o' peace she was dreaming of, though. Turned out that Niall was mourning the death o' his first wife, and once back home, he couldn'a see past her ghost, or so I heard. I think Sorley thought that having her sister wi' her might be the tonic Mailie needed. Instead it made her worse, wi' her fearing that Elspeth would be openly practising their ma's craft and bring down accusation o' witchcraft on them. That's why I understood why Elspeth and Alex left. It was no' the refuge they needed. I just wish they'd told me where they were going.'

"But you said Alex came back?" Gary asked warily. "Back to Argyll or back to here?"

Hugh gave an angry snort. 'Back to here!'

"And where was Elspeth by then?" Gary wondered even more cautiously.

'That's the rub,' Hugh fumed. 'All I could find out was that it was o'er Fife way, or mebbe just north across the Tay. No' exactly a small area to start looking in! And at the time I was still tied to the army.'

"Oh my God!" Anna gulped. "That's where some of my ancestors on my father's side come from."

Gary smiled at her. "So you could have links to Elspeth that way. That could account for a lot."

"Was it knowing that Elspeth was over there that made you even more willing to desert?" Anna asked Hugh.

Hugh's ghostly sigh was telling. 'Aye, it had a lot to do wi' it. But it was a couple o' years after I heard about Alex that I finally ran wi' Isobel.' It reminded Anna and Gary that there were two women to this tale. 'And I didn'a hear about Alex at the time o' his coming, but a fair while afterwards.

Heaven knows where Alex had been, because as I heard it, he'd long since left Elspeth and gone in search o' his folk, who had left Argyll some years before them. Yet he showed up in Dumfries just after Isobel left.'

"And roughly what year was that again?" Anna checked.

'That would ha' been 1679, too,' Hugh confirmed. 'The bluidy fool went into a rage and got into a fight wi' bluidy Thomas McBurney, o' all men – as savage a beast as walked the earth, and all kenned him as a dirty fighter. Plus McBurney was built like a bull by then, whereas Alex was thin as a lath after so long on the road, so I heard. Well McBurney killed Alex and claimed it was in self-defence. And wi' McBurney's temper, and his uncle having no' long stepped down as one o' the bailies, nabody was going to argue the point, especially as Alex had nae family here to speak up fer him and was the son o' two accused witches.'

"But why on earth would he pick a fight with this McBurney?" asked Gary. "Surely he wasn't another suitor for Elspeth?"

They saw Hugh's face darken with anger, even though he had no physical body to suffuse with blood. Clearly this was a very sore memory.

''Twas no' ma lovely Elspeth, his ain wife, he fought o'er,' Hugh ground out furiously, 'though I kenned even before we left that, long afore then, McBurney and his evil shite o' a brother tried to rape her.'

“Oh no!” Anna cried, both for Elspeth and fearing that this was another complication on top of Jonet’s rape.

‘They didn’a get her way back then or ever,’ Hugh immediately reassured her, ‘but that was ’cause she ran to the kirk here, and the nuns protected her. They thought that being a witch’s child, she would run to the Apostles’ Stones, but she didn’a. It’s led than a mile way across the fields, ye’ ken, and back then she was young enough to run all the way. But Tam McBurney always thought it was Elspeth as a witch who killed his brother Rab years later at the time we all left. It wasn’a. Rab cornered Elspeth at the Apostles’ Stones the day we were leaving wi’ Sorley, and this time ’twas the fae that came to her rescue. Sorley and Elspeth herself told me that. Mind, it didn’a help Alex’s temper that when he returned here, he got presented wi’ the bill fer his ma’s time in the tolbooth.’

“What?” Anna gasped, appalled. “They charged him? For what?”

‘Fer the pay o’ the men who stood watch o’er her.’ Hugh gave a bitter laugh. ‘It happened to me, too. As soon as the bloody kirk-men learned who I was when I came back wi’ the Highland army, I was billed fer my ma’s keep in prison, her being watched o’er, and the cost o’ the God-forsaken fire which killed her.’

“That’s appalling!” Anna exclaimed, horrified. “Please tell me you didn’t pay?”

‘I had nae say i’ the matter,’ Hugh said with a snort of disgust. ‘It was taken out o’ what little I got paid from the army wi'out me ever touchin' a coin. And it was fifteen pounds they took, too.'

"Bloody hell," Gary intoned. "No wonder you never got the money together to buy that croft you longed for." He turned to Anna. "Half the time the soldiers barely got what they were owed anyway, and to come up with that much must have wiped out *years* of Hugh's pay. I thought I came out of the army with not a lot, but this is far worse. And being asked to pay for what amounted to the murder of your loved ones…that's criminal."

'It was no' just me and Alex,' Hugh qualified for them. 'It happened every time there was a witch brought in fer questioning. If families didn'a pay, then they were assumed to be as guilty and could end up being questioned too. 'Twas no' quite as bad o'er here as in Fife, as I heard, but those God-curse-them presbyters couldn'a afford to pay fer the gaolers to watch o'er *all* o' the women they brought in, so the way they got around it was by making their families pay. Ye' can imagine the cost o' keeping men watchin a woman fer several months.'

Gary nodded. "And we're not just talking about a man sitting outside the door of one or several cells on watch, are we? There was more than one man in the room with her twenty-four hours a day, making sure she didn't sleep when her master, the Devil, might come to her. And I guess if the local kirk thought they needed to bring in a higher authority, then that would get charged to the poor suffering families too?"

'Aye, it did,' Hugh sighed. ''Twas another fear folk had on top o' the accusations, ye ken? Not only could ye' be shunned by all around ye', but ye' might even lose the roof o'er yer head if ye' couldn'a pay up to the kirk fer a woman who was taken fer questioning. And the cost o' a public burning was no' small. It crushed families for decades, and no' just the close members, because the kirk and bailies were determined to get the money off someone.

'If Alex had had half a brain, he'd ha' stayed well out o' Dumfries itself. Having taken a look around to see if he could find his ma and pa – 'cause that's who he came back to find – he should ha' got on his pony and left afore anyone else knew. But stupid Alex turned out to ha' held a torch years ago fer Isobel. Her pa had married her off awful young, so to Alex, she was out o' reach afore he was even an age to marry. Then he came back, discovered that she'd been widowed, and that Tam McBurney had sent her to work fer Auld John Corsan, and even worse, that she'd just run away.'

Hugh's expression by now had shifted more to exasperation and disgust. 'I never did find out if Alex discovered who she'd run wi', but he took his disappointment at missing 'his' woman – who wi' his dying breath, he called out was the love o' his life – on McBurney, who hammered him into the ground like a fence post. They threw Alex into an unmarked pauper's grave, so I only found out when someone I kenned told me as I passed by their croft.

'...I was furious! He'd left dear Elspeth wi' not only Mailie's two wee bairns, but his ain daughter, too, to pick a fight o'er a woman he'd long ago once had a young lad's passion fer. He kent nothing o' Isobel as a woman, or what kind o' life she'd led, 'twas just an auld obsession. He was just another man who wanted possession o' her, and the poor lass had had enough o' that to last ten lifetimes.'

"Is that why you felt you had to help her?" Anna asked gently. "You felt that she'd been disregarded and dumped in the way that Elspeth had been by Alex?"

Hugh nodded. 'Aye, I certainly felt a kinship wi' her o'er that. But she was also Elspeth's cousin – her cousin Margaret's daughter – and at times she reminded me awful sharp o' Elspeth, no' so much in looks but in her ways.'

"Oh Hugh, that's so sad," said Anna, finding herself filling up with tears, not just for Hugh, but for Elspeth and Isobel, who seemed to have had such a raw deal in life.

And seeing that, Gary guessed why, but also realised that Anna felt this so keenly herself because in her own way, Anna had been just as badly used by her idiot ex, Jensen. He might not have abandoned her with three kids, or sold her off into what was slavery in all but name to some religious zealot, but he had given scant thought to Anna as a person, other than merely as his 'plus one'. So he gave Anna recovery time by asking Hugh, "Do I gather from what you just said that Elspeth was looking after her sister's children?"

Hugh took a steadying breath, gave a nod, and answered, 'Aye. Mailie died just afore they left Argyll.' He gave another regretful shake of his head. "Niall, Mailie's man, had two boys by his first wife, and he never seemed to be able to see past them to see the two wee ones he had wi' Mailie. I would ha' taken them in wi' open arms had I had the chance wi' Elspeth. And then she had her own wee Marione, named after Alex's ma. I heard later that Niall, the bastard – saving your presence, Anna – had called his wee girl Jonet, but no' after Mailie's ma, but after his first wife.'

"Bloody hell!" Anna swore. "Talk about rubbing salt in the wound. If Mailie had fears about her mother's reputation following her north, her deciding to call a daughter after her would have been unlikely. But to have the name forced on her child, *and* have the same name hold the memories of the woman who still had her husband's affections…good grief! That's awful! They can't have been that short of names for girls that that was necessary, so it had to be deliberate. Poor Mailie."

'Aye. 'Twas deliberate. The wee boy, Jamie, who was the older, was named after the wife's brother, but I guessed that Mailie was fine wi' that because that brother had died a hero in the wars alongside her own man. It was when young Jonet was born that the truth hit her. And o' course, that was only a couple o' years afore Elspeth and her pa turned up bringing all the other memories wi' them.'

Gary gave a huff of disgust. "Those poor ladies – both of them. Mailie, for losing two children by her previous husband, and then finding that one of those by the current one was named after someone she could never replace, because she had reached almost saint level in Niall's eyes. And poor Elspeth, too, because it wasn't her fault that any of this happened. What it must have been like to lose her mother and cousins under such circumstances, and then to arrive at a place of safety only to be rejected by her equally damaged sister is just beyond belief. Did you ever find out what happened to Elspeth and the children?"

Hugh sighed. 'I heard from the same person who told me about Alex that he'd said something about Culross, but I couldn'a get there to look fer her. I was intending to do that after Isobel died, but never got there.'

Gary looked sympathetic. "That's tough. But if I can bring you back to our current problem, Hugh. We've got Elspeth's mother as one of the ghosts who can't bear to release her grip on the old kirk, in part because she wants to know where Elspeth is, or was. So if we are trying to trace her in our here and now, who are we looking for in the records? In your time, who would she be? Still Elspeth Allen? Or might she have changed her name for safety's sake? Only I think if we can tell the ghost of Jonet that we've found her, that will help her enormously."

Hugh was silent for a while, clearly taking Gary's words seriously, and making Anna grateful that she was dealing with the more reasonable of the two ghosts. Hugh would always consider the feelings of the women tied to the kirk as well as himself. She doubted whether Gideon ever could or would.

'I think,' he said very carefully, 'that if Elspeth and Alex took on Mailie's children – who would have been too small to recall or question what their family name was – then given that Elspeth's own daughter would have been a Black, she would probably have stuck with her own name. Being Elspeth Allan who wed Alex Black, and then had three children, would have united that wee family far more than if she'd had to explain that Jamie and Jonet were Munroes, while young Marione was a Black.

'Niall had made it clear by then that he didn'a care a jot about his children with Mailie, so Elspeth certainly wouldn'a have used his name for all o' them. She might ha' used her family name – Allen – but in a way, that might ha' aroused comment with people wanting to know what *her* family name was if the children were Allens. Do ye' see the conundrum? The implications then might ha' been that they were bastards when they weren'a.'

"Oh, I see that very well," Gary said instantly. "I'm old enough to have known what a stigma illegitimacy could be, especially in small communities. Thank God Anna's generation don't have that to contend with, and these days we try hard not to taint a child with its parents' 'sins', but we're not that far away from those times that an old bloke like me doesn't recall some of the taunts to other kids at school. It was bloody cruel. So yes, I can easily imagine that it would be easiest for Elspeth to use her husband's name for all three children, especially with people who didn't know them well enough for her to be able to explain all the details."

Anna had scribbled down notes and now looked at them with despair. "I have to say, Hugh, that while I'll do my best to find out what happened to Elspeth, I'm not hopeful. As you found, there's just too big an area to cover, and it's too far in our past to be sure of anything surviving in the way of records, meaning that although I can search faster, there might be less still around. …But can we ask you as well about the other ladies who died with your mum? We've got several of them lingering over in the old kirk, and while I know that Gideon is a sore point for all of them, how many of them are as deeply entwined in this as you and your family are?"

Hugh gave a huff and thought for a moment. 'Well ma Grandma Grissell lived down at Kirkcudbright, and Aunt Marione went as often as she could to help her out once Grandpa William died. It means that they knew several o' the others well.' He stopped and frowned. 'Ye're making me think, and now I recall that one o' the things which condemned them was that they were accused o' meeting wi' a black man.'

Anna's confused expression meant that Gary had to hurriedly explain to her, "That would be unlikely to mean a man o' colour, as we'd say these days, Anna. More like someone who was considered the incarnation o' the Devil himself."

"Really?" Anna was aghast. "They would think that? That Old Nick could manifest himself as a real person?"

'No' so much believe beyond doubt,' Hugh said dryly, 'as it being an awful good misdeed to add to their supposed sins. I've long since wondered whether it all started wi' some miserable auld besom spotting them talking to a relative o' Uncle Samwell's, 'cause there were Blacks living down there too, and it conveniently getting misunderstood.'

Anna gasped. "Oh! And Samwell himself had been taken in for questioning hadn't he? So whichever one of the two culprits really wanted your aunt and uncle's croft, then Samwell getting released without charge must have really pissed them off. Meaning that if they could still use his family against others of the women they wanted out of the way, you can see how that would happen."

'Ye' never got just one witch accused,' Hugh told them sadly. 'One might go to trial, but behind them could be a dozen friends and family who were regarded as suspect just fer being i' the same hoose as them, or buying seed or a fleece off them, and who suffered questioning as a result, but then had to be let go. Ye' only had to have that happen a few times in a small town fer people to be bluidy terrified, because everyone kenned everyone else in those wee places, so everyone could be suspect at some point.'

Gary grimaced. “And if the kirk was billing each of their families for the time they were being held – never mind if they ever made it to a trial – that was a nice little earned for the kirk, wasn’t it? You can’t imagine that the watchers came from the top tier of local families. Those folk would be too busy working their fields or out on their fishing boats, and because of that, paying vital taxes which nobody would want to stop coming in. No, it would be the roughs. The ones who might otherwise have been in the tolbooth themselves for vagrancy or the like, who could be put to work, in effect paying off what it would have cost the parish to keep them incarcerated, by doing the dirty work nobody else wanted. And if they got a bit too rough with the prisoner, well they’d deserved it for being a witch, hadn’t they? The kirk won at every turn.”

1681-82

Gideon

After his return home from the fight at Bothwell Bridge, Gideon did his best to change his life. His father's cronies were discouraged from calling around. Not all of them straightaway, mind you, and those he began with, not all at once – he wasn't that stupid. Instead, one would come and be told that Auld John was having a bad day, but be let in the next time or the time after, the intervals between them seeing the old man getting subtly longer and longer. At the same time, Gideon made sure that his vile father no longer got the best cuts of what meat they had. Those either went to him, or into the communal pot of stew that was kept going over the fire, and without Isobel's good cooking, that wasn't to his father's tastes either, meaning that he picked at it and complained. Isobel and McKay on their own with the old man might have become worn down, but not with Gideon there. Not with Gideon able to fight back, and McKay therefore no longer cowed.

Moreover, Isobel's disappearance was a blow Gideon hadn't remotely anticipated, and was something he could not find it in himself to forgive her for. Why had she vanished, seemingly with bloody Edward McCartney? What was it about that weakling that she found so appealing, when she treated himself with such revulsion? And much as he wished he could blame their escape wholly on Hugh Ferguson, subtle enquiries in the district revealed that Ferguson had marched off with a band of the Highlanders quite some time after folk had seen Isobel and McCartney with others, up at the fore of the Highlanders' exodus from the shire. It didn't please Gideon, and it didn't please Auld John, yet there wasn't a damned thing either of them could do about it. It had Gideon nightly cursing Edward's soul, because on top of his own misery at losing her, without Isobel his father was even harder to manage.

Given that McKay was getting more of a share of the decent stuff instead of the poor fare he'd had up until now, he, at least, was saying nothing in protest. Moreover, Gideon gradually learned that it had been come and serve Auld John or be homeless and starve, after old John had connived to get him thrown off the farm where he had worked. That the old man had done it to get a different man, who was already in his debt, ingratiated into the farmer's life – Auld John having an eye on the farm and wanting to dig up what dirt he could on the farmer – just made it all the more unfair.

Therefore Auld John's rooks were coming home to roost, as McKay would stand nodding mutely before visitors as Gideon wove his tale of his father weakening. Given that they all believed McKay to be wholly under Auld John's thumb, after Auld John had so often boasted of that, McKay's apparent agreement with Gideon made him believed when on his own they might have questioned him. And the more Auld John refused to eat what he was given, having limited appetite when he could do nothing, and having been spoiled by Isobel making him special dishes to tempt him (albeit out of fear), the more he weakened in reality.

Gideon knew it was far from Christian, but by Christmas he was praying for a good chesty cold to sweep through the district, because with any luck, the old man would catch the Winter Fever, and that would be the end of him. Often called 'the old man's friend' for the number of elderly folks whose lingering suffering ended when they caught it, Gideon was now thinking it would be his friend, too. Young John was as much of a drain on their resources as their father since his blow to the head, as he ate well but could contribute nothing. It meant that Gideon himself had to roll up his sleeves and help with the harvesting, ploughing, and then the planting of what would become the spring crops.

Not that that was new to him, given that he'd been shoved out into the fields as soon as he'd been old enough to be useful, with his father threatening beatings if he didn't report back as to who had shirked their share of the work, or maybe picked up some extra ears of barley or oats for themselves. For although the runrig fields should have had the strips of furrows redistributed every year, to give everyone on those communal fields an even chance of getting some of the good as well as some of the poorer soil, Auld John had ruled his crofters with a rod of iron, always keeping the best for himself. And with a Presbyter like Veitch in the nearest kirk to many of the crofters, they feared for their immortal souls if they crossed Auld John and Veitch heard of it.

Veitch might not have been the only man of the Kirk thereabouts, and as a vehement Presbyterian, he ought to have been solidly behind every man making his own choices, but in reality, that was up until that man ran contrary to what Veitch wished. Then he soon found out how little say he had if he wanted to stay on the right side of the local Kirk Sessions. And everyone remembered only too well how the local Sessions had been the primary movers behind women like Jannet Corsan, and Agnes and Margaret Clark being burned at the stake only twenty years previously. That was within one generation's memories, and most families had several living under the same roof, meaning that the eight women who had died had not been allowed to be forgotten, even if poor Bigis Cairns faded from recall having not survived to the actual day.

It was that lingering public memory which Gideon found the hardest to deal with, not least because it was only the truly desperate who would come and work for him. In the end, he found it simpler to sub-let out strips and fields that he couldn't manage himself in return for half of the crops, fleeces, or meat. After all, a small household, such as he kept these days, hardly required vast amounts of food, and he certainly had no intention of entertaining his father's old cronies at the croft – and the more they got used to that, the less likely it would be that they would come to *Blackpark House* once it was fit to live in, and he'd be free of their censure. As long as he had food on the table and sufficient to sell for him to pay the laird who actually owned the land if not the buildings on it, Gideon had too much else to worry about to care about making a profit.

The new house would have to be paid for out of what Auld John had hidden away – money which then could not be left to Matthew, when the middle brother had done nothing to help with either their father or the house. Young John might be a liability now, but in Gideon's eyes, he'd at least been there for as long as he'd been able, and that gave him some right to be fed and housed. Matthew had not. Yet the final touches were being put to *Blackpark House*, and Gideon dared to dream that one day he might be able to move into it.

The winter of 1681-82 proved to be the end of Young John's miserable existence. Unable to move around much, he succumbed to a chesty cough which got worse and worse, until one morning Gideon got up to find him cold and dead. Yet to Gideon's silent fury, the old man managed to shake off the same cough, and continued to linger, getting even more crabbit, if that were possible.

Then as Gideon stood beside the grave on a freezing cold February morning, as Veitch wittered and warbled his way through the funeral for Young John in his ancient voice, the unthinkable happened. Out from behind the old yew tree in the kirkyard at Irongray came a scarecrow-like figure – even more gaunt than Auld John, if that was possible – which gave him an almighty fright as he thought for one horrible moment that the old man had regained the use of all of his limbs. But it wasn't his father, it was Matthew.

Clapping his hands to his face to prevent himself from screaming in frustration, Gideon could only hope that the few bystanders would think it was in grief. He'd wondered, though not often, what had happened to his other brother, but only in as much to offer up heartfelt thanks that wherever he was, it wasn't here. But now he was, and going by his garb, which had the distinct look of being Veitch's cast-offs, he'd been hiding at the Manse.

Well, that figured. With Matthew being as much of a zealot as Veitch, if not more, if anyone was going to fly in the face of government edicts and hide a Covenanter rabble-rouser, it would be Veitch. And the cadaverous smile on Veitch's face as Matthew came up beside him and made the responses in the service confirmed that. Veitch and Matthew were in league with one another.

Dear God, why are you making me suffer like this? Gideon silently prayed, his mind now far from the burial of Young John. He, lucky sod, was out of this hellish situation, and all Gideon could think was to hiss at Matthew as they filed away from the grave, and the grave-diggers began filling it in, "Do not come to the croft! People have seen you here now. They know you're back, and someone will surely tell the soldiers. The croft will be the first place they look for you because of Father being there."

In July of 1680, word had come to Dumfries and Galloway that the leaders of the Remnant of the Covenanters had been captured, and then the remaining one who hadn't died in the fight was taken back to Edinburgh where he'd been gruesomely executed. Then a year later, last summer, a new leader and followers had suffered the same fate. With the King's brother set to succeed him to become James the Seventh (of Scotland) and Second (of England) when his time came, the government were making sure that those who might oppose him were removed from the picture. The Highland Host of soldiers might have long since gone back to their homes, but an army still remained in the area – now heavily under the sway of the mighty Douglases, because of the dreaded Colonel Douglas – and Gideon had seen them around and about often enough to have a deep-seated fear of them turning up and arresting him if Veitch, in his dotage, implied that the Corsans were staunch supporters of his own favoured cause.

"Do not fear, brother, God will watch over me," Matthew intoned, the same maniacal gleam in his eye that had scared the living daylights out of Gideon when he'd met him fleeing St Andrews back in 1679. But to Gideon's intense relief, this time Matthew vanished back into the hedgerows, presumably to slink back into the Manse, since he wasn't seen on any of the lanes leading away from the kirk.

Yet he knew his luck couldn't hold, and so straightaway he began making plans to move into *Blackpark House*. A bed was set up in the smallest of the ground-floor rooms in the tower-house. Its chimney was small enough that it could be heated, and Auld John cackled with glee as he was hauled bodily into the place by McKay. The serving man was more than happy too. He'd got the room next to the kitchen all to himself, which was actually warmer than almost any other room aside from the kitchen itself, and he was far enough away from Auld John to not have to listen to his endless complaints.

For himself, Gideon took the master's room up on the first floor – a generously proportioned room which got the evening sunlight, and if it was big enough to be chilly, Gideon was prepared to tolerate that for the bliss of having some peace. That it looked toward the remnants of the old nunnery was far from ideal, but he'd already planted some saplings in between to obscure the view, and soon, in summer at least, he wouldn't be able to see it at all.

All I need now, he thought to himself on the first night he lay on the rough mattress on the floorboards of his grand room, for he'd yet to fetch the bed frames from the townhouse, *is for Isobel to come back with her tail between her legs. Then I can bring her here, marry her, and be seen as a respectable married man at last. Surely the old man can't last another winter?*

Yet when Auld John died before the winter arrived, it wasn't through any effects of the weather or disease. Gideon had been into Dumfries on a family business issue he couldn't get out of, and returned home to hear voices in Auld John's room. The fact that he'd seen McKay pottering around in the kitchen as he'd walked around from the stables meant that it couldn't be him. So who was it?

Assuming it must be one of the old man's cronies come to inspect his father's rise up to the next level of society with the house, Gideon foolishly went out to the pump and washed the dust of the road off first, then beat it off his coat and took that up to his room. He'd actually managed to acquire some wine that didn't taste like vinegar to him, and had had the pin-barrel taken up to his room, determined not to share it with anyone, and now he poured himself a glass and sat at his chair by the window. Furnishing a place the size of *Blackpark* was going to take some doing, and for now the only rooms in the main house worth inhabiting were his room and his father's, hence him not going into the hall.

Indeed, he'd been looking at some rather fine work of a carpenter in Dumfries and had calculated that he too might commission similar pieces if he sold off the Black's old croft. Now that he didn't need to live in it, Gideon wanted the place disassociated with their family as fast as possible, and because Auld John could no longer sign his name to anything, the family man of law had finally got Auld John to recognise that Gideon's signature would have to be used for family business. That Gideon might use it for his own ends had been a worry for the old man, but necessity had forced his hand, and now Gideon knew that few would question whether Auld John would want furniture for his new house. Of course he would. It wouldn't be seen as strange at all, not when Auld John was such a social climber.

Therefore it was nearly an hour later when, fortified by a second glass of wine, Gideon descended the stairs (of which one day, the upper section would remain in the hotel as the housekeeper's stairs) and wandered into his father's room. He was braced for another old man to be blathering away to his father. He was not prepared to see Matthew, hands thrown skywards and praying almost incoherently, and to see a pillow still lying over their father's face.

"What have you done?" Gideon vaguely heard himself screaming, only to see Matthew turning to him with that terrifying maniacal gleam in his eye.

"I have rid the world of a truly evil sinner," his brother intoned with rather too much relish in his voice.

"W…Wha*aat*? …Oh God in Heaven! You've *killed* him?"

"I extended God's mercy to end a pitiful life," was the ridiculous response, to which Gideon could only stand open-mouthed in shock and horror.

Matthew returned to his wild praying over the rapidly cooling corpse of their father, as if it was the most natural thing to do, whereas when Gideon could scrape together what wits he had left, he fled the room. Running faster than he'd known he could to the kitchen, he grabbed McKay.

"You can ride, yes? Ride fast?"

"Aye, I suppose I could."

"Then for the love of God, saddle up Sorrel and ride like the wind to Dumfries."

McKay looked at him vacantly. "Why?"

"Because my idiot brother has just smothered our father. Go get the bailie's men! Hurry!"

"But your brother's dead."

"Not my youngest, you turnip-brained goat-tupper. The middle one! The God-botherer. He's gone mad. Thinks he's done God's work. Now for the love of Christ, get on the bloody horse and go and get help. I'll lock the lunatic in the house and try and keep him there."

Finally, the urgency of the situation percolated through to McKay, and in shock and horror, he ran to do as Gideon had instructed. Meanwhile, with shaking hands, Gideon went and found the house keys, which were hanging off an iron nail behind the front door. Making sure that he had locked the door between the main house and the servants' wing, he then went through into the main hall and locked the front door, sealing the still praying-aloud Matthew in the house alone with their father. No way was Gideon going to lock himself inside with that lunatic, for what might Matthew do in his madness if he could kill his own father?

It took what felt like eternity before a bailie and two men rode into the yard with McKay behind them. They found Gideon sitting on the front step with the keys in his hands and the front door locked.

"Is the heretic within?" Bailie Ferguson asked, and Gideon cursed his rotten luck that of the two bailies, it was this one who had come. In truth, he was probably the better man to deal with something like this, for his younger brother was rising through the ranks of the army, and was purported to be Colonel Douglas' favoured man, meaning that if further action was needed, Ferguson would be able to get it done. Yet the family name gnawed at Gideon's insides. Why could they not have been Murrays or Kennedys or some other-named family? In truth, he had no idea whether there was any link between Hugh or his wretched father James to Bailie Ferguson, but so many families around here did link up somewhere down the generations, Gideon could not disregard it.

"I locked the doors as soon as I'd sent McKay for you," Gideon said wearily, rising to his feet.

"There's no way out of the house on the other side, so he must still be in there. I've not heard his ranting for a while, and an hour or so ago I heard him rattling the door, trying to get out, but it's been silent since then."

He wasn't about to recount the curses Matthew had rained upon his soul through the door when he found it locked, nor his own screamed purging of all the grievances he had against Matthew back at the man he could not see.

"How dare ye' question a man o' God?" Matthew had ranted. "I curse your miserable soul, brother!"

"I'm not the one going to Hell for killing our father!" Gideon had flung back. "You're a blight on our family, Matthew! A carbuncle on all of our souls, not the saving of them."

But Bailie Ferguson didn't need to hear that. Instead, Gideon let them into the house, told them where his father's room was, and then stood back and waited for the fight. The suspicious continuing silence soon made him worried, though. And when Bailie Ferguson came out shaking his head, Gideon felt his guts turning to water.

"Where is he?" he almost squeaked in his disbelief. "He was in there! I know he was."

Bailie Ferguson sighed and shook his head, and then both of them felt a sudden gust of wind from further back in the hall.

"Seems like your brother might have gone out of the window," Ferguson said, but with little conviction in his voice, and Gideon's guts did another turn over as he realised that if they didn't think Matthew had ever been here, then he was suddenly the main suspect in his father's death.

"Out of the window? But it's easily a ten feet drop," Gideon said incredulously, stepping back into the main hall and looking towards the rear. "You could break your neck jumping out of that."

Yet to his intense relief, when they got to the open window and looked out, it was clear that that was exactly what Matthew had done. There'd been no time yet to worry about tidying up on this side of the house, and so there were several self-seeded fledgling bushes and a couple of two-year saplings below the window, some of which were broken in the shape of someone landing very hard and clumsily into them. Then in the damp soil there were footprints leading away from the house.

"He's dragging one leg," said one of the men with the bailie, who clearly knew a thing or two about tracking. "He won't be hard to follow, especially with the river being in spate at the moment. We'll either find his drowned body or catch up with him as the river loops back this way."

Trying hard not to breathe in great gulps of air in his relief that he wasn't suspected, Gideon managed to nod his agreement. Then he had to hold onto the door frame to stop his knees buckling completely, when the other bailie's man came out and told them that the pillow had still been over his father's face, but that in his father's clenched fist was a ripped piece of black cloth.

“Like the ministers wear,” the man said knowingly, and pointing to Gideon’s clothes adding, “not like his. And his aren’t ripped at all. If we catch the other one, at least one sleeve should be in tatters. The old man didn’t give up without a fight.”

And for the first time, Gideon was glad the wicked old man had had so much strength left in him.

CHAPTER 16

Gideon paused for breath in telling Phemie all of this. Rita had kept silent throughout as soon as he started talking, letting Phemie be the one to do what little prompting was needed, but now managed to keep her voice gentle as she asked him, "Did they catch your brother?"

'Aye, they did,' Gideon confirmed. 'He was sent to Edinburgh fer trial, being a kirk-man and all. I didn'a go. Couldn'a face it. I buried the auld man and cursed bluidy Veitch at every one o' his sanctimonious words as he stood at the graveside, 'cause wi'out him sheltering Matthew, he'd have had to leave the area long afore. People still kent his face, ye' understand, no' like some o' the outsider preachers who still came in to hold conventicles out on the hillsides.'

"Did he hang?" Phemie asked softly and got a nod. Then she and Rita were shocked as Gideon added, 'Aye, would ha' been faster if he'd ha' been shot out on the hillside like Veitch's son, but t' ma mind he deserved to go slow.'

"This Veitch had a son?" Rita exclaimed, too shocked to be quiet about it.

Gideon gave a huff of disgust. 'He wasn'a the man his faither was, but the auld man always insisted that Jeremiah would follow him into the kirk, and *our* kirk at that. Like Matthew, he was sent to St Andrews, and just like Matthew, that's where he fell in wi' the rabble rousers. I always reckoned that's why Veitch seized on Matthew when he came back. He'd already lost his son and acolyte to the cause, so Matthew was Jeremiah's replacement.

'Little good it did either o' them getting dragged into the auld man's twisted plots. By the time Matthew died, the government's hands were turned against him and his kind. Most o' us saw the Covenant's time had run out, except for Veitch and a few like him. It might ha' been the right way to God, no' like those bluidy half-Catholic Episcopalians, but ye' canna fight everyone at every turn.'

Phemie felt that this was a good point to bring up Gideon's death.

"Did you get buried as you would have wished?" she asked gently. "Did you want whatever the Covenanter service of your day was? Or did you get something else?"

'Me?' barked Gideon, his face turning sour. 'Me, I got nothing. Ma bluidy luck! Ma bones are probably still rotting down by the river, if they haven'a been washed away already. *I* wasn'a good enough for a grave, but bluidy Hugh Ferguson, he gets a hero's tomb. *I* saw them from here. I saw them from up here and what they did wi' ma body – and it was no' in some proper grave! Ma grave got pissed upon like I was a bluidy mad dog that had bitten its owner. And pissed on by one who should ha' done better by me too! I should ha' been buried properly i' the kirkyard alongside that evil auld goat o' a faither o' mine – no' that I wanted to be close to his bones, but at least it would ha' been on consecrated ground fer the sake o' ma soul.'

Both Rita and Phemie winced at this. Yet another wrong that they might need to right to get Gideon to leave.

"That's really harsh," Rita said, trying to follow Phemie's lead in being more outwardly sympathetic to Gideon, even if inside she still wanted to shake him until his ghostly teeth rattled. "However, I need to tell you that Hugh's grave out in the grounds is far from heroic. For a start off he was wrongly buried as a Covenanter – which rankles with him as much as that stone tomb does with you."

'Ferguson was never a Covenanter!'

"Gideon, you know that. We know that. And Hugh knows that. But the person who had that tomb built didn't, not least because he was over a century on from when you two died. He was just someone with a commission to fulfil. And on the subject of things being not what you think, you seem to have got the idea that a Ferguson now owns this hotel. Well they don't. Fergusons were a company who bought the place and sold it again earlier this year. So please stop…"

"Beating yourself up over that," Phemie interjected over Rita, sensing that she was about to tell him to stop being such an idiot. He was, but telling him in that tone was inviting him to go into another sulk. "In fact, why don't you tell us about the other Ferguson who you say got his hands on this place? You sounded very angry about that, so what happened?"

If Gideon had had feathers, you could almost have seen them ruffling up and then smoothing down. 'When bluidy *Hugh* Ferguson killed me, there were nae more men in our family close enough to take this place on,' he said with a huff. 'Or at least none wi' the money to finish what ma faither had started, and they were verra distant cousins indeed, anyway. I kenned that ma sister Jean had married Bailie Ferguson's brother, the captain, a while afore that, though I wasn'a pleased, and if faither had found out she'd married wi'out his approval, there'd ha' been Hell to pay. How a scullion got the attention o' a man like that I dinna ken,' said in such a way as to imply that she must have tricked him in some way.

It made Rita's hackles rise. If Jean had been more like the mother Gideon said so little about, maybe she had been a sweet-tempered, pleasant lass, who had swiftly moved from a lowly position into something higher within a household. Certainly high enough to be a respectable wife for a soldier who had risen through the ranks, as Ferguson seemed to have done. Yet Gideon seemed to have never bothered to even try to find his sister once she left home, as if she was beneath him caring about. Rita could see Phemie clenching the skirt of her dress where Gideon couldn't see, obviously as annoyed by his attitude as her, but managing to keep her tone kindly as she asked, "Just the one sister?"

'Er…no. There was Katherine, too.'

"And what happened to her?"

Gideon gave a ghostly shrug. 'Nay idea. I last saw her when I was a lad in my teens. She went as a servant somewhere just as Jean did. Ma arranged all that. Faither wouldn'a sully his hands wi' a girl.'

"So this was the same Ferguson you were telling us about with Matthew and your father dying?" Phemie managed to redirect him before he said something which would enrage Rita and herself. Gideon really was a miserable misogynist. "Because you said that those Ferguson brothers weren't related to Hugh? So why the anger against them? There was surely more than one Ferguson family in the district, and not all related?"

All they got from Gideon was a surly teenager shrug.

Yet Rita had a moment of inspiration. "For your own sake, Gideon, this has to stop," she said firmly, adding before he could dismiss her, "We want to help you move on from here. But you really don't want to be judged by God for persecuting people who have never done you a wrong, do you?"

She caught Phemie's covert nod of approval, with her picking up on that with, "If we can, we'll try to find your bones and get them properly interred at a kirk of your choice, but you have to work with us a bit on this, Gideon. We can't wipe away your sins for you, so you certainly don't want to be adding any more to what you already have." That seemed to get through to him, so she continued, "So let's stop this silliness about some descendant of Hugh's now possessing this place, eh? It's just a coincidence of name, that's all. Nothing to get all worked up about."

Gideon looked away, seemingly unable to meet Phemie's eye, but she and Rita got the feeling that at last the message had sunk in.

"Now then, tell us about how you died, and why your body didn't get a proper burial." Phemie saw him starting to bristle again and hurried on with, "We're not expecting you to give us chapter and verse. We know that there'll be some things you can't tell us. But even a few clues might help *us* to help *you*."

It seemed to mollify Gideon a little, but he'd clearly tired of answering questions and turned and vanished off into Crocus through the wall, Rita and Phemie having called him to them in Tulip, which being one of the smallest rooms in the hotel was more easily not used if Gideon continued to lurk there. The two of them got up from the chairs they'd been sitting on and stretched the kinks out of their limbs.

"Good grief, he's hard going," Cameron said from where he'd been sitting on the floor in the doorway to the two rooms. Hauling himself to his feet, he held the fire door to the stairs open for the two ladies and then followed them down, saying, "I'm ashamed to say it, but I probably wasn't much better than him when I was thirteen or fourteen, but like most other people, I grew up. Do you think he's regressing the longer he's trapped here?"

"I wish I could make that excuse for him," Rita said sadly, "but I fear this is pretty much who he always was."

"There is one thing, though," Cameron said thoughtfully. "It's quite possible that, if Gideon was so loathed locally that his body was thrown in the river, at some point in the intervening centuries it might have turned up. So rather than having to beat through the bushes the length of this river and the Nith, we'd probably do better looking at the local newspaper archives."

Rita spun to look at him with admiration. "That's a bloody good idea, Cam! There's a strong chance that he was reburied once whatever investigations which took place were done with him. That makes it a whole lot easier if we're going to try to call him to them. And if he's already in a kirkyard somewhere, then getting the local minister to say a few words over him will be much easier, especially if that will soothe that prickly soul of his."

Up in his eyrie, Gideon was feeling far from comfortable. What the feisty auld woman had said about sins had struck a chord with him, but by then he'd already told them an outright lie. He knew full well where Katherine had been by the time he died. It had been here, with Jean, or at least for a while.

Someone – probably the interfering Veitch – had let them know of their father's death, because at the time of Auld John's death, Gideon genuinely hadn't kept track of where his sisters were. And it really had been just him of the family at their father's graveside, because Jean and Katherine had been badly delayed and had missed the actual service. That delay, though, was a suppurating wound in Gideon's soul, the source of so much of his ire and grief.

The first he'd known of any of it had been two days after the funeral, just at the point when he'd felt a lightness of spirit. *I'm ma own master*, he'd been thinking. *It's all mine now. I can do as I please! No faither to tell me how I'm failing at every turn. Just me and McKay, and he's no' going to say anything, because right now he's better off than he's been for years.* And then he'd heard horses' hooves outside in the yard.

Puzzled as to who on earth would be visiting the house now, he'd got up and gone to the door, to see McKay coming to take the bridles of two shaggy garrons. Even more of a shock was to see two middle-ages ladies dismounting, and then he saw him, bloody Ferguson! He was sat on his own pony back at the edge of the bushes, and raising a hand in farewell to the two women, who shockingly waved back, before turning his pony and riding away. What were they thinking? And who were they?

He was prompted out of his stupor by the taller one of the two demanding, “Are ye no’ going to invite us in, brother? It’s been an awful journey to get here, and I’m no’ of a mind to be standing out here freezing to death!”

Stunned by the realisation, for a moment all Gideon could do was gawp at them. Granted, it was a chilly day for the time of year, but not that cold, until he realised that they were both drenched. Their heavy wool cloaks were weighted down with the damp, and it occurred to him that they must have been caught in the dreadful thunderstorms which had followed the afternoon of the day of the funeral and the day after. There was no other way they could have got that wet other than falling into one of the rivers.

“Ye’d best come in,” he managed to strangle out, though in truth that was the last thing he wanted.

As he led them into the main hall and realised how chilly that was, he was forced to walk them on through into the room their father had used. So far, all he and McKay had managed to do was to move the bed into the second of the smaller ground-floor rooms, and pull the chairs brought from the townhouse close to the fireplace. He'd been planning on bringing the rest of the furniture over in the coming week, but at least he'd had the forethought to bring the beds over, though in those first moments of his sisters being there, he was praying that they weren't planning on stopping with him.

There was a pile of seasoned logs and kindling in the hearth, put there in anticipation of the old man's calls for a fire long before the weather turned really cold, but that was fortunate now as it meant that Gideon was able to get a fire going with speed. Less fortunate was the growing realisation that there was hardly anywhere else they were going to go, for tonight at least, and if he'd stripped the townhouse of chairs and beds, then they could hardly go there tomorrow.

He was about to ask what brought them here, when he realised that would just make him sound stupid. It was bloody obvious what had dragged this pair out of the woodwork – the promise of an inheritance!

"I've to travel in to Dumfries on Friday to Faither's man o' law to hear the will," he said instead. There, that should shut them up before they started asking how much they had coming and when they could have it!

"*Mm-humph*," the tall one intoned, with Gideon still not knowing if this was Katherine or Jean, until the other one said, "I'm so sorry we weren'a able to be with ye' to support ye' at the funeral. Katherine travelled o'er to our house the night afore, and we set out in plenty o' time to reach here the day afore the funeral." She shuddered. "We might ha' never made it if it weren'a for the kindness o' Hugh Ferguson."

Gideon felt the bile rising up his throat. Kindness? Could the damned man not have left well alone, leaving Gideon to enjoy his first taste of peace in decades? There was no kindness towards himself, of that Gideon was sure. But what in God's name had Ferguson done now?

Rita and Phemie rejoined Anna and Gary in Gary's cottage to talk over what they'd each found out. Unsurprisingly, Anna and Gary had far more to tell.

"We got another bit out of Hugh as to why he was so furious at the Covenanters," Gary said after Anna had told them about Elspeth. "It turns out that at the start of the Killing Times, in the December of 1684, a hundred local men broke into the tolbooth at Kirkcudbright and set all the Covenanter prisoners free. Now from the government and army's point of view, that was the last straw, making them take a harsher stance than they might have against the men defying the government over the Covenant.

"But Hugh made a fair point, too. He asked why, if the unified men of the parish could break the place open, did they not do that for the women in 1659? It was only twenty-five years on. Hardly long enough for a massed change of perspective on things such as you might get over the course of a century, and we could see his point. I was telling Anna about how life for women in particular has changed in my lifetime, but within a similar period between the nineteen-nineties and now, it's not *that* radical."

Anna was nodding. "And I said that I think that the key factor was that too many people stood to gain from those women dying, along with a presbyter who – if we're right and he raped Bigis Cairns – had a vile attitude towards women which it probably wasn't easy to go against. Plus it was the shocking misogynistic perspective of those Covenanters in the tolbooth being primarily – and maybe even exclusively – men, and therefore other *men* being outraged by that in a way that they never were for the women."

"God, that's grim," Cameron said in disgust. "I've known a lot of blokes who aren't exactly feminists, but who would never act like that."

"A different time and different attitudes, sadly," Phemie said, reaching over and patting his knee consolingly. "And it was possibly worse in areas like this, where the staunchest of Protestants held sway. I've done a bit of reading about the medieval period, and contrary to what a lot of people might think, in the earliest times women were better off than later on coming into this era. It's as if when the Church broke away from Rome, some men saw the chance to grab even more earthly power for themselves, and as you're finding with the witch trials, a chance to rid themselves of women in the community who had any kind of standing or authority."

"Then thank God we don't live back then," Cameron said with feeling. "I'm not sure I'd be any good at keeping quiet over seeing women in my family treated like that."

"Same here, lad," Gary agreed, "so it's easy for us to see Hugh's point of view – it's close to our own. But I've been thinking that maybe Gideon isn't the total nightmare we've been taking him for, but rather more just a normal man of his time, willing to shut his eyes to what might otherwise make a tough life even harder."

Anna grimaced. "That's not a pleasant thought, but it makes a lot of sense."

"On the other hand," Rita said, "did you get the feeling, Phemie, that Gideon hasn't been entirely truthful with us? Did you notice how he got all squirmy when it came to his sisters?"

"Aye, I did. And I'm thinking that it's no coincidence that that was the point when he suddenly decided he'd had enough o' talking to us – especially as you'd just brought up the matter of his eternal soul and him accumulating further sins to be answered for. Gideon's got more secrets, of that I'm convinced."

CHAPTER 17

However, there was an immediate and positive outcome to the two conversations. Anna, Rita, and Phemie went into the old kirk, and were able to tell Jonet what Anna had found out from Hugh about her daughters. As she recounted Mailie's story, Jonet broke down in sobs, but they got the feeling that a large part of that was relief at finally knowing. Agnes and Margaret came up to beside the ghost of Jonet, all of them hugging in that other place, and the three living women felt that there was a sense of closure at last for them.

Anna very carefully didn't tell Jonet the full story of Niall's spiritual, if not physical, unfaithfulness to Mailie. She didn't need that burden. Nor did she tell her of Alex abandoning Elspeth for the same reason.

'Thank ye' so much,' Jonet managed to sniffle. 'So Mailie couldn'a have hated me that much if she named her wee girl after me. And it doesn'a surprise me that Elspeth would take care o' the two wee ones after her sister passed. Elspeth was always a kind soul. And she finally had a wee girl o' her own? Ach, I'm so glad o' that. I always thought she'd make a bonnie mother, but shock can do dreadful things to a woman. I feared that after what we witnessed, she might not conceive.'

"She did," Anna confirmed, hoping that the smile she'd pasted on her face looked convincing. She had talked with Rita and Phemie on the way over, and they'd agreed that Elspeth's life must have been bloody awful after Alex cleared off, with them all saying that they hoped that she'd found shelter and been cared for as she got older, because in those days that was far from a given. Moreover, it wasn't so much lying to Jonet as omitting to tell her what would only cause her greater distress, and all the worse for it still all being way too far back for anyone to alter. In this case, the small lie brought a greater kindness.

The level of comfort Hugh's words brought to the witches meant that all three then felt it only fair to go and tell Hugh that. If he was worrying about his mother and the others as much as they'd been fretting over the fate of their children, it seemed only right to give some happiness back. And one thing did come out in that conversation, which was that once the floor of the apse of the nun's kirk had been lifted and dispersed within *Blackpark House*, the nuns' ability to extend themselves further afield had been crushed. Where once they had been able to at least ravel as far as the Apostles' Stones, if not to do much other than speak, once their anchoring point of the place where they'd met their brutal end had gone, the blood link had been broken, and with it much of their strength. That answered the question which had begun to perplex Anna and Rita, and now they felt they understood more why the witches had not been able to reach out to Hugh when he died, because Gideon had already done the damage to the apse's floor – another thing the women held against him.

So heading back into the hotel, and saving their legs by taking the lift for once, the three modern women went into the housekeeper's room and relayed the news on to Hugh.

"Considering how little we've had to work with, that's not a bad day's results," Anna said cheerfully as Rita was about to say goodbye to Hugh. "Now if we can just find out how the heck Gideon's sister Jean ends up owning this place, and why that's such a sore point with Gideon, we might be well on the way to settling things down."

'Ach, I can tell ye' that,' Hugh said, swimming more fully back into view. He gave a ghostly chuckle. 'Aye but it fair ruffled Himself's feathers, that did!'

Despite their tiredness, that had Rita, Phemie, and Anna grabbing the chairs to sit, waiting to hear more.

''Twas genuine happenstance,' Hugh began. 'I had nae idea who they were at first. Ye' have to understand that this happened afore Isobel died by a few years, so I didn'a have that quarrel wi' Himself as yet.' Hugh had picked up on what Rita had said about not naming Gideon if they didn't want him butting in, and it clearly tickled Hugh's sense of humour to refer to his old enemy as 'Himself' as Rita had done a couple of times.

'I was in the army still and patrolling wi' others when we heard these women's screams. We went to investigate and found two ladies of apparent good repute being set upon by a gang o' five roughs, or so we thought. When we got closer, Gow recognised one o' them as a hedge preacher we'd been hunting a while. He and the other men set off like hounds after hares when the cowards took to their heels. Seems it was fine to accuse decent women o' being whores fer being out alone wi'out men, but they were no so keen to stand up to us.'

"Was that a problem?" Anna asked. "Women travelling alone, I mean. Was it frowned up in society?"

'I'd say 'twas more unwise,' Hugh clarified, 'but then the one woman said that they were travelling to their father's funeral, which made a bit more sense. That was what made me hang back and offer to escort them. I couldn'a fault them fer wanting to do something like that. Then when I asked their names and they said Katherine and Jean Corsan, I near fell off ma ain horse.'

"You knew them?" Phemie wondered.

'I wouldn'a say 'knew', but aye, I recalled them as girls playing wi' the sisters o' friends o' mine when we were all just wee. Now, though, it turned out that Katherine was a widow, living wi' her daughter whose husband was a sailor and so away a lot. The daughter had no' long had another babe, so was in no state to travel. But it was Jean who really gave me a shock. I kenned that Colonel Douglas had a Captain Ferguson amongst his officers, but I'd no' served under the man, and like we've said, Ferguson is no' such an uncommon name that I'd know everyone o' that name around here. So it was a fair shock to learn that Jean was his wife o' several years, and the mother o' his children.'

Rita had to know, "Were you in any way related to this Captain Ferguson?"

'Me?' Hugh laughed. 'Lord no, Mistress Rita. Captain Ferguson might no' have been a great nobleman like the Colonel, but his family were far above mine, and his father came from somewhere o'er towards Perthshire, so no' local. No' that he was likely to inherit anything, being the third son, ye' ken, which was why he'd been off fighting in Holland – I think – and could marry more as he wished. And while *I* might hate the bloody C…*them*, to an outsider, Jean was from a decent family, able to afford a townhouse as well as the farms which were a bit bigger than the average croft – and o' course the Captain wouldn'a have known the ill deeds Jean's faither had used to get those crofts. So she seemed no' that far below him in station.'

"And I suppose the witch trials were rather in the past by then?" Phemie pondered. "They'd be what…twenty years before? So not the talk of the town anymore."

Hugh nodded. 'Aye, and on top o' that, the Captain met Jean o'er where she worked, she having risen to being a proper lady's maid to one o' the Kennedys across in Galloway.'

"So not on the doorstep of where the scandal was," concluded Phemie. "Yes, Jean would have escaped the tarnishing she might have got if she'd been closer to home. …So what happened, Hugh?"

'Well, the pair had been a mite foolish in trying to cut the loop o' the coast road off fer speed, but I can understand that by the time they heard o' the auld man's dying, they were awful short on time. Not that it was out o' any deep seated love fer him that they were going. Once they kenned who I was, they talked more freely. Katherine especially said she was going to piss on the auld de'il's grave fer the misery he put them and their poor ma through. Wanted to make sure he was six-feet deep and never coming back up!'

It made Anna think of how superstitious people were in those days, and that that might not have been the joke it would have been in more modern times. It was possible that there was a real fear of someone coming back and haunting you. Then did a mental double-take as she realised that right now *they* were being haunted, so why couldn't it have happened in the past? What would people have made of something like this in an age when religion dominated their lives far more than now? Moreover, without modern medical knowledge to ascertain a cause of death, if someone went into a coma, with very little pulse, and then came around, it might well seem like the dead had come back to life. So with a father like John Corsan, it was credible that his daughters would want to be sure he'd really gone, because his retribution if he came back and they'd done something he didn't like, probably didn't bear thinking about.

'We set off,' Hugh was continuing, 'but we ran into a beast of a thunderstorm on the morning after, when we should ha' made it to the funeral, and it was moving in the same direction as us and no' likely to blow over. We had to take shelter in an auld shepherd's hut fer that night, but the rain was so bad it brought part o' the roof down. Heavens, we were drenched. 'Tis a wonder we didn'a catch our deaths o' cold, fer we were soaked to the skin. And fer the rest o' the next day we only managed to move on to a farmer's barn, because all o' the streams were in spate like I'd rarely seen.

'So sadly we didn'a get to the kirk in time fer the service, though I wouldn'a have set foot inside Irongray's kirkyard wi' Veitch there. I wouldn't ha' been responsible fer what I might ha' done to the auld villain! In that sense, I was saved the trouble o' having to make excuses, fer the two women had been fair glad to see someone they knew, and I didn'a have the heart to tell them that their de'il o' a faither had murdered ma' ma. 'Twas naught to do wi' them, ye' see. They'd been out o' the home long afore that. No' like Him.'

"I presume you got them here, though?" Rita asked.

"Aye. I'd already seen what they were doing to this place, and I'd heard that Himself and the auld man had moved in. And this was closer than taking them to the townhouse in Dumfries. Plus I wasn'a sure there was anyone at the townhouse anymore. I didn'a want to traipse all the way there to find a locked door. They were sopping wet, cold, and hungry, and they needed to get warm pretty quick. Over the years, I'd got used to drenching, but it was hitting those two ladies hard.'

"It's nice that you call them ladies," Anna said warmly, "and can separate out the blame. A certain someone flings blame around like confetti…err, petals."

Hugh gave a withering snort. 'Aye, he's good at that.'

"So does He know that you met his sisters?"

'Oh, aye. I escorted them right up to this place. They tried awful hard to get me to come in and have a meal at least, which forced me to admit that things were no' so friendly between me and their brother. I have to say they took that better than I expected.'

Phemie leaned forward expectantly. "So did the sisters inherit anything from their father? A share in this place, perhaps? Is that how Jean's name crops up in the records?"

Hugh shook his head, but then grinned. 'Fer once the auld man slipped up. Seems he'd forgotten his daughters even still lived. It might ha' been the seizure by then, o' course, but they'd each left home as children and never gone back, so him being him, he might genuinely have forgotten he'd ever had daughters. He never set much store by women unless he could use them to get his filthy hands on property or money.' This last was said with real bitterness – understandable since that was what had happened to his own mother.

He brightened up again, though, as he added, 'The will said that his estate was to be shared equally amongst his heirs. I ken that, because a week or so later there was a message came to our quarters, asking if I might be spared to see the two ladies back home. That was no' our usual duties, ye' understand, but coming from one o' the Colonel's officers it wasn'a to be refused and I was sent to collect them.' He chuckled. 'No' that I was let anywhere closer to here than the end o' the drive. The serving man here – poor sod – had to wait i' the rain to tell me to stay there while he went and told the ladies I'd arrived.'

"He was paranoid, wasn't he!" Anna exclaimed.

'More like fit to have an apoplexy o' his own by then. Ye' see, the auld man had thought he was providing fer his darling M…other son, when he said that Himself would get the hoose, but the money was to be split equally, and the crofts and townhouse would go to his 'other heirs'. I reckon he meant the youngest son who died just months afore him as well as the older two, and by the time John died, I doubt the auld man had chance to change his will. And o' course,wi' Matthew being done fer murder, he couldn'a inherit anything either.

'The distribution had been left to the man o' law, ye' see, no' Himself – no doubt because the auld man didn'a trust any o' his sons not to cheat the others out o' stuff. And the man was fair and even-handed in his breaking up o' the money and properties, much to Himself's disgust. Katherine was overjoyed. She had no intention of spending even a night in a hoose the auld man had made his ain, but selling the townhouse would let her buy a nice place in Stranraer fer her and her daughter's family fer when the sailor came home. Said there might even be enough so that he wouldn'a have to risk going to sea again. Made her right happy, that did.'

"And what of Jean?" Anna asked eagerly.

'Well, she was o' the same mind as to not sleeping in the townhouse or any o' the crofts, but aside from one small one which Katherine also got, she had the rest to sell. She was more cautious, though. Said she needed to sort things out before her husband learned o' her good fortune. Seems that, at the time, her husband was only a captain because o' the death o' another. He'd need money to purchase a full captaincy.

'Now Jean wasn'a totally against that, but she wanted to make sure that she had a place o' her ain, on account o' her being in rented rooms while she followed him around. She'd had enough o' that, and had her eye on a nice wee place just outside o' Dumfries fer her and the bairns. Her man could have his captaincy, but here in the militia, no' the fancy regiment she kenned fine he'd have his eye on if he thought he could afford it. I gather he'd gone through the money he'd earned fighting in the Lowlands wi' rather more speed than Jean was happy wi', if ye' get ma drift.'

"Fascinating," Rita breathed, "and I'm guessing that the lack of money was why *Blackpark House* wasn't fully finished by the time the two of you died? Himself had a fine house but none of the money to make it grand, or at least not enough if he only got a third of what was left after what it must have cost to do the building work here. Good grief, I can see why that would have been salt in his wounds. After all that time to be cheated at the very last by sisters nobody had remembered must have felt like the witches' curses had come home again."

'Yer no' wrong,' Hugh sighed. 'I saw nought o' him maself, but I got called in to the castle where the officers were the next time the Colonel and the Captain were there. Got roundly thanked fer saving his wife, so I did, and like a fool, I dared to think this gave me a bit o' protection against Him making any more wild accusations against me.'

"Did he do that?" Rita wondered.

'Oh, aye. I heard a few rumours that he'd been cursing ma name up hill and down dale, but given that it was fer dragging sisters back who might usefully – to his mind – have perished at the hands o' righteous men – that last being probably prompted by bluidy Veitch – he got scant sympathy.'

"Did they catch the men?" Phemie asked.

‘Shot them where they were found out on the hillside,’ Hugh said with a grimace. ‘That was something I was never comfortable wi’. There should ha’ been some sort o’ court hearing if men were to die, but the likes o’ me got nae say in the matter.’

“So did Jean ever live here?” Anna wanted to know.

Hugh shook his head. ‘Neither o’ them did, her nor her man. That’s why it took so long fer our bodies to be found. Or so I think.’

Rita frowned in thought. “So who was it who threw Gi…Himself’s body into the river?”

Hugh was shocked. ‘Who on earth told ye’ that?’

“He did.”

‘Well he’s a bluidy liar, then!’

The three women looked to one another, baffled.

“Hugh, how do you know that?” Anna asked gently.

‘Because I saw them take him out and bury him i’ the garden. …Or rather, as I am now I saw that. I saw Katherine directing men to dig the hole, and then them carry him out and stick him in the ground.’ Hugh gave a mirthless laugh. ‘And after they’d left, I saw her go out, lift up her skirts, and piss on his grave too!’

“But what of your body?” Rita asked. “Where did that go?”

Hugh shrugged. ‘I’m no’ sure. I have this vague memory o’ a very short while after we died o’ someone being near to me. A woman. Could ha' been Katherine, could ha' been Jean, but I doubt Jean would ha' come back here after Himself tried to throw her down the stairs.'

CHAPTER 18

The three women were aghast.

"He did *what*?" Rita fumed, outraged at Gideon's violence towards his own sister.

'She made the mistake o' coming to see him when she and the Captain were next in Dumfries,' Hugh explained. 'Jean was the one most like their ma in temperament, and she was a good and kindly soul who didn'a deserve the life she got. The Captain couldn'a go wi' her, so he asked that I go instead.'

"Hang on, Hugh," Anna begged him. "I'm going to get Gary and Cameron up here too. They need to hear this." She ran out onto the stairs and leaned over, seeing Hugh and Cameron down in the main hall below. "You two! Up here!" she called, making frantic gestures, to which they responded by taking the stairs two at a time to reach her. "I think we're about to find out what happened at the end."

As Anna led them back into the attic room, Rita was saying, “Can you go back a bit Hugh. At what point did Jean make this visit to her brother? Was it soon after they’d inherited or not?”

‘Apologies, Mistress Rita. After all this time, it tends to muddle together, being so long ago.’

“Oh, that’s quite understandable,” Rita agreed, finding it vastly easier to be forgiving with Hugh when he was trying so hard, compared to Gideon’s twisting of the truth all the time. “So let me prompt you if that helps,” knowing that she could give a swift recap for Gary and Cameron in the process. “The old man died in…?”

‘1682.’

“Right. And we know that Isobel died in 1685 and that you died some time after that. So I’m guessing that what went on with Himself’s sisters happened in those three years in between?”

‘Ah yes! So it did.’ The prompt seemed to clear Hugh’s mind. ‘Aye, so it must ha’ been early 1684 when He started trying to pressure his sisters into giving him some more o’ the auld man’s money. Of course, I didn’a ken any o’ this until I was riding there wi’ Jean. He had letters written to them by his man o’ law, implying that he might try to claim his inheritance back through the courts, women no’ being allowed to hold property, ye ken.’

“I bet he came a cropper with that,” Anna observed, then realised that Hugh wouldn’t necessarily recognised the Midlands expression. “It didn’t work, I mean. Jean and Katherine sound a bit too astute for that.”

Hugh smiled. ‘I ken what ye’ meant just fine. And aye, he did, but no’ from any connivance o’ the ladies. ’Twas the law man who did the selling o’ the townhouse and crofts, see? And he had every cause to do so on account o’ legitimately overseeing the auld man’s will. So all he did was hand on the *money* to the sisters, no’ the crofts themselves. Might ha’ been different if Katherine’s man had still lived and wanted to farm the crofts. Or had the Captain wanted to step away from the army and at least be a landlord o’ crofters, but that wasn’a the case. But that was why it took so long fer them to have anything handed to them that Himself could ask them fer.’

“That must have stung,” Phemie agreed. “He probably struggled to even afford to heat this place, let alone do it up without his father’s money. A couple of years of penny-pinching just to survive here wouldn’t have done anything for his health and temper.”

‘It didn’a. Katherine, as Jean told me, simply sent a letter back saying he couldn’a have back what she’d already spent, though we both thought it more that she’d cannily tucked a fair bit away rather than spent it all at once. But Jean hated that now they were quarrelling all over again, and wanted to try to reason wi’ him. I told her there was nae chance o’ that, but she still wanted to try, God bless her.’

Then he stopped and shook his head with a frown. ‘What am I thinking! I’ve got this amiss. I’m so sorry. That first time I went wi’ Jean, we got nae further than him shouting at us through the upstairs window. Said he wouldn'a let her in if I was wi' her. 'Twas *after* that that he tried accusing her and Katherine o' being witches.' Hugh's expression at that was understandably bleak.

'He got nowhere wi' that, mainly because at last that auld villain Veitch had gone to answer to God fer his many sins. Wi'out rabble-rousing presbyters like him in charge, the accusations against women got thankfully fewer. Oh, I ken in other parts o' Scotland there were still times when women were in danger, but no' so much around here, thank God.'

Gary leaned in on his chair to ask, "So I'm guessing you thought that the women were generally safe? But then you went to Sanquhar and found Isobel being questioned. Is that the right order of things?"

Hugh gave a pained wince. 'Aye, it is. Well ye' ken how that went. After what happened wi' Isobel, I staggered about a fair while, living rough and getting what food I could. But eventually I resolved to get back up to Argyll and the McAllisters. At least there I kenned I had true friends. And having absconded from the army, I couldn'a call upon the Captain to save me, or at least, no' wi'out dragging Jean into the mess – and after the way Isobel and the other women got treated, I feared what would happen if folk started remembering what a dyed-in-the-wool Covenanter their faither was. I couldn'a do that to either o' them.'

The modern-day listeners all nodded in understanding of that.

'I still had enough o' ma wits to also know that I needed to get back on ma feet before attempting a journey o' that kind. Himself, I knew, would ha' put the poison down about me wi' the bailies' men in Dumfries, Kirkcudbright, and Wigtown, so I went further west again. I found a farmer who didn't ask too many questions.

'Oh, I was honest wi' him as much as I could be. Told him the truth, that I'd been swept up i' the army fer many years, and was heart-sick o' fighting ordinary folk. Made it clear that all I wanted was a bed and food in return fer ma work, and that he and his family had nought to fear from me. And I stayed there over the winter after Isobel died. I reckoned that by the time a year came around I'd ha' been forgotten about, and some other poor soul would be the latest man everyone was watching fer.

'I wasn'a wrong, either. I called in and saw Katherine to ask fer Jean's new place so that i could go and say farewell – I kenned where Katherine was, ye' see, but no' where the house was that Jean had bought – and got told ma name wasn'a remembered. Well I got to Jean's house and she was home alone wi' the bairns, the Captain being away. She asked me if I would do her the one last kindness o' going wi' her to here, only this time fer me to sneak around out o' view so Himself wouldn'a ken I was there. She said she'd wanted to try one last time to make peace wi' her brother, but didn'a dare to face him alone.'

Hugh paused and gazed off into the distance. 'I had the feeling that all was no' so well between her and the Captain by now. Kind of like she didn'a want her brother telling him something he could use against her. I didn'a ask, but I suspect her putting the family before his wants fer the captaincy hadn't gone as easily as she'd hoped.'

"That doesn't surprise me," Gary said knowingly. "I've seen a few army marriages fail when the wives get sick of being dragged around the world like spare baggage. Jean's not alone in that. Men who just never grasped that small children can't be yanked here there and everywhere to suit their father's career, and then blaming their wives when they have to go on postings abroad alone – and that's with the ones where there even are married quarters available. I've seen things get very acrimonious."

Hugh nodded. 'Aye, I've seen that, too. Yet I didn'a think there was the depth o' animosity from him that she got from her ain family, so ye're probably right that they simply started pulling in different directions. Well we got here, and I tied ma pony up around the back. Jean gave me time to sneak up on the hoose, and then when I waved to her to show her I was as close to the front door as I dared get, she rode in up the drive and knocked. By then, even McKay was gone, so Himself had to answer his ain front door, and they stood on the step arguing fer quite a while. Then I heard him say that she'd better come in – something about papers.

'I didn'a like the sound o' that, especially as it was a sudden change o' heart. I feared the bastard had something nasty up his sleeve, and so as soon as they'd gone in, I ran to the door and eased the latch again.' Hugh gestured down in the direction of the current front door. ''Twasn'a like now. The front door led straight into the main hall, so I had to be awful wary. I stood listening and realised that he was leading her upstairs. I thought that odd. From what others had said, I thought his sitting room was off to the left o' the hall, no' upstairs. That made me even more worried, and I crept in and hid in the shadow o' the stairs.'

Hugh paused and shuddered. 'Thank God I went everywhere armed by then. I started to hear him shouting at her. Vile stuff about her being a witch's spawn, no' their ma's. A changeling foisted onto the family.'

"Oh, that's bad," Rita told the others. "Being a changeling was another reason people – and women in particular – got taken in for questioning. That was a charge he might just have got to stick if he got heard by the right people.'

'Aye, he could ha',' Hugh agreed. 'That's when I started to go up the stairs. I thought it was time I got her outta there.' He paused and took a deep, shuddering breath, while his audience were practically holding theirs. 'I'd just got to the first turn when she came flying back towards me. All I could do was try and break her fall.

'…I did, but I was in a heap up against the balustrade, wi' her on top o' me, when He came down and saw us. …He went mad, and I mean mad, as in totally lost his mind.' Again Hugh shuddered. 'I've never seen someone change like that. No' even in the heat o' battle. Such a vile temper, and calling Jean a witch and me a witch's get who should ha' died in the fire alongside Ma. I've often wondered since then whether something o' the auld man lingered here, and in the dark o' night in his years here alone, it crept into Himself, because there was something aye dark in that man that day.'

"Oh dear God," Phemie gasped. "That's it! This is why he's so all over the place. It's not just the soul of Himself. There's something of the old man warped and twisted around him too. Heaven's, Rita, we have to do something about that or we'll never get him to leave when the two parts of him are pulling in different directions."

Rita was nodding gravely. "We'll talk about this over the way," she promised., nodding in the direction of the cottages. "But carry on, Hugh, we're not disputing any of what you're saying."

For that Hugh looked grateful. "So…I managed to roll Jean off me. She was shaken and a bit bruised, but no' badly hurt. I told her to run, because he'd turned and vanished back into a room, and I was sure I'd heard a flintlock being primed."

"Did she get away?" Cameron asked anxiously.

'I didn'a see her again, but then by the time I died, he wasn'a in any fit state to chase her either, so I think so.'

"And he shot you?" Gary prompted.

'Shot *at* me. Didn'a hit me, though I got a fair few splinters from the stair rail that it ripped apart. I drew ma dirk and charged him, and fer a while I had him on the back foot. But the trouble was, he was always uphill from me. I was always having to come at him *up* the stairs, while he had the advantage o' being higher than me. …I wasn'a the young fighting buck I'd once been, and I started to tire. And then we were grappling, and somehow he got ma sword from the strap on ma back. So now I only had the dirk and he had the advantage o' reach wi' the longer blade.'

Hugh shivered. 'He ran me through, but then he made the mistake o' standing back to laugh at me. It gave me the opening. I struggled to ma feet and shoved that dirk straight up into his belly, and up into his cold, black heart. …I must ha' passed out fer a moment, because when I came to, collapsed on the stairs, he wasn'a in front o' me anymore. I grabbed the rail and pulled ma'self to ma feet and saw him. He must ha' toppled over the rail, because he was lying a three-quarter's turn below me, bleeding out, but swearing he'd be the end o' me before he let me pass and escape him. …That's when I crawled up here, and the rest ye' ken.'

For a moment there was silence as the others absorbed the story.

"So could he have crawled up the stairs to the bedroom we threw him out of?" Rita wondered. "Did he die there, or have we got it wrong and he died on the stairs?"

Hugh could only shrug, answering, 'I had a belly wound, which ye' didn'a recover from but wasn'a instant death, but I stuck that long dirk right int'a his heart. I'd be surprised if he could climb that many stairs with that wedge in him. I'd say he died on the stairs.'

"Someone must have come here eventually after that, though," mused Anna. "I mean, even G…He…must have had deliveries of stuff. And you'd think that Jean would realise that you hadn't come back to find her. She might not expect her brother to care, but you'd shown that you would protect her. So you not reappearing must have struck her as worrying."

Hugh had to think about that. 'Aye, now ye' say it like that, I do recall bits and pieces. I'd passed on by then and ma head was in an awful muddle – I've had time since then to get used to this in-between world now, but those first years were so verra strange. As I am now, I think I recall hearing voices in here. No' Jean's, though. Men's.'

"She probably told her husband that her brother had attacked her and you, and he sent men," Gary suggested, yet Hugh frowned.

'I dinna think they were soldiers, no' least because I have vague memories o' their shock over how much blood there was. But aye, I have vague memories o' seeing a body in a winding sheet being carried out o' here, and that's around the time I saw Katherine in the garden. I reckon Jean was too shook up to come back and must ha' sent for her sister.'

"Was that the same body you saw being buried out in the garden?" Phemie wondered.

Hugh suddenly shot bolt upright in shock. 'Jesu God!' He was rigid. Stunned by what he'd clearly remembered.

"Take your time, Hugh," Rita said gently, going into dealing with combat veterans' mode.

'Ma plaid. …*Ma* plaid was wrapped around the body they took away. Aye, and in another sheet, too, no doubt to cover up the blood. That's no' me out i' the garden!'

And suddenly it was Cameron who guessed what had happened. "It's Him," and he jabbed an urgent finger in the direction of Gideon's lair. "Hugh's not talking about the rough grave Katherine pissed on, but the fancy tomb. Hugh's not in *there* – that's why he was barely aware of it until we mentioned it. There's no reason why he would have a connection to it. But Gideon knows, and that's what *Gideon* meant about being shoved in down by the river, while he thinks Hugh got the grand memorial, even if it's not his tomb. The river might even have run a bit closer to here back then, if it's silted up over the centuries on this side. *Gideon's* the one not on consecrated ground, and maybe not even in the commemorative tomb! And that's why he's so outraged at being despoiled."

"Especially if he saw his sister literally peeing on his grave!" Anna gasped. "Jean may not have ever had the nerve to come back here, but I bet she sent for Katherine in a hurry after the fright she got, and it was Katherine who came back here with men, took your body away for burial, Hugh, and dumped her evil shit of a brother in an unconsecrated grave in the garden. I wonder if we can find a grave for you-know-who somewhere, because that's likely to be where you got given a Christian burial in his place, Hugh. Blimey! What a revenge his sisters took on him. And the tomb-maker was right – there *is* a Covenanter in there, it's just not Hugh!"

They gave Hugh time to recover before leaving him alone, and then retreated back to Gary's cottage for much needed drams after all the excitement.

"Jeepers, that was a bit exciting, wasn't it!" Phemie said, collapsing onto a sofa with a sigh of relief. "Goodness me, Anna, my other excursions into the spirit world weren't anything like as complicated."

"Sorry, Nan," Anna apologised, feeling bad for having called her for help now. Asking a lady of her age to cope with all of this was probably a bit much to ask, so it was with relief that she heard Phemie's answer of, "No, don't apologise. This is more excitement than I've had in years. Just wait 'til I tell Davey!"

"To be honest," Rita confessed, "this is getting in a bit deep for me, too. How on earth we disentangle Gideon from whatever residue of his father's malignant spirit is entwined with his, I do not know."

"Would the nuns know?" Anna asked. As all eyes swivelled to her, she blushed and hurriedly added, "I know that might be a naïve question. I just thought that with them being *within* the Church, so to speak, that back in the day they might have had more experience of dealing with that sort of thing?" She saw them all looking at her agog and cringed as she hurriedly tried to explain further. "I mean, they must have had mental illness in those days, mustn't they? But without the recourse to modern drugs and stuff, there must have been a fair few folk dying who wouldn't rest easy. …Erm…stupid thought I know, but…"

"No, no!" Rita said flapping a hand towards Anna to make her stop. "No, not a stupid thought at all. This is far more in their realm than ours. Tomorrow morning we'll go and ask them. And well done, Anna for thinking that way, because it's just occurred to me that we'll have thirteen nuns, and nine witches, and the three of us. They might not have been able to deal with Gideon simply because they couldn't reach him, but with us in the present acting as a conduit and working together, they may be able to do more than we can."

CHAPTER 19

The following early morning's conversation with of all of the ghosts in the old kirk was enlightening. All of them confirmed that it was a matter of reaching Gideon, not dealing with him, which had stopped them resolving things long ago. Moreover, once it was suggested to the witches that old John Corsan's spirit might in part be lingering within Gideon's, they were swift to say that they could feel something of him, but had mistaken it for his paternal connection within Gideon. Them having known him in the flesh, this was the confirmation the others needed.

''Tis no' all o' him by any means,' Margaret Clark told them, 'but there's surely some o' that evil auld goat twisted around his son. I feel bad now fer always blaming Gideon fer the evil I felt rolling out o' the old hoose all these years. We should ha' picked up on the possibility long ago.'

"No, please don't blame yourselves," Rita said firmly. "In all of my time dealing with restless spirits, this is the first time I've ever come across one infesting another spirit – rather than someone living – with evil intent. And I think it's fair to say that the only reason old John got the chance to do this to Gideon was because they are close blood relatives. Whichever way you explain that link – whether by science as we do, or by spiritual link as you might – I think that Gideon was so damaged by his wicked father that it was easier than it might have been for the old devil to latch onto him."

"So we were thinking," Anna said tentatively, "that you might know of a way to separate them out? Because we think that if we can get rid of old John, then Gideon won't put up as much of a fight." And she went on to explain what they'd discovered about the tomb in the garden. "Cameron, here, is going to apply to the council to get the tomb opened up under the guise of getting some restoration work done. That way, we can open it up and find out if Gideon's bones are really in there. To be honest, we're praying that they are, because then it should be relatively simple to get them taken to consecrated ground and leave this as just an empty memorial. Do any of you have any memory of bones being put in there?"

None of the witches did, but the prioress and two of the other nuns said that they could recall someone coming and digging up a body.

"That was back closer to the time these ladies died," the prioress added. "But I have no recollection of the body going back into the ground around here," hurriedly qualifying that with, "It's not that we could reach so far as to be able to watch, you understand, but it calls to us when people nearby are praying. We hear more than we see."

Phemie nodded. "That makes sense. If Gideon died in or around 1685, and then someone came along in say the 1770s and found him, even in those days you wouldn't just dump a body back in the ground. Not when it isn't a consecrated graveyard. Yes, some wealthy people were able to have special places made into their family burial areas, but that would have to have been done with the express consent of the main Church of the time."

Gary agreed with her. "Even the Kirk – the one without bishops – hung on to its right to claim the burial fees for a community. Sorry to sound jaded, Prioress, but the high-up men in the Kirk kept a very earthly eye on the coffers in any age. That probably means that Gideon got taken off to an unmarked pauper's grave, and thrown in with a lot of other anonymous people. But it also means that the local folk of the time would have wanted the local priest, or minister, or presbyter, to do his job and say the appropriate words over him. Folk were very frightened by the prospect of unquiet spirits hanging around. So if you never heard or felt someone doing that, then I think it's safe to say that we have a simple memorial out in the grounds, not an actual tomb."

"It won't hurt to make absolutely certain," said Cameron with a nod, "and what you've said about the late eighteenth century as a date, Phemie, makes me think that looking in the archives at the local newspapers of the day might still be a worthwhile effort. There can't have been that much going on in a small county town like Dumfries that the discovery and re-interment of a body would go uncommented upon. It has to have been worth a column or two on one of the inside pages, if not headline news."

"So do we try and get rid of old John now?" Anna wondered. "Or do we wait until we have more information? I guess what I'm trying to ask is: if we separate them out now, can we be sure we can despatch old John to the hereafter so that he can't worm his way back to Gideon? Because one or the other of them is going to have to go the moment we separate them."

Rita heaved a sigh. "Bloody good question. For what it's worth, my instinct is to not do the separating until we can be sure of sending Gideon off pretty swiftly. Indeed, I'm wondering whether we weakened Gideon when we broke his link to the bedroom, because despite what Hugh said about Gideon's wound, I reckon Gideon did manage to crawl up to that room to die. And very much like our nuns being weakened by the stone slabs they died upon being dispersed, maybe chasing Gideon out of his room has left a chink in his armour for his father to surface a bit more? If he's not here, then there's nothing for old John to try to bounce back onto. And I don't know if you ladies on the Other Side agree, but I don't think there can be enough of old John left that he could hang on here on his own. If there was, I think we'd have seen him manifesting as a nasty and violent ghost all by himself – he wouldn't have needed to piggy-back onto Gideon."

With there being a general agreement over that, Rita had another question for the witches. "Are there any of you who would like to leave now? I give you my solemn word that Gideon will not be left to harm any others. If the worst comes to the worst, we will do a proper exorcism with a priest, but that could be very rough for those of you on the periphery. I've only ever been involved in two of those, and they were horrible for the living involved. I have no idea of what one might be like for nearby spirits who might feel the backlash of one."

The witches and the nuns went off into a ghostly huddle, with Agnes Clark eventually coming back to tell them, "We've agreed that Jean and Janet McGown will help you take Bigis through to the Light – they lived close to her in life and have always been the ones who could calm her after we died. Bigis is the most fragile of all o' us, and we dread to think how it might affect her if Gideon and Auld John really fight you back. And Janet McNaught and Jennat Callen will help you to take Helen to the Light, for she is another who was no' in her right mind even afore the torment she suffered, and they too lived near to her."

Anna did a quick tally in her notebook. "So that will leave you, Agnes, and your sister Margaret.

Also, your mum, Geillis – who is also Jonet's sister-in-law and Hugh's beloved Elspeth's mum – and Jonet herself. And with you will be Hugh's mum, Jannet Corsan, and Grissell, who is Hugh's grandmother."

Rita was counting, and with a glance to Phemie, said, "Hmm, shame we can't have seven of you. Seven is a number with some power, but I agree with what you've said about getting those others to safety before we start. But I also think there might be some power in the fact that Geillis, Grissell, and Jonet make a trio of those who died from being questioned or as a result of the evil old John did. While Agnes, Margaret, and Jannet are three who died directly at his behest. If we combine that with the three strongest from amongst you ladies, Prioress, then we have three times three on your side, and that is *really* powerful."

At this point Anna, Gary, and Cameron had to leave to go to work, but Rita and Phemie stayed on to discuss methods. Sometime later, Rita came to tell Anna that she and Phemie were heading into Dunfries for 'supplies' but didn't enlighten her further. However, when she got in from her shift, her cottage was full of the scent of herbs and spices.

"Blimey, Aunty, Nan! It smells like an alchemist's shop in here," she said, shrugging off her smart jacket, and coming to the kitchen table where the two older ladies had bundles of herbs spread out, and a couple of mortars and pestles in use.

"We're brewing up two separate lots," Phemie explained. "The first one, which we've made in quantity, will ease our six lady ghosts to the Light but also weave a web of protection around them, just in case it starts Gideon and his damned father off on a shouting match. For them we've added in things like lavender and rose so that it feels loving and warm. Some of it is a paste that we'll make protection symbols with on the walls of the kirk, but we'll also water it down and filter it to make a spray we can use on the doors and windows. We're making this now so that it has time to infuse and blend in the pots."

Rita nodded, shoving a stray strand of hair back off her face and creating a streak of green from the herbs in the process. It made Anna smile, because Rita looked the epitome of an eccentric kitchen witch, with her stained apron and shoved-up sleeves, totally regardless of her own appearance. In contrast, Phemie had somehow managed to stay clean and tidy, and could have been a poster advert for a modern witch, standing there in her trendy trainers and Scandi-style wrap-around pinafore, which hardly had a mark on it. Yet both of them looked in their element, and Anna could almost feel the power rolling off them as they worked.

"When are we going to do it?" she asked, going to the kettle to make herself a cup of decaf and the other two ones as well. "I presume you've picked some suitable auspicious date?"

Rita nodded, putting the pestle down and decanting the paste she'd been making into a jar, which she screwed the top down on again as soon as she'd done. "This coming Thursday for the ladies. It's Lammas, or Lughnasadh, and so a time for celebration. It's one of the fire festivals but also one of the harvest celebrations, so it's got that element of things coming to fruition, which I think is appropriate for ending those poor souls' time of lingering here. We'll have the kirk full of candles and light. Nowhere for anything to lurk unseen in the dark."

"And Gideon and old John?"

Rita accepted her mug of coffee off Anna, answering, "On Saturday night. It's a new moon. You should know by now that that's good for new beginnings, and there'll still be some residual positive energy left from Thursday night."

"But we also thought," Phemie added, accepting her own mug off Anna, "that doing it on a Saturday night might be more easily explained away if things get rowdy in the hotel. We're going to have to tackle the two male ghosts in the hotel itself. There's no way around that. So on a night when you can say that you had some noisier than expected guests, it might deflect any comments from guests."

"Good thinking, Nan. Luckily we're in that weird mid-summer slight lull, when all the kids are on school holidays – both north and south of the border – and with us not having much to offer modern kids, we don't really get many families in. Plus a family of four or more for a whole week would work out a bit pricey with us. And our older couples avoid the school holidays like the plague, so we're quieter with them. So it's mainly business people coming in at the moment.

"No weddings for another two weeks, either, which is good – nothing to set Gideon off and no need to use the honeymoon suite. Friday night we're rammed with people in transit between holidays and home, but Saturday we've far fewer people in, and I've put all of them in the back range of rooms or the round tower as a precaution, anyway. We're not so quiet that folk will think it odd if things do get noisy, but none of our guests will be in any danger…I hope! But we've a slew of weddings in late August and early September, so having this place peaceful by then would be a blessing."

Come the late Thursday afternoon, Anna handed over at the hotel to Brenda, who had been told of what was happening and guaranteed that Anna would not be called upon. Together with Rita and Phemie, they went around the inside of the old kirk's nave, anointing symbols as directed by Rita, and repeating three versions of the Lord's Prayer – one in Latin for the nuns; one in Gaelic, which was the nearest they could source a version for the witches; and one in the King James Bible version, which they hoped would resonate with Gideon and old John without being too inflammatory.

They'd had to resort to practising with YouTube videos to get the pronunciation right on both the Latin and the Gaelic, the Gaelic being by far the harder. Only Rita had heard much in Scottish Gaelic for all that Phemie had lived most of her life in her homeland.

"I'm afraid I never watch the Gaelic TV channel," she confessed. "I've never really had much interest in the language. I think I'll be going home and dragging Davey off to a few language classes after this, though."

"Good grief, Nan," Anna protested as she followed Rita around the kirk, lighting the candles and tea-lights Rita was setting out. "At your age that's going it a bit – no disrespect meant – but learning a new language in your eighties won't be easy. I'd struggle at that."

"You're never too old to learn," Phemie said with a wag of her finger as she prepared the little dishes with charcoal discs in, which would have incense resins put on them when lit. This time there'd be no cheap incense sticks – Rita had raided her supplies of genuine frankincense, myrrh, and Palo Santo for this.

Rita had also consulted her lunar calendar and so once the kirk was prepared, they retreated to Anna's to prepare themselves. They weren't going across to the kirk again until just after midnight to be there for moonrise around one a.m., and so they had a light meal and then Rita led them in a meditation to calm them and get them into the right state of mind. Gary and Cameron were on standby in Gary's cottage, but had agreed to stay out of the way unless something went very wrong and for some reason the ladies needed their help. And as

Rita had confessed, that might be more in the case of a medical emergency than anything they could do physically.

They went across just after Anna's old mantel clock struck midnight and began by lighting the candles, then the incense. Once more they repeated the three versions of the Lord's Prayer, and then Rita and Phemie opened up the portal with Anna only able to join in where told.

"I call you to come forward now," Rita said gently. "I call the first three who are going home to come to us."

"Janet McGown, are you ready?" Anna called, and a woman swam into view and became more distinct until she was almost in front of Anna.

"Jean Thomson, are you ready?" Phemie called, and the second woman hurried forward so eagerly that Anna felt she must have been aching for this day for a very long time.

"Agnes Cairns…are you there?" Rita called gently. There was a faint swirling, but no real definition of a woman. "Come on sweetheart," Rita urged her. "Time to rest. Time to let all this pain go."

'Come on, Bigis,' Jean called, holding out her hand, as if to a child, and Janet did the same.

Even so, the figure of a small and distressed person only lurked on the edge of the portal. Behind her the other witches and nuns lined up, gently shooing her to head towards it, but Bigis was resistant.

"They aren't here, Bigis," Anna said, guessing what might be holding this damaged soul back. "They're over in the big house. They can't touch you if you come to us. We've made sure of that."

The little figure shuffled forward a bit more.

'He ain't on the other…?' and she made a vague gesture with her hand towards where Rita had already opened the way to a beautiful white light.

"Who, sweetheart?" Phemie asked. "Gideon?"

There was a strange sort of shrug and shake of her head, so it seemed that Bigis wasn't afraid of only Gideon.

"Old John?" Rita guessed. "He's not here, either."

But then it was Jean who guessed who it was. 'Oh Lord, she's afeared that being a kirk-man, Thomas Wylie, is waiting fer her on t'Other Side!'

"The man who raped you?" Anna gasped. "Oh, Bigis, no! A man that evil would surely never have made his way to where you are going. Just because he was a minister here on earth in his day, it doesn't mean he got the heavenly reward he might have expected." She was grasping at straws here. After all, she was the last person here who had a clue as to what Heaven might look or feel like. She'd barely set foot in a church throughout her life, let alone studied the Bible. But something deep in her soul was saying that a man who had committed such evil during his life would surely not be able to prey upon his victims again in the afterlife.

Then Anna thought back to what she knew of Bigis' trial. She'd had ten men accuse her, so had any of those testified to her being a witch to avoid her naming them as further rapists? And of course, Bigis had committed suicide, which in her day had been thought a mortal sin.

"Bigis," she began softly, getting up and taking a couple of steps towards the witches' portal, but not enough to break their own circle. "Come to me, Bigis. Please." The sad little figure shuffled a few feet nearer. "Did those men threaten you? The ones who testified against you?"

She got a miniscule nod of the head, but Bigis still wouldn't turn her face to Anna.

"Bigis…did those other men rape you too?" This time there was a more positive nod. "And was one of them Thomas Milligan, the man whose house you lived in?"

There was another nod, at which Margaret Clark came right to the fore. 'If ma evil shite o' a husband is around when I reach the Other Side, I'll have more than a few words to say to him!' she snarled. 'Dinna you fret, Bigis, he'll regret ever doing what he did to you and me.'

It wasn't quite the reconciliatory tone Rita had been hoping for, but her former mistress' words seemed to reassure Bigis somewhat. She was still hanging back a little, though.

"Are you worried what will happen because you took your own life?" Anna wondered, keeping her voice gentle.

'Ah didn'a! Ah *didn'a*!' Suddenly Bigis was right there, close to them with Jean and Janet. 'I *wouldn'a*! 'Tis a sin. I kent that. I *always* kent that.'

And suddenly Anna remembered something she'd read about the trial. "You said that the Devil strangled another woman in Kirkcudbright Tolbooth when you were questioned, didn't you? …But they misunderstood what you said, didn't they?"

Bigis nodded.

Probing very carefully, Anna asked. "Did you mean a real man? A man you thought was the Devil incarnate?"

At last Bigis' shattered gaze turned up to Anna's, making Anna realise what a small little soul Bigis must have been, because very few people had to look up to her, normally it was her getting a crick in her neck looking up at them. And her first thought was what an innocent face it was, even after all she'd been through.

Then like a bolt from the gods, it pounded in on her what the attraction of Bigis had been. That almost winsome expression, and the big eyes lacking any guile. No obvious breasts, and Anna had to believe she appeared in the afterlife as she had in reality. She was like a child! A little *girl*, not simply a small woman. They had been paedophiles who had raped her, taking an underdeveloped and naïve woman when they couldn't get an actual child to satisfy their warped fantasies.

"Oh Bigis!" Anna gasped, tears suddenly streaming down her face. "Those bastards. To cover what they did to you under the cover of the Kirk. You're only little now, but did this start when you were still a child?"

Bigis nodded, and behind her, Anna heard Phemie and Rita's gasps as they too realised what Anna was talking about.

"A paedophile ring," Anna said over her shoulder to them, though she couldn't see them through her tears. Turning back to Bigis, she said, "And I'm guessing that you were already so frightened that when the men carried on once you were grown up, you didn't dare tell anyone?" She got a tiny nod. "Did one of them come to you in the tolbooth after the trial?"

'He said I mu'nt call out in ma pain,' she replied. 'Said I had t' go now. I were a shameful thing. No' to be brought int' the light o' day.'

Behind Anna there was a horrified gasp of, "Oh!" from Rita as she realised Bigis' muddling of the Light to which they were trying to draw her, and the wicked man's reference to light. Getting up from her chair too, with Phemie rising up as well, Rita took steps forward to come alongside Anna.

"Sweetheart, the Light we're talking about is a wonderful thing. What that evil man said about you staying in the dark…it doesn't mean *this*."

'He said Ah was too wicked a thing to be seen i' the light,' Bigis said in such a sad voice that all three women were now in tears. 'He said ma sins were so great, good Christian folk mu'nt ever look upon me fer fear o' the De'il taking their souls too. That if I came int' the light, the sight o' ma face would send other t' Hell just looking at me.'

"No!" Anna, Rita, and Phemie cried in unison, with Phemie adding, "What an evil, wicked lie to tell you."

Cuffing her eyes, Rita said, "You have a sweet little face, Bigis. No decent person could take offence looking at you. He said that to hide *his* sins, and probably to hide the sins of his cronies, too. Just the sight of someone can't do that kind of harm – if it could, then Presbyter Veitch's congregation would have been dropping like flies given the amount of sins hanging around *his* neck. You can go into the Light and be completely safe, my lovely."

'I'll no' drag anyone t' Hell if they go wi' me?' she asked hopefully, looking at Jean and Janet, who were on either side of her.

They all shook their heads, and suddenly a smile broke out on Bigis' face, probably the first one in decades, and she held out her hands to Jean and Janet.

After that, the flesh and blood women had to resort to tissues to sort themselves out, but then it was comparatively easy for Rita to open the way fully for the three. With one backward glance and a smile from each, the three tormented women walked forward into the Light and vanished from view. It was then little surprise that the other Janet and Jennat hurried forward eagerly, bringing Helen Moorheid with them.

Helen was very different to Bigis, more what the modern women would expect of someone who had received a brain injury in an accident. She seemed merely distracted, as if struggling to focus at all, rather than Bigis' level of distress. She certainly wasn't worried about drawing near to the Light, and she walked through with her friends without a backwards glance.

"Good grief, that was traumatic," Phemie said afterwards, as they gratefully collapsed onto the sofas at Gary's, while he and Cameron plied them with herb tea and biscuits.

Rita nodded. "And well done Anna for picking up on what happened to Bigis," she said, then explained to Gary and Cameron.

"Christ almighty," Gary swore when she finished. "Poor wee Bigis. What a terrible thing for her to have lived wi' all this time. It's too late to be able to set the score straight over those other men, not least because we don't know who they were, and we don't know whether the preacher man and Margaret's husband were part o' that ring, or just nasty bastards into rape o' the more normal kind – though regarding rape o' any kind as normal makes me want to puke."

"If there actually is such a thing as Hell," Cameron said with feeling, "then I really hope those men are rotting in it."

CHAPTER 20

Anna was grateful that they had arranged for her to take the late shift on Friday. It meant that despite getting to bed in the early hours of Friday morning, she managed to get a full eight hours' sleep, although she woke several times after nightmares of terrified small girls being pursued by crow-like men in flapping clerical garb. So she was grateful when Cameron came around with Harris and Lewis at midday, and asked if she'd like to go for a drive before her shift started at four o'clock.

"That would be lovely," she immediately agreed.

"Where would you like to go, then?"

"Well we can't go too far afield in the time we've got, but do you know what? I'd like to see what Lagg Castle was like." Cameron looked surprised, forcing Anna to explain, "I had the completely wrong impression that it must be over

Wigtown way, but it isn't. It's not that far down the road from here."

Cameron blinked in surprise. "This is the bloke known as Cruel Lagg? The one who the crows wouldn't leave be until he was buried?"

"That's the chap. But get this, Cam – I've discovered since then that he also had a pet monkey who he named after a famously tried witch, one Major Weir. I think these days we'd diagnose Weir with some kind of PTSD, meaning he was sleep-deprived and hallucinating even before they got their hands on him, because the poor soul seems to have ranted on about having sex with the Devil and stuff. Mind you, he was getting on a bit at the time – especially for that era – so it could equally have been dementia, and he dragged his poor elderly sister into the mire with him. She supposedly confessed, but given everything we now know about how such confessions were obtained, I don't think either of us would put much store by that, do you?

"But as for Grierson, it's a bit freaky, calling your pet after a supposed warlock who got burned to death, isn't it? If anything gives credence to the idea that Grierson had a bee in his bonnet about witches as well as Covenanters, and that's why Hugh's Isobel and her companion Grissell died such gruesome deaths with the other two women at Wigtown, then that surely does. And also may explain why they died witches' deaths, not dissenters'."

"So why on earth do you want to see where he lived?" Cameron asked, slightly worried that this was taking too much of a toll on Anna.

She gave a huff, and sat back in her sofa. "It's not that I'm obsessing on the grim, if that's what you're worried about. I just want to see how much higher up the food chain the Griersons of Lagg were to the Corsans, that's all. Were they way above him, or just a whisker higher? Was Gideon creeping around someone high above him, or appealing to a man of a similar status? Because I can't think of anything still standing and being adverised on the tourist routes that would count as a *major* country pad close to here, can you? So if we get a chance, can we go and have a look at the Douglases' pad at *Drumlanrig Castle*, too? I know we haven't got time to go around it today. I just want to see for myself what it looks like and how *much* bigger it was. Why they had such a hold over this area."

"Fair enough. Get your coat. We're going exploring – but you'd better have had some map reading lessons off Gary, because I'm not sure my sat nav will find this castle at Lagg."

Sure enough, the tower at Lag or Lagg, depending on where you looked it up, was just north-east of the tiny village of Dunscore, just a bit north of where they were. All that remained was the ruined finger of a tower, pointing skywards in a leaden sky, which was promising a good downpour before too long. It loomed gloomily above a farmhouse, and in its day must have dominated the surrounding landscape and the small cottages most folk would have lived in, but it certainly wasn't huge as castles went, and even on a lowering day like today, wasn't that threatening.

"I thought it would be bigger for such an influential man," Anna mused as they stood outside of Cameron's car taking in the scene, holding firmly onto Harris and Lewis who were more interested in the sheep. "Granted, most of it is probably ruined now, and once upon a time it might have had a house tacked onto the side, but don't you think that the footprint of it isn't *that* big?"

Cameron stood back and surveyed the tower for a moment.

"What are you thinking, Cam?"

"Well in Gideon's shoes, and thinking about the size our tower-house must have been, do you think that Gideon thought himself not that much below the Griersons by the time it was done and he fully inherited it?"

Anna took her time digesting this. "Yes, I see what you mean. This is older, and would have been an established house of note when *Blackpark* was just a building site, but size-wise, *Blackpark* had to be coming on for the same once completed. Are you saying that this affected how Gideon behaved?"

"I think it might have. If he thought he was the new big kid on the block, for want of a better analogy, then maybe the whole reason he took Isobel towards where Grierson held court was because he thought he could sway his opinion?"

"Oh, God! Then he *was* trying to save her. He was taking her to somewhere where, in his admittedly mistaken and arrogant view of the world, he thought he could influence people to look more kindly on Isobel."

Cameron dared to add what he'd been thinking, which was, "Don't forget that by then, Gideon was a widower, and after Edward died his gruesome death up at Sanquhar, so was Isobel – a widow, I mean. Did he think that if he offered to marry her and keep her under control, that Grierson would spare her life?"

Anna turned to Cameron, appalled. "Dear God, that's a twisted way of looking at things, but heavens, Cam, I think you may have the right of it. Yes, after so many conversations with him, I can imagine that that might have been the way he would think. Let's face it, he can't have been ignorant of the size of Lagg Tower, when it's virtually on his doorstep, can he? It's not that far from Irongray, either. Do you think that Gideon might have dared to hope that old Veitch's rule might have held sway as far as here, and that thing going on between Veitch and old John might then sway things his way here? I guess I'm saying, did Gideon think that Grierson was as afraid of Veitch as he was?"

Cameron sighed. "It's a thought, isn't it? I definitely think that we have to stop thinking that Gideon was acting malevolently towards Isobel, because if we show a bit of understanding of what he was trying to do, that might be one of the ways we can separate him out from his father. And I think we have to ask him if he came with Isobel to Lagg *first*, and finding that Grierson wasn't at home but at court, *then* rode for Wigtown? Because that puts a rather different slant on things, doesn't it? He wasn't dragging her straight to a court at all. And if Hugh was tracking them, this detour might have confused him as to where Gideon was going, as well. It would explain why he didn't try to cut across country to catch them up if he couldn't make sense of where their tracks were going."

Anna looked at him worriedly. "Heavens, that's quite a thought, Cam, and I have to say that I think you have several damned good points there. We have to tell Aunty Rita about that. So how much above Gideon and Grierson of Lagg were the Douglases, then? I think we need to go and see *Drumlanrig Castle* more than ever, now."

Yet both of them were rendered nearly speechless when they pulled into the car park there. The house was open, but they didn't go in, instead taking the dogs for a walk around the gardens to view the place from the outside. As Anna said, "The folk we're dealing with wouldn't have got any closer than this. They'd hardly be invited inside, would they? So we'll know as much as they did from out here."

But what a place *Drumlanrig* was! Vast compared to Lagg or what the tower-house at *Blackpark* must have been, it was also obvious that this was heading into a totally different architectural era. Lagg was a relic of the previous age, a fortification for repelling raiders. And if *Blackpark* had been an effort to create one of the newer style tower-houses, nonetheless it was still backwards looking to a time when great houses needed to be fortified. *Drumlanrig* imposed itself on the landscape through grandeur alone. 'How dare you question my right to rule you?' it seemed to challenge all who saw it.

Four storeys rose all along the building, with the towers adding fifths where they rose higher, and the endless tall windows spoke of incredible wealth in a time when glass was expensive and beyond the means of ordinary folk. It wasn't quite as grand as somewhere like *Chatsworth House*, which just predated it, or *Blenheim Palace* which would be completed within fifty years of it, but it was having a damned good go at evoking the same level of luxurious living, late-seventeenth-century style.

Anna took in the huge building from one of the garden terraces and observed, "In the medieval era, down in England they used to call the earls of Warwick the king makers. Well I reckon up here and in their time, the Douglases must have held the same kind of power. In that respect, Hugh was much more astute about the men of power, wasn't he? He reckoned that the Captain Ferguson who was no relative of his, but the husband of Jean Corsan, would have enough sway to protect him, because if you were the favourite of a man of *this* family, you can see that he was quite right. Whereas Gideon – warped by his father's way of power-playing – thought he could bluff and connive his way into getting Grierson to be lenient with Isobel, and lost badly."

Cameron agreed. "Gideon played his cards totally wrong, didn't he? And I can appreciate now what Hugh always knew – which is that the Douglas family were so high above everyone else in these counties that they were effectively a law unto themselves. No wonder Colonel Douglas literally got away with the murder of Covenanters. Who around here would dare to tell him to stop if his own family didn't? Even if you got as far as having the courage to ride here to protest, I reckon you'd get as far as the gates, take one look at this place, lose all hope, and turn around."

They returned to the car to make the drive back, the oncoming rain doing nothing to raise their spirits in what had turned out to be far from the uplifting morning Anna had hoped for. However, Rita and Phemie agreed that what they'd surmised would be helpful when they came to deal with Gideon. Gary had gone to Dumfries, because after they'd finished the night before, Phemie had rung home, and hearing her distress, Davey had said he'd be on the morning train over, from which Gary was now collecting him.

When he arrived, Anna's grandfather turned out to be the kind of grandfather she'd always dreamed of. Slightly portly, wearing well-worn jeans and a battered army-surplus sweater, he swept her into a hug without hesitation, wrapping her in a scent of new-mown grass and wood-smoke. Like some real-world Tom Bombadil, Davey Clark was a man of the earth, kindly and full of common sense, and it was instantly visible how he and Phemie complemented one another.

"Ach, I can see your cousins in you," he told Anna with a grin.

"I have cousins?" she gulped. It was ridiculous. Of course she must have cousins with her mother having older siblings. It was just that never having heard of them, the idea of them came a bit out of the blue.

"Ten of them," he answered with a laugh, "though we'll be kind and not introduce you to them all in one go. They're a bit of a handful when they all get together, but I can tell you that Paige is dying to meet you already. She's probably the nearest to you in age. Then there's our Holly. She, poor lass, has had a bit of rough time o' it after our William – her dad – died in a car crash. We never set much by his wife. Nice lass but a bit of a fluff-head, if you get my meaning. She's our other granddaughter we've long wanted to get up here and closer to us. Finally meeting you gives me hope that we might manage that too."

However, the rest of the family history had to wait because Anna had to go to work, and Phemie and Rita wanted to bring Davey up to date on what was happening on Saturday. Yet after that, they both felt the need to go and tell the two ghosts what Anna and Cameron had come up with, because easing Gideon's guilt and giving him time to take it in might make all the difference to how he felt about leaving. Together they went up to Gideon with Phemie taking the lead, and with the intention that they would swop over when it came to Hugh.

As Phemie explained what they'd been guessing, Gideon's face was a picture.

'Ye' didn'a think I took Isobel to Lagg wi' the *intention* o' him punishing her, did ye'?'

Phemie sighed, "Well you didn't exactly bother explaining things to us or anyone else, did you, dear? So all we knew was that you rushed in and took Isobel and young Grissell, and the next thing we hear, they are being tried by Grierson – we know nothing of what went on in between."

Gideon moaned in distress. 'I took them to Lagg first, like you said. Ach, Grierson liked t'play the big man, but Lagg was no' better than here by then. I was o' half a mind to bring Isobel back here and wait fer him, but then I heard that Veitch had had word o' Isobel being taken fer a witch, and I was scairt he would come here looking fer me to join in a hunt fer her. So the quicker I got her away and pardoned, the better. When I got to Wigtown, I tried to say I would marry Isobel and keep her in order, but Lagg wasn'a listening. Instead he was crowing to the others about how they would make examples o' these degenerate women, on account o' him now being in somehow wi' the Duke o' York, or was it King James by then? I canna recall. Damn him, Lagg was as bad as bluidy Veitch!' And he covered his face with his hands and sobbed.

'I kept saying to him, that they were no' that bad, but every word got twisted. When I said they were no' Covenanters like the other women, he turned it around to say that they were Godless, and must be witches. And when I then said they were no' witches, he asked if they'd been questioned to make sure o' that? Asked if I had been enchanted by them to come and make a plea on their behalf. Nothing I said got taken as it was meant,' and he sobbed again.

"Oh Gideon, I'm so sorry," Phemie consoled him and meant it. However much of a pain in the neck Gideon was, his was truly a case of the road to Hell being paved with good intentions. "It must have been terrible to watch Isobel being flogged through the town."

''Twas dreadful. Too many soldiers to get to her. All I could do was shove my way through the crowd to keep pace wi' her. Then when she fell…by the shore…when I saw all her blood…all I could do was wait until the soldiers had marched the others out to the stakes, and then pick her up. Oh Lord Above, she was light as a feather. There was naught left o' her. And even though I ran wi' her up to the tolbooth, by the time I got there she was gone. I couldn'a even get that right. Couldn'a get her there fast enough to bind her wounds and save her.'

"Gideon," Rita now chipped in firmly. "Listen to me. Anna went to where Isobel fell. Just like we're talking to you now, she made a connection to Isobel." She and Phemie saw his head come up. "Gideon, Anna felt Isobel die down there by the river bank. You didn't fail her. She was dead by the time you could even get to her. Her dying wasn't your fault."

Granted, Rita felt she could have made a fair point for it being Gideon's fault for being daft enough to take her to Grierson of Lagg in the first place, because Grierson sounded a right nasty piece of work. But she wasn't going to say that now, because Gideon's whole demeanour was changing.

'It wasn' ma fault? She was deid already?' The weight of that guilt was almost visibly lifting from him. So Cameron had been right – having been blamed for everything for all of his life, finding he truly was guilty through his own actions and nobody else's had been more than Gideon could bear.

"You can rest now," Phemie said gently. "You won't be punished for this," and Gideon faded away into his lair, for once weeping in relief.

Hugh's reaction was more as they expected.

'The bluidy fool!' was his first response. 'Why in God's name did he think he could sway a man like Grierson?'

Then as Rita explained in more detail, her own exasperation now able to be expressed, Hugh reached a point where he too was simply shaking his head in disbelief.

'Ye' say that Anna had a connection to Isobel at her last?' he asked when they'd got through the tangled story.

"She did," Rita confirmed, "and I think it sorts out why Himself thought Isobel loved you. You see, Anna felt her calling out to Grissell to hold on, and that you would come, but I suspect that with Himself being not that near to her, all he heard was your name. That's been salt in the wound of his guilt all these years. He never gave poor Grissell Asman a second thought once the women were in Wigtown tolbooth. All he thought about was Isobel. Whereas Isobel was the kind soul you knew her for, and her thoughts were that even if you couldn't save her – because Anna says she knew she was dying – she wanted to give Grissell the hope that she might yet live."

They both saw Hugh's bleak expression.

"No, Hugh," Phemie said urgently. "Please don't blame yourself any more on that account. As we've said, you couldn't possibly have guessed that your old enemy would be daft enough to go to Lagg and then on to Wigtown. And we may not have to do things the hard way as you did when trying to find someone, but we do know enough to know that all you could do was follow the ponies' trails when you were so far behind, and hadn't a clue what he was planning. He's still at fault. We're just giving him a bit of consolation so that he isn't scared out of his wits over what will lie on the Other Side for him."

Rita agreed. "We wanted you to know what Anna and Cam came up with, because having confirmed what really went on with Isobel, we're hoping that we might get Gideon to leave." Then she took a deep breath and said, "But if his father has enough left of him that he can resist going with him, telling him this might be the thing that releases the son's iron grip on this place if not the father's."

Hugh took a deep breath, then huffed it out and gave a nod. 'Ye're right. Even he doesn'a deserve to be condemned fer something he didn'a intend to happen, though I could still cheerfully wring his neck over everything else. Thank ye', ladies. I wouldn'a want to go to ma rest wrongly accusing a man.'

And that, as Rita and Phemie said to one another after they left the hotel, showed the difference between Hugh and Gideon in a nutshell.

CHAPTER 21

Thankfully, the start of Anna's shift was suitably mundane, allowing her to autopilot her way through her various managerial jobs, such as renewing the hotel's insurance, paying some invoices, and trying to source a supplier for some specific ingredients Emilio had asked her to try and find. But then the doors to reception swung open and a woman, of the sort Anna had never expected to see in a hotel like this, stalked in. In one hand she carried – no, displayed – an expensive-looking handbag, and in the other held the hand of a squalling little boy of about five. Tottering on her blood-red high heels, she yanked the kid through the door before it could swing shut and whack him one, but only just.

For a moment Anna's customer service skills deserted her. The leopard print leggings hugging skeletally thin legs, topped with a sweat-top on which the word 'Gucci' was emblazoned in sequins, all screamed 'knock-off' and 'tart'. Indeed the last sort of customer Anna had ever expected to see at *Nuns' Kirk Haugh*, not least because she ticked every stereotype Anna had ever seen on TV of a prostitute, right down to the bright red lipstick layered on so thickly it couldn't possibly survive kissing or consuming even a cocktail, let alone food.

"How can I help you?" Anna managed to splutter, while fumbling with the duty phone and dialling the emergency number for Gary. If anyone could handle booting some scruffy street-worker out, it was him.

"We've come to see Gaylord's daddy," the nightmare said with a pout.

"I think we need a little more to work with than that," Anna croaked while desperately trying to maintain the professional smile.

"The *owner*," the women stated, as if Anna was as thick as a brick for not knowing that.

Swallowing hard, Anna managed to ask, "Which owner? We've just changed hands, in case you didn't know."

Behind the woman, beyond the glass doors, Anna saw Gary skidding to a halt, and him mouthing his unheard exclamation of, "Fuck!" as he saw what was standing there. He had a ringside view of the skinny legs, high heels, and bling-encrusted sweatshirt, topped with bouffant hair that was so uniformly and densely black, it could only have come out of a bottle, and was now held rigid by more hairspray than Anna thought she had ever possessed in her life. Even unflappable Gary had to visibly pull himself together to encounter this one.

"Cameron," the woman answered with another pout of her cosmetically filled lips, which would have done a fighting gourami fish credit. "The. Owner!" she emphasised as though Anna was particularly thick.

"Ah, so not *Ferguson Holdings*," Anna responded frostily. "Just one moment please."

She was about to put a call though to Cameron and fudge it somehow to tell him to make himself scarce until they could sort this out, when he strolled out of the dining room.

"Hello, Cameron," the young woman said, hanging on to the screaming brat. "I've brought your son for you to look after for a bit. Thought it was about time you faced up to your responsibilities," and she smiled nastily at him.

Anna and Gary turned in shock to look at Cameron, only to see him go grey in the face and look as though he might have a heart attack on the spot.

"Oh look, Gaylord," the nightmare gushed, as the child tugged her hand and distracted her from Cameron. "A staircase with a banister you can slide down! Oh, what fun. Go on! Show Daddy what a big boy you are."

"No!" Gary snapped in his best parade-ground voice, halting the snivelling child as it was about to stomp up the first steps. "No sliding down banisters! It's against health and safety."

The young woman turned her petulant stare onto Gary, looking at him as if he was something she'd just scraped off her six-inch heels.

"It's Gaylord's daddy's hotel," she positively spat back. "And if my baby wants to slide down the banister, then he bloody-well can."

"No, he cannot!" Gary roared, catching the child's hoodie as it went past and summarily hauling it back to its mother, coming to stand almost nose-to-nose with her. "It doesn'a matter a rat's arse who *owns* the hotel. This is the law! Now take charge of your child, madam, or I shall be forced to ask you to leave."

And something about Gary's manner made the woman stop. Implacable and fully within his rights to stop her, she had run into someone who wouldn't budge an inch, no matter how many tantrums she threw – and Anna was half expecting her to lie down on the floor, and start drumming her heels and holding her breath. She spun around to demand that Cameron back her up, but he'd vanished, and she returned her irate pout back on Gary. Little Gaylord had stopped snivelling and was looking up at Gary in awe, clearly never having come across anyone who could shut his mother up at speed like that before, and Rita, who had puffed her way in in Gary's wake, seized the chance.

"Come with me," she said firmly, taking his hand. "Let's go and find you some ice-cream, eh?" She shot the mother a look which ought to have killed her stone dead, but certainly froze her to the spot.

"Allow me to find you a room for the night," Anna said, taking her cue from Rita, and adopting her iciest customer service manner. "I'm sure we have a room *somewhere*," and was gratified to see Cameron grasp the moment of distraction to dive out of the other door from the bar which he'd dived into, and escape towards the billiard room. "Yes, here we go, you can have Sloe for the night. You'll have to have your son in the bed with you, but I'm sure a devoted mother like you will want to comfort her child in a strange place, anyway." She gave what she called her 'suck on that, you prat' beaming smile, which she had perfected over years in the supermarket. It was one which defied any customer to say she had been in any way offensive, and at the same time was so blatantly false that they knew that they hadn't won the argument – whatever it happened to be.

"May I just take your name for the purposes of the guest register…in case of fire, you understand. We wouldn't want to leave you burning to death because nobody had bothered to check you in properly."

"India Hackstone," the woman ground out through gritted teeth, knowing she'd been outmanoeuvred.

Seeing Polly coming in from the service kitchen, Anna called, "Oh Polly? Could you *show* Mrs Hackstone up to Sloe, please? …And what time would you like to dine Mrs Hackstone? I presume quite soon for the sake of your son? Shall we say six-thirty?"

"It's *Miss*, not Mrs! He wouldn't marr…"

"Lovely, *Miss* Hackstone, so that's dinner at six-thirty for you and your son, which gives you an hour to get settled in. We'll serve it in the *front* dining room so that he won't disturb other diners if he runs around. Here's your key." Anna held the key out which Polly took, oblivious to the situation, just reading this woman as being a particularly difficult customer and adopted her best manner, too, taking her lead from Anna.

As Polly chirpily chivvied the fuming India across to the lift and vanished from sight, Anna and Gary collapsed into the chairs on either side of the reception desk.

"Bloody hell! Wherever did he find her?" Anna asked rhetorically.

After taking a couple of deep breaths, Gary said, "I'd better go and find him. Did you see the dreadful colour he went? That's no' just a guilty conscience. That's a bloody nightmare come to haunt him!"

"Do you think the kid is even his?" Anna wondered. "That's not wishful thinking on my part, by the way. I'm not being taken in. It's just that that little lad has to be easily five years old, and yet I can't see a single thing about him that resembles Cameron."

"Aye," Gary said thoughtfully. "By that age you'd have thought you'd start to see something. In a baby it's hard to tell, but without seeming to be prejudiced, that wee lad's skin is way darker in colouring than either his witch o' a mother – even with her bottle black hair – or Cameron. Both o' them are definitely very fair-skinned, even if her is covered with so much make-up you have to look at her neck to see her real colour."

"Be careful who you call a witch around here," Anna warned, casting a worried eye upwards.

"*Sheesh*!" Gary fumed. "Bloody forgot that, didn't I! …No, Hugh or Gideon, if you're listening, she's no' a witch in the way you think, she's just a nasty wee baggage who's using her own son for blackmail."

"Do you think it is?" Anna asked worriedly. "Blackmail, I mean?"

"I think it stands a fair chance."

At that point, Polly emerged from the lift, clearly glad to have made her escape from the clutches of India.

"Holy-moly!" she gulped, coming to grab the seat in front of the computer so that she couldn't be asked to leave again. "She's a piece of work, isn't she?" And that, coming from Polly, was quite a condemnation. With Rita bringing a much calmer little boy through from the service kitchen along with a bowl of chocolate ice-cream, Anna told her which room his mother was in, told Polly that she was in charge of reception and not to answer any demands from Sloe room, and that she and Gary had something to attend to.

Together they went through the bar and onwards to the billiard room, seeing no sign of Cameron. Nor was he in the tackle room.

"He's made a run for the cottage," Anna guessed, "and who can blame him?"

Grabbing their outside coats, she and Gary hurried off down the fork of the drive which led to the self-catering cottages, glad that the dogs were safely tucked up at Gary's. At Cameron's door, Gary knocked firmly and then marched in without waiting for an invitation. For a moment, Anna feared that Cameron would yell at them to get out, but then saw what Gary had already guessed at – Cameron was sitting on the sofa hugging himself, ashen-faced and shaking, too stunned to react to anything.

With a sympathetic glance, Gary went straight to the kitchen and put the kettle on, dumping a teabag in a mug and a hefty spoon of sugar. When the water had boiled and been poured, Gary made sure the tea was good and strong, sloshed a splash of milk in, and then poured a goodly slug of whisky in too.

"Bloody waste to do that to a good single malt," he sighed, "but this is an emergency. …Here, lad. Drink that as hot as you can," and he made sure that Cameron had both hands around the mug before he let it go.

When the tea had had chance to work its restorative effect, Gary began with, "Who in the flaming world is that wee besom? Please dinna tell me she was really your girlfriend?"

Immediately Cameron shook his head vigorously. "God, no! No! Not that! …She was…is…Mum's…best friend's…daughter."

"Oh, good Lord," Anna groaned as he struggled to get the words out, already suspecting that this was another situation where Cameron had been manipulated to near breaking point by his mother.

Cameron looked up balefully at Anna and Gary, clearly expecting to see angry faces but only seeing sympathy, at which point his face crumpled and the tears began to stream down his face.

"I don't know what I've done to have two good people like you believe in me," he hiccupped, but with some of the shake having left his voice.

Gary leaned over and grasped his wrist reassuringly. "Just tell us the truth, lad, what happened?"

It took a couple of false starts before Cameron could string something intelligible together but eventually he told them,

"I'd come home from uni after graduating. …Found myself a decent job. …Got a little flat with one of everything."

"I thought you'd been left your aunt's flat in Edinburgh," Anna questioned gently.

He snuffled into a tissue as he nodded. "I had. But this first job was in Glasgow. Would have cost too much to commute every day. So I rented Aunty's out – gave me a bit extra income, you see? Especially back then with my student debt still hanging over me at that stage."

Talking to them seemed to be calming him down as he carried on, "Mum kept pestering me to return to Edinburgh to live, but Dad saw that it wasn't viable and stood by me. That went on for a good few years, because although I applied for jobs back over in Edinburgh I didn't get them, so there wasn't much she could do about that." He gave Anna a wobbly and rather watery smile. "Didn't occur to me *why* she wanted me back until after I'd talked to you. I just thought she was being a bit of a clingy mum, because she'd hated me being at uni in Newcastle, even though it was only a short train ride away."

"Oh dear," Anna sighed. "You probably loved uni and the freedom you got there, but never twigged at the underlying reason."

He nodded. "At eighteen I was just glad to get away from the growing rows around Austin. I'd chat to Dad on the phone, and assumed that I didn't get many conversations with Mum because she was too taken up with looking after my brother. …And then of course, when I graduated, I had to take a job where there was an internship – I didn't have *that* many choices of good places." He suddenly cringed.

"What?" Gary asked gently.

"It's just hit me. The 'I miss you' routine was actually her way of saying, 'I want to you to come back and start caring for Austin with me.' I never saw it quite like that at the time, though. And she always made it seem like I was out partying all the time while 'poor Austin' would never get to do that."

"I'm guessing you weren't," Anna sympathised.

"No. Too busy putting in the overtime so I'd seem keen to the bosses."

"So when did yon' floozie turn up?" Gary wondered.

Cameron cringed again. "Oh God! That was a party that Mum and Dad dragged me off to – or rather, *Mum* did. It was at India's parents' house. By a year later those two were divorced, but at the time they had a big house out beyond Leith. Austin was in a week's respite somewhere, and Mum bamboozled me with pleading, saying that just for once she wanted to be able to take a child of hers to show me off in the way her friends could do."

"Holy crap!" Anna muttered. "That sounds like something my parents would do! Well did, actually, now I think of it."

Cameron gave her another weak smile, but her comment seemed to give him encouragement.

"Well, India and some of her friends were there. She's always been wild.

"You mean bloody spoiled," Gary interjected darkly.

"Suppose so," Cameron agreed, relaxing a fraction more as he remembered that for once, these were friends whom he could speak honestly and openly to. "A total brat, if I'm being frank. I saw them popping pills and getting very loud. That didn't appeal to me, but one of them must have slipped me something, because I truly don't remember much of anything of the rest of the night."

"Oh shit!" said Anna, already guessing where this was going.

He nodded. "I woke up the next morning with India next to me. In her bed. I was horrified! Got dressed and legged it out of there before she woke up. Went to the STD clinic as soon as I could to get checked out, because she had that kind of reputation, and then knowing I was clean, thought nothing more of it. I went back to Glasgow and got on with my life for three months.

"Then all of a sudden I got these hysterical calls from Mum, accusing me of treating India badly. I honestly hadn't got a clue what she was talking about. Then it turned out that India was pregnant, and insisting that it was mine!" He gave another shiver. "God! She played the innocent virgin for all she was worth, when in truth everyone knew she hadn't been that since she was thirteen.

"Mum went into full overdrive, accusing me of wrecking her friendship with someone she'd known since school. Kept on and on at me to 'be a man' and come back to Edinburgh and take on my responsibilities. Thank God Dad took a different view. He totally backed me up then, especially when Mum started talking about solicitors to get me to pay what I ought." He gave a shudder. "Christ, Anna, it's what you said, isn't it? Mum wasn't worried about backing *me* up. She was more worried about what her friends would say.

"Thank God Dad believed me. He said he wouldn't pay a single penny in maintenance for the kid on my behalf, not even if it was a loan – which was something Mum tried as well. I guess she knew I wouldn't leave a debt to Dad unpaid. And Austin playing up was for once to my advantage, with *him* saying why should he pay for my cock-ups with the money from his inventions? I think in part it was because right about then, he was forced into paying part of the money towards his next big project himself. It paid off in the end, earning him many times what he'd put in, but it did mean that he didn't have much to spare at that time.

"And then the firm I was with heard that the company I've now recently left had an opening for someone to do a year over in Dubai. It was a great chance for someone, but their own best candidate was a girl, and she took one look at the conditions of work over there and said no. And although my old firm did compete with them in some areas, they had also worked together on some big projects, where each had people with skills the other didn't. So they offered it to me, and as my old boss had a nephew he needed my job for, I got to go."

He sighed. "I probably did things all wrong, but I packed my biggest suitcase, jumped on a plane, and didn't tell Mum and Dad until I was over there. Made sure it was too late for Mum to get Dad to drive her over to Glasgow and give me the full performance, because even then I knew I was being manipulated – I just never understood how much and how badly. I just thought, 'Mum's going to flip when she knows I'm in the Middle East!' Then India gave birth earlier than expected by a good couple of months, but the midwives kept telling her mum and dad that it was a full-term baby.

"Her dad believed them and told my dad that, and that it couldn't be mine because she had to have been at least a couple of months pregnant by the night of that awful party. But that was the final straw for him – her dad, that is. Years of India and his wife bawling at him all the time, and then all the lies about the pregnancy…he'd just had enough and filed for divorce. It saved me, though, because suddenly her mum didn't have the money to get shyster lawyers chasing me for paternity payments for a kid that wasn't even mine."

"So why has India come here telling everyone that the child is yours?" Anna wondered. "Did you never demand a DNA test?"

Cameron rolled his eyes. "I was a fool. A total bloody fool. I got back from Dubai and moved into Auntie's flat because I was now working in Edinburgh. Never thought anything about India, to be frank, because nobody had mentioned it after the first couple of months I was in Dubai. Then this year, out of the blue, when I started going through Austin's accounts, I came across this whacking big payment to India some months after the birth. I couldn't believe it!

"I asked Dad about it, but he was as shocked as me. I'm still certain he didn't know a thing. But when I collared Mum, she went all tearful on me, and told me she'd siphoned the money off from Austin when he was having one of his hazier days, and she could just get him to sign the cheques without arguing. And by then he'd had a big payout, so there were funds available. She said that she wanted to be friends with Rowena again, and that since the divorce, Rowena and India had been struggling."

He screwed his eyes up at the painful memory. "I didn't think that was true for a second. But what could I do? I couldn't ask for the money back, because I knew it would have long since been spent. I was over my ears in sorting out the rest of Austin's financial mess. And if I'm honest, just the thought of speaking to India and her mother ever again was enough to have me breaking out in hives! So I thought if Austin hadn't noticed it in nearly five years, why rock the boat? Never in a million years did I think it would come back to haunt me like this!"

"But how did she find you?" Gary wondered, then grimaced. "Of course! Your mum. This is her payback for you leaving her with Austin again, isn't it? She told that young besom where to find you. She told her to come and make a scene so that you'd be embarrassed and all at sea. I bet that once her spy is in the camp, your mum will turn up, full of how you have to take India and the lad on because 'you' have already paid maintenance to them once, proving your guilt – or some cock-and-bull story of a similar sort. And also, it won't be long before she brings your brother over here, and before you know it – or so she thinks – they'll be living here free of charge."

Cameron turned ashen again. "Christ! No!"

"Too right, no," Gary said forcefully. "If we have to dip into the petty cash to get her a train ticket, that wee witch is out o' here tomorrow. End o' story! And I'm taking you into Dumfries to find a solicitor first thing – oh bugger. Tomorrow is Saturday. Nobody will be open. What a pain. Monday then, first thing, and before anything else. You need proper legal advice, and although I know you've got good business solicitors to hand, I think this situation requires someone who knows every trick in the book where family law is concerned. You need someone who knows all the ins and outs of paternity suits, and how to break them. I'm a bit surprised your dad didn't help you with that far earlier, but I suppose he thought that if you were over in Dubai, you were out of harm's way.

"Well Anna, Rita, and I will testify that she turned up here trying to blackmail you, and this time, son, you are going to demand a DNA test. I feel awful sorry for wee Gaylord – what in God's name possessed her to give the poor lad a name like that? He must get the crap kicked out of him at school being called that! But it'll be worse for him if he keeps getting used as his mother's bargaining chip. It's one thing stepping up if you were his real dad, it's something else being conned into a world o' misery you had no part in creating."

"Stay over here, Cam," Anna said firmly. "These cottages are far enough from the hotel that she won't see even your car, and in those heels, she'll never manage the track up to here. We'll field her enquires and say you've gone away on business and won't be back for a few days. That way, if she starts making trouble, we can boot her out as a troublesome guest without it getting personal."

"Thank you," Cameron said from the heart, as he showed them out.

As they walked back down the track, Gary observed, "What a bloody mess. Poor lad. He was being twisted and tugged at on every side."

"I've known women like her," Anna said bleakly, "or rather *of* them. Connected to people I worked with, you understand, and they're always trouble. She's not some poor lass from the wrong side of the tracks who's got into trouble and needs help. She's a spoilt brat who doesn't see why she should have to take responsibility for her own life and mistakes. I pity the little lad, though. He doesn't stand an earthly chance of growing up to be a decent man. Not with the way she's shrieking and performing around him. I bet he doesn't know whether it's Christmas or next week most of the time."

Gary was just nodding and saying, "Aye, it's always the kids you feel sorry for," when a car came bombing down the drive, far over their recommended speed limit, and screeched to a halt in the drop-off area right in front of the front door.

"*Hoy*!" Gary yelled. "…You, there! …Ye canna park there, and what the hell were ye' doing driving like a lunatic up the drive? We have wild fowl and folk wi' dogs walking up and down there."

The man who had practically fallen out of the driver's seat turned to face them, and instantly they knew that this was Cameron's father.

"Bloody hell, did someone light the fiery cross summoning the clan?" Gary muttered darkly.

"Mr Wiseheart?" Anna called, and he paused in his move towards the door. "You are Cameron's dad, aren't you?"

By now Anna and Gary had jogged up to him, so he could hiss urgently at them, "Is *she* here? Has that bloody wee madam turned up yet? Please tell me I've made it in time to warn Cam?"

"Sadly not," Gary said, taking his arm and firmly steering him towards the tackle room and out of sight of the front room, where even now a table was being set up for India and Gaylord by the window. "But she doesn't know that Cam's actually here. We're about to tell her that he's just left on business. She caught sight o' him, so she might believe us if she thinks he's run from her. It might give us a bit of manoeuvring room."

Mr Wiseheart all but collapsed against the doorway in relief. "I can't believe that Helen would do something like this to him. It's just too cruel. But then I'm coming to realise that when it comes to taking it out on others when she doesn't get her way, Helen can plumb depths I've never really accepted, and I'm a fool for that. I should have stood up for Cam long ago."

"I'll go into reception," Anna said, "and distract her if necessary."

Gary nodded and took Mr Wiseheart's arm again. "Come on. Stand by the door. I'll get into your car and turn it around to here. You get into the passenger seat and I'll drive you around to Cam's cottage. I think he'll be very glad to see you, and he's got a second bedroom over there, so you need never set foot in the hotel while she's here."

Leaving Gary with Jeff Wiseheart profusely thanking them for their help, Anna walked into the reception as if she had returned from some minor clerical duty, not emergency damage control.

"All okay, Polly?" she asked brightly, but with a drift of her eyes towards the front room.

Polly grinned. "She's not down yet, thank God. Rita's chewing the carpet in the service kitchen over the way that woman's treating her kid. Seems the poor little lad could do with a good bath amongst other things. It's a good job you said to set her up in the front because he's a bit hard on the nose, if you get my meaning."

"Flaming hell, some mothers," Anna muttered, thinking that however much of a nightmare her own had been, at least she'd always kept her children clean-clothed, washed, and properly fed.

They managed to get through the evening without too many disasters by virtue of keeping the front room door firmly shut, so that young Gaylord could tear around making as much noise as he liked, and through several inches of heavy oak door, he caused no problems with the other guests. Anna had shoved India into Sloe in an instinctive move to put her into the least luxurious available bedroom in the hotel, so that she wouldn't want to linger. But it turned out to have been an inspired move, because Sloe backed on one side to the main first-floor landing, and had the narrow corridor from that through into the round tower on another, and the tower's landing on a third, meaning that sound-wise it was isolated. As Gaylord was hauled off to bed, when Anna firmly told India that they were closing up the front room, and that, no, Gaylord could not play in the main hall, his screams echoed down the main staircase until they were muffled by the fire doors, making Polly say, "Good grief, that kid has a pair of lungs on him."

Polly put her coat on to go home and Gary wandered in for his night shift, waiting until Polly had left before telling Anna, "All's well. Cam was delighted to see his dad. They're consoling one another over a few Macallens."

"She doesn't have a clue they're here," Anna informed him back. "She did ask at dinner, but I told her that Cam had already told us he was leaving on business this evening for an early business meeting tomorrow morning – or rather that Mr Wischeart is. I kept it very formal."

She gave a little shiver. "I hate to say this Gary, but do you think that there's a weird atmosphere in here tonight?" She looked up to the mezzanine landing. "Young Gaylord had a right paddy up there. If Aunty Rita is right about conflict drawing you-know-who like a moth to the flame, then that kid isn't helping us."

CHAPTER 22

They got through the night without any full-blown battles, but Gary said that in the small hours Hugh had come down to report to him that Gideon was on the prowl, clearly on edge after all of India's shrieking. Unfortunately, any thoughts of getting her out first thing were soon shown to be hopeless. Breakfast service came and went without her showing her face, and finally Rita took a master key and went and hammered on the bedroom door, Gary behind her for added emphasis. If anyone had to go in with India in a state of undress, it was going to have to be another woman, and Rita was adamant that it wouldn't be Anna.

"If she flies at you, it might just provoke Hugh's protective instincts," Rita warned, "and if he shows up, you know that Himself won't be far behind. Sloe was definitely the right choice for the business, isolating her from the other guests, but it's one wall away from Himself's domain, and that's not good. Damn it, why did the daft lass have to show up today of all days?"

Anna knew what she meant. They'd hoped to keep the hotel calm in the build-up to dealing with Gideon late this coming evening, but that had gone out of the window with India's appearance. Nor did things get any better when Rita finally let herself into the bedroom when Gaylord told them through the door that his mummy was still in bed. An almost empty bottle of vodka stood on the bedside table, and from the smell of her, India had probably drunk most of it last night. She was certainly still slurring her words when Rita shook her awake.

"Get up!" Rita snapped. "What's the matter with you? It's getting on for midday and your son hasn't even had his breakfast, and yet you're lounging in bed like you're some princess who's going to get waited on hand and foot. Well you aren't. You're his mother. Start acting like it!"

Feeling sorry for the little lad, Gary had followed Rita up and now had him firmly by the hand, and went to take him in for a shower. One look at the state of the bathroom, however, and he was snatching up the small case which was clearly Gaylord's, and marching him out to where Sally was cleaning Pippin across the hall. As he and Sally got Gaylord washed and into what few clean clothes he seemed to have, Sally agreeing to take the rest and put it on a fast wash and through the tumble dryer for his sake, they could hear the ranting and raging as Rita got India moving.

Knowing that Rita more than had this in hand, Gary took little Gaylord down and through to the front room, and then got Sarah to keep an eye on him while he went and rustled the lad up some brunch. Half an hour later, India tottered in through the front room door looking considerably shaken, her previously bouffant Amy-Winehouse-hair lying flat and damp, not a scrap of make-up on, and with a red mark on her cheek showing that she'd tried Rita's patience once too often.

"Breakfast," Gary said tersely, pointing to a couple of croissants and pot of yoghurt. Gaylord's eyes had nearly fallen out of his head when Gary had brought him through a mini version of a full Scottish. Clearly he never got that at home, and had tucked in with gusto, but Gary had no intention of cooking the same up fresh for a woman who couldn't be bothered with her own child. He did go and get hot coffee for her, though, but only because he was getting a mug each for Rita and himself too.

"We've had chance to speak to Mr Wiseheart now," he said as he plonked the mug down in front of her. "So I'll make this plain: you are not welcome here. Whoever the father of this wee boy is, it's blindingly obvious it's not Mr Wiseheart, so what you are trying to do is nothing more nor less than blackmail. We will not aid and abet you in this. If you persist, we will inform the police. Do I make myself clear?" What she didn't know was that Gary had put the knife and fork that Gaylord had licked clean into fresh food bags and sealed them. Gaylord's DNA should be extractable from them, he hoped, and that would put this nonsense to rest once and for all.

"I not going to live in the castle?" Gaylord asked innocently.

"Sorry son," Gary said, ruffling the lad's now considerably cleaner hair, and getting a grin in return. "No castles for you, I'm afraid. Your mammy's been at the falling-down water a bit too much if she told you that."

Gaylord didn't seem too distressed at that. "We go home now?" was all he said, but adding hopefully, "More sausage?"

"Aye, I reckon I can rustle you up a square sausage bun or two for the journey," Gary laughed, only for India to shriek,

"You've given him *meat*?"

"Oh for God's sake," Rita growled. "What *do* you feed the poor lad on, then?"

As India rattled off a list of trendy foods, mostly vegan, all of which she no doubt bought as ready meals, Rita cut her off with, "So that's why the poor wee soul is batting off the bloody walls! You're stuffing him full o' preservatives and synthetic sweeteners in bloody diet food meant for adults, not kids. Give the lad some real food, for pity's sake. Something *fresh.* If he's a handful, I'm not surprised with that diet. Heaven knows how many colourings and E-numbers are in those things." She shook her head despairingly. "Did your own mammy not teach you better than that?"

However, the mention of her mother provoked a different reaction to any Rita and Gary might have anticipated.

"Well you can ask her yourself when she and Aunty Helen arrive," India said with a smirk. "You won't be so free with your hands then, you old witch! Aunty Helen will throw you out."

"Who the fu…fudge is 'Aunty Helen'?" Rita demanded. "I can tell you straight, young lady, she's not on any board of directors here. So whatever authority you think she has here, she hasn't."

"She's Cameron's mother," India sniped back with savage glee, "and she'll *make* him behave. You'll see. She will!"

"I think you'll find that the wool is no longer being pulled over his eyes," Gary was just saying, when he caught Rita's horrified expression, and she cut across him with the question,

"Please tell me she's not bringing Austin with her?"

"Well given that Cameron cheated his brother out of ownership of this place, err…*duh*…yeah!" India riposted sarcastically with a nasty smirk on her face. "If Cameron can afford to pay Austin back, he can bloody-well pay me maintenance, and if he can't then he's stolen this off Austin, and Aunty Helen will have something to say about *that*." And she smirked at them again.

"Ach, don't you give me that attitude," Rita warned her in a tone which, if India had known Rita half as well as Gary did, should have had her shutting up and retreating at speed. "You haven't the faintest idea of what's going on here, and if we don't stop this, you may end up needing a change of underwear every time you think back on your time here."

All she got from India was dumb insolence. However, Gary had caught on as to why Rita was now so worried. If Austin had mental health problems, and was frequently unstable and volatile, that was a dangerous mix to bring into the hotel right now. It would have been bad enough with a guest, but at least then they'd have had some control over the situation, in as much as they could have made sure that the guest was in the most distant room from the ghosts, and never came down the main stairs, but used the lift. And of course, guests rarely stayed beyond three or four nights unless they were working in the area, and so they could have planned to delay dealing with Gideon, whereas this was open-ended. With Cameron's mother and India's mother about to descend on them along with Austin, suddenly they were now going to have four unstable adults in the mix, and even if they got them out in terms of sleeping here, there was little doubt that they could keep turning up like bad pennies for many days.

"Come on, sup up," Gary told India, gesturing to her coffee mug. If he could at least get her and the lad out of here before all hell broke loose that would be one less nutcase in the mix, and it was the boy he was thinking of more than anyone. The little lad didn't deserve to be scared out of his wits because his mother was too daft to take a hint.

Yet fate was against them. Outside they heard a car pulling up, and then a waspish woman's voice demanding very loudly, "Where are you? Cameron Wiseheart, you come here right this minute. Don't you dare ignore me!"

As India began to laugh hysterically, Rita and Gary exited the room, Gary producing his set of master keys and locking the front room door, preventing India's escape and Gaylord further trauma.

"Jesus, what a bloody mess," he swore, picking up the phone and trotting out down the corridor towards the billiard room, where he wouldn't be heard, to make the call through to Cameron's cottage to warn him. For her part, Rita was whispering urgently to Sarah and then shooing her out of the way towards the kitchen. Anna followed Sarah to warn the rest of the staff of the nightmare about to descend. So when the two mothers flounced in through the reception doors, it was Rita they were greeted by, not a younger woman they might have bullied.

"Which of you two pathetic excuses for mothers is which?" Rita demanded before they could get a word in, sitting back in the receptionist's chair with her arms folded disapprovingly. "Because I have to say that I'm not impressed with either of you."

Her confrontational approach from the outset rather took the wind out of the sails of the pair, who'd come in expecting to ride roughshod over all and sundry.

Rita jabbed an accusing finger at the woman on the left. "You have the look of that equally useless young woman who canna even keep her wee lad clean," she said acidly, "so I'm guessing you're her mammy? Well shame on you! You should have sorted her out long ago. …And you!" She spun in the chair to face Cameron's mother. "You are a disgrace! What mother backs a friend against her own child? Do you have any concept of what a fine young man you have there? Any right-thinking mother would be singing his praises to the skies. But not you. Oh no. All you can think of is what he can do for you."

Then the double doors banged open and a truly huge man of around forty barged in, demanding, "When are we having dinner? I want my dinner *now*!"

"Oh God," Rita intoned, because this had to be Austin, and he looked way more of a problem in the flesh than she'd imagined from Cameron's descriptions, and she'd expected him to be bad. For a start off, he was vast. It was all fat, but there'd be no easy wrestling him out of the way, even if Gary, Cameron, and Jeff got stuck into the task. Topping six feet by a couple of inches at least, Austin also had to weigh twenty-five stone if not closer to thirty.

Worse, everything Cameron had said about Austin being given his own way for years suddenly became clearer when seen in person. Reasoning would not work with this man – and he was a man, not a child – because he'd not had to comply with anything or give way to anyone for so long, he simply didn't know how to anymore.

"It's only one o'clock," Rita said firmly. "Chef doesn't start serving the evening meal until five-thirty. I can offer some light refreshment now, but not a full meal."

"I *want* my DINNER!" Austin bellowed, coming to loom over Rita and pounding his fist on the desk, which shook alarmingly under the assault. Given that it was a solid old mahogany thing, it said a lot for the amount of power Austin was expending, and for the first time in many years, Rita felt a frisson of fear.

"*Hoy*! Pack that in." Gary's voice came from behind Austin, and the ferocious growl it had been issued in was enough to percolate through to him. Lurching upwards, Austin swivelled his ungainly weight around to face Gary, his fists bunched.

"Fuck! Off!" Austin spat. "Mine!" And he waved a fist to encompass the hotel, narrowly missing Gary only because he was on full alert and easily ducked out of the way.

But Gary now saw Austin as a very dangerous threat indeed. One swipe from those huge hands, however unintentional, and he could badly hurt one of the younger members of staff, not least because the force would send them flying, and Gary knew full well how lethal being flung against something like the stone inglenook fireplace could be. Taking that in in a trained instant, Gary acted, jabbing a well-placed rabbit-punch at Austin to temporarily disable him. There was too much belly fat protecting Austin's diaphragm for a belly punch to wind him, and a kick to a knee to get him sat down could well snap it like a twig with that much weight on it when it twisted, meaning they'd need a special ambulance and god-knew how many paramedics to get him out.

Instead Gary aimed higher, and although Rita didn't see quite where or how he hit him because of the speed, Austin thumped to the floor, gasping for air, but still conscious. The thud of him hitting the floor made Rita and Gary glad that this part of the hall had the old flagstones under the carpet, because even the huge old oak floorboards closer to the dining room would have groaned with that impact.

"You hit my baby!" Helen screamed, launching herself at Gary, fingers hooked to claw at his face, but Rita was no shrinking violet either. Already up on her feet, she grabbed Helen's one arm, spun her around, and administered a sharp slap.

"Pack that in!" she commanded, the old skills from being a colour sergeant's wife in barracks, and needing to break up cat-fights among drunken young army wives and live-in girlfriends, kicking in. Austin she might not manage, but with the two women she was on familiar territory. "He's not a baby at all. And if you'd been half the mother you should have been, you'd have instilled some restraint into him."

"He's disabled!" Helen screamed, but with more of a wail as she tried to loosen Rita's grip.

"Of course he is," Rita snapped back, "but I've known kids with worse damage than him who, with a bit of patience, could be better behaved when a quarter of his age. He's had no triggers here – there hasn't been time. No shocks. No frights, nor people shouting – apart from you two harridans – to disturb him. So him coming in and throwing his fists around is him just being a brat."

Through the front room door there was now a wail of, "What's happening? What's going on? Let me out! Let me out!"

"India! Baby!" shrieked her mother, who the others guessed must be Rowena Hackstone.

"Bloody hell," Gary growled as Rowena clattered over to the door on designer kitten heels, and started shaking the doorknob. "Move!" And he put the key in the lock, shoved the door open so fast that Rowena tumbled into India, sending both of them stumbling backwards, and then shut and locked the door again before either of them had realised what had happened.

"One nightmare at a time," he said firmly and got a nod from Rita.

At that point Phemie and Davey appeared beyond the glass doors in the outer hallway, worried because they'd been offering sympathy and support to Cameron and Jeff when the call had come through of Helen and Austin's arrival.

"No! Don't come in." Gary called in warning. "He fights," he added, pointing a finger at the still wheezing Austin. Two people in their eighties coming into contact with Austin's random fists was enough to worry him sick.

"Can you deal with this one?" Rita said, hauling Helen bodily through the double doors and into the hallway to them. "Take her into the billiard room and try to talk some sense into her."

Rita's mind was running at full tilt, working out that Gary had had little choice but to shut the two Hackstone women in the front room, but that they needed to swiftly get Helen and Austin beyond the footprint of the old tower-house, and Gideon and Hugh's reach.

"Are you hungry?" she asked Austin and got a sullen nod. "Well then, you're going to have to get up."

It took some instruction and pulling and shoving from her and Gary, but they got Austin onto his knees and then his feet, and guided him over to the far end of the main hall, away from the old tower-house footprint. The dining room they deemed far too dangerous, because the tables were already set for dinner, meaning too many knives to hand. Austin might not have a clue as to how to wield a knife, but his brute force could turn a butter knife into a dangerous object.

"Now then," Rita began as Gary stood guard, ready to pounce if Austin dared to harm a hair on Rita's head, and a doorstep sandwich was handed out of the service kitchen to Gary to quieten Austin. "I think we need to get some things straight. Yes, you did make the initial purchase of this hotel." As Austin made to interrupt, she raised a warning finger and waved it at him. "*Aah-aah-no*. Wait. I haven't finished."

Something in her firm but even tone seemed to be filtering through to him, and if not fully listening, then he wasn't arguing back yet, either.

"Now do you remember back at the end of last year a young woman calling you up and upsetting you?" Austin's brow furrowed, but after a moment he nodded. "Right, well that was the woman who was the manageress here at the time. Not a nice person, I gather." Austin shook his head.

So far so good.

"Well she left," Rita continued explaining, "and Anna came. She's nice. You'll like her. Your brother was trying to sort out your money so that you'll be taken care of…"

"…Don't need taking care of," Austin interrupted. "Not a baby. Know what I want."

"I'm sure you do," Rita said through gritted teeth, but keeping her tone soothing, "but you want to focus on your tech stuff, don't you?" She got a nod. "And you find it annoying to have to do the financial stuff." Another nod. "So all Cameron was trying to do was set things up so that you could do just that."

Now came the hard part. "The trouble is, your mum wants to keep control of you, but have other people do the messy parts." She got a perplexed look at that.

"What messy parts?"

"Austin, you wouldn't want to be bothering to do your own clothes washing, or food shopping, would you?"

"Got better things to do."

"Yes, and from what Cameron has told us, you can do such amazing things technically, you really should be focusing on those. But that means you need people around you to do things like your washing, cooking, and cleaning the place where you live."

"'S what Mum's for."

Rita and Gary exchanged despairing looks. Clearly Austin had trouble with any emotional attachment, even to his own mother. On the other hand, because of that, it might be easier to extract him from her influence than if he'd been deeply bonded to her. It took Rita a good deal more patient explaining, but finally Austin grasped that Cameron hadn't been robbing him at all. During this time, she and Gary had seen Anna flitting across the hall to reception, then out of the door, and coming back.

Now she came across to them and told them, "Sally and I have done a bit of juggling. Thank heavens we'd been doing up the cottage next to Cam's anyway, with the long-term intention of his dad coming to stay there, because I'm moving India, her mum, and little Gaylord over there. Cam's coming to my cottage with the dogs, and Helen and Austin can sleep at his. The only thing is, Aunty, we need Gary's spare room for Jeff. That single I've got in my spare room isn't big enough for a tall man like him, and anyway, I'm going to have to sleep there because it isn't fair to force the dogs to sleep with the ghosts around. Cam and the dogs are taking my room with the small double bed."

She saw Gary duck his head away so that Rita didn't spot his grin of triumph at finally getting Rita into his bedroom, and though Rita looked dismayed, she could see that it was the only sensible solution. Phemie and Davey were already here in the hotel, so there was no bedroom they'd been using which could be rearranged. And come hell or high water, they had to get these volatile people out of the hotel before nightfall. Neither Gideon nor Hugh had so far been active during the day, except when called to by Rita. The disruption always came at night, and Rita didn't need it pointing out to her, that with this being a potent time, the risk of things getting out of hand was considerable.

"I think we need to get Austin over there first," Anna said, with a knowing nod towards the front room.

"Oh yes," Rita agreed. "I gather you don't like screaming children, Austin?"

"Hate kids," was his instant response. "Too noisy. Hurts my head."

"That's not unusual for someone like him," Rita sad very softly to Gary and Anna. "They can have hyperawareness of noise and distractions. It's as if the mental filters that we use to cope just don't kick in for them. It's genuinely painful for them."

Anna nodded. "That's why I've put Austin at Cam's because of the quiet downstairs bedroom.

It's on the far side of the cottage to where it joins where Gaylord and his family will be. And Gaylord will be up in the tiny third room in that cottage anyway, which is on the far side of that one to Austin."

"Well played," Gary congratulated her. "Come on then, Austin, we're just going to go for a wee walk." As Austin looked horrified at the prospect, Gary took his cue from Rita, keeping his voice even as he said, "It's no' far. Just a wee bit up the path, then you'll be nice and quiet and cosy. You can even have a log fire going if you want."

"Hate log fires! Dangerous. Don't like the sparks. Don't like the noise they make."

"Ach well, you dinna have to light one," Gary brushed it off with. "There's some nice modern radiators in there too if the weather turns chilly. Come on, now." He went to take Austin's arm, but caught Rita's urgent signalling not to do that.

"He might not like a stranger's touch," she whispered at him as she moved out of the way. "Just be patient and tell him what to do."

Grimacing before turning back to Austin, Gary nonetheless did a masterful job of sheep-dogging Austin out of the hotel and onto the drive. Leaving him to do that, Rita and Anna hurried into the billiard room to find a glowering Phemie standing over a very subdued Helen Wiseheart – or Ferguson as she might chose to call herself if she stuck to the Scottish tradition and her maiden name. The fight seemed to have been crushed out of her, and Anna thought it was a fair indication of what a nightmare

Helen must be if Phemie had lost her temper with her.

"Gary's walking Austin over to Cam's cottage," Anna told her grandparents. "Do you think you can take this one there too, but keeping her well back from him so that she doesn't set him off again?"

"There'll be nae problem wi' that, will there?" Davey said with a quirk of his bushy eyebrows, which Helen looked at and squirmed with embarrassment. Anna couldn't wait to hear what had gone on there, but for now all she wanted was these dreadful arrivals out of the main building.

"Right, Aunty, let's go and see what chaos we've got going on in the front room," Anna was just saying as they walked ahead of Phemie, Davey, and Cameron's mother, when they saw some of the other guests coming in through the front door. The guests just smiled and waved at Anna, which she returned, but Helen chose that moment with an audience to say loudly as the reception doors were both open,

"Of course the hotel is owned by *Ferguson Holdings*. My *son's* hotel." She saw the guests turn and give perplexed glances her way before carrying on to their rooms, but the damage had been done, especially when she called loudly after them, "*I'm* a Ferguson, you know," trying to adopt a superior pose, as she passed the glass doors herself, and before they'd fully closed on their dampeners.

'A bluidy *Ferguson* in ma hoose?' Gideon's voice came from the staircase, and he swam into view. 'I'll soon see about that!'

CHAPTER 23

Gideon was furious. 'Ye lied! Ye' told me there were nae Fergusons here,' he ranted.

"She's a *visitor*," Anna told him, desperately trying to deflate the situation, as Helen was hustled outside, and she and Rita made sure that there were no other guests around. "We're not allowed to say, 'no Fergusons'. Sooner or later we were bound to have a guest with that name. You're reading more into the name than exists."

'Then why did she say she *owned* the place, huh?' Gideon riposted.

"Shit," Rita softly swore from behind Anna. "Why did he have to pick up on that?"

Anna glanced over her shoulder and grimaced in sympathy. Turning back to Gideon, she could only say, "Some folk have delusions of grandeur. They think a clan name makes them one of the lairds."

From behind Gideon there came a loud click, and looking to the stairs, Anna and Rita saw Hugh standing further up, his musket trained on Gideon.

'Leave them alone, Corsan,' Hugh said menacingly. 'I dinna want t' fight ye' again, but I will if ye' give me no choice.'

'Ye'? Fight me?' Gideon snorted. 'I'll show ye fighting, Ferguson, you come here and face me.'

But instead, Hugh made a rude gesture and retreated up to the mezzanine landing. With a roar of rage, Gideon spun around and began charging up the stairs, at which point Hugh gave a small salute to the two women and set off further up, Gideon's taunts echoing down but fading the higher they got.

"God bless Hugh," Anna said from the heart, "he's got him out of the way. Quick, Aunty, the keys. Let's get the other nightmares out of here before they can say something to make this even worse."

There was a lot more hissing and spitting from India and her mother, Rowena, when the door opened, but them frightening Gaylord into a sobbing fit helped to shut them up, especially as he clung to Anna when she picked him up to comfort him, and wouldn't go to either of them. With Anna leading the procession out of the hotel, Rita only waited to tell Brenda – who'd come on duty in the middle of all this – that the coast was now clear, and then hurried to catch Anna up.

To their surprise they met Phemie and Davey walking back down, which was quickly explained by Davey as Helen being unable to walk in her ridiculous shoes, and so he'd bundled her into her car, which had been abandoned in the turning circle, and had driven her to the cottage. While Phemie had escorted Helen inside, Davey had hauled their cases out, and then they'd passed Gary still chivvying Austin up the track, and had to come to help Anna. It meant that they joined Rita in escorting their other unwelcome guests, leaving Anna free to go and check on Cameron and Jeff.

By the time she'd told them all of what had gone on, Cameron was hugging her in thanks, and Jeff declaring, "You've got a diamond there, son. Don't let her get away or *I* might never forgive you." He laughed. "Of course, your mum won't forgive you anyway, so I'm probably the lesser of two evils."

"Dad, you're no evil at all," Cameron said, tugging Anna across to Jeff so that he could hug him with his other arm.

"I'm going to get Hannah and her assistants to plate up meals for the cottages, and then ask Gary to drive them up so they get here hot," Anna said, "but that means you two are more than welcome in the restaurant tonight."

"I think we'll lie low here," Jeff said tactfully, "but if you can send across one of those yummy puddings, I think I can cope with frozen pizza for my main."

"I'll bring it over personally," Anna promised with a laugh, "and two more proper meals won't tax the kitchen that much." But she was grateful that Jeff was being so considerate. It would only take one of the women to decide to head back to the hotel and spot them, and all hell would break loose.

When they were all back at the hotel, Rita and Phemie were in agreement that it just wasn't worth the risk trying to doing something with Gideon tonight.

"Not now," Phemie said with a sigh. "It doesn't matter how auspicious tonight is, all riled up like that, Gideon will fight us every step of the way. And if his damned father is entwined around him, we're just feeding his paranoia and aggression. We'll never disentangle Gideon until he's calmer too."

"It's just a shame that we ideally need to wait six weeks until Mabon comes around in late September to have a similar conjunction," Rita sighed. "A full moon not a new one, but still a good combination when teamed with an equinox."

"Do we have to wait that long?" Anna asked worriedly. "We've got four weddings coming up on successive weekends in between now and then. That's a heck of a potential for Gideon to cause chaos."

"If he gets really bad, we'll have no choice but to go down the exorcism route," Rita said regretfully. "I don't want to be that brutal, but if he gives us no other choice, then I will find a priest willing to do it."

"What about Austin?" Phemie asked. "I'm worried about him. You only had to see how much better he was when you and Gary were with him, Rita, but that mother of his is a total hysteric."

"Narcissist," Rita and Anna corrected her in unison.

"I doubt you'll ever get her in front of a mental health professional," said Rita regretfully. "As far as she's concerned, she's the sane one and we're all just deluded. How on earth we might separate Austin out from her I do not know."

However, Anna thought otherwise. "He's pretty determined, isn't he? Knows what he likes and what he doesn't. Let's face it, he's near genius IQ when it comes to electronics and stuff, so he's the complete opposite of subnormal. It's personal interactions he can't cope with. I did some looking up online about people on the autism spectrum, because I have to confess to being woefully uninformed, and I think I have an idea."

Her aunt and grandmother looked at her with anticipation.

"Well it's lovely and *quiet* here, isn't it?" Anna pointed out. "And there's that semi-derelict farmhouse just a bit further down the dead-end track where Cam's cottage is that's still within the hotel grounds. The roof's still on, so it's water-tight even if it could do with a new one. So it's largely a case of getting some decent windows and doors in, and a plasterer to skim plasterboard where the old stuff is failing. With Austin's money, how long do you think it would take to convert that to somewhere where he could have his own support staff taking care of him? It's got five bedrooms, so enough to create a staff lounge, even if we end up extending it later. Give him a few days here, and then offer to let him stay in the one cottage until the farmhouse is done, and I reckon he might decide he wants it. It's got to be quieter than Edinburgh, that's for sure."

Anna gave a huff of disgust. "With Helen being his mum, and Jeff only his step-dad in the eyes of the law, at least, we can't ask for Jeff to made Austin's guardian without Helen going completely psycho-mum. So we have to manoeuvre things so that it's *Austin* who *chooses* where he lives, not Helen telling him. Because as an adult with a good income of his own, it would be hard for a court to argue that he couldn't or shouldn't have a place of his own, as long as there were appropriate carers on hand – and Austin can afford those if we give him a strong motive to want them. We just need to show him how good things can be here for him to dig his heels in and show that stubborn streak to his mum for once."

"That's sneaky and cunning and I like it," Rita said with a grin, and Phemie and Davey agreed.

Over in Anna's cottage, Cameron and Jeff were having much the same conversation.

"I know he's not my son," Jeff was saying sadly, "but I've had so many years looking after Austin, it's harder than I thought to turn that off."

Cameron felt a surge of affection for his dad. "That's because you're a good person, Dad. And to be honest, if Mum had let you do more to sort Austin out, we wouldn't be in this mess now, because he'd have been kept on an even keel and been taught some basic skills for life. Nor is that your fault, so don't you dare go feeling guilty over that. While we were both kids, you worked your socks off so that Austin could stay in that special school, and even after that, you did so much to support him until his inventions started bringing the money in. I bet Mum's never once suggested that he hands some of that insane amount he's earned back to you in thanks?"

"I don't need him to pay me back!" Jeff exclaimed, horrified at even the thought.

Yet Cameron was making a point. "But actually, you rather do need him to, don't you? You're broke, Dad, or as near as makes little difference. Every penny you've earned down the years has gone into the family home, getting it equipped for Austin. The extension. The special equipment he needed before he could buy his own. I may not have lived at home for over a decade, but I do remember you wanting to go on a cruise for your thirtieth wedding anniversary, and then having to call it off, because Mum had already spent the money on something for Austin." He looked at his dad affectionately. "How much *have* you got in savings?"

Jeff winced and looked down, unable to confess to having nothing.

"That's what I thought," Cameron sighed. "But now you've left – and God knows how you've stayed this long – and that means *you* need somewhere to live. Your pension won't get you a mortgage, and I know full well what rents on anywhere decent are like. That's why I want you to come and live in the cottage next door to me here. I don't want to drag Mum through the courts either, but it's not fair that she won't sell the house and give you half. That's taking everything for herself after she's hardly paid anything towards it all, and leaving you who did with nothing."

"But what's the solution?" Jeff asked, and Cameron could see how mentally exhausted from this constant fight his dad was. Mercifully, he'd been more distant than that, and even he hadn't realised the depths of his mum's manipulations until he'd met Anna. Now he knew he had to save his dad.

"There are more buildings on this site, you know," he began. "Granted they aren't fully habitable at the moment, but with Austin's money, we could easily get them done up to a very high standard. …For Austin himself," he added hurriedly as he saw his dad drawing breath to protest that he couldn't take money from Austin.

"Oh." Jeff said, sitting back and letting that sink in. Then, "Oh!" as he realised what Cameron fully meant. "So if Austin's over here, and we're keeping an eye on him…"

"An 'eye' be buggered," Cameron laughed. "I'm talking about him having live-in carers. You're not wearing yourself out in your retirement, Dad. You deserve to have a life. No, we can get a house fully kitted out for Austin, complete with lab and staff. He can afford that. You move in next to me, and then we get a smart lawyer onto Mum and force her to be more reasonable. And no, that's not cruel, it's far less than she's already tried to do to you."

Jeff was visibly choking up. "I don't know what I've done to deserve you, son. Not after the way you spent your whole life being shoved onto the sidelines."

Cameron gave his dad an affectionate dunt with his elbow. "Ach, don't be daft. *You* did a lot with me. I remember you taking me up to Gran and Grandpa's in Fife in the school holidays. I had a great time there! And I know you had to go back to work in the week, but you came up to be with us at weekends." His smile faded a little as he recalled, "I see now why Gran and Grandpa wouldn't have Austin there, though. Mum would never even *try* to stop him wrecking places, and Gran and Grandpa must have worked so hard to get what they had."

Jeff nodded sadly. "My pa spent so many years in heavy industry his lungs were shot. That's why they moved to the coast and the fresher air once he'd got sick, and why he died so young. And then Ma had to make do on her State Pension, because Pa never had much in the way of any work's pension. I felt so bad that I couldn't help her out more. If I could turn back time, I'd spend less on Austin once he left school, and give more to Ma."

Cameron now reached over and gave his dad a full hug. "No. Please don't do that to yourself, Dad. Gran understood. In fact, thinking back now, that she understood more than we realised – especially about how you were being manipulated by Mum.

Just the once I recall hearing her say what she thought of Mum, and she didn't know I could hear, because I was upstairs in the cottage and she was outside talking to a friend. It just happened that the window was open. I never let on that I heard, but she said that you deserved someone so much better. She was worried about you, Dad, not angry at you."

That was the final straw for Jeff, though, and he completely broke down. Everything that had been building up for years and years had reached breaking point, and while Cameron felt dreadful that all he could do was hug him, at the same time he was beyond glad that his dad had managed to hold out until he was here, not go through this alone in his dreadful temporary caravan.

Anna must have stopped by at some point and then tactfully refrained from coming in, because she came with Gary to deliver the evening meals, and waited for him to let her in, whispering, "Is he okay, now?"

Cameron could only shrug. He had a feeling that there would be a few more sessions like that before his dad started to heal. However, the way Jeff's eyes lit up at the sight of Emilio's game pie with colcannon and seasonal veg, plus the jug of rich aromatic gravy, was encouraging.

"I thought you might like Emilio's special rhubarb and strawberry crumble with blackberry and port sorbet for afters," she added, and his eyes followed her all the way to the kitchen where she popped the sorbet into the freezer to keep cold.

Clearly there was no danger of Jeff fading away from lack of appetite.

"You're spoiling me," he said with a genuine smile, leaving Anna not knowing how to answer without risking setting him off again.

"Bon appétit," she said cheerily, and left them to it.

The meal was received less graciously by India and Rowena, though young Gaylord obviously thought all his Christmases had come at once by the way he grabbed the plate off Gary, and shot upstairs with it before his mother could protest. Gary managed to smother his mirth at the fact that India hadn't spotted what the pie on the plate was, being too busy criticising her own food. Nor was there much gratitude from Helen, but Austin looked at the food Anna had carefully picked for him after some judicial questioning, and then warily tried it. The fact that he then began eating it with relish was, Gary thought, a small victory. Anna had sat holding that plate in her hands as he drove up, because Austin apparently had a thing about the different foods on his plate not touching, and Anna had gone to a lot of trouble to make sure that she gave him a larger plate to make that possible and him still have a decent portion.

Therefore breathing sighs of relief, Anna and Gary returned to the hotel, and went into the dining room with Rita, Phemie, and Davey once most of the diners had gone, and they could sit and talk without disturbing anyone. They were in here because, with it being a Saturday night, the bar was busy and so was the billiard room, and they wanted to be well off the footprint of the old tower-house so that they could speak freely.

"Can you feel it, Phemie?" Rita asked, as she slumped back in one of the more comfortable carver chairs. "The whole place is twitching like someone blew psychic itching powder over it."

Phemie gratefully took a sip of her tea, and let it sink into her, restoring her equilibrium before answering. "I think that's a very good way of putting it," she agreed. "Dear me, it's a wonder that poor Cameron is still sane let alone the nice young man he is, with all that going on around him for so long. No wonder he doesn't seem to know what to do for the best half of the time. You have to give him some leeway for that." She gave Rita a look that said that she'd caught on to Rita thinking that Cameron was sometimes something of a wet lettuce. "It takes more courage and backbone than people think to survive mental abuse."

"I know," Rita replied just as pointedly. "I hadn't a clue that he'd been through *that* much. And rather more, now that I *do* know how damaged he's been, I really think he shouldn't be part of our expulsion of you-know-who. Someone with those internal scars could be a bit too much of an invitation to the old one if he feels we've booted him out of his own damaged son."

Anna gave a squeak of horror. "Bloody hell, Aunty! You don't think old What's-His-Name would try and get into Cam, do you?"

Yet it was Gary who wisely replied, "That's something I don't think any of us want to put to the test, lass."

"Point taken," Anna sighed. "Cam and his dad have been put through the wringer enough without risking that. …But is there *anything* we can do tonight, Aunty? Going by the way those chaps on their way to the friendly match up in Glasgow tomorrow are chugging lager, and taking the mickey out of one another in the billiard room, we've got a perfect excuse for things getting a bit rowdy, as long as it doesn't go on for too long after midnight."

"I'd rather not chance it," Rita confessed, and so they settled back, intending to have a quieter night than expected.

That all changed when two women of a party of eight teachers, heading home from a hiking holiday in the Highlands, came hurrying into the hall having been outside to the smoking area declaring, "There are ghosts out there!" rather excitedly.

"Was that really a roll-up you were smoking out there, or a bit of the wacky-baccy?" one's fiancé teased, and got a rude gesture in response, though both women laughed.

"No honestly! We saw them. Three nuns," her friend insisted, and Anna – who of all of them was closest to the door and heard her, sat up with a squeak of dismay.

"We forgot the ghosts!" she hissed to the others. Then when she got blank looks, jabbed a finger in the direction of the kirk and added, "*Those* ghosts. Outside!"

"But we were going to set an alarm for them," Rita protested, "So how would they know what time it is?"

"Because I *did* set my alarm in the spare room where they'd hear it," Anna insisted.

Rita looked at her perplexed. "Why on earth did you set that this morning when you knew that we weren't going ahead with things?" They had agreed that the easiest way to coordinate things with the lady ghosts was for Anna to set one of her alarm clocks for ten p.m.

Yet Anna groaned. "I didn't set it *this* morning, Aunty. It's a twenty-four-hour clock with a repeat. I set it *yesterday* morning and just clicked it off when it went off last night. I totally forgot that it would ring again tonight unless I fully cancelled it. So it must have gone off a quarter of an hour ago, and our ladies are warming things up for us. Oh God. This is all my fault!"

CHAPTER 24

Davey reached across and rubbed his granddaughter's back consolingly. "It's no' your fault Anna. If it's anyone's, it's those daft women turning up here and causing chaos. Ye' canna remember everything."

"Thanks, Grandpa," Anna said with a watery smile, "but that doesn't get around the fact that the ladies over the way are riling Gideon and the old man, because I forgot to tell them not to."

"Then let's not waste that," Rita said decisively. "Our ladies have waited too many centuries to give that old man a taste of the misery he handed out to them, so let's try to do *something*."

Anna grabbed her mobile and rang across to Cameron, explaining what had happened, and asking him to go ahead with the preparations over there. They had always intended to give Phemie the least exhausting of the three roles, making her the conduit between Rita up on the second floor of the hotel, and Anna out in the grounds with the nuns and witches. So now Phemie and Davey went through to the front room. They'd been going to lock the front room to keep guests out beforehand, but with all the kerfuffle with India and Gaylord, it had been left open, not least because Anna had had to plead with one of the young waitresses to give the room a thorough clean after crumbs and split drinks had been scattered around it by Gaylord and the even worse behaved adults. Now they were hoping that none of the ordinary guests had gone in there for a bit of peace and quiet.

"Oh, thank God," Anna sighed, as they went in and found it empty.

"Lock yourselves in," Gary instructed them. That was easy enough to do, because although it required a key on the outside, inside there was simply a knob which had to be turned, installed so that nobody could get locked inside in the event of a fire – only when dead-locked with the key, as Gary had done when India and Rowena had been in there, was it immovable. So they knew that Phemie and Davey would be able to get out if they needed to, but it would stop some poor unsuspecting soul walking in on them if things got a bit hairy with the ghosts. Making sure that the two most elderly of their team were set up with hot drinks and the heating on, Rita and Gary now headed upstairs towards Gideon's lair, while Anna grabbed her heavy fleece and set off up the track.

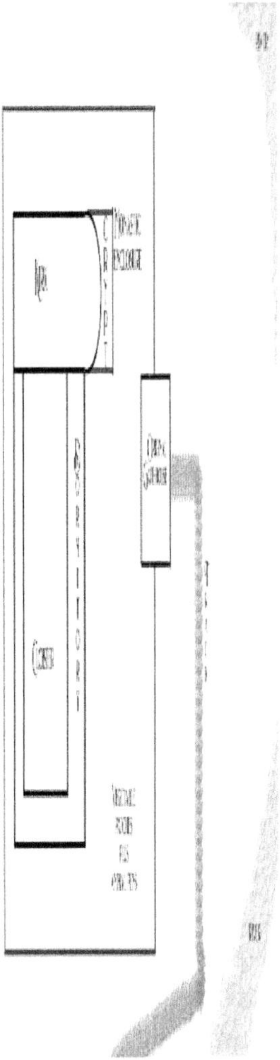

When she got near her cottage, she saw a bemused Jeff standing outside of her front door and watching as Cameron marked out a pentagram in what grass there was before the rhododendrons took over, on the space where – as best they could tell – the old crypt had possibly been, or at least begun.

Gary, as the one with the best skills at marking things out, had paced out where the points should go, and they'd been previously marked with some upturned plant pots to make them inconspicuous to the curious. Ideally, Rita would have had it marked out all in salt, but Gary had pointed out that using enough salt for it to be visible would kill the grass stone dead. So they'd have to wait for the winter rains to wash the salt away, and hope that the grass would re-grow in the spring, and for nobody to ask why there was a nine-foot pentagram in the dead grass in-between times. Instead, he'd come up with the solution of doing the lines in perlite – the white tiny beads usually incorporated into compost – then they'd just dribble some salt over the top of the perlite, which Gary could later clean up with the leaf blower.

"Better to not be killing anything off in the process," he'd pointed out to Rita, "even if it is only grass," which had earned him her surprised approval.

So now Cameron was pouring the perlite out in a steady trickle. The lines were a bit wobbly, because he was working fast, but at least the shape was coherent. Rita had decided that the top point of the pentagram, which represented 'spirit', should point towards the hotel. That meant that earth and fire points were anchoring the pentagram at the kirk, and she hoped that that would help if they were trying to haul a recalcitrant ghost that way.

Anna went and got the salt and followed Cameron around as they tried to explain to Jeff what they were doing and why. That was made rather easier as the six witches came into view, hovering about as far as they could get towards the hotel from the old kirk via Anna's cottage.

"Dear God, what happened to them?" Jeff gulped, looking at their ravaged faces.

"That's what a seventeenth century witch trial looked like," Anna told him sadly. "These ladies were strangled with a nasty piece of linked metal called a 'wirreit', which is the awful scarring around their throats, and it was done when they were already tied to the stake as the first of their punishments."

"Stake?" Jeff gulped. "You mean, like burning?"

Anna and Cameron nodded as they worked, leaving Jeff staring in horror as he realised why the witches seemed to have patchy skin.

"Their remains were thrown into this area, or rather beneath it, which at the time was the crypt of a dissolved nunnery," Cameron told his dad, as he came to stand by him as Anna stepped into the centre of the pentagram. "Gideon, who is the ghost we've had real trouble with, witnessed their deaths while still a teenager. Unfortunately he laughed and said some pretty vile things, egged on by his evil father. That's why the accused women really loathe him. We didn't think anything of old John Corsan, his father, was still here until very recently, but now we're as sure as we can be, that he's part of the reason why Gideon can't leave or rest in peace."

He pointed to the rhododendron bushes and trees beyond the rectangle of grass where Anna was. "There's a memorial tomb in there, which we thought Hugh's remains were in, but now we think that he's elsewhere. Gideon, though, may have been dumped in a shallow grave around here. That's why our helpful nuns are as far forward as they can manage – they're not hampered by rhododendron roots like we are, and can get right over the end of the old crypt. They said they want to feel what happens when we drag Gideon and/or old John out here. If they get a real sense of him, or them both, being anchored to something in the ground around here, then heaven help me, I'm going to have to fund a dig here and get him properly buried. We cannot go on with him causing this much chaos in the hotel."

By now there was the sensation of a strange breeze swirling around them which seemed to centre on the pentagram and Anna. Then they heard them. The six women began calling to Gideon and John Corsan, and if the modern listeners didn't catch every word of the old dialect, they were still sure that the six women were calling the pair some pretty awful names.

'Come on, ye' weasel-faced toad!' Jonet Clark called. 'Come and face us. Or are ye' scairt?'

'No' the big man now, are ye?' Agnes Clark taunted, not caring which of the two male ghosts took the bait. 'Oh, ye'd batter and burn women when ye' had yer bully-boys wi' ye. But ye'll no' face us alone. Coward!'

‘Come on, ye’ manky auld man!’ jeered Margaret Clark. ‘Or are ye’ scairt o’ us in death now?’

‘Frightened o’ this, are ye’?’ Grissell laughed, raising her skirts at the front and giving a wriggle of her behind, and making Cameron recall that underwear wasn’t the universal thing back in the women’s day, and glad he was viewing them from the back. ‘’Tis no’ a merkin, I have here but the real thing, and I’ll eat your scrawny wee manhood alive.’

“A merkin?” Cameron said, looking to Jeff in shock.

“A pubic wig, I think,” Jeff said with a startled laugh. “Or at least I think that’s what it is, but I’m going on episodes of *Blackadder* for that.” The women were continuing with the taunting, making Jeff add, “Jeez, I’m glad I didn’t get on the wrong side of these six. They’re formidable in death, heaven knows what they were like in life.”

Yet Cameron clarified with a sad sigh, “I think it’s more because they *weren’t* formidable in real life, Dad. These poor souls died with the few friends they had too terrified to help them for fear of ending up on the pyre themselves, and as women they had no voice in the court they were tried in.”

It felt like an eternity, but could have only been a minute or two later, when they heard a disembodied male voice shouting, ‘Hold yer whist, wuman! Dinna gi’ me that!’

"I think that must be the old man," Cameron whispered to Jeff. "That's not Gideon's voice as we've heard it before."

In amongst the dark branches of the rhododendrons, they could now see the shapes of the three nuns, and they seemed to be pulling at something unseen.

"Cam," Anna said urgently through gritted teeth. "Phone Gary. Tell him to tell Aunty to pull old John back her way. We're getting more of Gideon's spirit, even if it's old John who's mouthing off. If she tugs hard at old John, we might separate them out."

Cameron immediately did as she asked, and then rang Davey's phone as well to let Phemie know.

From up by the hotel, they now heard Gideon's voice calling, 'Elspeth? Where are ye'? I can hear ye' calling me. Where are ye'? Wait fer me. I'm coming!'

"Bloody hell," Cameron whispered shakily to his father, "Gideon thinks Anna is Elspeth – the daughter of one of our ladies there who he was obsessed with. We knew they could feel the echo of Elspeth in Anna, but we didn't think Gideon could."

The three nuns were suddenly joined by the shades of the other nuns, who drifted out of the old kirk, singing some sort of ancient Benedictine plain chant, and up at the hotel end, they could vaguely hear what must be old John shrieking at the top of his voice,

'Cut that caterwauilin', ye' papist whores! Stop that! Stop that or I'll set Veitch ont' ye'. We'll have ye' excommunicated, so we will! Shut up. Shut up!' and he continued to rant on in this way, but never coming closer until they heard him give an almighty shriek and start shouting, 'Let go o' him ye' vile witch's get! Stop callin' him. …Let me go, ye' vile auld wuman. …Gideon. You come back here! …Ach ye' were always too easily taken in by bluidy wumen. One flash o' a pair o' paps and ye' were dough in some doe-eyed wench's hands. Ye weakling! Man up, Gideon.'

Then suddenly there was a weird sucking sensation followed by the feeling of something snapping, as of elastic stretched too far.

Hurtling through the rhododendrons came Gideon's shape, wailing, 'Elspeth! Elspeth, wait fer me…I'm coming. I'm coming,' only to vanish towards the river, while from the top floor of the hotel came a howl of fury.

Cameron's phone rang, and Gary's voice was saying urgently, "Tell Anna to tell the nuns and witches to stop. Stop now! Rita's passed out and old John is somewhere in the hotel, but I don't know where."

"Stop! Stop!" Cameron yelled to everyone around him, and to their credit, the female ghosts did and listened to what he said.

As Anna stepped out of the pentagram, the nuns clustered around them, the prioress telling them, 'Gideon is now anchored in his bones, which are somewhere over there. We felt him go to his remains. They are further over than we thought, so the body that we felt being moved some hundred years after our ladies died couldn't have been him.'

"Probably some poor old tramp…err, vagrant," sighed Cameron, remembering just in time that the term 'tramp' wouldn't be one the nuns were familiar with. "Just an unfortunate soul who died out in the open. Oh bugger, so that means we really will have to find Gideon's body."

"I need to go to Aunty," Anna said worriedly, looking exhausted and with her hair plastered to her with sweat from her efforts.

"We'll come with you," Jeff said, coming to take her other arm to the one that Cameron came and supported.

Together they walked as fast as Anna could manage to the hotel. By the time they'd got there, Davey was waiting for them at the main door. "Rita's come around and she and Phemie are in the dining room with Gary," he told them, holding the door open for Anna and looking worriedly at her.

In the dining room they found Rita telling Gary not to fuss over her, but looking very pale, and sipping on a large glass of whisky. Phemie looked dog-tired, but not the kind of washed-out that Anna and Rita did, making them glad that they'd positioned her where they had.

"Nan, please go to bed and get some rest," Anna begged her. "As soon as Aunty feels up to it, we'll be heading back to the cottages and our beds too. We can do the post-mortem on what happened tomorrow over breakfast," and for once Rita didn't argue, which in itself said how much this had taken out of her.

As they walked out into the main hall and towards the stairs, they saw Hugh waiting for them at the bottom half-flight.

'Ye' did well tonight,' he said. 'The auld man is lurking up in the top rooms, but wi'out his son, he's no' as strong as he was. I doubt he could manifest anything right now.'

"Thanks, Hugh," Gary responded, but noted the qualification of 'right now'. That meant that at some point old John Corsan might scrape himself back together enough to become a minor pest, even if he wouldn't be tearing around the hotel firing off muskets.

Once he'd seen Rita tucked up in bed, with Jeff promising to call across to the hotel if she became unwell, and Anna in her cottage being looked after by Cameron, Gary went back to the hotel and resumed his more normal duty of night porter. Luckily, the rest of the night was peaceful, with no late-night guests returning, and Gary, too, was able to get some sleep on the folding bed in the back office. Thankfully, the cottages where India and her mother and Rowena were, and the one with Austin in, were too far down the track to have heard what was going on, or if they had, must have assumed the faint sounds were late-night revellers at the hotel, so Gary even had a quiet night from them. In the morning he handed the trial of organising breakfasts for the unwanted guests in the cottages over to Brenda, and then made his way home.

Happily, Rita was up and drinking coffee while Jeff and Cameron made them all quantities of bacon sandwiches. She still looked more drawn than Gary liked, but was enough of her old self to be fuming over the intransigence of their two ghosts to just give up and go to the Light. She was much intrigued by what Cameron and Anna reported hearing Gideon calling though.

"Well, well, so Gideon *was* triggered by you coming to the hotel, Anna. It's not exactly consoling for you, but it does mean we were right to think that something had changed for them to get so active all of a sudden." She turned and gave a watery smile to Cameron. "I don't think you need to worry about permanent infestations with ghosts after this. The likelihood of this happening at all was incredibly slim, and I'm now thinking that over time, even Gideon might have just faded away if nothing brought him back." Then she growled, "That old man, though, is even more frightened of what will happen to him than Gideon is. He really needs to be got rid of."

"With good cause," Anna added around another mouthful of bacon. "He has a lot to atone for, I'm thinking. And without Gideon to ride around on, we should be able to contain him until we can force him out."

"I know it was a rough ride for you last night," said Rita warily, "but I don't suppose you noticed where Gideon vanished to?"

Anna sat back and thought. "I don't think he's within anything of the old monastic enclosure. From what the nuns have told us, that didn't go much further north than a thin strip around the northern side of the kirk, although obviously it extended out to the hotel if that was the old gatehouse to the enclosure. I think he headed more towards the riverbank, but that's going to be a nightmare to find."

Jeff cleared his throat. "I know I'm the late arrival here, but can I make a suggestion?" Getting nods all round, he continued, "Well I think you're making this more complicated than it needs to be. Those huge rhododendrons around the back and down along the river paths are the same kind of thugs I used to help clear out rhodo'-bashing, to remove them from things like riverbanks and where they were choking native plants, and we burned them. They're invasive, not protected species or anything. You don't need permission to hack them right back, just a couple of lads with chainsaws and a chipper to get rid of the rubbish.

"At this end of the summer, I bet you could get a landscape firm in here fairly quickly. So if you get them to sweep the area clean of top growth, then you'll be able to walk over it if you're careful. And am I right in thinking, Rita, that you know the feel of Gideon well enough by now, that if you're virtually standing on top of him, you'll know it?"

"Oh yes," Rita said confidently, "and I suspect Anna will, too."

Cameron heaved a sigh of relief. "Well that's all very achievable. I'll get on the phone first thing tomorrow morning. In fact, if I can get someone who'll run a mini digger over the site, fetching out the roots, we might even unearth Gideon in the process. That would be a lot easier on everyone concerned. …Now what the hell are we going to do about the living nightmares?" and he jerked his head towards where his cottage lay.

CHAPTER 25

It was at this point that Gary revealed the packet with the knife and fork in, and explained his idea of getting Gaylord's DNA.

"Excellent idea!" Jeff immediately agreed, making everyone recall that he'd effectively been entrapped into marriage with Cameron's mother, and why he would be extra determined for that not to happen to his son.

Rather more of a surprise was for them to walk around en mass to the cottages, and find Austin just standing outside in the small garden, perfectly still.

"You okay, Austin?" Jeff asked carefully.

"Birds!" Austin answered with the biggest smile. "Birds in the trees. Had birds in the trees at school. I like birds."

"Would you like to come and live here?" Anna asked gently, and all of them were taken aback by the way Austin instantly said yes.

That was one obstacle removed, hopefully, because if he was this taken already, his feelings might only strengthen. They then went into the kitchen and realised that Helen had decamped to next door to be with her friend and India. Leaving Jeff to sit quietly watching Austin, the rest of them went to find the women. It turned out that none of the three had bothered to go and find Gaylord; clearly some country air and food that didn't stuff him full of chemicals had resulted in the little boy finally getting a proper night's sleep. Growling under her breath, Rita went to make sure he was all right.

"What do you think you are playing at, Cameron Wiseheart?" was Helen's opening rant. "How dare you ignore me!"

Yet she was unprepared for the way Cameron looked at her wearily. "You never stop trying to manipulate us, do you, Mum?"

"Manipulate? Now you just…!"

"Shut up!" Anna overrode her. "That's enough. You've twisted things and turned them around so that they look nothing like the truth anymore, so you stop it." She turned to India. "We're not so different, you and I."

India gave a snort and looked Anna up and down in disgust. "I'm nothing like you. I wouldn't be seen dead dressed like *that*, for a start off."

As Rita reached the bottom step of the stairs and prepared to wade in on Anna's behalf, Anna herself waved to Rita that she'd got this. "I didn't mean clothes or anything like that. I meant we're both products of our mother's aspirations."

India looked at her blankly.

"Mrs Hackstone," Anna began again, addressing Rowena. "You know full well that Cameron isn't Gaylord's father." Then as the woman took a deep breath, about to start screeching, Anna snapped, "Stop it. You *know*. You knew when India went into labour months too early for the child to be Cameron's, and the nurses told you that Gaylord was full-term. Frankly, I don't give a damn whether you made that clear to Mrs Wiseheart, and the two of you cooked this idea up to make India respectable by forcing Cameron into the role of father. Or whether you kept your so-called best friend in the dark, and lied through your teeth to her so the outcome was the same."

A glance to Helen said that she probably had been in the know, but Anna wasn't about to debate that. They were as bad as one another in that respect. "You need to know that what you are doing is blackmail," she said firmly.

"No it isn't!" was Helen's outraged squawk.

"It bloody-well is," Anna insisted. "And the proof of that is in the fact that you did it to extort money from Cameron. Money which, when you couldn't get it out of him, you stole from your older son." She waved aside Helen's blustering. "Yes, it was theft. Austin had no idea of what you did."

Jabbing an accusing finger at Cameron, Helen snarled, "Well then *he's* as guilty." "He's *stolen* this hotel off Austin! That's more money than I took to support his bastard."

Cameron physically reeled back at the savagery in his mother's tone, making Anna truly angry. "Cameron stole *nothing*. It all went through banks and solicitors, and every last penny was repaid into Austin's accounts. We have proof. So don't you dare accuse him of that. And is that what you think of that poor little boy upstairs? Is that all you can call him? A bastard? Shame on you!"

By now Rita was building up to a full head of steam, and the word 'bastard' tipped her over the edge into full Glaswegian outrage. "Right you, ya manky bitch," she fumed, directing her first tirade at Helen. "Comin' here tryin to pap that wean on him! You're a fucking disgrace. No' fit to be called a mother." And turning to Rowena she continued, "And you, ye' scheming tramp…ye' really think he'd go near a wee whore like *her*?" She jabbed the finger of blame at India. "She's even mankier than you!"

Rita managed to take a deep, steadying breath as the other two older women were momentarily stunned. Clearly women with aspirations of grandeur from Edinburgh didn't often get the full Glasgow Fury speaking her mind to them.

"You be awful careful," Rita now carried on, still seething and only fractionally calmer. "All three o' you, actually. The state of that wean when he arrived here, and with other members of our staff independently witnessing it, means we could have Social Services onto you for child neglect. Do you really want to be dragged through a families' court? Because I have the contacts to make sure you do."

She turned to India specifically. "Do you want to lose your son? To have him taken into care? Because that's a real possibility if you keep on the way you've been going. …Jeez-oh-day, do ye' have even a scrap o' mother's love for him?"

Yet far from any frantic protestations that she would never want to lose him, all India did was give another of her sulky shrugs. That all by itself had Anna welling up on Gaylord's behalf. She knew how it felt to grow up being the unwanted addition in a family. That sense of never being 'enough', or sufficient compensation for having lost something nobody ever made clear to you, was something she wouldn't wish on her worst enemy; nor the endless striving to get a meagre demonstration of the affection which other parents gave without thinking twice.

Rita was equally disgusted with Rowena and Helen. "And as for you two tramps…there are women who would love and adore a wee grandson like him, yet you two…" Words temporarily failed her for something sufficiently disgusting. "You canna summon up an ounce of love or affection for him. But then if you'd been decent women and set a proper example, then this miserable scrawny baggage wouldn'a be the total failure of a mother *she* is."

"You are leaving first thing tomorrow morning," Gary said, taking control of the situation before one of the daft trio said something that had

Rita truly raging and getting physical. "I'll not have you running off the road on the way back to Edinburgh because you've set off in a temper this late, but tomorrow I shall be over here and putting your cases into the car, packed or not. All of you. Not Austin though. He's staying here. Right now Jeff is out there offering him a permanent place here in the peace and quiet, and Austin has already said yes in principle. He's a grown man, you harridan, and without you yanking him here, there and everywhere, he's perfectly capable of making his own mind up."

"Don't be ridiculous you stupid man!" Helen spat at him. "Austin needs care! Not being left in the hands of some…some decrepit wannabe *Outlander* hero and a shrivelled old shrew."

She never saw the slap that toppled her backwards in her chair. As she lay on the kitchen floor sucking in air like a landed fish out of water, Rita stepped forwards to loom over her. "Old shrew, am I? Then how come Austin is happily out in the garden listening to the birds and completely calm? It's you, you vicious botox-stuffed hell-cat. You're the one who winds him up like your own mechanical toy, and then sits back laughing while he causes chaos. But you dinna think, do you? You're too full of how everything revolves around *you* to worry that he might get hurt in the process."

"You can't take my baby," Helen wailed. "He needs *me*! How dare you…you…*bastard*. You can't take him away from me. I won't let you! He's *mine*, do you hear me? Mine! Don't you dare tell him what to do. You don't control my precious boy. I'm the only one who understands him. He can't help being what he is. Stop blaming him. Stop making him out to be a monster."

"Nobody called him a monster," Rita growled. "Pull yourself together, ye' daft bitch. All anyone's tried to do is warn you how dangerous it could be for Austin himself if he lashes out at people."

"Dad and I have tried to warn you about the danger of not teaching Austin how to remain calm over and over again," Cameron said, recovering enough to come to stand shoulder to shoulder with Gary. "We've said that one day Austin could really hurt someone and end up in court over it. But would you listen? Did you care? No, you didn't, because all you've ever done is use Austin as a weapon against us."

There was a high-pitched wail from Helen, and she flung herself dramatically down into one of the chairs and began sobbing hysterically, the effect rather spoiled by the fact that she couldn't quite wring out any real tears.

"I see through you now, Mum. I see all the attempts to guilt-trip Dad and me, just like you're trying to do now. And do you know the worst of it? I see that we could have done everything you asked of us on every occasion, and it still wouldn't have been enough. It wouldn't have been enough, because if you'd once said that you were happy with what we'd done, it would have meant that you lost what you see as control over us. While you have us turning ourselves inside out trying to jump through your impossible hoops, you're calling the shots all of the time. There's nothing in it for you if we succeed. Only by failing do we feed your endless need to be centre stage and have control over us in a vice-like grip.

"Well we're done. Both Dad and I. It's taken us far too long, but we're not playing this game anymore. If you want to see anything of me ever again, then you can start by being reasonable towards Dad. He's supported you and cared for us for all these years, and you wanting to keep everything you've ever had in your marriage and let him have nothing, is beyond selfish. It's arrogant and cruel."

Helen had by now lifted her head up off the table where she had collapsed in a ridiculously dramatic flop, and was glaring at everyone but Rowena and India. "Selfish, am I?" She gave a nasty laugh. "You wait. I'll drag your precious father through the courts and he'll be lucky to have the clothes on his back by the time I've done with him."

Rita's hoot of derision shocked her into silence. "You think that, do you?" Rita snorted with savage glee. "Oh, I can't wait to see you try. The women who get those kinds of settlements are ones who've been in the position Jeff's been in – the ones giving their all for nothing in return. But you? You're the other face of those abusive husbands. Not every case of cruelty that goes to court is about physical violence, and these days, courts recognise that men can be as much the victims as women can. It's not a one-way street."

There was something in the certainty with which she said this that shut Helen and Rowena up – though on later reflection, they did wonder whether the pair had remembered that Rowena's divorce hadn't gone the way she planned.

"So tomorrow, you are leaving," Gary repeated. "For today, you do not come across to the hotel. Not for *anything*. We shall send you a meal across tonight, and if you even think about causing trouble, you should know that I have the local police on speed-dial and I won't hesitate to call them."

"I's hungry," a little voice from the stairs said.

"Oh are ye'?" Gary said, his tone of voice immediately changing to warm and friendly, and coming to sweep Gaylord up in his arms. "Well then we'd better go upstairs and get you dressed and take you to breakfast."

It didn't take him long. Time in which a sullen silence hung over the cottage's kitchen, Rita and Anna glaring at the other women, and Cameron looking at his mother in a way that said he was wondering why it had taken him so long to see what she was really like. Rowena went to sit by Helen, making a great play of rubbing her back and saying soothing words, while Helen sniffed and glared, but had run out of steam after her Oscar-winning paddy. When Gary came back with Gaylord, they headed back to Gary's cottage, with Cameron briefly detouring to tell Jeff what had happened.

Even so, they were surprised when Jeff appeared a bit later with Austin. Harris and Lewis were happily watching Gaylord's every move as he ate the square-sausage bap Gary had made for him, ever hopeful that they'd get some. Yet Austin also seemed to be happy with the big dogs and them with him, and even Lewis was less bouncy and approached Austin with a soft sniff, not a slurping lick with his paws up on him. The fact that Gaylord was also calm, and quite happy to sit on the floor afterwards while Gary told him a story, meant that there wasn't even any friction between him and Austin.

"Dogs have an awful good sense of when someone needs them to be gentle with them," Gary said softly to a surprised Jeff. "It goes for little kids, old people, and the disabled. It's only abused dogs that turn on people, and that's the fault of the owners, not the dogs."

Later on, Phemie and Davey walked over, and all agreed that those two needed to go home and rest up after all of the excitement.

"You can always come back in a week or two's time," Anna said firmly when Phemie made to protest. "I don't think any of us intend to try anything without taking time to think it through. We can always confer with you over the phone."

Therefore the day passed without any further repercussions. Both Gaylord and Austin seemed to be all the better for a short afternoon walk in the fresh air, and by the time Anna went on shift afterwards, a strange sense of peace had descended.

The following morning, Davey's last act was to help Gary chivvy and harangue Helen, Rowena, and India into Helen's car and to watch them leave to make sure they didn't turn back. In fact, Gary drove Phemie and Davey to the station, tailing Helen all the way to the Dumfries bypass where they turned off to Edinburgh, and then after the station, did a long loop to come back to check other roads and make sure the dreadful trio really had left. The only thing that tore at all of them was the way Gaylord sobbed at leaving his new best buddy in the form of Gary, and to her own surprise, Anna as well. But then she grasped that being picked up and cuddled when distressed was going to have much more of a profound impression on him than a child who always got that. The little boy twisted in his car seat and waved frantically to Gary until they disappeared out of view, making Gary wish that they'd been able to remove him from the toxic trio. It might be time for Rita to get in touch with that contact in Social Services, he thought bitterly as he drove back. No child deserved to be stuck with that neurotic trio as the adults in its life.

Cameron was as good as his word, and by the end of the week a landscaper, who reckoned he could fit most of the job in before he started another contract, had appeared with wagons, chainsaws, and a chipper. As the rhododendrons along the stretch of garden up from the river path disappeared in short order, they realised that Jeff had been right – there was nothing here that couldn't be cleared away. At this stage, all that was happening where the memorial tomb lay was a tidying up of the rhododendrons, not least because clearing around the tomb would need to be done more carefully, and because once stripped of the tangle of bushes, the garden beyond looked more post-apocalyptic than decorative.

"If we can get that stretch looking a bit better, then I'll get some of the closer bushes cut down," Cameron said to Anna, as they watched yet another huge pile of branches and twigs get munched up and spat out as chippings, "but it's a bit of an eyesore as it stands."

Anna agreed. "And we've got those weddings to get through yet. We can hardly have a garden like a war-zone when they've booked it with how it looked before. The only people who come along this bit at the moment are the fishermen, and they don't give a stuff about the pretty plants." She surveyed the expanse of stumps sticking up out of bare earth. "Even the best of photographers can't make this look good. Mind you, this does give you the chance to have something rather nice put in over the winter to cater for wedding photos in the garden. We can make something positive out of all of this."

To their relief, the weddings over the following weeks went off without disasters. Hugh had confirmed that wherever Gideon was, he hadn't returned to the house, and it was only Hugh's worry that Gideon might now be even closer to his mother and the other women that had him lingering. That and the relic of John Corsan. All of them said that they felt him like a nasty oil-slick on the air when they walked up through the fire doors onto the second floor's landing, but rather more concerning, more often on the mezzanine landing. Why his ghost should linger there, they weren't sure, but Gary, for one, was definitely attributing the odd atmosphere in the small sitting space to old John more than Gideon, now.

Jeff had declared himself more than happy to help with some of the research, and so once he'd been back over to Edinburgh and brought some more of Austin's things over for him, he and Cameron took it in turns to keep an eye on Austin, and when he wasn't doing that, Jeff headed into Dumfries and the local archives. Austin was soon found a carer in the person of a former mental health nurse not much older than him, who, after a nasty brush with Covid-19, had found work on the wards too exhausting, and so was more than glad to come and live in with Austin. That Austin liked Mike was a blessing for both Cameron and Jeff, and Austin seemed to enjoy the more peaceful life, which as Gary pointed out, might mean that after years of Helen's screeching, he was as exhausted by her as Jeff was.

It took the best part of August before Jeff had anything to report, but when he did, it was eye-opening. With Phemie and Davey back over in Fife, he had made a point of sharing his meals with Cameron in the cottage they were now both in, and most of the time Rita joined them. But when the rotas allowed, they had family meals there which included Anna and Gary, and this Friday was one such occasion.

"I have news," Jeff told them with a gleam in his eye. "I've found a newspaper article about the garden."

"Ooh! Do tell," Anna said as she poured them all an after-dinner coffee.

Jeff's grin got broader. "Well this is actually a piece about the production of the tomb in the garden, which is dated 1851, but it refers back to the discovery of the body. Listen to this…

"Mr Patterson was prevailed upon to create a tomb for one of the hitherto unrepresented martyrs to the cause of the free Kirk. With the house in near ruins, there were no ladies whose sensibilities might have been offended by this disturbing of bodies, for the current owner, Sir Robert McCartney, lives in Edinburgh for the most part. He recalls that his great-uncle, Edgar McCartney, told him of the hunting of a renegade Covenanter called Hugh Ferguson, with the insistence that if ever the said Ferguson was discovered, he should be taken immediately to the justices at the nearest tolhouse. Sir Robert was also told that the house was a refuge for Covenanter preachers, and that it was in the taking of one of these that Ferguson was killed.

Upon investigation, the bones of the dead man were not found, but the memorial has gone ahead in his memory. A local woman said that one of her ancestors saw the Covenanter being buried in a shallow grave near the river. This obviously pre-dates Sir Robert's ownership of the house, but he believes that shortly after the event it was bought by his family from a Captain Ferguson, who had inherited the place through his wife. At the time, Captain Ferguson was at pains to point out to Mr McCartney's ancestor, that he was no relation to the renegade who had died there, for at the time this would have placed him in a perilous position, and in danger of being taken himself. Happily, the Earl of Douglas was able to confirm to Sir Robert's ancestor that Captain Ferguson was a loyal soldier of the Crown.

Captain Ferguson said that the house had only bad memories for him, and since it had nothing to do with his family was glad to sell it. Sir Robert said that his family were told that Captain Ferguson had been driven out by the ghosts, and that the reason nobody wished to live in the house now was also because of the unquiet ghosts. The stairs in particular were a place where they were seen, and Sir Robert's wife has declared she will never set foot in the place again. Therefore upon appeals from the local minister, Sir Robert is willing to have the memorial placed so long as it is not visible from the house, should he wish to sell it."

"Oh thank, God," Cameron breathed in relief. "So I don't need to start applying to open up the tomb. To be frank, knowing how long things like planning applications can take, I was worried that it could take months to get through."

Anna gave his hand a reassuring squeeze. "And the contractor is coming back with the digger this week to start getting the roots out."

"Hmm," Gary added. "I think Mr McCartney was a bit adrift in saying it was his great-uncle, though, don't you? If this piece was in 1851, even if this Robert McCartney was in his fifties, meaning he'd been born around the turn of the century in the eighteen-hundreds, it's stretching it a bit to think that someone of an age to be his grandpa's brother would himself have been old enough to be actively involved in 1715.

"Even being rough with the calculations, it's unlikely that his father was born before 1760…and his grandfather not before 1720. So neither he nor a brother are likely to even have been alive in 1715, let alone old enough to be doing much of anything. Didn't the ladies tell us that the dreadful John McCartney, who was in league with John Corsan, had an older son quite aside from the Edward who ended up with Isobel?"

He got a nod from Anna. "Then I'm going to suggest that the McCartney who bought the house off Captain Ferguson was that older son's child or even grandchild, who could certainly have been alive in 1715, making him a great-great-uncle, or even a great-great-great-uncle. Let's not forget that the purchaser had to be someone mature enough to have that kind of money to splash around – not a young chap in his twenties, say, unless he'd suddenly come into money, which there's no hint o here. So let's not take it as gospel that they searched that hard for a body.

"The 1715 McCartney might well have known something of what old John McCartney did alongside John Corsan, and been warned not to get people asking too many questions. Regardless of what they did to those poor women, they clearly did some dodgy land deals to get their hands on places, and in 1715 there'd be enough local families who'd still have some memory of what went on in 1659 for him to want to not rock the boat too much. So I think we need to keep our search fairly broad because of that. But on a more positive note, I'm wondering whether the roots of those huge bushes might, over time, have brought Gideon's bones a bit closer to the surface? We may not have to go down that far to find him if we keep an open mind as to where he might be," which was a comforting thought to all of them.

The initial clearing of the rhododendrons had happened very fast, but then the contractor had had to go to his other job, and it would have been hard to explain to him that they needed it cleared to go and look for a body. The first week the top growth had been taken off, it would have been foolish to even try walking over the site, because there were stumps everywhere, and hardly a place to put a foot down evenly. A sudden dry spell had worked in their favour, though, and what greenery there had been left had now died down, showing just where the main stumps were.

But it was also something of a surprise to all of them just how big an area the rhododendrons had covered – even to Gary, who had to confess that he'd not paid them much mind, being more interested in the fishing than gardening. From where the memorial tomb lay – which nobody called

Hugh's anymore, since he wasn't in it – there was quite an expanse where a grave could have been dug. It covered a loop in the river's bank, and from there went back many yards further than they'd appreciated, almost up to the driveway.

"What a pity that the roots will have disturbed everything so much, there's not much point in asking the nearest university with an archaeology department if they'd like to use our site to train some students with ground-penetrating radar," Gray said regretfully.

"It makes a difference?" Cameron asked.

"Oh yes. They look for things like air pockets in the ground, and different moisture levels," Jeff answered. "I love watching the old re-runs of *Time Team* and seeing what the Geo-Phys team come up with. And I know what Gary means. They could cover this area far faster than we can, and scan it for where we should actually dig."

Rita gave an amused snort. "You boys with your mechanical toys. We don't need a machine to scan the place. We dowse!"

"You can do that, Rita?" Gary asked in amazement.

"You just stand back and watch me," she said with a grin. "All I need is to be able to walk over that lot without breaking both ankles and I'll soon sort it out."

CHAPTER 26

Once the contractor had spent two days with the mini digger, the area was considerably safer to walk over if still not exactly level, and it was time to start hunting for Gideon's bones. Rita produced two sets of metal rods, each one with a right-angle bend in it to create something to hold, while letting the horizontal bit move.

"It's all about letting go and allowing the rods to do the divining," she explained to Anna. "You can't force dowsing. It happens in its own time. But when it works, it's remarkably effective. What you are waiting for is the two rods to suddenly meet and cross over. At that point, you're onto something. Where the uninformed go wrong, is them forgetting that dowsing can only show you 'yes' or 'no'. So asking complicated questions will get you nowhere."

"So I need to ask, am I getting closer to Gideon?" Anna guessed, holding the two rods like they might bite her.

Rita shook her head. "No. 'Show me when I am standing over Gideon,' is more how you should phrase it. 'Getting closer' could happen when you step within a radius of several yards, but that won't help us much, will it? We know he's *somewhere* under what was that tangle of bushes, it's getting right up to him that we need to know."

"So, 'Tell me when I'm within two yards of him', might be even better to start refining things down a bit?"

"Excellent!"

They started off at the most uphill point, largely because Rita had taken on board Cameron's point of the river having silted up on this side. Given how far the rhododendrons had crept to beyond the old kirk, they thought it unlikely that Gideon would be even further from the river than the driveway, but also that for him to have lain undiscovered for so long, he must be somewhere where the bushes had kept him covered. So working towards the river over the uneven ground gave them the best chance of finding him.

For an hour or two, Rita and Anna went back and forth along the turned-over earth, taking it in turns and going slowly for safety's sake, but finding nothing. They stopped for a break and then began again, grateful that Gary had used some twine and canes to mark the area out in sections to make sure that they didn't cover the same ground twice. Yet even Rita's certainty of finding Gideon had taken a beating by the time four hours had passed and not as much as a twitch of the dowsing rods.

"Where is the pestilent man?" she muttered darkly, as they got to the start of Gary's final row of squares before the river path. "You definitely saw him heading this way?"

Anna shrugged. "As sure as I can be, but it was all a bit fraught that night, and of course the bushes were still standing." She picked up the rods and went to stand in the lee of the old kirk's north wall to get out of a sharp easterly wind that had picked up, needing to warm up a bit before starting again.

All of a sudden the rods twitched.

Whatever Anna had thought it would feel like, she hadn't expected anything quite so vigorous. "Aunty?" she called, her voice wobbly. "I've got something."

"Ach, will you look at that," Rita declared with satisfaction as she came around and saw what had happened. "I told you the rods would find him. But what the heck is he doing here?"

She took them off Anna, and now Anna had a clear view of how the rods really worked as Rita narrowed down the spot with careful questions.

"My goodness," she said, as they stopped at a spot which must have been far enough away from the kirk for the nuns not to feel him, especially with his spirit still anchored in the house, but close enough that if his spirit *had* been with his bones, he could have seen the kirk, and possibly heard the nuns praying. "Katherine must have truly hated her brother."

"Why?"

"The north wall," Rita said, as if that was explanation enough. Then seeing Anna's blank expression, realised she'd better explain. "You almost never get a north door in a kirk or church, because that's where the Devil is supposed to be able to enter. In some churches, even the windows on the north side are smaller. It's also why, when you find an old church building that's been expanded by putting a side aisle on, it's inevitably on the south side. If there is a north aisle, it's often later than the south one, and only put in when the church *really* needed more room."

"Wow! So Katherine was treating Gideon as though he was her own personal demon?"

"Something like that. But do you know what, Anna? I think there was also an element of wanting to make him suffer by being that close to the old Catholic kirk, not a place like Irongray, which had been Protestant for a longish time by their lifetimes, and Presbyterian for many of those. She must have known what their father had been like as a supporter of men like Veitch, and presumed Gideon was the same."

"I would have thought it even more likely that Gideon told them about Veitch hiding their brother Matthew," Anna suggested. "Jean and Katherine might not have loved their father, but having him murdered might have been more than either of them could just shrug off. They may well have thought that if Gideon had given Matthew up earlier, he'd never have had the chance to kill the old man. They may have loathed their father, but that doesn't prevent them for blaming his death on both of their brothers."

Gary, Cameron, and Jeff agreed with her when they told them of their success, and that they now had a location to start digging. However, Jeff, as the most recent arrival, had a question.

"How did these kirk-men get to have so much power?" he wondered. "I just don't get how men like Veitch came to have such a grip on his parish that they could terrorise people like Gideon. Surely everything you've told me points to his father being a powerful man in the community if people were afraid of him?"

"Ach, you have to understand that most folk were illiterate – or at least might be able to read a wee bit for things like bills o' sale, but not much more – and even men like John Corsan wouldn'a have found reading that easy," Gary explained. "In a world with no newspapers except for a few in big cities, no TV or radio, let alone the internet, the place where news was passed out to the people was from the pulpit on a Sunday. You learned of the outside world from what the minister *chose* to tell you, which had been passed down to him from the bishop or the laird. The local laird wouldn'a stoop to coming to address his tenants, and half the time he probably didn'a live on the estate anyway. So he'd get word passed to the minister and leave it to him."

He sighed. “That’s where it got so messy around here, because when the government finally woke up to the propaganda being preached, and told the local lairds to put a stop to it, it was a bit like trying to put the genie back into the bottle. The locals didn’a know the laird, but they did the minister or presbyter. And them putting, quite literally, the fear o’ God into you for what would happen after you died, was a lot more convincing than anything the laird’s man could say.

“The local minister could even excommunicate you – and in those days, that was the very worst thing that could happen to you, because everyone ‘believed’, and to be cut off from Heaven for eternity was unthinkably bad. That’s why old John thought his threat of having someone excommunicated was so powerful. Your life here on earth might be dire, but what got most people through their grim days was the firm belief that there was something better waiting for them once they died. But it’s why the Stuart kings desperately needed control o’ the clergy. Have them on their side, and they could discourage rebellions and encourage loyalty to the crown.”

“Oh!” Jeff now caught on. “But if the minister thought that the King was ungodly, against their version of the Church, and preached against the King…”

Gary nodded. “You have it. After all this started, I got interested and started reading up on this era. Turns out the reason why Fife in particular was such a hotbed of dissent was that a lot o’ ministers went to St Andrews University, just as Gideon's brother did, which was heavily Presbyterian. If you think about it, with all its little harbours and the east coast trade across to the Continent, Fife was ideally placed for contact with very Protestant countries like Sweden and what are now parts of Germany. Back then it was the Holy Roman Empire, mind, made up of independent places like Saxony, Bavaria, Burgundy, and Swabia, and by the time o' the Thirty Years War, which is just before our Civil Wars, the Empire was split by religion into two, but no' in a neat line, every state was different.

"It's one of those weird twists o' fate that at the very same time, the noble families in Fife and southern Perthshire had the highest concentration o' officers serving as mercenaries over in those Continental wars. It was nothing new for younger sons of noble families to go abroad to get military experience, it happened all the time. It was just that at that particular time, they weren't in wholly Catholic countries like France or Spain, but right in the heartland of Calvinism and the birthplace of the Protestant church. So all of a sudden, you have verra experienced military men, who have personal experience o' fighting in, and for, a Protestant army wi' their chaplains and stuff. But at home, their local ministers are preaching the same things, and pretty vehemently, which obviously, if they then became the lairds, they weren't going to do much to stop if left to their own choices."

"That must have been a dangerous mix," Cameron, who had been listening to Gary's explanation, observed. "You can understand why a government loyal to the King would roll out that Highland army Hugh was in to try to squash dissent down here. I didn't get the full significance of that until now. But if Charles the Second and his brother were leaning towards Catholicism, then I assume the Highlands would be where they'd hope to have more support. And conversely, Fife would be the danger zone. …But why here? Why Dumfries and Galloway?"

"I suspect it was because it just happened that there was a hardcore of St Andrews-trained ministers around here. That university produced some real fanatics around that time. There were other universities, but the preachers down here hadn't gone to them. It's a pure fluke that it wasn'a Glasgow university that the majority came from – because Glasgow churned out just as many preachers – and although it did have a few radicals, it was nothing like as many as St Andrews."

"Didn't Hugh tell us at some point that he'd heard Gideon ranting about Matthew being part of the group who murdered the archbishop over there?" Cameron got a nod from Gary. "Well if you can bump off an *arch*bishop – so not just any bishop but the head honcho himself – I suppose it's not such a big step to killing your own father if you were of Matthew's frame of mind. I'm beginning to see why Gideon lived his whole life looking over his shoulder. I'm not saying that Hugh had it easier, because he clearly didn't. But in one way, being forced out of the area did him a strange favour in that he had room to breathe in a way that Gideon never did."

"And I think that has much to do with why Gideon has been such a recalcitrant ghost," Rita now added. "He's not likeable, but good grief, you can feel sorry for him."

"So once we've dug him up, where do we put him?" Anna wondered.

"I doubt that will be up to us," Gary answered. "The minute we find bones, we have to inform the police, even if they are clearly ancient. After that, it will be the county archaeologists coming out and lifting him. We can suggest Irongray, but it will be up to the county in the end as to where his bones are put to rest."

"Would it help if I offered to pay for his reburial at Irongray?" Cameron wondered. "If we keep it simple, and say that we think his are the bones of the Covenanter for whom the tomb was made, it'll seem less odd than trying to demand that a random set of old bones from someone else go there."

"That's a really good thought," Rita praised him. "Yes. Especially if we say we're not looking for him to have any grave marker, since he effectively has that here already. A parcel of bones will be more easily slipped into a spare bit of ground than him taking up a whole plot with a headstone."

The following day, Anna and Cameron went to a local garden centre and bought some rose plants, thinking that it would be a lot more convincing if it looked like they were just gardening than searching for something they shouldn't have known was there. Gary went and got several bags of farmyard manure, and so it gave a strange air of normality when the three men began digging a fairly deep trench in a straight line, some twenty feet out from the kirk's wall, which then got a goodly layer of manure worked in, and a rose over the top at regular intervals. For a horrible hour or so, they dug deep, got three roses in, and found nothing, then Cameron stuck his spade in and heaved, and up came a skull.

"Bloody hell! Hello, Yorick," he laughed nervously.

"I don't think we're quite into *Hamlet* territory yet," Gary said, taking the skull carefully off him, "or at least not unless you have some secret plot to murder your mum going on."

Cameron's laugh this time was less strained. "I might dislike her intensely at the moment, but no, I'm not at that point yet. And there's no step-dad lurking in the wings, either."

"Just don't let Harris and Lewis off their leads out here," Anna warned. "I really don't want to be pursuing those two around the grounds, trying to get a thigh bone back off them!" which elicited nervous laughter from all of them at the thought.

Gary went off and did the ringing of the police, and then all they could do was sit around and wait for them to arrive. Happily, even the keenest of detectives couldn't have argued that the bones were modern enough to warrant an investigation once the forensic team came and began uncovering them. The state of them made that clear even to a layperson. Therefore the body swiftly migrated from being a police issue to the county archaeologist's, and guests arriving to see the white tent over the spot were easily told of the discovery of an old body, possibly attached to what had once been a small kirk. The county archaeologist was quite happy for Cameron to pay for the re-interment at Irongray, and so on a rather bleak Friday afternoon in mid-September, the five of them plus Phemie and Davey, who had come over especially, found themselves at a smaller than normal graveside in the kirk-yard.

A very earnest young man was filling in for the resident minister, and had taken Rita's point about the body being an ardent Covenanter to heart. So there would be no eulogy – which would have been difficult in the circumstances even if it had been something which went into a normal Presbyterian service. The young minister had queried what they would like for hymns, and Rita had been about to say that none of their modern hymns would have been known to the deceased, when Gary suggested 'Abide with me.'

"It's got a good minor key – so it doesn't sound too modern – and has the right sentiment," he pointed out in their planning session in the bar. "I've got a portable speaker I can attach to my phone, so it won't be just us warbling along. I've got a good Welsh choir version that will do nicely."

Seeing that Jeff was about to ask Gary why on earth he would have such a thing to hand, Rita gave his foot a nudge under the table and shook her head. She knew that this came from Gary attending too many funerals of men he'd known – something she quietly explained to Jeff later on. Gary had come up with last-minute music for a few where he'd been one of only a handful attending, when PTSD and other demons had driven their families away, and some funeral director had come up with something the man in question would have cringed over. Being able to plug his phone into a chapel's sound-system had saved the day more than once.

At this point Gary became their expert on funerals, and so in short order they came up with Psalm 23 – the Lord is my shepherd – which they thought was pretty universal and must have been known in Gideon's day, especially the King James Bible version. And for the same reason, Gary suggested Psalm 121 – I lift up mine eyes unto the hills – which around here was more than a little apt. Teamed with a few traditional prayers, they thought that this would be a short but sweet funeral for Gideon, and as Anna said, "It's more than he's got in over three centuries, so he ought to be grateful he's got this."

What they didn't tell the young minister was that once he'd said goodbye to them, they were returning to the grave for Rita, Phemie, and Anna to call Gideon home. It took a few attempts, but then suddenly Gideon's ghost was there with them. What shook Anna was how different he was, almost cowed, and once he could see the Light, his sad cry of relief tore at all of them as he vanished towards it at speed.

'Ye' weren't there, Elspeth,' he wept. 'I thought ye'd be there by ma bones, but ye' weren't.'

"She'll be on the Other Side," Anna told him gently, though none of them were that sure that if he did meet Elspeth in the afterlife, that she'd be any too pleased to see him. "Elspeth and Isobel are already there."

'Oh, thank God. At last,' Gideon sobbed. 'I'm so weary. So tired o' *him* always at ma' heels,' though he didn't expand on whether that was Hugh or his father.

At this last, Gideon was glad to be going to his rest.

Thankful that at least part of the job was now complete, everyone piled back into the cars and headed home for some warm drinks and a celebratory tipple and cake. With Cameron driving Phemie and Davey with Jeff back to the hotel, it left Anna and Rita in Gary's truck, and now Anna said what had also been bothering Rita.

"That was a very different view of Gideon, don't you think? So how much of our trouble has been his father in the driving seat? We've still got that wicked old man's spirits loitering in the hotel, don't forget."

Rita sighed. "I hadn't forgotten, hen. Damn it, that one's like bloody glue for the way he sticks around. I'm sure Hugh has already figured it out too. Once John Corsan is gone, then we can deal with the others quite easily. But that old man is worrying me."

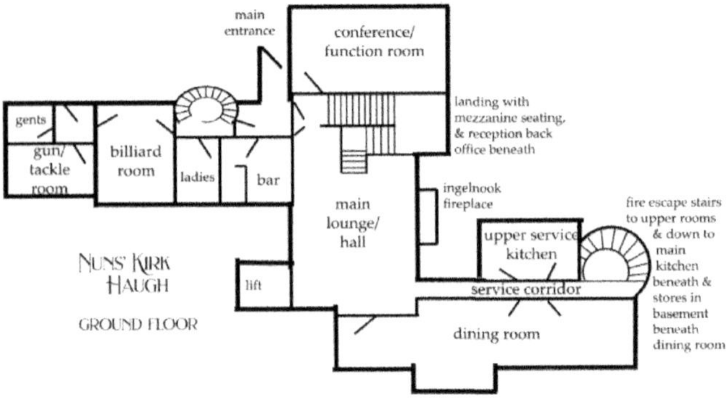

CHAPTER 27

They took the chance of a quiet Wednesday evening, close enough to the equinox and the full moon to satisfy Rita's criteria, to attempt to rid Nuns' Kirk Haugh of old John Corsan once and for all. Rita had dowsed all around the hotel, trying to find the right spot to focus on him specifically now that Gideon was gone. She half expected to find some residue of him in the Rosemary suite, but didn't, making Anna wonder, "I think we were right to assume that the reason why Gideon seemed weaker when we separated him out, was down to it being him who had the strong attachment to this room? Was this really his anchor point, which we broke and allowed old John to come to the fore again? Was Gideon telling us the truth when he said the room was his?"

"Goodness, that's a thought," Rita replied. "I hadn't considered it in quite that light, but you could have hit the nail on the head there. Didn't Gideon say that the old man had to have his room downstairs, in which case maybe he never came up here in life? Yes, if Gideon's strength was tied to his attachment to this room, when we broke it, we broke some of his own strength too. He may or may not have died here, from what Hugh said, but he could have had a very strong emotional attachment to it."

"Do you think that it was because it was the one space he ever managed to make his own?" Anna wondered. "We're so used to everyone having their own bedroom these days, we forget that it would have been abnormal in his – a totally new experience for him. It might have been the first time in his entire life that he had a place where he could be at peace without someone hounding him. That might explain why he effectively barricaded it against Hugh in the afterlife too."

"Aye. Couple that with the effect of us sending your dreadful late father-in-law's spirit off to the Light after Gideon had dived into him, and we might well have been chipping away at Gideon more effectively than we thought. So all of the strength we've suddenly feared might come from his father could actually be our misconception."

"That's reassuring," Anna said with relief, yet there was a definite black spot on the mezzanine landing, making her recall, "Didn't Gideon tell us something about his father being obsessed with having an oriel window?"

Gary, who'd been perched at the top of the flight of stairs leading down from Rosemary to the mezzanine space, watching Rita work, said, "I must admit, I thought this window here was later than that era. But rethinking that, it's possible that it was simply remade when this staircase was put in. If the house in its *Blackpark* phase was near derelict when that Major Grant chappie bought it in 1870-something, it's possible that much of the external stonework here was good, and they tidied it up when this staircase went in, putting in some new fancy tracery and the stained glass. That tracery is very Victorian."

Anna came to perch beside him, and looking at the window wondered, "But wouldn't this appeal to old John? In his day, affording stained glass like this would have been out of the reach of someone even as wealthy as him. Yet when it did go in, if he was watching, I bet he was chuffed to bits at getting something that grand in what he no doubt thought of as 'his' window."

"Aye, I reckon you're right, there," Gary agreed. "Well, well, he's the miserable sod who doesn't want anyone else sitting there and enjoying this spot, is he? Hopefully that weird chill Cam and I felt when we sat there will go for good once he's gone."

When it came to the night itself, Rita thought that they might cope with just her and Anna and Gary, with Cameron and Jeff stationed to keep any curious late-night guests out of the way. She really didn't want to expose Phemie to the old man's malevolence unless they had absolutely no choice, not after the way she and Anna had been drained separating him from Gideon – but then hopefully now he was weaker too. They didn't even start until midnight to give all the guests chance to get off to sleep, and aside from them the hotel was silent.

Thinking that while John Corsan might not be up to much manifesting, he could be capable of blowing out her candles as fast as she lit them, Rita made sure that the main ones were in the glass lanterns they'd hitherto only used in the old kirk, plus some more she'd bought for the occasion. Anna had collected up water tumblers from the restaurant for the tea-lights, since they were in their own metal cups and wouldn't ooze wax everywhere, and now there were tea-lights on either side of each step leading up to the landing from the hall and onwards from it up to the fire doors. They were leaving no dark corners for Corsan to lurk in.

The main nine candles that Rita had lit were on the landing's coffee table in a circle, and she'd chosen nine to represent the nine women whose lives Corsan had condemned at the trials. Three dishes with charcoal disks and incense burning in them were in the centre of the circle, and were already filling the space with the scent of frankincense, rose, and lavender – scents which Rita hoped would convey healing, not conflict.

"John Corsan," she began by calling. "It's time for you to answer for your life."

'Ah'm no' answering to ye', ye' auld besom,' a voice replied from higher up the staircase, making Jeff take a startled step back out of the way.

"It's not me but a higher authority who calls you now," Rita said firmly. "You cannot lurk here forever. I am not the one who will decide what price you have to pay for what you did."

'What I did? Ha!'

"John Corsan, I call you to answer for the trial and death of Margaret Clark, the woman you accused and sent to the pyre to be strangled and burned on the fifth of April 1659."

There was something like a shudder on the air.

"John Corsan, I call you to answer for the trial and death of Jean Thomson, another woman you accused and sent to her death on the same day."

Rita and Anna had carefully worked this list up, taking each of the accused women in the order that they had originally been brought to trial. They wanted there to be a building sense of his guilt. Janet McGown was listed next, but when they came to the fourth woman who went to trial, Rita was more specific.

"John Corsan, I call you to answer for the death of Agnes Bigis Cairns…"

'Ha! She didn'a burn on ma account. Got ye', ye' lying auld witch!'

"She *died* on your account," Rita snapped. "Stop nit-picking over your guilt. If she hadn't been brought in to be questioned, if she hadn't had to endure that travesty of a trial, then she wouldn't have been taken on that Saturday back to Kirkcudbright Tolhouse to await her death. And if she hadn't been *there*, then she wouldn't have been waiting like a tethered sacrificial goat for one of those who'd repeatedly raped her to silence her. Did you know that? Are you a rapist, too?"

There was a sullen silence, making Anna speak up, "*Someone* feared what she would cry out in her pain and fear. If that wasn't you, you surely knew who did fear that amongst those men who stood in the same room as her, and lied through their teeth."

'We didn'a lie! We swore on the Bible. Veitch held the holy book and we swore on it, so damn ye', ye' whore!'

"Veitch was the most corrupt of you all," Gary snapped. "Dinna give us any o' your blame-shifting excuses, Corsan. And dinna expect to be handing out his name on the Other Side and getting any leniency on account of it, either. He's probably been stoking the fires o' Hell all these centuries already."

The temperature dropped drastically, as if echoing Corsan's fear.

"So," Rita began again, "I call you to answer for your part in Bigis Cairn's death. You do not get to pick and choose who you answer for, and in many ways, hers is the worst case, because of the torment she suffered throughout her life, not just at the end. And you couldn't even leave her body to be buried where she'd lived, could you? Because you, or one of your cronies faked her suicide, the poor woman couldn't be buried on sacred ground, according to your blinkered beliefs. So you dragged her poor body all the way up to Dumfries, then shovelled the remains of the burned onto her, and carted her along with them to the kirk here. Disrespectful doesn't begin to describe that, and you *will* answer for your part in it."

She took a deep breath, and when he didn't answer back, continued, "John Corsan, I call you to answer for the death of Janet McNaught…"

Helen Moorheid, Jennat Callen and Agnes Clark's names all followed, all with the demand that he come and answer for them. In the background they could hear him chuntering on to himself about how unjust this was, and that he wasn't to blame. Yet when she came to the final name of Jannet Corsan, another form swam into view.

'I wasn'a old enough or strong enough to call ye' to answer fer ma Ma's death in life,' Hugh said, 'but before God, I call ye' to answer fer her now. I bear witness to the fact that she never put a curse on a soul in her life, nor did harm to anyone. Yet ye and yer cronies tormented her, tortured her to gi' ye' names o' other innocent souls, just so that ye' could grab their goods and chattels, and their crofts.

'Ye left whole families shiverin' in fear and doubt, always wondering' whether ye' were coming fer them next. Ye crippled women's hands, made it impossible fer them to earn an honest living, then called them witches when they traded what cures and potions they could still manage to make in order to buy a wee bit o' bread that they might no' starve. Ye defiled their most private parts wi' yer evil instruments o' torture, and fer what? What did it achieve that they could no longer feel the love o' their husbands, beside yer own warped fantasies? Ye're an evil man, John Corsan! Evil through and through, and I call ye' now to answer fer that.'

Perhaps because Hugh was in the same dimension as old John, finally he seemed to be dragged forward to where they could see him. Hugh and Gideon had always manifested as men who appeared younger than they must have been at the time of their death, and the same happened to old John. His appearance was of a mature man, but with no sign of the paralysing stroke he'd lived with for years before his death. But it gave the watchers a good view of how he must have appeared to the women at the trials. His was a cruel face, hooded eyes and a thin mouth above what seemed like a habitually clenched jaw, with sallow skin tight over his skull, and all topped by black hair. It was a face you wouldn't want to see facing you when accused, because there wasn't a shred of compassion or kindness there.

'She deserved what she got,' John Corsan said with a wave of his hand in dismissal.

"No," Rita said firmly. "You are the one who is going to get what you deserve, and I hope and pray that whoever on the Other Side decides what happens to you next, that they are not in a forgiving frame of mind, because you've never shown a drop of that to another being. None of these women deserved what you and your cronies handed out to them. None."

Then just when Corsan must have thought she was done, Rita added, "And I call you to answer for other deaths, that were your doing as surely as if they had stood in that court and had been sentenced. I call you to answer for Jonet Clark, Grissell McCartney, and Gellis Morisone."

'Ah didn'a kill *them*!' Corsan protested.

But Rita was implacable. "All three of these women died from the effects of being questioned, and died knowing that those they loved and cared for were in danger from you and your associates. You helped set them up for the questioning they endured, and you must take your share of the guilt. You were a blight upon their lives, John Corsan, and if those that stood alongside you were here now, I would be calling for the same for them. This is not vengeance, as I'm sure you would like to paint it to diminish it. This is justice."

The last word seemed to hit Corsan's ghost and it shivered.

Rita turned and began opening the way to the Light, while Hugh stood between Corsan and the way back up to his secondary lair, Anna now moving to stand by the way down, holding a candle to ward him off, so that Corsan could not escape the landing.

As the Light grew brighter, Corsan's ghost began to shiver and shake, glancing around trying to find some way, any way, out of there except that. Then as Rita began to gesture him towards it, a candle in her hand, suddenly he shot upwards, twisting and writhing to wedge himself up on the highest point of the window. Somehow he was managing to cling to the stone tracery, though for a real person there was nothing deep enough to have got a hold on and bear their weight.

Believing he was beyond their reach, Corsan began laughing nastily.

'Think ye' can drive me out o' my ain home just like that? Ye're naught but a wuman!' He spat that out as though it was the worst insult.

However, Anna had an idea. Running downstairs, she went into the back office and retrieved the brush they used for removing cobwebs. Of itself it wasn't going to make the slightest difference to Corsan, but it had plastic bristles and an extending handle, and coming back upstairs, Anna liberally sprayed the brush with the holy water Rita had used to seal the main hall and the upper stairs off to Corsan. Extending the pole to its limit, she jabbed the damp brush as high as she could towards Corsan, but he simply laughed.

"Allow me, lass," Gary said, taking the sprayer off her, pumping the pressure up more and turning the spray to a tight jet instead of a mist. Holding it like a pistol, he took aim and squirted. The jet still didn't quite reach, but as Corsan laughed again, he suddenly choked it off as Gary leapt nimbly up onto the end of the wooden bench-seat, giving him the necessary height.

As the jet of water shot upwards, Gary's aim being deadly accurate, Corsan scuttled like a malevolent spider across the top of the window, then realised to his horror that he was now closer to the portal of Light that Rita had open and waiting.

He also hadn't reckoned on Hugh, who beckoned to Anna to come closer to him. When they were almost face to face, he reached out as if he wished he could hold her hand.

'Ye' have been such a comfort to me,' he said wistfully. 'Ye' remind me so much o' my dear Elspeth wi' yer kindness. I truly hope that she is on the Other Side waiting fer me, but will ye' do something fer me when I'm gone?'

"Absolutely," Anna agreed without having to think twice.

'Will ye' go over to Fife and see if ye' can find her? If her spirit lies over there, tell her I never forgot her down all these years, and maybe if she can come towards her old home, we might meet again. I would so love to see her again.'

"I promise. And I'm sure she never forgot you. But am I Elspeth's daughter's descendent or Mailie's? Is it her daughter who grew up in Fife who is my ancestress?"

'Both,' Hugh said with a sad smile. 'Mostly Elspeth, but I feel Mailie in ye' which must come from her daughter who Elspeth raised, and a wee bit o' Margaret too – that's why ye' could connect to Isobel when ye' stood where she passed. I couldn'a tell at first when ye' asked, but the longer ye've talked to me, the better I could feel them.'

He looked to where Gary was harrying John Corsan back and forth with the water, but never quite getting the wretch to let go. The water in the bottle was getting very low now.

Hugh heaved a deep sigh, then calling back over his shoulder to Anna as he moved, 'Tell Ma I love her, and thought o' her at the last,' he flung himself at old John.

The two ghosts wrestled and tumbled, but Hugh had the momentum, and in a tangle of limbs the pair fell rather than walked through the portal. For an instant the Light flared even brighter and then closed with almost a snap.

"Jeez, Rita!" Gary gulped as he staggered, having nearly fallen towards it himself, having had to duck out of the way of the flailing ghosts. "I know we wanted shot o' him, but you didn'a need to close it quite that hard. What if I'd have fallen through?"

Rita shook her head, looking shaken. "I didn't close it. They did from the Other Side."

"Bloody hell," said Gary, sitting down hard on the nearest seat.

"I don't think you were ever in danger of falling through," Rita tried to reassure him, though she came to sit beside him and held his hand tightly. "I reckon they've been waiting to get him to come through for a long time, and weren't about to let him back out."

Anna looked at her worriedly as she, Cameron and Jeff came to join them on the seats. "I thought you said he couldn't come back?"

Rita huffed. "Come back once fully through? No, he can't, but how many near death experiences have you heard about from people who were on death's door? I've never done anything like this before, so I'm no expert, but I'd say someone over there was making sure even a scrap of him couldn't worm its way back before he was fully there."

"And God bless, Hugh," Gary said solemnly. "I know he said he wanted to see his mum and the other women safely on the Other Side before he left, so he's put a lot of faith and trust in us to see that done."

"We will," Rita said, giving his hand a squeeze. "We won't let Hugh down."

CHAPTER 28

Pulling themselves together, they got up and began the clearing up.

"Do we leave the candles burning?" Jeff asked.

Rita grimaced. "Ideally, yes, but there's no way I'm risking leaving this many flames burning unattended, and even the tea-lights have a few hours left in them yet. No, blow them out and clear them up."

Anna went and got a couple of oven gloves from the kitchen, because all of the holders were hot by now, and while Cameron went around blowing them out, she and Jeff picked them up once the wax had cooled enough not to spill, and they took them all through into the back office. There they carefully used some metal kitchen tongues to lift the tea-lights out, and then Anna took all the glasswear through to the kitchen and put them through the dishwasher, which she'd asked to be left on.

At that point they all staggered off to their beds, but in their morning meeting over breakfast, which for once they all took in the front dining room, being glad of a full cooked one, Cameron began by asking Anna what Hugh had said to her. It reduced her to needing a tissue as she relayed it, and even Gary and Jeff were choked up by his words.

"He was a faithful one, wasn't he?" Gary said with admiration. "Never wavered down the centuries."

Cameron wrapped an arm around Anna and said, "We'll take some holiday time over in Fife. I'd love to show you where Dad's folks lived, and we can easily explore a bit further afield. And don't forget, we have an open invitation to your grandparents' now, and that's in Fife, too. It's not an impossible task, even if we have to take a few goes at it."

Anna nodded and had another sniffle into a tissue.

"And we'll hold to the promise of seeing our ladies to rest, too," Rita promised. "They'll have felt Corsan's evil leaving the place, but also Hugh. I can't go and deal with them today, but tomorrow when I've had a rest I'll go and tell them what happened. Maybe on Sunday we can help them move on."

However Cameron had another thought. "Wouldn't it be good if we could find out where Hugh's bones truly lie? So we can tell Hugh's mum before she goes, and hopefully she can tell him? We've been so taken up with getting rid of the bad that I'm worried we haven't done enough for the good person in all of this."

"That does you credit," Gary praised him, but it was Jeff who said,

"Then you and I had better head back to the library and the archives, son. We were rather the bystanders last night, so now it's time for us to do our bit."

Luckily, Gary wasn't rostered in for the coming night either and was able to get some rest, but Anna had to do her bit come the evening, while Rita simply headed back to bed, wiped out. And the first day's investigating yielded nothing for Cameron and Jeff's efforts. Yet at the end of Friday afternoon, Cameron suddenly hit gold.

"Good grief, Dad, I think Hugh must be watching over us from wherever he is, because talk about last minute!" They only had half an hour left before the library closed. "I've found it – a reference to Gideon being buried. Total chance. Turns out someone from Australia came back and was hunting down his ancestors. I think he must have been one of Katherine or Jean's descendants, but he was interested enough to go hunting for Gideon. Something to do with him being a lay preacher in a church over there, and thinking that Gideon was an unsung martyr to the Covenanting cause."

"So where is he, or should I say Hugh, since we now know he's the one in that grave?" Jeff came to look over Cameron's shoulder to read the article in a local paper. If he'd been expecting something modern-day, he was much mistaken, because this had happened in the Edwardian era. "For those days, that's quite the journey he made to find his forebears," Jeff observed.

Cameron gave a snort. "I'm just bloody glad he's not around now, so we don't have to answer any awkward questions, because reading this, he thought Gideon was quite the hero."

"So where is Hugh? I don't recognise that place-name."

Cameron turned and grinned up at his dad. "It's the old graveyard where we found the modern memorial. Hugh's in an unmarked grave there. They found it through some crumbling parish records, not a tombstone. And I reckon that's a document that's felt the effects of time, which is why I didn't find it before. It's only in this article that we get a reference. So he *is* on hallowed ground, and it's *not* at Irongray."

The relief that everyone felt when they got back with the news was considerable.

"I was really worried," Anna said, as they toasted Hugh's memory with a glass of prosecco each, "that Katherine and Jean would have had no choice but to put him in Irongray's kirkyard. That would have been absolute torment for Hugh – not because of it being Presbyterian, but because of it being Veitch's and so very close to the site where Veitch had tortured women."

Cameron smiled at her. "I'm afraid I can't give you an exact spot, but I think it would be perfectly acceptable to go and place some flowers there for him."

It earned him a beaming smile from Anna. "That would be lovely. Yes, I'd like that."

"And I can tell Jannet that on Sunday as well," Rita said with relief. "I couldn't have lied to her about it, even if it might have given her some peace. She'll be knowing the truth too soon for me to be comfortable doing that. I don't want any of them thinking that we've been underhand with them."

On Sunday afternoon, they all assembled in the old kirk's nave, including Phemie and Davey, who once again had wanted to be part of this.

"Ladies, it's time for you to leave," Rita called gently, and was rewarded by the sight of the six remaining witches coming forwards, but also the thirteen nuns.

'We can go now,' the prioress told them with a grateful sigh. 'We only waited this long to be with these women, who have become dear friends down the years. Now that the evil is gone, we shall be glad to rest. We'll all go together now.'

Rita turned to Jonet Clark. "Before he left, Hugh asked Anna to visit where he last heard of your Elspeth. I'm not going to guarantee that we will find where she died, but we'll do our best, and hopefully she'll already be on the Other Side to meet you when you go through."

"Aye," Gary agreed, "and I know the part o' Argyll where she and Mailie went to with Sorley

McAllister, so we'll go and lay some flowers for Mailie too."

'Thank you,' Jonet said gratefully. 'Even if I canna find them on the Other Side, knowing what I know now has been such a comfort after all these years.'

"And Jannet," Rita said, "Hugh told Anna to tell you that he loves you and is waiting for you."

Jannet was wiping away ghostly tears, but they were ones of relief and happiness at the thought of finally being with her family, not ones of sadness.

Anna had been into Dumfries and brought back bunches of autumn flowers, and now the little kirk was full of asters, dahlias, and chrysanthemums, in warm, glowing colours, the scent of their greenery underlying the rose and lavender fragrances of the candles. She and Rita had been determined to make this a celebration and to make it uplifting. This was not a banishing but a releasing of these women from what had been captivity in all but name.

As the final six of the Dumfries women walked towards the Light, Jannet and her mother Grissell leading the way, followed by Jonet with her sister-in-law Geillis, and sisters Agnes and Margaret bringing up the rear, the watchers thought they could see seven faint figures on the Other Side waiting for them.

"Our other ladies and Hugh," Anna whispered to Cameron, whose hand she was holding tightly. "I'm so glad they're there to welcome them. I hope that Margaret reunites with Isobel, and that what I felt at Wigtown of Isobel helped to make this possible." She turned to Rita. "Is it worth asking whether I need to be doing something about Isobel?"

However, Rita was immediately shaking her head. "I think that was about delivering exactly the message we gave to Gideon and Hugh. Once you'd made contact with them, if you'd needed to do more it would have been apparent by now. No, Anna, that was a message pure and simple, even if it was a shock at the time. And if you needed further proof of that, it worked with Gideon, didn't it? I don't think he'd have let go half as easily without the knowledge that Isobel died before he reached her. Someone over there realised that and saw you as the way to finally tell him after all these years."

As the six women stood at the edge of the way onwards, Jonet turned back to them. 'I can never tell you how much you've done for us. What it means to finally leave.' She looked at Anna in particular. 'I feel enough of ma Elspeth in ye' to know that ye' will do as ye've said, and try to find my girl. But please dinna feel guilty if ye' canna find her after all this time.'

Anna smiled back. "Thank you, and for saying that."

'And Anna…'

"Yes?"

'Dinna make Elspeth's mistake. We kenned Hugh loved her more than Alex. And Rita, I ken ye' were being kind when ye' told us what had happened, but afterwards, when we talked o' it amongst ourselves, we kenned that something wasn'a right by the end. Ye' only spoke o' Elspeth, no' Elspeth and Alex.' She looked to Cameron. 'Dinna waste time, make the most o' what ye' have, fer none o' us ken what's coming fer us. Ye' may be ma Elspeth come again, but just because yon lad isn'a Hugh come again, dinna wait to try and find him, fer ye' never might.'

Anna felt herself tearing up. "I will, I promise," and she squeezed Cameron's hand tightly.

Then seeming to collectively take a deep breath, the six walked into the Light and vanished.

"Bless them, they're at peace," Phemie said with relief, and Rita agreed.

The nuns now lined up in pairs behind the prioress, and were already singing a plainchant. None of the modern people had a clue what it was, but it sounded joyful, or maybe that was simply the inflection the nuns were putting on it. Then just as the prioress reached the Light, one of the nuns towards the rear gave a cry of dismay and shot back out of sight. Everyone exchanged worried glances, but a moment later she was back, cradling the form of a ghostly cat in her arms.

'Anselm!' she explained. 'We couldn't go without Anselm. He wasn't with us at the beginning, but he's stayed with us for so long now.'

Without hesitation, the nuns now processed forwards and out of earthly sight. This time the Light shimmered and then softly dimmed to nothing. There was no slamming shut of the way, but then none of those who had passed through were fighting to come back, but welcoming what they'd been waiting for for so long.

For a while, everyone stayed sitting on the chairs in silence. It seemed too profound a moment to just get up and leave after. When they did move, it was to head over to Cameron's cottage and a small celebration they'd left waiting.

"I can't believe we've finally done it," Cameron said with relief. "No more worrying about couples in the honeymoon suite or ghosts setting muskets off."

"I am glad about that," Anna admitted, "but the longer this has gone on, the more I'm relieved that we've given those poor ladies the peace they deserved, and Hugh as well. I wish we could make sure that everyone who suffered like they did is resting in peace. I doubt it, though. Going through what they did, it couldn't have made for them slipping quietly away. The sheer violence of their deaths would be bound to leave its mark."

"You're not wrong," Rita agreed. "I think every time I've been called to help with a haunting, there's been that element of violence in the departed's death, so heaven alone knows what happened with those women."

"Were there a lot?" Jeff asked, and was horrified when Anna and Rita told him that from the late sixteenth century through to the early eighteenth, there were over three thousand documented cases, though many of them were little more than a name, and who knew how many more names had simply been lost.

"The worst of it is," Phemie added, "I went to the museum of witchcraft in Leven after getting home the last time, and the owner told me that there was a point just after the Restoration of Charles the Second when all of the Scottish records were sent to London for scrutiny, but the boat sank. It means that virtually none of the records for easily the ten-year period before then survive – and that includes our ladies. Who knows how many others of the women accused in Scotland suffered and died under questioning without every reaching a trial? Even if a modern day government has shown willing to issue an apology for what happened, so many will forever go unnamed."

"Which makes it all the more precious that we've done what we can for those we know about," Rita said firmly, determined to keep today positive. "What's more, I know of some cases up near where I've been living which I think I might be able to bring to light a bit more. But right now, I need some breathing space."

However, Anna had latched on the words 'been living'. Had her aunt finally realised that she should be here with Gary? She wasn't going to say anything today, but she was mentally crossing her fingers that she had.

The kitchen door opened, and Austin wandered in, but this was a much calmer person than the angry and confused man who had worried Rita when he'd first come storming in. He still had no social skills at all, but although he didn't ask if he could join in, he didn't disrupt the gathering either, which Cameron and Jeff felt was a huge step forward in such a short space of time.

"We have a family," Anna said, looking up at Cameron and smiling. "We're a bit of an odd assortment, but we all fit together."

EPILOGUE

It took some months to get the farmhouse fully fitted out for Austin, and it was well after Christmas before he was finally able to move in. By this time, Cameron and Jeff had held several meetings with the banks, and had got Helen removed from having access to Austin's money, not that it had been anything like easy. As they had warned Gary and Rita, Helen's response to being separated from Austin was bitter and vicious. Solicitors got involved and then Social Services, but what none of them could have predicted was Helen having a total tantrum in court and trashing her own claim.

It had been at a stage when Cameron and Jeff had begun to fear that they might lose, because Helen was really pulling out all of the stops convincing the social workers that Austin was incapable of looking after himself or making decisions for himself. Luckily, Jeff and Cameron had convinced the social workers to come and see

Austin at the cottage where he was still staying for the time being. By the time Austin had proudly shown them his new home under construction, they were rapidly revising their opinions. Then when Jeff and Cameron showed them that Austin had written several cheques for the work all by himself in his near-illegible handwriting, it was harder for Helen's claims to withstand scrutiny.

That was the point when they got into court, and as the judge began commenting on the legitimate and constructive expenditure of Austin's money on himself, that was when Helen lost control.

"You stupid old fossil!" she screamed at the judge. "Are you fucking retarded or something? What do you think *I'm* going to live on if I don't have Austin's money?" Her tirade went on in graphic detail, with nobody else able to get a word in over her screams – not even her own solicitors, who were desperately trying to get her to shut up before she did more damage. But damage she did, and after she had been escorted from the court by two burly officials, the judge had had no hesitation in both handing over Austin's support to Jeff and Cameron, but also ruling that Helen should be excluded from all financial access too.

It meant that another two carers were able to join Mike to look after Austin in shifts, one of whom was technically capable enough to assist him with his work, even if he openly admitted that Austin was working at such a rarefied level that he hadn't a clue what he was aiming for. One lived locally and the other lived in, but the four bedrooms were converted into one for Austin and a two-bedroom flatlet for the carers, with what had been a huge main bedroom as their lounge and kitchenette, giving them some privacy and personal space when not on shift. A couple of prefabricated offices had been joined onto the farmhouse to create a workshop-lab for Austin, and he was already deep into planning his next project.

The reassuring thing to Cameron and Jeff was that in the peace and quiet, and with people around him who didn't stress him out, Austin was turning into a totally different person. They didn't need to worry about him turning up at the hotel and causing chaos, however unwittingly, because he gratefully avoided people as much as possible. Gary had even managed, with the help of the carers, to get him to start taking daily walks, and that combined with a better diet mean that the weight was falling off him, and he was healthier all round. What amused everyone was that Gary had gained enough of Austin's trust that he would let Gary use his clippers to give him a short haircut once a month, getting rid of the ragged mane which he hated having brushed and washed. At that point, Austin also became fascinated with Gary's collection of flat caps, insisting that he had some of his own, and so for the first time in his life, Gary found himself in the role of fashion guru to someone.

When Jeff was able to take over the second cottage fully for himself, Anna moved in with Cameron. There had been more than enough pieces of furniture in storage from his aunt's flat that – despite leaving plenty for the buyer – they needed next to nothing extra. It meant that since Anna's flat had been furnished from second-hand shops, she could look at getting most of it cleared and not brought up here. What she did want would fit into a hire van, and Gary volunteered to travel down with her in the spring and empty it out. Cameron had at first said he wanted to do this with Anna, but Gary explained that he wanted to visit the site of the fallen Scots at Powick where his ancestor had fought, and since somebody in authority needed to stay with Brenda to run the hotel, Cameron agreed to stay and hold the fort.

Much the same was going to happen to Rita's rented farm cottage. For the moment she was travelling up and down, but spending more time with Gary. The only hold-up to their plans was doing Gary's cottage up a bit more so that chef Harriet could move across to that, and then what had been her middle cottage could be joined with Anna's to make a place a better size for two people to live in. Put together, the two cottages were making a lovely bungalow with plenty of room for the two of them.

Less happy was trying to sort out Anna's legal entanglements. In a grim echo of Helen's behaviour, Jensen's mother had turned into a nightmare haunting her. Mrs Coleborn seemed incapable of grasping that her adult son might have made a decision for himself, and had left of his own accord. For her, Anna was the one and only villain of the piece, causing the death of her beloved husband, and sending her son off into the wilderness where he could be lying dead by the side of the road with nobody to notice. It was clear as the months went on that the tone of Mrs Coleborn's solicitors' letters became increasingly weary, and nobody doubted that they probably cringed every time she came pounding in through their door with yet another point she wanted raising. Yet there was still the matter of Anna's divorce.

At first Anna had expected Jensen to serve her papers from some other solicitor in whichever town he'd moved to. But time dragged on, and eventually Anna decided that she was going to have to be the one to get the ball rolling on their divorce. Gary came with her to a solicitor who specialised in family law, and with Anna being honest and upfront that she had been the one to leave, and that she wanted nothing at all from Jensen except her freedom, it should have been straightforward. Except no-one could find Jensen to serve the divorce papers to.

At that point even Anna and Gary began to get worried about him, yet the police could do nothing because, from their perspective, Jensen was a capable adult.

"It's a weird echo of when I left and ran to Aunty Rita's," Anna said sadly at the next family Sunday lunch. "Back then I was so grateful that the police couldn't make me go back to Worcester to answer to my bloody parents and his, even if they couldn't have forced me to return to being Jensen's wife. Well now I'm on the other side of that. I'm the one who doesn't know where he's gone, and I can't do any more about it than he could."

"Aye," Gary said, reaching out to put a comforting hand over hers, "but you ran to someone you knew. It didn't take your father long to figure out where, either. I don't like the fact that even those people you thought were friends of Jensen's don't seem to know where he's gone. You'd have thought by now that he'd have rung one or two of them and said, 'please don't tell Mum where I am, but I'm in…'. The fact that he hasn't makes me wonder whether he had a rougher reception when he went home from failing to drag you back from here, and that was the final straw and he's had some kind of breakdown."

"It would certainly explain why his mum is desperate to shove the blame onto you," Jeff agreed. "In her heart of hearts, she must know the truth of what happened between Jensen and his dad, even if she wasn't as bad, and she's probably having a hard time facing up to that."

Anna smiled faintly. "Thanks for the support, but for all that I left him, I can't help but be worried for him. I never wished him harm. I just didn't want to be married to the life that came with him thanks to his overbearing parents."

"And it stops you moving on with your life, too," Cameron said regretfully. Everyone there knew what he meant, and that he would propose to Anna the moment a wedding became possible.

Right now, though, he didn't want her to feel pressured anymore than she was over the divorce.

Therefore it was a relief when at Christmas a card came for Anna, and when she opened it, it turned out to be from Jensen. Against everything she expected, he had only thanks for her making him wake up and take control of his own life, and the note inside told her that he was living in Brighton in a bedsit for now, but that once he'd been in his job a bit longer, he was intending to buy a flat down there. The fact that he included a photo of him out in a bar with his arm wrapped around another young man made Anna think that he'd been suppressing an awful lot of his own desires in the face of his ever-demanding parents.

"I'm not going to push him straightaway," Anna announced. "He deserves the chance to get his life back on track every bit as much as I did. He hasn't given me an address – perhaps because he fears I'll pass it on to his parents…Oh God! Do you think he even knows his dad is dead? Oh bloody hell, I hope that's not the case."

"I think a call to the Brighton police is in order," Gary said. "I know Brighton isn't that small, but it's no' that big either. By the sound of it, he's still using his own name if he can access his savings accounts and stuff, so he shouldn't be hard to find. All we need to do is ask for someone to go around and make sure he knows about his dad. We're not asking them to drag him back in handcuffs."

Reassured by that, Anna was able to celebrate with everyone else, because there was someone else who was coming to join them. Gary and Rita had had several intense conversations on the matter of little Gaylord, and the moral duty they had to inform someone of the state he was living in.

"I can't just pretend I didn't see what I saw," Rita often said, and after a few weeks she made the trip back up north to speak to her contact in Social Services in person. That set a ball rolling in Edinburgh which resulted in them contacting the hotel and getting statements from everyone who had seen the state little Gaylord had been in when he arrived. Yet it was when Rita's contact got back in touch with her to tell her that those she'd spoken to in Edinburgh had made a courtesy call back to her to tell her that Gaylord was being taken into care that gave everyone pause for thought.

"I feel awful for the poor lad," Gary confessed, with Jeff saying much the same.

Yet it was Anna who tentatively suggested what they'd all been thinking, which was, "Do you think they'd let him come and live here?"

"Would you want him to?" Cameron asked her in surprise.

Anna blushed. "I'm getting older, Cam, and the older I get the less time I've got to have kids of my own. It wasn't really something I'd thought deeply about until he was hanging onto me and crying that he didn't want to leave. That really gave my hormones a boot into life, I'm afraid, and since then I've been thinking that while I can't guarantee to have a baby of my own, knowing what it's like to grow up with parents who don't care about you, I could be a good mum to that little lad."

"I think you'd make an amazing mum," Cameron said, looking at her with adoration. "But I think it would probably be easier if I said that, despite us knowing that he's definitely not my sons – thanks to Gary and the DNA test – that for his sake I'd be willing to step into the role of dad for him." He turned to Jeff and grinned at him. "I don't have far to look to find a good role-model for the difference a step-dad can make, because without you, Austin would be in such a bad place by now."

Therefore the night before Christmas Eve, Anna and Cameron made the drive over to Edinburgh and picked up Gaylord while Gary and Rita held the fort back at the hotel. Beyond excited to be coming back to *Nuns' Kirk Haugh*, and at Christmas too, everyone knew that Gaylord wasn't going to let them get much sleep, but the joy of watching him open the pile of presents they'd all bought him on Christmas morning was worth it. The hotel was open on Christmas Day, but Anna had been considerate with the rotas, giving the mums on the staff the day off, and drafting in extra help for the kitchen, dining room and bar. She was beginning to really get to grips with the managerial side of her job, and realising that she didn't need to do everything herself, but could hire and delegate as long as she kept an eye on the budget.

On Christmas afternoon, they all went to walk the lunch off with a stroll around the grounds, coming back over the newly levelled garden and path to the kirk. Nobody was suggesting that the kirk be made into a living space. Instead, as part of the refurbishment of the gardens, a driveway was being created from the turning circle outside the hotel to the former west door, which got reopened, and the kirk restored so that they could hold weddings in there if wanted. They had at first thought of just a path, but it had been Rita who pointed out that given what most modern brides wore on their feet, and the length of some bridal gowns' trains, it was unrealistic to expect a bride to walk from the hotel to the kirk.

It wouldn't become a full church again, but there was something lovely about the space now which just invited celebrations. The old windows were opened up again and glazed, and what had been the stable doors cut into the old walls were replaced with sealed glaze units with normal doors in them. The ones facing into the courtyard were frosted at the lower levels to give Gary and Rita the privacy to create a garden space beyond there, while the north side now had a lovely view over the gardens to the river.

"If ever I feel up to taking the risk on another wedding," Anna said as they wandered past, "this would be the place I'd want to do it. So much nicer than that bloody awful place my father picked out for me. Who'd have thought that that would end up with me being here?"

"Well, I hope you intend to stay for a very long time," Cameron said, realising that much as he would have loved for theirs to be the first wedding in this new space, Anna was going to need much longer before he could make this a reality. One thing was for certain, though, he wasn't going to let this lady get away – his dad was right, she was a diamond and he was going to treat her like one.

As soon as Christmas was over, he and Anna took a week's break over to Fife to stay with Phemie and Davey – Gary and Rita, along with Jeff, revelling in their new roles as adopted grandparents and the chance to have Gaylord all to themselves. The charming little villages on the south Fife coast all had associations with witch trials, but in none of them did Anna feel so much as a twitch of a connection for Elspeth. Only when they took a day trip further south to the historic town of Culross did Anna suddenly feel a connection.

"It's as if I know this place," she said to Cameron, as they walked hand in hand up the cobbled street leading away from the coast. "And it's more up here, rather than down by the old medieval palace and the grander buildings."

They had reached what had once been a Cistercian abbey and was now the parish church.

"Look," Cameron said, pointing to the information board. "It became the parish church at the Reformation, so if Elspeth was here, this would have been the church she came to. I wonder if she was buried here?"

Yet Anna found that just as at Wigtown, the churchyard held nothing for her, and it was outside of it that she felt the strongest link.

It was to take them several more trips over to the east coast, gradually working further north, before Anna again felt anything, and that was largely thanks to Jeff. With his new-found peace in retirement, Jeff had taken to being their historical researcher, and was getting very skilled at it.

"I think I've found a link for you," he told them triumphantly, just as they were planning a summer long weekend away. "We worked out the Elspeth must have had her daughter Marione in the early 1660s, didn't we? And that her surname would have been Black. ...Well I've found an old will that I think must relate to her."

"Come on then, don't leave us in suspense, Dad," Cameron chivvied him.

Jeff laughed, as similar comments came from Anna, Rita and Gary, who were sitting around the dinner table with him.

"Okay, so the will is for a James Black, who had a small farm outside of Brechin. The disposition of his goods and property is made to his daughter, Elspeth, but also to the son of his widowed cousin, and another cousin's daughter. He's pretty specific, and the way it reads is that he got the farm via his late wife's family, but that he himself was the son of a woman widowed in the aftermath of the 1715 Jacobite rebellion, when his father, James Black senior was killed. He and she would have starved without the kindness of his father's sister's family, he says, and he names her as Jonet Black. But get this, Jonet's son who's also in the will is called Alexander Sorley McAllister

Gibbons – because of course, while she remained a Black, the son took his dad's surname."

"Good grief, that's a bit too much of a coincidence," Anna gasped.

Jeff nodded. "It was that name which convinced me that I was on the right track. So our lad, who was named in part after Sorley, is the dad of the second woman in the will, also called Elspeth but known as Eliza."

"I'm starting to see a pattern here," Gary said. "They all must have thought the world of Elspeth for her name to keep being honoured like that."

"Wait 'til you hear this," Jeff said. "The son of the widowed cousin? He sounds younger and his mum was called Mailie, though of course she wasn't a Black because if I've got this right, she's the daughter of Marione who married a Gordon, and so Mailie is a Gordon, and in the next generation who inherit, the lad who inherits is…Sorley James Black Gordon."

He got a round of applause for that.

"I think you've done them proud," Anna said. "Now the only other thing you need to tell us is, were they all in the same area? Had any of them moved away?"

Jeff shook his head. "They're all in the general Brechin area, and get this: the Jonet who we think must have been our Elspeth's adopted daughter, her husband, and her son Alex, were all in service to the Erskine's up there. Now that makes me wonder whether our Elspeth was there too?"

"It has to be worth a look," Cameron agreed, and that was how, a couple of weekend's later, he and Anna ended up taking a tour around the beautiful mansion of *House of Duns*, between Brechin and Montrose. All the way around the main house, Cameron kept looking expectantly at Anna, but she kept shaking her head. Then when they finished the tour and got outside, suddenly her eyes went wide and she grabbed Cameron's hand.

"I can feel her! She was here. Out here, in the working part of the house. …Elspeth? …Elspeth? Can you hear me? Your mother is waiting for you, and so is Hugh. You can go to them now. They're with you on the Other Side." And just for a moment, Anna swore she heard a sigh of relief and something soft brushing her face, as if a ghostly hand had touched her, and then it was gone.

"We did it," Anna said happily. "Mission accomplished. All of our ghosts are at rest."

"Then it's time to go home and start focusing on *your* life," Cameron said, as they went and retrieved Harris and Lewis from the car.

"Yes," she agreed. "There's so much I find I want to do, and all of it is with you."

If you enjoyed reading this book, please leave a review. I'm an independent author without the backing of a big publishing company, and reviews are the best way to help others find this book. You don’t have to write an essay, just a star rating can be very helpful.

AUTHOR'S NOTES

Firstly, I'd like to thank you for staying the course of Anna's story, but I would also like to clarify where I was coming from with Austin's strand of the story. I have a good friend whose adult son is high on the autistic spectrum and have heard first hand from her the struggles they have faced. Most relevant to the book is the very real problem of coping with meltdowns when it's a grown up, not a child, having them. My friend was for a while a Special Constable (these are volunteers who work alongside the police), and she found it heartbreaking to go out to calls to violent incidents and find that it was an autistic adult who was involved.

So it is from her that I heard a lot about the difficult balance between catering to the needs of someone with a disability, and yet keeping other people safe from them. The police she went out with had a duty to keep members of the public safe, and when you have a grown man flinging fists about – however much it's just expressing frustration or fear – it doesn't lessen the danger they pose to others. In the end, she had to give up volunteering, because it was just too hard to keep dealing with situations like this. Given time, she knew from her own experience as a mum, that the situation could have been deescalated, but at the time, there simply wasn't *enough* time to allow this to happen and *safely*, and all too often she saw people like her son being arrested as the only way to get them away from those they posed a danger to. It's a horrible decision for anyone to have to make, and she understood fully why the police had no choice, but at the same time she was torn because she could see the other side of the problem too.

Sadly, while autistic children are now getting more understanding and better treatment within schools, the moment they leave school, the world becomes an absolute minefield for them. Few if any people give them any leeway. They are simply expected to 'grow up' and 'fit in', which they can't, and which leads to all sorts of problems. If you have a family member who is on the spectrum, I hope you don't hold Gary's actions against me – I was trying to give a balanced view and show both sides.

The genesis of this story was finding the records of the very real women who lived and died in Dumfriesshire all those years ago, and as Phemie points out, their official records were lost in the early 1660s. So we have to rely on what can be pieced together from parish records and local government passing references, and the survival of those records is very much at the mercy of damp, mould, and mice! Parish records were normally kept quite literally in the parish chest – probably a stout oak box – which inevitably suffered the ravages of time, and was far from impervious to the wet, and rodents being attracted to documents written on parchment or paper. This fate is far from unique to the women accused primarily during the seventeenth century, but in their cases it really hinders our ability to put the records straight, let alone calculate the true number of women who were persecuted.

I also have to point out that in the course of my research for these two books, I came across some truly gruesome details. For the sake of my readers, for whom this is intended to be a pleasurable read, I have left some of the worst out. That hasn't been to in any way sanitise what happened to them. Rather it's that it's so vile that I really didn't want to leave anyone having nightmares after reading this the way I did during researching.

While writing this, I visited the museum of witchcraft in Leven, run by Leonard Low, and saw some of the implements he has managed to collect and they are gruesome. Some of what was done to the accused women leave you wondering what kind of person thought that it would achieve anything other than getting that woman to agree to pretty much anything to make the pain stop. But then I suspect that in the cases where their accusers had their eye on very earthly gain from their deaths, that was the point – get them to reveal lurid details which had been suggested to them when sleep-deprived and wracked with pain. Details which came more from their accusers' imagination than anything those women had seen or done, but which were guaranteed to condemn them. If you are anywhere near the south Fife coast, it's worth visiting the museum in Leven, if only to thank your lucky stars that we don't still have such barbaric punishments, inflicted simply on someone's accusations. Perfect, our own time might not be, but things aren't quite this bad.

It is one of those quirks of fate that while writing this second book, I also learned of Grierson of Lagg owning a pet monkey named after Major Weir. I already knew of the case of Weir, who was seventy at the time of his accusation, and who was one of the few men who got strangled and burned as a witch, along with his unfortunate sister. Some of his story was the inspiration behind the fate of my fictional Edward McCartney and Isobel, though Weir's trial was in Edinburgh, not Sanquar where my character died. The women who died at Wigtown are also real historical figures apart from my fictional Isobel and the young Grissell, and Grierson was the leading justice they were brought before. Yet I had written that episode before I found out about the monkey, so Grierson really did have an obsession with witches as well as for punishing Covenanters. He and his family were not to enjoy being in royal favour for long, but that was scant consolation for the families of those whose deaths he ordered while in a position of power.

Two other men of power feature in this book who are also real historical characters. John Graham of Claverhouse was very much the soldiers' soldier as portrayed in the book. There is a surviving letter in which Claverhouse wrote to those who had sent him and his men to Dumfriesshire to maintain order, complaining of the difficulty in tracking the Covenanters down, especially when they easily moved across shire borders, while his orders limited him to Dumfriesshire itself. His later name of Bloody Clavers comes from the time of the Jacobite rebellions, not this period.

In contrast, Colonel James Douglas, being part of the incredibly powerful Douglas family, could afford to flaunt the law. It's hard to appreciate the level of influence this family had in Dumfries and Galloway. In places like Edinburgh there were other families of a similar status, but out in the western shires the rest of the nobility and gentry were so far below the Douglases as to be unable to challenge them in any significant way. So James did indeed have men shot where they were found, without any reference to a higher authority, and without any repercussions to him personally. Their seat of Drumlanrig Castle is open for a limited period every summer, and is every bit the grand place I have described it as. Even just seen from the outside, all by itself it illustrates the dominance of the Douglases over the whole of the south-west, and there really isn't another place like it in terms of size or grandeur in the county.

The memorial to the Covenanters which Anna and Cameron visit is as described – and every bit as hard to find! I'm used to map reading, but like them, we went in and out of Thornhill trying to find it. It is a lovely spot, and there are some fascinating old headstones there of the late seventeenth century. And like Anna, I'm always surprised at the different 'feel' to the various graveyards and cemeteries I visit in the course of my research. Dalgarnock is certainly one of the very peaceful and lovely ones. Yet the point made in the book holds true: where are the women on that memorial? We know that women were prosecuted for attending conventicles, and yet as you go around looking at the memorials and dig into records, too often the only women's names you come across are as the wife of X.

Therefore the point I had Anna making stands: if Dumfries and Galloway was such a hotbed of rebellion, and wives at the time had little choice but to follow their husbands' leads when it came to religious observances, where are the women on the Covenanter memorials? Don't they warrant a mention? And similarly, if men were supposed to have so much control over their wives that in other instances they could be held accountable for them, where are the husbands who should have been held accountable for their witches?

This is a question which I feel has been ignored by historians of the era. Was it simply that those women who fell afoul of the authorities were more easily disposed of without needing to go through the expense of a trial by accusing them of witchcraft? As I had Phemie say, the level of misogyny in the seventeenth century was far in excess of what you find in the earlier medieval times. This is not something carried forward out of the past, but something which rears its ugly head with some of the more severe iterations of the Protestant faith, which is perhaps why the witch trials in Scotland were far more numerous and went on for far longer than any did down in England. The Covenanters tried several times to get their Covenant accepted as the form of religious practise in England in return for their armed support during the Civil Wars, and you can't help but think it was fortunate that they failed for the sake of the women of the time.

A sad reality connected to this is that the families of those women detained, and often tortured, as witches were indeed expected to pay for the cost of gaolers and other expenses. Therefore if the kirk wanted someone to pay for imprisoning and questioning a witch, then the men had to be *able* to pay, not be incarcerated alongside their wives, so there may have been an unpleasant financial element as to why so few men got taken in for questioning. There was no such recompense to the authorities for the men held as religious deviants when the Covenanters fell out of political favour. So was there that financial element to women not being imprisoned for breaking the law by attending conventicles, and the reason why the men who did get caught were too often simply shot where found? It would bear considerably more historical research.

Sadly, it is true that the ship carrying huge numbers of Scottish documents for inspection in London sank, with everything lost. It leaves a huge gap in the documentable history of the mid-seventeenth century, because it was far more than just the witch trial records which went down with the ship. This is why so many women cannot be traced further than the odd mention in a parish or town document – further records simply no longer exist.

The coast around Wigtown is very quiet and peaceful these days, and Wigtown itself is Scotland's book town, holding an annual literary festival. However, walking down to the site where the two real martyrs drowned is a sobering experience. When the sun is out, it's a beautiful spot, but the clouds only have to come up a bit for you to imagine what it would have been like for someone being dragged out to the estuary. The tide comes in very slowly along the wide mudflats of the Bladnoch River, with there being no point at which there would have been a sudden rising of the water to end the women's suffering. For me, on balance I think that this probably did happen, but there is enough doubt that you can decide for yourself whether you think it did or not.

The Keithock standing stone near Culross still stands, and is as I described it when Elspeth visits it. Not part of an actual circle, it nevertheless is part of a group of stones. I leave you to make up your own mind as to the interpretation of their placement.

The women of Culross whom I made friends of Elspeth's are taken from the records of witches, and did die in Edinburgh for their 'sins'. I couldn't come up with a story for them of their own, but this was a way to honour their memory. If you've watched the first series of *Outlander*, then you've seen part of Culross, because it was the setting for the witch trial scene. Please don't let that put you off visiting Culross. The medieval palace is a stunning example of a high status medieval home, and the painted room is worth seeing to get a glimpse of how houses were decorated before wallpaper. The abbey church has been much altered, but is still a lovely old church to visit if you enjoy exploring them as much as I do.

This is the end of this particular story, but I hope to let Rita and Gary each have their own tale to tell in subsequent books – with a bit of help from Anna of course.

About the Author

L. J. Hutton lives in Worcestershire and writes history, mystery and fantasy novels. If you would like to know more about any of these books you are very welcome to come and visit my online home at www.ljhutton.com

Also by L. J. Hutton:

Time Will Tell

She's broken ...this house needs fixing. Can they banish one another's ghosts?

Fliss' career has broken her, but her uncle has a plan to save her. Restoring Sytchampton House to its former glory is the kind of job he regularly does, and doing nothing more stressful than wielding a paint brush alongside side him seems just the therapy Fliss needs – except the house itself has other ideas!

Why does Fliss keep finding hidden caches of letters leading back to the earlier family who owned the house? And why do they play on her deepest desires so strongly? Her grief over not having a child of her own keeps getting tugged at by the abandoned children of the past, and when she starts speaking to someone in the past, Barry fears Fliss is going to do something rash which might crush her future forever.

Yet those in the past have a voice and a mind of their own too, and trapping Fliss isn't in their plans – they just need her help. Can righting the wrongs in the past, and proving the innocence of those long dead, give Fliss the fresh start she desperately needs in the present?

Witches' Brew

Angelo is bad news, the kind Fleur doesn't need. But is he truly evil, is the past leaking into the present, and is he acting alone?

Cataloguing Angelo Vance's latest acquisition is the last job Fleur wants, but his mother insists that it's her and her alone he wants for the task. Yet arriving at *The Rookery*, alongside the books Fleur discovers a treasure trove of old grimoires. Worse, something is very wrong in this old house. Who is the shadowy figure she keeps catching glimpses of, and hears? If it's, Angelo he's not just bad but mad, and if it isn't, is he in danger?

As Fleur digs into the family who owned *The Rookery*, ever darker secrets start coming to light and worryingly, seem to be impacting on the present. Could the lethal recipes from the grimoires be still in use, and if so, why? As violence towards her and others erupts, the police get involved and Fleur needs all her skills to make sure the wrong man does not get arrested …and the right one lives to tell the tale!

Published by Wylfheort Books

Copyright 2024 L. J. Hutton

Copyright

The moral right of L. J. Hutton to be identified as the author of this work has been asserted by her in accordance with the Copyright, Designs and Patents Act 1988.

Aside from actual historical persons, all characters in this book are fictitious, and any resemblance to actual persons living or dead is purely coincidental.

All rights reserved. No part of this publication may be reproduced, stored in a retrieval system or transmitted in any form, or by any means, without the prior permission in writing of the author, nor to be otherwise circulated in any form or binding or cover other than in which it is published without a similar condition, including this condition, being imposed upon the subsequent purchaser.

Printed in Dunstable, United Kingdom

64824876R00306